WEAPON OF FEAR

WEAPON OF FLESH TRILOGY II
BOOK 1

BY
CHRIS A. JACKSON
AND
ANNE L. MCMILLEN-JACKSON

ILLUSTRATIONS BY
NOAH STACEY

Dedication

This novel is dedicated Anne's mother, Marge McMillen, and Chris' father, Robert Jackson, both of whom passed away during the writing of this story.

Acknowledgments
We would once again like to thank Noah Stacey for agreeing to do the cover art for this second trilogy in the Weapon of Flesh series. We owe Noah more than we can ever repay.

WEAPON OF FEAR
WEAPON OF FLESH TRILOGY II
BOOK 1

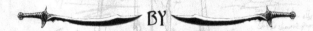

BY

CHRIS A. JACKSON
AND
ANNE L. MCMILLEN-JACKSON

ISBN-13 978-1-939837-10-3

JAXBOOKS.COM

PRELUDE

The assassin's kick splintered Hoseph's ribs like kindling, knocking the breath from his lungs. The room spun around him as he tumbled back over something cold and hard. He landed in a heap, pain lancing through his chest. A gasp for breath brought the tasted of blood.

A growled curse and the clash of metal from beyond the stone slab caught his ear. Hoseph blinked away the darkness edging into his vision, forcing his mind to focus on the here and now, on the fight, on the unbelievable mayhem these assassins from Twailin had unleashed.

The guildmaster and his Master Hunter had turned out to be more than anyone bargained for, daring to challenge the Grandmaster of the entire Assassins Guild, the very emperor of Tsing. They had even managed to kill two of his bodyguards, blademasters of Koss Godslayer, a feat unheard of…until now. The Grandmaster was immune to their attacks, protected by his ring from any guild assassin, but Hoseph couldn't rely on the three remaining blademasters to contain the situation. His own attempt to kill Guildmaster Lad had proven disastrous. He needed help.

Clutching the tiny silver skull that dangled from his wrist on a thin silver chain, Hoseph called upon his patron goddess: Demia, Keeper of The Slain. Dark tendrils curled about him, her chill power infusing his flesh. The stone walls of the interrogation chamber faded away into shifting veils of gray—the Sphere of Shadows. At once, the pain of his injuries vanished. Here, in this place without physical substance, his incorporeal body could feel nothing, hear nothing, taste nothing. Grateful for the release, Hoseph was tempted to linger, but he dared not. He pictured his desired

1

destination in his mind and invoked the skull talisman once again.

Hoseph staggered upon the uneven footing, gritting his teeth against the renewed pain. A long, torch-lit stairway rose before him and descended behind. This was as far as Demia's magic would take him, for magical wards of immense power shielded the rest of the palace from any kind of magical transport. The imperial guards stationed at the top would rally aid. They were sworn to protect the emperor. Of course, they had no idea that Emperor Tynean Tsing II was also the Grandmaster of the Assassins Guild. Only five people in the city of Tsing were privy to that truth.

And soon, two of those five will be dead.

Hoseph smiled grimly. As a high priest of Demia, his role was to usher souls from the realm of the living to the afterlife. He would take great pleasure in doing so for Lad and Mya. He pushed himself up the steps, gasping for breath as his splintered ribs ground against one another. Blood dripped from the wound in his upper chest where Mya's dagger had pierced him during her surprise attack, though how she had survived the Grandmasters dagger thrust, he couldn't fathom. No matter. Demia's grace would heal his injuries, but not quickly. In the meantime, he had a long flight of stairs to climb.

With one arm clutching his chest to stabilize his shattered ribs, Hoseph lurched forward. Lightheaded, he leaned against wall until his dizziness eased. *Hurry...I've got to hurry.* If the traitors escaped, the Grandmaster's wrath would be terrible. He started up the stairs.

Though his legs were uninjured, his progress was slow; each breath felt as if he were being stabbed with a ragged blade. His foot missed one step and he nearly tripped. As he caught himself, the torchlight danced in his vision, then dimmed. *No...don't pass out!* Forcing the darkness aside by sheer force of will, he climbed on.

How could he have underestimated the assassins so badly? He knew that Lad had been created for Saliez, the former Twailin guildmaster, as a magically enhanced weapon. *But Mya...* Hoseph wondered if Saliez had commissioned more than one weapon, conveniently neglecting to inform them. It would explain her uncanny speed and battle skills, but didn't make sense. Mya was an incredibly competent young Master Hunter; her record in the guild was clearly documented.

It doesn't matter. They can't touch the Grandmaster, he reminded himself with cold certainty. His only worry was the Grandmaster's reaction. Hoseph's proposal of Mya as the perfect choice as Twailin guildmaster had precipitated this whole situation, and Tynean Tsing was not a forgiving master.

The priest stumbled against the thick, iron-bound door at the top of the stairs. Reaching for the handle, he bit back a curse as he realized that he had no key. Only the emperor and the jailor had keys to this door. As usual, the jailor had been dismissed once the preparations for the meeting were completed, retreating to a dark corner of the dungeon with a bottle of rum until summoned to dispose of the bodies and clean up. Hoseph had no time to go back down and find him.

He pounded on the door with his fist, shouting as loudly as he could, though each word cost him pain and blood. "Guards! Guards! The emperor is under attack! Assassins!"

"What?" came the voice from beyond the door. "Who is this?"

"High Priest Hoseph! Listen to me! Assassins in the dungeon! Summon the guard and break down the door!"

Hoseph fell back against the wall, his chest afire from his efforts. "Thank Demia", he murmured as shouts rang out beyond the door.

Pounding feet and clanking armor soon announced the arrival of troops. Moments later, a heavy blow struck the door. Hoseph stumbled back as a second blow shook the door in its frame. The pounding continued, heavy implements cracking against the wood, with an occasional clang against the iron bands and hinges. The door, however, was too well built to submit to mere brute strength.

Hurry... Covering his ears to ease the racket, Hoseph tried to gauge how long it had been since he had left the torture chamber.

The pounding stopped.

Have they given up? Surely they wouldn't—

A screech of tortured metal and the crack of crumbling stone shivered the air. Hoseph backed down another step, staring as the door's iron bands, hinges, lock, and handle all glowed eerily, then crumpled inward. Wood splintered and rivets popped. Hoseph flung up his arms to defend against the shrapnel as the stout door collapsed in on itself, as if a giant's hand had wadded it up in a ball.

Beyond the heap of twisted iron and shattered oak stood a slim

3

man in silver robes—Archmage Duveau. The phalanx of imperial guards and knights hung back, fearful of getting caught up in the fierce enchantment.

"Archmage Duveau! Thank Demia! The emperor's in danger!" Hoseph gestured down the long stair. "Hurry!"

"Where?" Guards surged forward.

"The interrogation chamber." Hoseph was about to choke out directions when he saw several of the senior guards and knights exchange knowing, unsettled glances. They knew where to go. Commander Ithross led dozens of his imperial guards past him down the steps, followed by several knights and their squires. Hoseph pressed himself against the wall to avoid being overrun. As their clatter passed into the distance, he concentrated on trying to breath without fainting.

"You're injured." Archmage Duveau stood before him, his robes shimmering like quicksilver in the torchlight.

"Yes. I tried to intervene. One assassin kicked me in the ribs, and the other stabbed me with a dagger." Hoseph wiped blood from his lips and tried unsuccessfully to straighten without wincing.

"Here." Duveau pulled from a pocket in his robe a small dark sphere about the size of an olive. He held it out to Hoseph between his finger and thumb. "Swallow this."

"What is it?" Working with assassins for years had bred in Hoseph an unshakable habit of distrust. Though he couldn't imagine why Duveau might want to harm him, he accepted nothing at face value.

The archmage sneered in derision. "It's called a fleshforge. It will cure your injuries, since your death goddess apparently has little regard for the health of her priests. Now swallow it. We haven't time for reticence. We must aid the emperor."

"Of course." Steaming at the offhand insult, but reluctant to anger the archmage, Hoseph popped the sphere into his mouth. It was cold and tasted of iron. He swallowed forcefully, and the sphere slid down his throat. He tensed as heat pulsed outward from his belly, but then his pain began to ebb. The ends of his broken ribs shifted, not grinding now, but moving together and knitting. The knife wound closed and the split skin sealed. Even the ache in his thighs from the long climb vanished. Before Hoseph drew another breath, he was healed.

"That was—" A sudden wave of nausea gripped him. He retched, bending forward with the force of the convulsion. The small sphere surged up his throat and out his gaping mouth.

Duveau caught the fleshforge, wiped it on Hoseph's robe, and tucked it away. "There. Now, we must hurry."

The two men hastened down the stairs. About halfway down, Duveau stopped and seemed to sniff the air, then grasped Hoseph's arm as if to steady him.

"I can walk. You needn't—"

"No time for walking." Duveau murmured arcane phrases and pressed a hand to the wall...*into* the wall. The stone swallowed his hand as readily as Hoseph had swallowed the fleshforge. But the archmage didn't stop there. He strode forward, dragging Hoseph along with him.

With no time to panic, Hoseph found himself pulled into the wall and utter darkness. Though he knew it was solid stone, he felt like he'd stepped through a gentle waterfall. A moment later, they emerged just down the corridor from the interrogation chamber.

Hoseph tore his arm from the archmage's grasp. He was unaccustomed to being on the receiving end of a spell, and didn't like it in the least. A clatter from down the hall drew his attention as the crowd of guards and knights arrived, clearly astonished to see Duveau and Hoseph there ahead of them. But they didn't stop, continuing their headlong dash down the corridor.

Hoseph wanted to rush right behind them, eager to see the two assassins laid out in pools of blood. Duveau strode after them at a slower pace than Hoseph would have preferred, but he refused to cede his own dignity to the archmage. The collective gasps and cries from the warriors spurred them forward into the chamber. They found no fighting, no clash of arms, only a closely packed crowd of guards and knights around the spot where he'd left the emperor.

"Your Majesty!" Hoseph shouted as he hurried forward.

A young squire stumbled back from the crowd of guards, fell to his knees, and vomited. With a cringe of disgust, Hoseph side-stepped him and shoved his way through the strangely quiet assembly of warriors. "Your Majesty! I've brought—"

Hoseph stopped, blinking in shock, for a moment disbelieving his own eyes. Instead of Lad and Mya, the emperor's five blademasters lay pale and dead in a veritable lake of blood. One was missing a head and a hand. A steel spike protruded from the head of another.

A middle-aged knight, Sir Fineal, knelt beside yet another body stretched out on the floor. Blue and gold robes streaked with blood, silver hair, a golden circlet inlaid with blood-red rubies. But all Hoseph could stare at was the emperor's own hand clutching the hilt of the kris that had been thrust up into his brain.

No... Demia's high priest stared in shock, unable—unwilling— to accept what his eyes were showing him. *How can he be dead? They couldn't touch him! He wears the ring!* Hoseph suddenly realized that the gold and obsidian band of the Grandmaster of Assassins no longer glinted upon Tynean Tsing's finger. The ring—the Grandmaster's last protection from his own guild—was gone.

"Our emperor has been slain." Sir Fineal reached down to close the dead sovereign's eyes.

A disbelieving voice broke the silence. "He...he killed himself?"

Idiot! thought Hoseph. "But how..." *Lad and Mya* couldn't *have killed him.* Hoseph only realized that he had spoken aloud when he felt every eye in the room upon him.

With narrowed eyes, Sir Fineal stared at the priest as he rose. "How this could have happened is *indeed* the question, High Priest Hoseph. You say that you were with His Majesty. What occurred here?"

"I..." Hoseph glanced about the room. Everyone stared back, expecting answers. He caught sight of the open iron maiden near the emperor's corpse. It had, only moments ago, held the captain of the Twailin Royal Guard. *Empty?* Hoseph caught his breath. *Where is Norwood?* The captain had signed his own death warrant when he begged audience with Tynean Tsing, believing that a spy posed a lethal threat to the emperor. The man had discovered that the emperor himself was the threat. But now he had vanished.

"Pardon, Sir Fineal." Commander Ithross stepped from the crowd. "First squad, search the entire dungeon. Whoever did this didn't pass us on the steps. They must still be down here. Find these assassins!"

The order sent a jolt of urgency through Hoseph. There were

prisoners down here who had seen him in the company of Lad and Mya with the emperor. Allowing them to be interrogated would be disastrous.

As the squad of imperial guards hastened off, Ithross took up position next to Fineal. "High Priest Hoseph, please continue."

Hoseph's mind spun, parsing the facts into things he could tell them and things he most certainly could not. His eyes fell on the six slabs of stone arrayed around a heavy iron drain. Only one was occupied. Kiesha had been a beautiful woman once, an excellent thief, and a competent operative. Unfortunately, she had decided to think for herself instead of obeying orders. Though she had been alive—barely—when he left the room, her chest no longer rose and fell. A story clicked into his mind. He pointed toward Kiesha's corpse.

"I was summoned by His Majesty to aid in the passing of that prisoner's soul to the afterlife."

"You did that to her?" Fineal interrupted.

"I did not. As you undoubtedly know, His Majesty preferred to conduct his own interrogations." Hoseph suppressed a smile as the man shifted uncomfortably. A knight doesn't like to be told that his master was a sadist, even if he might suspect it. "As I did my duty, two assassins appeared from nowhere." He couldn't very well tell them that Lad and Mya had come at the invitation of the emperor himself.

"They just *appeared?*" Ithross asked. "The way you and Archmage Duveau just appeared down the corridor?"

Hoseph shrugged. "I don't know. My attention was on my task. His Majesty's blademasters defended him, but the two were preternaturally skilled."

"Skilled?" The knight loomed over Hoseph, staring down at him with flinty eyes. "Two assassins kill *five* blademasters, and all you can say it that they were *skilled?*"

"Sir Fineal, please," Ithross protested. "We need answers, not accusations, and this investigation falls under the jurisdiction of the Imperial Guard, not the knighthood."

The knight clenched his jaw, muscles writhing under his close-cropped beard. "Of course, Commander. Please. Ask."

Ithross turned to Hoseph. "Can you describe these two

assassins?"

"Yes. A young man and woman, both slim and light-skinned. His hair was sandy colored, and hers was red and short." He didn't see a problem with giving accurate descriptions. If they had escaped the palace, he could have the entire city looking for them in no time. "That's about as much as I could tell in the furor. I tried to intervene, but I was badly injured, as you saw."

"So you ran." Sir Fineal sneered.

"Of course, I ran." Hoseph stared at the knight without quailing. "If I hadn't, I, too, would be dead, and none would know what had transpired here." Hoseph longed to sneer back, but maintained his equanimity.

"An amazing story, High Priest Hoseph." Ithross turned to the archmage. "Archmage Duveau, we have seen by your own example that the dungeons can be accessed by magical means. How is that possible, considering the palace wards prevent magical travel?"

Duveau glanced sidelong at Hoseph, obviously disgruntled at having questions directed his way. "The dungeons are not protected by the wards, Commander."

Ithross looked skeptical. "I was told that the wards extend around the *entire* palace."

"And His Majesty explicitly instructed me to maintain only those wards already in place, which does *not* include these lower reaches. There have been no wards on the dungeon for longer than I have been archmage."

For one day longer... Hoseph remembered the day Tynean Tsing ordered a reluctant Archmage Venron to remove the dungeon wards. Hoseph had made it look like a natural death, of course, and the following day the emperor appointed an oblivious Duveau.

"Why would he do *that*?" Ithross sounded incredulous.

"I have no idea, Commander. I didn't *question* my orders, I merely followed them." The archmage raised an eyebrow. "Were *you* in the habit of asking an explanation from His Majesty?"

Ithross ignored Duveau's sarcasm. "Can you use magic to find the assassins?"

"Perhaps. It would require something personal of theirs. Hair, a nail clipping, or even some token that they held dear for some time."

"What about the blood on this blademaster's sword?" A knight lifted a stained katana. "The assassins apparently didn't get away without injury."

"Alas, no. Blood is a fleeting thing in the human body. I would require something more substantial."

"We'll have to search." Ithross waved over his lieutenant. "Rhondont, send a runner for the emperor's healer. Master Corvecosi may be able find something in this mess that didn't belong to one of the blademasters, and help us piece together just what happened here. And Prince Arbuckle must be informed of his father's death."

"I'll inform the prince personally." Sir Fineal gathered his two squires and they tramped out of the room.

Hoseph bowed to Ithross. "If it please you, Commander, I'll be off to clean up and rest. Archmage Duveau has healed my injuries, but I am weary and heartsick at the emperor's demise."

"No, High Priest Hoseph, it does *not* please me." Ithross looked stern. "The emperor is dead, and all we have to go on is a vague description of two assassins who apparently can pop in and out at will. You may not remember much, but Master Duveau's magic can compel you to supply us with details you may not readily recall." He'd stopped just short of calling Hoseph a liar. "I know you won't mind."

Hoseph's mind spun. Under Duveau's spells, Hoseph's mind would be laid bare. They could ask him anything, and he would be compelled to answer truthfully. That he could not allow, not if he hoped to get out of here alive.

"High Priest Hoseph?" Ithross' expression shifted to suspicion, and his hand drifted toward his sword.

Hoseph smiled wearily. "Of course, I'll do whatever I can do to help in the investigation, Commander. However, as the late emperor's spiritual advisor, I have been entrusted with certain...personal confidences. It would be disrespectful to inadvertently reveal anything in"—Hoseph glanced around at the lingering guards and knights—"this company. Perhaps I could answer your questions someplace else? Someplace *private?*"

"Very well. One moment." Ithross turned to his lieutenant. "Rhondont, secure this room. No one should be touching anything until Master Corvecosi examines the scene."

Hoseph strode for the door without waiting for Ithross or Duveau. He had no time to waste, not with so many loose ends to tie up before he left the dungeon. Lengthening his stride, he flicked his talisman into his hand as he turned the corner, and invoked Demia's divine power. All Archmage Duveau and Commander Ithross would find when they stepped into the corridor would be a few dissipating tendrils of black mist.

CHAPTER I

The tap on the door snapped Prince Arbuckle's eyes from the book he was reading. He glanced at the ornate clock on his mantle. It was late. While it wasn't unusual for him to read in bed until the small hours of the morning, a knock on the door at this hour was unheard of.

"Yes?"

The door opened and his valet, Baris, stepped in, shutting the sturdy oak portal firmly behind him. The man's glazed eyes and slightly askew jacket roused Arbuckle's curiosity. In all the years that Baris had attended him, he had never seen the valet less than sharp-eyed and impeccably attired, much less knocking on his door in the middle of the night.

"I'm sorry to disturb you, milord, but there is a knight here who insists on speaking to you."

"A knight?" This was getting interesting.

Arbuckle didn't know many of the knights beyond the few younger ones who sparred with him as part of his martial training. The older, more experienced knights were often away keeping order in the provinces or commanding troops in the field. Perhaps one of these had arrived with an urgent question of military convention, an issue requiring historical precedent. Arbuckle warmed to the prospect. Though he'd never studied at a formal university, he'd had tutors aplenty, and the palace boasted one of the best libraries in the empire. He was a true scholar of history, though few ever sought his knowledge or opinion.

"Which knight?"

"Sir Fineal, milord."

"Fineal?" Though Arbuckle had met Sir Fineal, he didn't know

11

him well. "Very well."

By the time Arbuckle had put his book aside and slipped his feet into a pair of slippers, Baris held his robe ready. Shrugging into the sumptuous garment, Arbuckle tied the sash tight and ran his fingers through his unruly hair. "Good enough. Let's go."

"As you wish, milord." Baris bowed and opened the door.

Arbuckle stepped into the sitting room, the two blademasters stationed at the door slipping quietly into position behind and to either side of him. Bright lamp light reflected off Sir Fineal's armor. Two squires hovered behind the knight, and all three bowed low as the crown prince entered.

"Milord Prince," Fineal said as he rose, "I bear tragic news."

For the first time since the knock on his door, apprehension trumped Arbuckle's curiosity. He noted a red stain on the knight's knee and boot—blood. Dread knotted Arbuckle's stomach.

"There's been violence. What's happened?"

"I regret to announce, Milord Prince, that your father, the emperor, is dead."

"Dead?" The news was so far from what Arbuckle expected that the word didn't register at first. "Dead? How?"

"We were told there were assassins, Milord Prince, in the...dungeon."

For a long moment, Arbuckle felt nothing. He remembered being grief-stricken by his mother's death when he was only ten years old, so why didn't he feel anything now? He welcomed the wave of emotion when it finally washed over him, but instead of grief he felt...what? Relief? Liberation? The second wave was guilt for his lack of sorrow. But then, he and his father had never been close, the chasm between them widening year by year. A son's love can withstand only so much derision and ridicule. Arbuckle had long ago realized that he didn't even like his father, let alone love him. Duty, however, he understood.

"Take me to him."

Sir Fineal's mouth tightened and he seemed reluctant when he said, "Milord, it's dangerous. In addition to your father, these assassins killed five of his blademasters, and they've not yet been apprehended."

Arbuckle felt a trickle of fear down his spine like a cold finger or a drop of icy water. *Five blademasters...* The notion seemed ludicrous. *Impossible.*

The two blademasters at Arbuckle's sides stirred. Glancing back at one of them, he was amazed to see a flash of disbelief in the man's eyes before it was secreted beneath the customary blank expression. The flash of humanity there surprised him as much as the notion of regicide in the palace.

"Has the Imperial Guard been mobilized, Sir Fineal?"

"Of course, Milord Prince, and the entire knighthood and Order of Paladin as well."

"Then I daresay my safety is not at risk. I *will* go to see my father." He turned to his valet. "Baris, some clothing, quickly now!"

"Yes, Milord Prince." Baris dashed into Arbuckle's bedchamber.

"Milord Prince, I would feel better if your other bodyguards also accompanied you. May I summon them?"

"Of course."

Fineal flicked a hand toward his eldest squire. The young woman bowed and quickly exited, her footfalls echoing as she ran down the corridor.

Arbuckle retired to his bedroom to dress, his mind spinning. *Who could kill five blademasters?* The entire situation seemed surreal. *The dungeons...* He suddenly remembered one day when he was quite young, his father insisting that he accompany him down to the dungeons on the pretense of playing some sort of game. The faces of the prisoners and the stench of human confinement had sent Arbuckle running. That had been the first of many occasions when he had resisted his father's attempts to "educate" him. What the education entailed, Arbuckle never knew. Finally—thank the gods— Tynean Tsing had stopped trying and left Arbuckle to his books.

What if this is just a ruse to get me down there? He wouldn't put anything past his father.

Arbuckle emerged from his bedroom into a sitting room crowded with agitated warriors. Three more knights and their squires shifted impatiently. In contrast, the additional blademasters stood absolutely still save for the flicking of fingers as they conversed amongst themselves in their indecipherable sign language. Arbuckle swallowed. He'd known since his youth that blademasters didn't speak, but had not learned until later that their tongues were cut out as part of their training. In a corner stood the imperial scribe, apparently summoned from his bed, surveying the scene and scribbling notes in his big book. All snapped to attention and bowed.

Arbuckle jerked his surcoat straight and twisted his neck to relieve a persistent kink. "Take me to the emperor."

"Yes, Milord Prince!"

The entourage strode swiftly through the palace corridors and down myriad stairs, the knights' armor clattering, and the blademasters as quiet as death. The sumptuous tapestries and rugs of the residential wing gave way to the ostentation of the public galleries, then an isolated corridor as bleak as Arbuckle's memory of it. Instead of the impressively stout door he remembered, however, a heap of splintered timber and twisted iron lay aside.

"What happened here?"

"Archmage Duveau breeched the door with magic, Milord Prince," Sir Fineal explained. "Only the jailor has a key, and he couldn't be found."

"I see." The thought of such power made Arbuckle's skin crawl. He had read about the havoc wreaked by magic in battles, but the most extravagant description of destruction paled beside first-hand observation. All the blademasters in the palace couldn't protect against something like that. *Thank the gods that Archmage Duveau is on my side.* "Lead on."

The long, dimly lit stair led to a dungeon worthy of nightmares. The thick air reeked of refuse and excrement. As Arbuckle followed the knights down a corridor, he spied within several of the barred cells forlorn figures huddled upon straw-strewn floors without so much as a blanket for comfort. His gut roiled. He understood that the empire had enemies, and that those arrested for crimes must be punished, but such squalor was inhuman.

They turned a corner. A crowd of knights and squires stood before a doorway, facing a line of imperial guards who blocked the entrance. Though the heavy double doors were open, Arbuckle couldn't see through the mass of people to the room beyond.

"Milord Prince." Sir Fineal held up a forestalling hand. "I must warn you that the scene is...not pleasant to view. The...interrogation chamber is a grim sight."

"Very well. I've been warned." Arbuckle clenched his jaw, resolving to be stoic, though the sickly scent of blood now permeated the air as well. "Proceed."

"Yes, Milord Prince." The smell grew stronger as they approached the line of imperial guards.

One turned to call into the room. "Commander!"

The knights and squires moved aside, but the imperial guards held their ground.

"Move aside for your lord prince," Fineal said.

Arbuckle peered past the guards, the light of a dozen torches gleaming on the burnished metal racks, spikes, chains, and other implements that furnished the room. "Good Gods of Light!"

"Sir Fineal, I told you that—" Commander Ithross stopped as he caught sight of Arbuckle, and his eyebrows shot up, then he bowed low. "Milord Prince! I didn't expect you to come down here."

"Sir Fineal has told me that my father is dead, Commander. I *must* see him." The guards stepped aside at Ithross' wave. Arbuckle entered, looked with revulsion at the burnished machines of torture, then turned his gaze to the imperial guard commander. "What is this place?"

Ithross swallowed forcefully. "The emperor called this his interrogation chamber, milord."

"You mean *torture* chamber, don't you?"

Ithross lifted his chin and gazed steadily back at the prince. "His Majesty always referred to it as the interrogation chamber, milord."

"And who conducted the interrogations?" Arbuckle forced the words out, afraid that he already knew the answer.

"I don't know for certain, Milord Prince, but it's rumored among the guards and knights that…" Ithross glanced questioningly at Sir Fineal and received a nod of acknowledgement in return. "…that the emperor took a…special interest in the practice."

Arbuckle felt ill. He'd known for years that his father was a heartless tyrant. That Emperor Tynean Tsing had actually participated in the torture of prisoners, however, turned his stomach. Arbuckle fought to maintain his composure, speaking through clenched teeth.

"Show me my father, Commander."

"Yes, milord." Ithross led them around the room's thick central pillar, and a cordon of guards parted.

Blood... It was everywhere, the scent so thick that he could taste it. Arbuckle stopped at the shore of a congealing crimson lake strewn with carnage. He had watched the blademasters spar many times, always amazed at their skill and stamina. Trained to be the best, inured to pain, blessed by their god, and pledged to defend their charges or die. These five had died.

"Good gods..."

A figure to his left stood from a crouch—Master Corvecosi, the imperial healer—and Arbuckle saw rich blue robes at the man's feet. He knew instantly who lay there.

Father... Arbuckle skirted the thick pool of blood, compelled by an unnerving yet unrelenting need to see this man whom he had *thought* he knew. Closer, he couldn't avoid the blood, and his shoes squelched in the spattered gore underfoot.

The healer stepped aside, bowing low. "Milord Prince."

"What are you doing here, Master Corvecosi?" Arbuckle couldn't take his eyes from his father's body, the bony hand clutching the dagger that had been thrust up beneath his chin into his brain. He tried to feel pity or sorrow, but all he could think was that the old man's cold eyes would never again stare disdainfully, his lips wouldn't twist into a sneer, his harsh voice wouldn't chide and berate, the hands would never again torture... He realized with a start that Corvecosi was speaking.

"...summoned to examine the scene and lend my expertise, perhaps to determine exactly what occurred here."

"What have you determined so far?"

"I can unequivocally say that your father did not, as it may appear, take his own life. His hand gripping the dagger was very nearly crushed. Something very strong grasped His Majesty's hand and thrust the blade that ended his life."

"I see."

"I have just begun examining the scene, Milord Prince, but I have already noted a few peculiarities."

"More peculiar than five dead blademasters?" Arbuckle stared at the carnage again. "How many assassins does it take to kill *five* blademasters?"

Ithross mistook the rhetorical question for an inquiry. "Milord Prince, we've been told that there were two assassins."

"Two?" Arbuckle couldn't imagine anyone capable of such a feat. "How in the Nine Hells could two assassins overcome five blademasters?"

"We don't know, milord. The only person who saw the fight has...vanished."

Arbuckle stared at Ithross. "*Vanished*? What do you mean? Who saw this happen?"

"Master Hoseph was apparently here when the attack started. He escaped to summon help, though he bore injuries of his own. I was about to question him further, with Archmage Duveau's aid, when he..."— Ithross looked uncomfortable—"vanished."

"Vanished. You mean he actually, *magically* vanished? I thought the palace was warded to prevent that."

"According to Archmage Duveau, the dungeons are not included in the wards."

"Why not?"

"We don't know, Milord Prince."

Arbuckle shook his head in stunned silence. *Mysterious assassins, dead blademasters, vanishing priests...what next?* "What else is peculiar, Master Corvecosi?"

The dark man gestured to the blood pooled beneath the hanging cage. "I at first assumed that this blood was from the emperor, being so close to his body. Upon closer examination, however, it appears that someone was recently restrained in this device." He touched one of the gruesome screws. "This blood is fresh, yet there is no corpse here bearing wounds so inflicted."

"A rescue?" Arbuckle's mind whirled. "What prisoner would precipitate such a rescue?"

The healer shrugged. "That is an interesting theory." He strode to one of the corpses, apparently unfazed by all the blood. "And here, this man, unlike all the others, has barely a mark on him." Kneeling, he pressed a plump hand to the blademaster's brow and muttered under his breath. "Yes, as I suspected, he was killed with a lethal toxin."

"Toxin?" Arbuckle knew from his reading that poisoned weapons were commonly used in some cultures. "You're sure?"

"I'm quite sure, milord." He rose and nodded his head absently. "Quite sure."

Arbuckle had no reason to doubt him. He had always liked Corvecosi, one of the few imperial attendants not stifled by formality or unduly cowed by the late emperor's imperious attitude. As a boy, the prince had appreciated the man's quiet bedside manner, his cool hand on a fevered forehead, gentle words, and the sense of peace that followed his visits. Evidently, there was more to the healer's art than mere knowledge of illness.

"Continue your examinations, Master Corvecosi. I want to know how everyone here died. Use whatever resources you—" Turning, ready to be away from all this death, he spied one more victim, and choked on his words.

What lay on the stone slab didn't look human—at least, not anymore. Arbuckle stared at the corpse, willing himself to believe that the person had been dead when the skin had been peeled away in strips, the joints twisted, the bones exposed, the pearly nerves bared by careful dissection. But deep in his soul, he knew that she had been alive. This was his father's depravity flayed and displayed for all to see.

"Good Gods of Light..." Arbuckle strode to the side of the table, heedless for the first time of the blood. There however, with the scent of death in his nostrils, staring down at her tortured body, bile burned the back of his throat. "Oh..." Arbuckle turned away and fell to his knees, heaving painfully, as if expelling any hope that his father had been a decent man. A hand touched his shoulder.

"Milord Prince, you must go." Ithross waved, and blademasters came forward.

"No!" Arbuckle wished with all his might that he could retreat to his room and his books—his sanctuary—but he had already disgraced himself enough. This was the emperor's doing. Only a son could atone for a father's sins.

Wiping his chin with his sleeve, Arbuckle lurched up to stand over the slab where the poor woman lay. *Had she been beautiful? Had someone loved her? Were they waiting for her to come home?* He welcomed the rage that burned away the last thread of feeling that he had for his father. It straightened his back and stiffened his resolve.

"Your cloak, Sir Fineal." Arbuckle held out a hand, and the

knight immediately unclasped his cloak and handed it over. The crown prince carefully draped the deep-blue cloth over the woman's mutilated corpse. Bowing his head, he mumbled a prayer that the gods would ease her tortured soul. "Master Corvecosi, take care of her."

Master Corvecosi bowed. "As you wish, Milord Prince. I'll also see that your father's body is properly attend—"

"No!" Arbuckle glared one last time at the heap of dead flesh that had been his father, then looked deliberately away. "Divest him of any accoutrements of his former office, then burn his corpse and cast the ashes down the nearest cesspit!"

The crowd shifted and Corvecosi seemed struck dumb, standing with his mouth gaping. Only Ithross summoned the courage to speak.

"Milord Prince!" the commander stammered. "To disrespect His Majesty's body would be...tantamount to treason."

"No, Commander Ithross, *that* is treason!" Arbuckle pointed to the shrouded form on the slab, his hand shaking with rage. "That is an *abomination!*"

"But, Milord Prince! The nobles... They will expect a royal funeral."

"Then we'll bury an empty casket! I'll not have the House of Tsing or the soil of this empire further contaminated by his corpse."

"Milord Prince, your father was—"

"My father was a living piece of *shit*, Sir Fineal!" Arbuckle rounded on the knight, biting back his rage, though he could not suppress his disgust. "It's only fitting that he spend eternity amongst his peers."

Ignoring the shocked murmurs, Prince Arbuckle headed for the door. A last thought stopped him in his tracks, and he turned back.

"After Master Corvecosi's investigation is complete and the bodies have been removed with all due reverence, send for me. I'll see every vile machine in this room destroyed and the door sealed forever. Is that clear, Commander Ithross? Sir Fineal?"

"Crystal clear, Milord Prince." Fineal bowed low, then rose with a grim smile on his chiseled features. "It will be my pleasure."

Ithross glanced about the room in disgust and nodded. "It will be done as you command, Milord Prince."

"Good." Arbuckle turned and strode from the room. Blademasters took position around him, forming a five-pointed cordon as they matched his stride. *Five blademasters—the emperor's contingent.*

I'm going to be emperor. The thought was nothing new, but had always been suffixed by "someday." Now the inevitability of his future came rushing in, and with it, one more dreadful realization. *I'm not ready for this!*

Ready or not, he had no choice in the matter. As he mounted the stairs, Arbuckle swore to all the Gods of Light that he would be a better emperor than Tsing's last.

Mya toweled her hair dry, barely able to keep her arms aloft, so weak was she from the evening's trials. She cast the towel aside in frustration, and sat on the bed.

"Quit bitching, Mya. You're alive." Few people could survive being stabbed in the gut—*Twice!*—nearly eviscerated, and hacked from shoulder to chest. Blood loss had left her weak, but her runic tattoos had healed her wounds. Only an injury to the heart or decapitation could truly end her life. Her heart ached, but not from a sword thrust. "Alive…and alone."

Forcing herself up, she grabbed her wrappings, the long strip of enchanted black cloth that she wore under her clothes. She used them to hide her tattoos, her secret, but the magically self-repairing cloth had saved her life only hours ago, holding her chest together long enough for her to heal before she bled to death. She submerged them in the murky water filling the tub, and began to scrub.

It had cost her a silver half-crown to convince the proprietor of *The Prickly Pair* to send up a tub and a meal at this late hour. The water and the food had been tepid, but plentiful. She was still a little light-headed; it would take time to recover from the blood loss. The memories of the fight, she was sure, would take much longer to banish.

Sitting back on her heels, she focused on a pleasanter memory…kissing Lad in the carriage. Mya closed her eyes as she

20

remembered the warmth of his lips, the scent of him. A little smile twitched her lips, then fell. He had kissed her back, just a little, but it was a kiss goodbye. Lad was out of Tsing by now, and out of the guild, headed back to Twailin and his family. She doubted that she would ever see him again. Her heart ached anew.

Don't, Mya! Love was a weakness, and weakness would only get her killed.

Pulling the wrappings from the tub, she wrung them out and draped them on the back of a chair to dry. Better to focus on their other kiss, on Lad's betrayal. Her cheeks flushed as she remembered how he'd tricked her, letting her think that he shared her feelings, then slipping the Grandmaster's ring on her finger.

Mya held up her hand and examined the ring: obsidian dark against her pale skin, filigreed gold bright in the lamplight. It was beautiful, she had to admit. More distinctive than the band of unadorned obsidian that she had worn as Master Hunter, and more ornate than the black-and-gold ring that Lad had worn as Twailin Guildmaster. There were six guildmaster's rings scattered across the empire. *This* ring was unique. There was only one Grandmaster of Assassins.

And that's me. With a scoffing laugh, she leaned wearily against the tub and closed her eyes.

"Godsdamned Grandmaster… Lad's crazy if he thinks I can do this." She tried to be angry with him, but knew she couldn't lay all the blame at his door. She'd chased power her whole life. To a frightened girl on her own, joining the Assassins Guild made sense. Strength, skill, and power meant safety. She had been ambitious and ruthless, prepared to sacrifice whoever got in her way.

Until I met Lad.

"You're the perfect Grandmaster", he had told her. Mya didn't believe it for a second. "You think like an assassin, but you have a good heart." Lad was naïve. That was one reason she'd fallen in love with him.

"He has no idea what's in my heart." Mya heaved to her feet. Catching sight of herself in the mirror, she stopped and stared. Her dark tattoos writhed in the lamplight, a tapestry of magic engraved on her flesh from neck to wrist to ankles. They'd kept her alive tonight. Imbuing her with strength and speed, sharpening her senses, and healing grievous wounds, they made her nearly invincible. They also made her a monster.

"No wonder Lad sent you packing."

Stop it! If Mya expected to survive, she had to forget about her unrequited feelings for Lad and do what she did best.

"Think like an assassin, Mya." Whirling away from the mirror, she went to her trunk and rifled through the contents, drawing out a comfortable silk shirt, a pair of supple trousers, and clean scanties. She considered her situation while she dressed.

Lad had killed Emperor Tynean Tsing II. She had no doubt that a massive manhunt for the emperor's killers would ensue, that descriptions of her and Lad were being distributed to the city guard. Of course, that led to her next problem.

The emperor of Tsing had also been the Grandmaster of the Assassins Guild. In helping Lad to kill the Grandmaster, she had cut the head off a very large snake. Now *she* was the head of the snake, the master of a guild that didn't even know she existed. Could she control it, or would it turn its fangs on her? That would most likely depend on one person.

Lady T…

The Tsing guildmaster had not been overly impressed with either Lad or Mya, but the woman had seemed frightened when she escorted them to their meeting in the palace dungeons, giving Mya the distinct feeling that Lady T feared the Grandmaster. Not surprising, considering what a monster the man had been. So, would the lady welcome Mya as a liberator or revile her for a usurper?

Mya began to pace, and to think. Everything depended on how Lady T reacted. The assassins of the Tsing guild would follow her lead, and Mya had no doubt that the provincial guilds would fall in line behind the Tsing guild, the strongest of them all.

And if she doesn't accept me?

Bound by blood contracts signed when they joined the guild, no guild assassin could even attempt to harm the wearer of the Grandmaster's ring. Nothing, however, prevented them from hiring someone outside the guild to kill her. A chill ran up Mya's spine as she realized that the guild wouldn't have to hire an outsider to kill her.

"Hoseph…" Glancing around the room as if just saying his

name might summon the priest, Mya swallowed hard.

Hoseph had called himself the Right Hand of Death for two very good reasons. The priest had been the Grandmaster's intermediary with the guildmasters, able to travel vast distances in an instant. He had also been the Grandmaster's personal executioner, able to kill with a single touch of magic. Mya had her own experience with his less lethal magic, the pulse of darkness that had filled her with utter despair, incapacitating her with every dark act and thought of her life. Mya's past was full of darkness. If not for Lad, she would have died without raising a finger to defend herself, so overwhelmed had she been by Hoseph's spell.

Admittedly, such skills would be invaluable to her as Grandmaster.

If I could control him…

But how would Hoseph regard her unseemly ascendance? After serving an Imperial Grandmaster, would he submit to her authority? *Not likely.* Even if he did agree to serve her, could she ever trust him? Hoseph wasn't a member of the guild. He could kill her, and probably would try if for no other reason than revenge. Until she knew for sure, she would assume the worst. Hoseph had no way to know she wore the Grandmaster's ring, but he'd find out soon enough.

Then he'll try to kill me.

"He can't know where I am," she murmured as her eyes flicked to the shadowy corners of the room.

Neither she nor Lad had detected anyone following them, but this was a person who could materialize out of thin air. Underestimating Hoseph could prove lethal. She glanced at the band on her finger. Could he somehow track the ring itself? Obsidian and gold danced in the lamplight as panic trembled her. She shoved it aside. Exhausted and blood-weary, her fears were easily roused. She needed sleep, but sleeping rendered her vulnerable.

"What I need is someone to watch over me…someone I can trust." Unfortunately, the only person she trusted had just ridden out of Tsing in a carriage bound for Twailin.

Mya stopped pacing and dug her two favorite daggers out of her clothes trunk. She scraped one of the blades along her arm, pleased to see tiny hairs fall to the floor. They were clean and sharp. If Hoseph popped in, she should be quick enough to gut him. *If I'm not asleep.*

"Sleep lightly, Mya, or wake up dead." She blew out the lamp, backed into a corner, and slid down the wall, her daggers ready.

Feeling slightly safer in the dark, her nervous energy waned even as her doubts waxed. Was this to be how she spent the rest of her life, hiding in the dark, afraid of death hidden in every shadow? What choice did she have?

"Have someone cut it off." Lad's simplistic solution came to her, and she seriously considered the option.

Mya raised one of her daggers and placed the edge at the joint of the finger that wore the ring. She drew the razor edge across her flesh, and blood welled from the tiny cut. *No pain...* She tried to apply pressure, but her hand wouldn't respond. She couldn't do it herself. The ring's magic wouldn't allow her to take it off or even cut it free. She wiped the blade on her trousers and sucked the blood from the already healed cut.

"That doesn't mean I can't walk down to the kitchen in the morning and pay the cook to do it." The simple solution steadied her. She had an out. She could, quite literally, cut and run.

Mya had a choice to make: flee, take control of the guild, or destroy it. It was that simple. Regardless of her final choice, however, she had to survive until morning. Cold resolve steeled her fear, and she realized that Lady T, Hoseph, and the guild also had a choice to make.

"Join me or die."

CHAPTER II

Hoseph woke to darkness and the dry, musty scent of parchment and leather. His back ached and he was chilled from sleeping on the stone floor with only a threadbare blanket, but he took no heed. Demia's chosen cared not for luxuries. What he coveted were life's intangibles: power and influence, order and control.

Despite the utter darkness, he knew innately that it was morning and time to rise. Calling on Demia's gifts, a pale glow emanated from his palm. He rose, stepped to the table and struck a match, lighting the lamp there and illuminating his surroundings. The room was not large, and bookcases packed with old leather-bound volumes and racks of scrolls made it seem even smaller. The history of the Assassins Guild was recorded here, unnumbered years of murder and conspiracy. This was also the repository of the blood contracts. Every assassin signed one, binding themselves forever to the guild, submitting to their masters' control, signing their lives over to be spent if necessary. This secret room—with the death of the Grandmaster, known only to Hoseph—represented the power and influence that he wielded as the Right Hand of Death...power and influence that had been disrupted by Lad and Mya. Anger and frustration tensed his muscles and clouded his thoughts.

"Blessed shadow of death, sooth me..." Hoseph recited the mantra until his pulse slowed and his mind eased. Dealing with death every day had taught him temperance. Hoseph hated being forced into hasty action as he had last night. The threat of questioning under compulsion had forced his flight, rendering him guilty in the eyes of the imperial guard. He'd fled a second time an hour later when he heard soldiers approaching his room in Demia's temple where he had been gathering his meager belongings.

What he needed now was a concise plan of action. The first step, of course, was to change his appearance, for he had little doubt the city guard would be looking for him. Of course, a disguise wouldn't fool his fellow priests and priestesses. They knew his soul. Demia, sorter of souls, gifted all her clergy with the ability to see the peculiar ethereal essence that made each person unique. This talent—useful when comforting the dying during their transition to the afterlife—made disguises superfluous. He would not be able to go back to his own temple until his name was cleared.

Doffing his distinctive crimson robe, Hoseph spread it on the floor. Then he selected a gleaming razor from his bundle of personal items, and stropped it to a fine edge. It had been decades since he had performed the ablutions of an acolyte, but old habits returned easily. Kneeling on the robe, he deftly shaved his head, letting the shorn hair fall. Unfortunately, he lacked water, resulting in a few nicks and cuts. He would have to stock the room with some essentials until he resolved this situation. When that was done, he shaved his face.

Hoseph bundled the robe to contain the hair and gazed down at his bare chest. He ran his fingers over the unblemished skin that last night had been split by Mya's dagger. Duveau's fleshforge had healed him completely, but there were scars that no spell could heal. An unfamiliar frisson of fear shook him. Not of death, his long-time acquaintance and ally, but of failure.

I won't fail, he insisted. *I've worked too hard, accomplished too much…*

From the bag of possessions he had managed to escape with, he withdrew his old acolyte's robes. The coarse gray wool scratched his skin, so unlike the smooth felt of his high-priest's robe, but it didn't matter. Anonymity was more important than comfort. Flipping the tiny silver skull into his hand, Hoseph invoked Demia's grace, and the room melted into mist.

Moments later, he materialized in a luxurious sitting room. The golden morning light glowed through sheer curtains. It was still early. Lady T was not present, but he hadn't expected her to be up at this hour. Nobles were notoriously late risers. Usually when he visited, he pulled the bell rope and waited until a servant arrived to summon the lady of the house. They were used to his comings and goings. Today he was in no mood to wait. He knew that she would still be abed, so he simply knocked on the door that he assumed led to her bedroom. He'd never seen inside the room, so couldn't use Demia's gift to travel there. Doing so would have been dangerous anyway; assassins tended to be jumpy.

The door to his left opened suddenly, and Hoseph found himself staring down the shaft of a crossbow bolt aimed at his heart. Lady T stood behind that crossbow, her fingers on the trigger and her hair disheveled from sleep. She wore only a silk nightshift, confirming his supposition that she'd still been in bed, but her eyes shone as sharp as the tip of the crossbow bolt that could end his life with the twitch of her finger.

"Put that down, Tara. We've got trouble."

"Hoseph?" Her eyes widened, and her fingers lifted off the weapon's trigger, though it didn't point away from his heart. "I hardly recognized you! What the hell are you doing here? What's wrong?"

Hoseph saw no reason to beat around the bush. "The Grandmaster is dead."

"*What*? How?" She lowered the weapon, the surprise on her face undeniably genuine.

"The Twailin guildmaster and his Master Hunter." Hoseph still didn't know exactly how they'd managed it, but the who certainly grabbed the guildmaster's attention.

"Gods of Light and Darkness..." She whirled through the door without another word.

Hoseph pursed his lips in mild irritation and followed her through a lavish dressing room and into an even more extravagant bedchamber. The bedroom was dim, the heavy curtains still drawn, and Hoseph paused to allow his eyes to adjust. The crossbow thumped down upon the expansive four post bed, and Lady T reached for a robe. With three steps, the priest reached the nearest window and pulled open the curtain. He turned to the glaring guildmaster as she tied the robe tight around her waist.

"But the emperor's blademasters—"

"Also dead."

"*Five* blademasters?" Lady T's brow furrowed as if she didn't believe him. "I knew that Lad was a weapon, but..."

"Mya also possesses some impressive skills. She's more than we thought." *More than I thought*, he admitted to himself.

"But to kill the Grandmaster...it's unbelievable. They had blood contracts! They wore *rings*!"

"Lad never signed a blood contract. It was the Grandmaster's plan to force him to sign one at this meeting. He did, however, wear the guildmaster's ring." Hoseph nodded solemnly. "I don't know how they managed to circumvent the magic of their rings, but the Grandmaster *is* dead. I saw his body."

Lady T's eyes narrowed as she gazed at the priest. "And where were you when this happened?"

Hoseph waved an impatient hand. "I tried to intervene and was sorely wounded. I went to summon the Imperial Guard."

"And you couldn't," she wiggled her fingers in the air, "magic him out of harm's way?"

Hoseph breathed deep—*Blessed shadow of death...*—before answering. His conscience had pummeled him with this question all night. He didn't need her to remind him that he had failed to save his master. "As you said, they wore their guild rings. There was no reason to think that they could lay a hand on the Grandmaster."

Lady T frowned, twisting the ties of her robe in thought. "So what are we going to do? The Grandmaster held the reins of the empire. Now those reins are cut. We've lost our political influence, our future."

"Not so." Hoseph had already thought this through. "There's no reason why we can't gain back everything we've lost. Crown Prince Arbuckle put off marrying only to spite his father, but now he'll *have* to produce an heir; the nobility will insist."

"We don't *know* what Arbuckle will do once he's crowned emperor."

"He's a weak-willed fool, Tara." Hoseph's lip curled in derision. "He's more interested in his books than in ruling. Have you ever known him to take a vested interest in governing this empire or interacting with the nobility?"

"He hasn't taken part because he hasn't been allowed to. We don't know what he'll do."

"I disagree. Arbuckle has done exactly as he's been told for his entire life. If he's told that the people with experience governing this empire are willing to take the reins for him, that he need do nothing but read his books and produce an heir, he'll do as he's told. If he needs additional incentive, we still have the provincial dukes under our thumb. They'll do our bidding, or suffer."

"*Our* bidding?" She cocked an eyebrow at him. "You forget that you're not in the chain of command, Hoseph. You were the Grandmaster's intermediary, not his second in command."

Blessed shadows of death, sooth me. As much as it chafed him, his position *had* changed; he would have to cajole and compromise to get his way. But in the end, it would all work out. Hoseph bowed his head to Lady T in silent acknowledgement.

"Once we have an heir, Arbuckle will be eliminated, and we'll ensure that the child receives the proper upbringing and training. It worked once, it will work again."

"And who will be Grandmaster in the interim?" She narrowed her eyes at him. "I sincerely hope that you don't think it will be you."

So that's what she's worried about. He smiled in contrition. "Don't be ridiculous, Tara. I'm no assassin. My place is in the shadow of power, offering guidance. I consider *you* the obvious choice, of course."

A wry smile spread across the lady's lips. "Until the royal heir is trained up, then you kill me to give *him* the ring. I'll certainly serve as interim Grandmaster, but I'll not wear the ring, except on a chain around my neck."

"That would suffice. By the time the child is grown, you'll have a duchy and be the Emperor's closest confidant, if we play our cards right." The priest rose and gave her a significant look. "But first we have to find and execute these two rebels. They took the Grandmaster's ring."

"They'd have been fools not to. But that raises a new problem. One of them has undoubtedly put the ring on. No assassin can touch the wearer."

"I can." Hoseph lifted a hand, the pearly glow of Demia's death magic radiating from his palm. "You find them, and I'll kill them. But be wary. For the attack to succeed, it must be a complete surprise."

"Of *course* it does!" She glowered at him. "Don't deign to teach me my business, Hoseph!"

"You haven't seen them *fight*, Tara." There it was again, that trill of fear up his spine. *Failure*...

"Some of my people encountered them night before last. I'm aware of their prowess." Her glare remained undiminished.

"Very well." He nodded respectfully. "Find Lad and Mya. They can't have gone far or fast. They took an injured prisoner with them."

"A prisoner? Who?"

"The captain of the Twailin Royal Guard." Hoseph quickly explained the sequence of events that had brought Norwood to Tsing, including Lad's association with the man while searching for his wife's killer. "Find the traitors. I'll inform the provincial guildmasters of the Grandmaster's death and our plan to pressure the provincial dukes to manipulate Arbuckle."

"Can I ask you a question before you flitter away?"

"Of course."

"Why the disguise?"

"I was...implicated in the emperor's death. They were going to question me under magical compulsion, which would risk exposure of the guild. I couldn't let that happen, so I fled. I'm sure they took that as evidence of guilt, and that the entire constabulary is searching for me."

Lady T cocked her head and scrutinized him, a lopsided smile on her lips. "I can arrange a better disguise for you."

Hoseph stiffened as he drew the hood of the acolyte's robe over his head. "Though I must forego my high priest's robes for the immediate future, I would not insult my goddess by disavowing my allegiance altogether." He looked deliberately around the room, committing the space to memory. If their relationship didn't work out, he might have to pop in someday...or night. "I'll be in touch."

Clasping the silver skull hidden in the sleeve of his robe, Hoseph called on Demia's power, and the room melted into shadow around him.

Arbuckle wasn't sure which ached more: his hands or his eyes.

He flexed his fingers, wincing at the blisters on his palms. He had wielded an axe for more than an hour, along with several knights and squires, demolishing the vile instruments of torture in his father's interrogation chamber. Afterward, he had watched with grim satisfaction as the doors were sealed and the keys destroyed. There would be no torture during the reign of Tynean Tsing III.

Except for paperwork, he lamented as he gazed at the parchments strewn across his desk. Ignorant of the intricacies of the running of the empire, Arbuckle had insisted he be brought up to speed. Most details were handled by functionaries, but he had to know how things worked. He'd been studying since he had woken after too few hours of sleep, and his eyes were bleary. A knock at the door startled him to attention.

Tennison, his father's secretary—*my secretary now*—his ever-present ledger and pen at the ready, hurried over and answered it. "The crown prince is busy. I can fit you in…well, not until after he lunches."

Arbuckle leapt at the chance to escape the paperwork. "Tennison, who is it?"

The secretary stepped back into the room, his sharp features pinched and his eyes wide. "Milord Prince, it's Captain Otar of the Imperial Guard, and Master Corvecosi. I told them—"

"Relax, Tennison. I'd like very much to speak with them."

"Very well, milord."

Arbuckle gestured to the seats opposite the desk as his visitors entered. "Gentlemen, come in please. Would you like some blackbrew?" Servants hurried forward.

"No, thank you, Milord Prince." Captain Otar bowed stiffly and stood at attention, declining to sit.

Corvecosi looked longingly at the silver tray laden with cups and a steaming pot, seemingly fought a private battle of propriety versus need, and acquiesced. "Thank you, milord." He sank into the chair and sipped the dark brew, sighing in bliss. The man looked exhausted.

"I daresay we've all spent a sleepless night." Arbuckle waved for another cup himself, though his head was pounding already with it. "Captain, you first."

Otar remained at attention, his gaze fixed over Arbuckle's head.

"I apologize for not being here last night, Milord Prince. I was out of the palace on personal business and didn't hear of your father's death until I returned. You have my condolences."

"You can't be everywhere at once, Captain, and Commander Ithross did very well." He sipped blackbrew and put down his cup. "Thank you for your condolences, but I'll not grieve my father's passing after finding out what a vile creature he truly was."

The captain stiffened, but didn't reply.

Arbuckle wondered how much Otar knew about the emperor he had pledged his life to serve and protect. Was his discomfort umbrage, or was it unease with the secret he'd kept for so long? "What progress have you made in your investigation?"

Otar clenched his chiseled jaw. "Not much, milord. We have no identification of the woman found in the interrogation chamber. There's no record of her arrest or how she came to be in the palace dungeons."

"That's rather strange, don't you think?"

"Indeed, milord. According to the guards, no one but the jailor, His Majesty, and his blademasters have entered the dungeons in weeks."

"Archmage Duveau contends that the dungeons are not warded against magical intrusion. Do you think she may have been brought in by magical means?"

"It's possible, milord." Otar shrugged. "You would have to ask the archmage about that."

"And we have no theories why my father tortured the woman?"

"The emperor conducted many *interrogations*, Milord Prince. She may have been a spy. I would not deign to question the actions he took for the sake of the empire."

"Yes, few would have confronted my father on *any* matter." One incongruent fact suddenly struck him. "You said that only the jailor, emperor, and blademasters have entered the dungeons in weeks, but Hoseph was there when the emperor was attacked, *inside* the dungeon."

"I understand from Ithross' report, milord, that High Priest Hoseph disappeared from the dungeon to evade questioning. They assumed he used some kind of spell."

"Invocation," Corvecosi said with a mild smile. "Priests employ

32

invocations, not spells."

The muscles at Otar's jaw bunched and relaxed. "Perhaps he entered using the same *invocation*."

"And maybe he brought the woman in with him," Arbuckle mused. "His disappearance certainly makes him appear guilty of *something*."

"I regret to inform you that he is still missing. His rooms at the temple were searched, and a guard was stationed there in case he returns."

"Anything else, Captain?"

"There are some...irregularities in the palace visitors' log for yesterday." Otar's eyes flicked to Arbuckle's for a moment before reassuming their distant gaze. "A Captain Norwood of the Twailin Royal Guard, along with his sergeant, were granted an audience with His Majesty, but there's no record of either of them leaving. The carriage they arrived in is still in the stables."

"I remember them." Arbuckle frowned. "The captain wanted to see my father about a matter of security, and insisted that they be alone. I guess they were right about the danger. Or...maybe they were the assassins. Have you tried to find them?"

"Of course, Milord!" Otar sounded put out. "We've searched the palace, and I alerted Chief Constable Dreyfus to seek them. We're also watching all the city gates for them, as well as your father's assassins from the descriptions provided by High Priest Hoseph."

Arbuckle cock an eyebrow. "The descriptions he provided right before he vanished into thin air? Do you think we can trust that?"

"They are suspect, but it's all we have to go on."

Arbuckle sighed. *So many questions and so few answers.* "Very well, Captain. Master Corvecosi, you mentioned some peculiarities at the scene. Anything new?"

Corvecosi nodded. "Several things, Milord Prince. The first is that the unfortunate woman—she was young, by the way—died not from her wounds, nor by being eased into the afterlife, as Master Hoseph said."

"How did she die then?"

"Poison. The same poison that killed the blademaster I showed you."

"So…" Arbuckle tried to make sense of what the healer was saying, "…the same assassins who apparently killed the blademasters and the emperor, also killed the woman he was torturing?"

"So it would seem, Milord Prince." Corvecosi sighed and rubbed his eyes. "There were some other clues, milord, that suggest the prowess of the assassins." The healer pulled from his pocket a slender metal spike. "This was completely embedded in a blademaster's skull."

"What is that?" Arbuckle peered at the four-inch steel spike.

"An implement of torture, milord. We found others scattered about, and one in the thigh bone of the woman."

"Gods…" Arbuckle's stomach roiled.

"This one was thrown or magically propelled with extreme force. Inhuman force, one might say."

"Inhuman? How?"

"Magically enhanced strength is not unheard of, milord." Corvecosi gestured to Arbuckle's blademasters. "Your own bodyguards are blessed with it by their deity. These assassins must have had *some* kind of magic to accomplish such feats."

Arbuckle leaned back in his chair and blew out a frustrated breath. "So, these unknown assassins have not only the ability to appear and disappear, but also inhuman strength. What next?"

"Aside from those in the…" Corvecosi glanced at Captain Otar, "interrogation chamber, four other bodies were found elsewhere in the dungeon."

Arbuckle sat up straight, his eyes snapping to Otar's. "What? Who else was killed?"

"Your pardon for not mentioning it earlier, Milord Prince," Captain Otar said with a bow. "They were just prisoners, by the look of them, though they wore simple smocks rather than prisoners' attire. They were found in a small room at the far end of the dungeon, behind a locked door. The room was outfitted as a dining chamber, but there was no food to be found, and the men appeared to have been ill-fed for some time."

"How did they die? Master Corvecosi?"

Corvecosi shrugged. "I don't know. They bore no wounds, and they weren't poisoned. The remaining prisoners are alive, but in ill health, malnourished and infested with various forms of vermin."

Arbuckle clenched his jaw, recalling the poor wretches he'd seen. "Please see that they're cared for. And I want every square inch of that filthy place cleaned."

The healer nodded. "I took it upon myself to assign that task to my apprentices."

"What about the jailor? Isn't that his job?" His attention shifted back to Otar. "Has he been questioned about all this?"

The captain looked stricken, stammering out his reply. "Not yet, milord. We found him out cold in an unlocked cell, drunk. And not for the first time, if the pile of empty bottles is any indication. We'll question him as soon as he is capable of answering."

Arbuckle wondered at captain's agitated reply, then recognized the man's fear. Under Tynean Tsing II, he would have been punished for failing to have all the answers. *I'm not like my father!* "My apologies, Captain. Do carry on, and keep me informed."

"Of course, Milord Prince."

"Master Corvecosi, thank you for your insights."

"It's my pleasure to serve you, milord." The healer stood, then nodded to the prince's hands. "Would you like me to heal your blisters before I go?"

Arbuckle shook his head. "Thank you, but I'll keep the reminder of a deed well done for a while longer." Arbuckle flexed his hands, remembering the satisfying crash of the torture devices shattering under his blows. *My father's legacy...*

A smile flashed across Corvecosi's lips before the two men bowed, then left.

Arbuckle flexed his hands again. "So, Tennison..."

"Yes, Milord Prince!" The secretary hurried to the prince's side, his ledger already open and his pen poised above the page.

"Relax, Tennison. It's nothing urgent. I only wanted to ask your opinion."

"My...*what?*" The secretary looked startled.

"Your *opinion.*" Arbuckle had always considered Tennison an pretentious prig, but now the truth shone clear in his pinched face. *He's frightened. This is my father's true legacy—fear.* "I must announce my father's death, but I'm wondering how to do it. I'll draft an announcement to be sent to the nobles, of course, but simply posting a notice to inform the commoners seems...insufficient."

"It is dire news. They will be…devastated."

"*Devastated?*" Arbuckle fixed Tennison with an incredulous stare. "Is that *really* what you think the common folk of this city will feel at the news?"

"I…" Tennison swallowed with effort.

"Tennison, *relax!*" Arbuckle stood, but the man remained rigid with terror, obviously unconvinced that he wasn't being lured into a trap. *Time to change that.* "You needn't be afraid of me. I'm *not* my father! I need you, above anyone else, to tell me the *truth.*"

"I…" The man blinked and swallowed. "I will, milord."

"Good. Now, tell me how I inform the commoners of the emperor's death. They deserve something more than a mere statement. An apology, an explanation…something."

A boyhood memory flashed in his mind, the face of a pretty young girl, the daughter of the chambermaid who had cleaned his room since he was a babe. The girl had accompanied her mother to work one day, and a young Prince Arbuckle had been delighted to meet another child. His father had nipped the friendship in the bud, lecturing his son on the impropriety of nobility mingling with commoners. "Subjects are to be subjugated, not befriended!" Arbuckle never saw the girl again, and a new chambermaid cleaned his room the next day. He wondered where the girl and her mother had disappeared to, and tried not to picture the poor tortured woman in the dungeon.

"They deserve more." Arbuckle began to pace. "They've been through hell at my father's hand, and need to know they can expect better from me."

"So…tell them that, milord."

Tennison's simple solution struck Arbuckle like a thunderbolt. "Of course!" He flicked an impatient hand at the secretary's leger. "I'll personally announce the emperor's death! We need someplace public, and large enough to accommodate many!"

The secretary's brows arched in surprise, his feather quill quivering over the leger. "Milord, I didn't mean—"

"No, it's *perfect!*" Arbuckle warmed to the proposal. "Draft posters to be distributed throughout the city immediately. I will appear at the Imperial Plaza this afternoon to make an important announcement. See to the details for transportation and security."

"Yes, Milord Prince." Tennison still looked horrified, but there was something else there, too.

Hope? Arbuckle wondered. The thought brought a smile. *Yes...that's what the commoners need. They need hope.*

CHAPTER III

At the chime of the doorbell, Dee dropped his polishing rag. With Lad off to Tsing, there wasn't much for him to do. The continuing investigation into the murder of Lad's wife was running without much help. Collating the information in preparation for Lad's return was his only real guild-related duty for the time being. Desperate to be busy, Dee had resorted to touching up the silver. Answering the door came as a welcome break.

Peeking through the lens mounted in the center of the door, however, Dee thought the break might not be so welcome after all. A hooded acolyte stood on the stoop, probably seeking a contribution.

"I'm so sorry, good brother," Dee said as he opened the door. "My master's out of town, and I'm not authorized to give donations in his stead. Perhaps if you come back when—"

"I know your master's not home, and I'm not here for a donation. I'm here on guild business, and I'll not discuss it on the stoop." The man's scowl was clearly not intended to entice generosity, and his face was unfamiliar.

Dee had been fooled once before by a spy in a clever disguise, and had vowed that would never happen again. However, if the man was actually a guild messenger, this certainly was not something to discuss on the stoop.

Stepping back, he waved the visitor in. "I have no idea what guild you're talking about, but if you have business, you may come into the foyer." If this was a trick to get entry for some nefarious motive, the man would be in for a surprise. Dee could summon two Enforcers in seconds. He closed the door and confronted the alleged acolyte, his arms crossed. "Now, what's this about?"

"Who's in charge of the Twailin guild?" The demand came without warning, and in a tone intended to intimidate.

Dee wasn't.

"I don't know you, sir, and I don't know what guild you keep referring to. I'll have your name and business, or you'll be out the door this instant."

The acolyte pushed the hood back off of his head, giving Dee his first good look at his features. The man's pate was shaved smooth, his features were angular, and his eyes cold. When he spoke, his tone came as sharp as a newly whetted razor.

"My name is Hoseph. I'm the personal assistant to the Grandmaster of the Assassins Guild. You are the assistant to Guildmaster Lad of the Twailin Assassins Guild. *You* need to tell *me* who's in charge of the Twailin guild in your master's absence."

Dee tensed, but maintained his long-practiced composure as his mind raced. *Personal assistant to the Grandmaster!* The claim seemed incredible, but rang true, given the man's knowledge of Lad's identity. It also explained why he seemed unaccustomed to being questioned. "Master Blade Sereth was put in temporary command."

"Very well. Have him here at this time tomorrow so that I may speak with him."

That didn't sound good at all. Why would the Grandmaster's assistant be here in Twailin when Lad was visiting the Grandmaster in Tsing? Had something happened to Lad and Mya? "May I tell him what this is in regard to?"

Hoseph stared for a moment, his eyes as blank as a viper's. Finally he said, "Tell Master Sereth that the Grandmaster of the Assassins Guild has been murdered by Guildmaster Lad and Master Hunter Mya. These traitors are to be sought and apprehended. I'll give Master Sereth the rest of the details tomorrow."

"What the—"

Before Dee could complete his question, his visitor flipped a gleaming silver trinket from his sleeve, uttered a word, and dissolved into a swirling cloud of black mist.

"Gods of Light and Darkness!" Dee staggered back as the last of the vapor dissipated, the implications of the man's visit and startling exit struck him. *Black mists...* Hoseph was the priestly assassin Lad had warned them about, the man who had twice interfered in the investigation of Wiggen's death, once by killing Baron Patino, and again when he tried to kill Lad's informant.

The thought worked like a key in his agile mind. Details fell into place like a row of tumblers. Kiesha—*click*! Patino—*click*! Black mists—*click*! Hoseph—*click*! The Grandmaster dead... The key stuck there, refusing to open the door on the final truth.

Dee tried to work it out. *If Hoseph didn't want Lad to solve Wiggen's murder, and he works for the Grandmaster, then...did the Grandmaster have something to do with Wiggen's death?*

Lad had vowed to kill whoever was responsible, and Hoseph had said that Lad and Mya had killed the Grandmaster. The theory made sense, but in reality, Lad and Mya couldn't lay a hand on the Grandmaster. The rings they wore wouldn't allow it.

It doesn't matter. The Grandmaster was dead, and the guild blamed Lad and Mya. *Oh, there's going to be all Nine Hells to pay for this.*

Dee hurried to the back of the house. The two Enforcers sat at the table drinking blackbrew and flirting with the pretty kitchen maid, who promptly curtsied and scurried off.

"I'm going out for a while." Dee grabbed his suitcoat. "Don't allow anyone into the house." He dashed out before they could ask any questions.

Outside, Dee slowed to a dignified stroll. He was a gentleman's assistant, and he had to maintain that image. At this time of morning the streets were bustling, so he had no trouble flagging down a hackney. Sereth's fencing salon wasn't far, just on the edge of Barleycorn Heights, but Dee hadn't taken the time to change from his house shoes to walking shoes. Truth be told, the hills in this part of town wore him out. Years spent working for Mya, and now Lad, had softened his muscles. But then, he'd always been more assistant than assassin. He gave the driver the address and climbed aboard.

Leaning back against the carriage cushions, Dee' mind wandered to his two masters. He'd enjoyed working for Mya. The Master Hunter was intelligent, sharp-witted, and unfailingly loyal to her people. The youngest Master Hunter ever in Twailin, she had earned their loyalty in return. Secretly, Dee had harbored a decidedly unprofessional infatuation for his boss, even though he knew nothing could ever happen. He had often watched her cast glances at Lad and wondered if something might be going on between them, but he now knew that Lad was utterly devoted to his family.

Lad... Being the guildmaster's assistant was an entirely different experience. No less gratifying, but challenging. There was an intensity to Lad that Dee found both unnerving and thrilling to be around. Working for someone who could snap you like a twig—a living weapon in emotional agony, no less—was daunting. Still, Dee's empathy for the man who had lost his wife firmed his resolve to help him in any way he could.

The hackney pulled up in front of Sereth's studio, and Dee was out the door before it even came to a halt. He tossed the driver a silver crown.

The driver caught it deftly. "Thank'e, sir!"

Sereth's assistant, Lem, answered the door and let Dee in. The Master Blade was sparring with a student, so Dee stood out of the way, forcing himself to relax and consider what he knew about the man.

When Mya had been warring with the other guild factions, Dee had dug up all he could about the masters and their people. As Master Blade Horice's bodyguard, Sereth had been high on the list. Though an accomplished swordsman, he preferred short blades to long, was hard-working, and until recently lived in a dreary apartment in the Docks District. More recently, he'd discovered that Sereth had a wife who had been held hostage by the Thieves Guild. Lad had helped free her, and had sworn Dee to silence about the entire affair. For that alone, Sereth owed Lad his loyalty.

The pace of the sparring shifted. At first glance, the fencing master and his student had appeared evenly matched, but suddenly, in a lightning exchange, Sereth scored several touches, one to each leg, one wrist, and a fourth that cracked the student's wire mask hard enough to snap his head back.

"Enough!"

At Sereth's command, the student immediately stopped and took off the wire mask. A shock of blonde hair and sweetly rounded face proclaimed that the student was, in fact, a young woman, not a young man.

"Very good, Lady Racine, but you're guarding your core overmuch and leaving openings elsewhere."

"You're so *fast!*" She was breathing hard, her face glowing with sweat. "I couldn't cover everything."

"Then get faster." Sereth noticed Dee. "I'm afraid we're out of time for now, but remember; speed comes with practice. Practice at home with a metronome as I showed you, and keep increasing the tempo. I'll see you in two days."

"Thank you, Master VonBruce." She saluted and racked her practice sword, and Lem helped her remove her thick plastron.

"Master VonBruce." Dee strode forward and executed a respectful bow. "My master sends his regrets that he'll be unable to attend his upcoming lesson. He'd like to reschedule if possible."

"I'll have to check my appointment book. Come with me." Sereth led Dee from the studio into a small office, closed the door, and offered him a seat. "What's happened?"

"Do I look that upset?" Dee prided himself on his ability to maintain an unruffled façade.

"No, but you never just pop in unexpectedly. I figured something was up."

"Something is. I just had a visitor." Dee quickly related the story of Hoseph's visit and his ideas of the priest's involvement in recent events.

"Mother of..." Sereth's oath trailed off, and his eyes drifted down to his hands.

"How could they kill the Grandmaster? Is it even *possible*?"

Sereth glanced up. "If anyone could do it, I'd bet on Lad and Mya." To Dee's raised eyebrows, he said, "You didn't see them at Fiveway Fountain. They fought like...nothing I've ever seen before."

"But what about the Grandmaster's ring? How could they even touch him?"

"I don't know, but there was Saliez..."

Of course, Dee remembered. *The Grandfather.* According to rumor, the former Twailin guildmaster had been killed by Lad, despite magical constraints that prohibited him from harming the man who had contracted him to be made.

Dee took a deep breath. "What are you going to do?"

"Meet with Hoseph." The Master Blade seemed surprised at the question. "I would be foolish to refuse."

"If I can point something out without getting killed..." Dee crooked a smile to make sure Sereth knew the comment was in jest.

"Go ahead."

"We owe no allegiance to this Hoseph fellow. He's not in the chain of command. If the Grandmaster truly *is* dead, our loyalty is to Lad."

Sereth pursed his lips. "It's more complicated than that, Dee. If Lad and Mya did somehow kill the Grandmaster, then they're traitors to the guild."

"But if the Grandmaster's dead, who's calling the shots?" Dee couldn't believe he was hearing this. "Your life doesn't belong to Hoseph, it belongs to Lad."

"I need to think about this before I make a decision."

"But he saved your—"

"Enough!"

Dee tensed. He'd expected more loyalty from Sereth, but he couldn't flout his orders. Lad had put the Master Blade in charge.

Sereth stood and opened the door, a clear signal that their meeting was over. "I'll see you tomorrow morning at Lad's house."

Dee nodded in assent, unsure whether he had masked his apprehension, and left. To him, the matter was simple. His loyalty belonged to Lad, not some nebulous dead Grandmaster in far-off Tsing. But he didn't dare alienate the Master Blade. Should Sereth be appointed guildmaster, Dee would have no choice but to work with him.

Or die.

Arbuckle strode into the Great Hall, his blademasters in tight formation around him, and stopped short. The cavernous chamber seemed to have shrunk, so filled was it with imperial guards, knights, and squires, all clad in gleaming armor and weapons. The herald announced his entrance, and the entire room bowed as one. A flutter of apprehension mixed with pride filled him. These men and women were sworn to him, and with them he would banish his vile father's shadow.

Struggling to maintain a composed mien, Arbuckle announced, "It's time, Captain Otar."

"Milord Prince." Otar stepped forward and lowered his voice.

"This is unwise. You put yourself in peril needlessly. Your father would never have—"

"I am *not* my father, Captain. The sooner you accept that, the better we will get along. Besides," Arbuckle tugged at the hem of his dress doublet, a bit snug now that he wore a fine chainmail shirt beneath it, "with all of you around me, I'm well protected."

"Heralds could just as easily announce the emperor's death, milord," Otar argued.

"No, Captain, they couldn't. Heralds and posters are impersonal. I must *show* the populace that things will change." Arbuckle smiled to the captain. "But thank you for pointing out that my father would never do this. Now I'm certain it's the right thing to do."

"If you say so, Milord Prince, but I'd have my objection to this foray noted." Otar nodded to the imperial scribe hovering just outside Arbuckle's cordon of blademasters. The man's pen was busy as always, recording every word.

"So noted, Captain. Now, I'll say a few words before we leave." Arbuckle stepped up onto the gilded dais at the head of the room and scanned the assembled crowd. "Ladies and gentlemen." Every eye snapped to him, and Arbuckle felt a twinge of apprehension. He was unused to making speeches.

Just tell them the truth.

"This the start of a new era. For more than forty years, Tsing has been ruled with an iron fist. That reign of tyranny is over. I am *not* my father, and things are going to change. We will maintain order, but we will institute justice as well. Every citizen of Tsing deserves the same rights. With your help, I intend to give them those rights."

Armor rustled as they shifted. He saw surprise on some faces, resolve on others.

"Change will not come easily, but is necessary. History tells us that oppression leads to rebellion and the death of empires. We— you and I—must show the common people that there is no need for rebellion. Today we bring them hope."

Several in the crowd nodded, though a few frowned. Arbuckle hoped that was simple worry, not rebellion.

"I expect that they will welcome the news. They may even get rambunctious, *but,*" Arbuckle lowered his voice, aiming for a stern but unthreatening tone, "your mission is to protect me, nothing more. There is to be no offensive action. The constabulary will deal with any unrest. Any questions?"

A single cricket would have seemed loud in the ensuing silence. Surprise wreathed every face, guard and knight alike. Their reactions brought a smile to Arbuckle. They were used to being ordered to action, with no questions allowed. They were learning that he was not his father.

"Very good." He gestured to the towering doors that led to the palace foyer and the courtyard beyond. "Let us proceed."

The clatter of metal echoed through the Great Hall as the troops parted to allow the crown prince passage, then followed him outside. Arbuckle boarded his carriage and settled into the soft seat, his scribe tucking into the opposite corner. The carriage shifted as his blademasters leapt into place with the driver, atop, and on the rear. Within minutes all were ready, and the carriage lurched into motion.

Arbuckle peered out the window, but could see little beyond steel and horseflesh. A cordon of knights and squires rode around his carriage, and the Imperial Guard marched behind. Arbuckle had envisioned a more discreet contingent.

It's like an invading army…

Arbuckle slouched into his seat, disgruntled at the thought. He despised his father's brutal policies, and had tried to dissociate himself from them whenever he could. As crown prince, he had stood beside Tynean Tsing II during audiences and attended social functions he couldn't get out of, though he refused at every opportunity. The emperor had long ago stopped trying to instruct his only son and heir in governance and statecraft. Arbuckle had tried instead to learn his duty from books, gleaning what he could from historical successes and failures. But reading was no substitute for experience, and he felt ill-prepared to rule the vast empire.

I thought I'd have more time…

After what seemed an interminable duration, but was probably less than an hour, the procession halted, and Arbuckle's mood brightened. It was time for the people to meet their future emperor, time for them to learn that he was not his father. A buzz rose over the clatter of hooves and armor, the voices of the commoners gathered in the plaza.

"We've reached the Imperial Plaza, Milord Prince!" Captain Otar opened the carriage door. "There's quite a crowd. I'll say again that I don't think this is a wise thing to do."

"Then I'll go down in history as Arbuckle the Unwise, Captain. This plaza epitomizes my father's injustice. This is where I need to be." He swallowed hard and stepped from the carriage, pausing a moment in the door.

The Imperial Plaza was as horrific as he remembered. Rows of pillories and whipping posts surrounded a cluster of gallows, an appalling number of them occupied. Above it all, the imperial flags snapped in the breeze. The deep-blue crested banner fluttered upside-down, proclaiming a death within the imperial family. Constables and mounted lancers girded the perimeter punishment area in a solid wall of steel.

The buzz of voices rose as the crowd caught sight of Arbuckle. Commoners by the thousands craned their necks to see him. Though notice of the gathering had been last minute, it seemed as if half of the city's population had attended.

"Milord Prince!" Chief Constable Dreyfus approached with a squad of constables, grim men and women in tarnished mail with hands on swords. He waited until Arbuckle's blademasters allowed him through their protective cordon. Bowing, Dreyfus got right to the point. "This is a dangerous place. This rabble could go off at any moment!"

"This *rabble*, as you call them, Chief Constable, look fairly calm to me."

"For the moment, yes, Milord Prince, but so does a tinderbox before it goes up in flames." He looked around, obviously nervous. "Trust me. They're like curs. Toss them a morsel and they'll turn around and bite the hand that feeds them."

"A dog that has been beaten for forty years has good reason to bite, Chief Constable!" Arbuckle forced down his temper. Dreyfus and his constables dealt with the dregs of society every day. No wonder they were jaded. "I respect your opinion, but please refrain from disparaging the people you are sworn to protect!"

Dreyfus looked stunned, but recovered quickly. "All I'm saying, milord, is that I can't guarantee your safety."

"That's not your concern, Chief Constable. The Imperial Guard will see to my safety. Your job is to maintain order. Protect the city and the populace from harm. I want no brutality here!"

"As you wish, milord." Dreyfus bowed and retreated to command his constables.

"Good. Now, where…" Arbuckle scanned the field of punishment and saw what he needed. "There." He pointed to one of the gallows. The platform was high enough that he would be visible to the entire crowd. "There! I'm going there."

"But to expose yourself—"

"Captain Otar, how can I address the people if they can't *see* me?" He glared at the man and pointed again to the gallows. "We're going *there*!"

"Yes, milord." The captain clenched his jaw and shouted orders.

The Imperial Guard formed a double row from the carriage to the gallows, shields facing outward. Arbuckle proceeded down the passage between lines of guards, his blademasters tightly knotted around him.

Good Gods of Light! Beneath the gallows dangled the body of a woman, a rope cinched tight around her neck. *I can't change my mind now.* He mounted the steps of the gibbet, his footsteps hollow on the well-trodden wood. A breeze fluttered his robe, wafting the scent of blood, infection, and death through the air. Arbuckle struggled not to gag as he gazed out across the sea of people.

"People of Tsing!" he shouted, hoping his words would reach to the edge of the crowd. "I am Crown Prince Arbuckle, heir to the throne of Tsing. The emperor, my father, is dead!"

Surprisingly, the people remained silent. Arbuckle had expected cries, maybe catcalls, perhaps some cheers, but not a sound reached him beyond the shuffling of feet and the clatter of armor and hooves on stone. He examined the crowd, looking from face to face. A few glanced sidelong at the squads of constables, but not a single eye met his.

Fear… Ice water trickled down his spine with the realization. *They're terrified.*

A lone shout of, "Good riddance!" rang out from the crowd, and a squad of constables surged forward.

"Stop right there!" Arbuckle bellowed. "I'm here to speak to the people. If they choose to speak back to me, they have the right. No one here will be punished for speaking out. There will be justice under my reign!"

"What justice?" A man surged forward to the cordon of constables, his accusative hand thrusting between the shields to point. "How dare you speak of justice standing above my wife's *corpse*! There ain't no justice for common folk. Only for you nobles!"

A murmur swept through the crowd, and Arbuckle could hear the rage in it. He looked back at the rope trailing down through the trap door in the gallows, and realized that the man was right.

What a hypocrite I look.

"There *will* be justice!" He raised his hands. "I pledge to you, there will be the same justice for all, noble and commoner alike."

The murmurs grew louder and the crowd shifted, a few more catcalls and epithets ringing out. The constables fidgeted, but remained in place. Arbuckle had to demonstrate his sincerity, but how? *Show them you're not your father.*

Turning to his nearest bodyguard, he held out a hand. "Give me a dagger."

The blademaster immediately handed over the dagger from his belt.

"Captain Otar! I'm going to cut down this poor woman. Have your men catch her. They are to treat the body with *respect*, do you hear me?"

"Milord Prince! Why?" The captain stared up at him with wide, questioning eyes.

Otar's surprise made Arbuckle realize that he had misinterpreted the captain's mindset. He hadn't been upset to learn that his former master was a sadist and disagreed with the notion that commoners deserved any consideration whatsoever, let alone respect. *Time to educate him,* Arbuckle resolved

"Because it is her due! Now do as I say or I'll have you removed from your post, Captain!"

"Yes, Milord Prince." Otar's voice was sullen, but he gave the requisite orders.

Arbuckle leaned out over the open trap door and gripped the rope, sawing the keen blade through the strands. The prince realized his mistake as the rope parted and the rough hemp ripped through his blistered palm. A hand grasped his shoulder, and another snatched the rope beneath his fist. One of his blademasters had saved him from dropping the body, and maybe tumbling after it.

"Thank you. Lower her gently." Arbuckle released his grasp, his hand bloody.

Another murmur swept the crowd as the blademaster lowered the body into the arms of two imperial guards waiting below. Easing the woman to the ground, one removed the noose while the other unclasped his own cloak and wrapped the forlorn figure in a makeshift shroud.

"Very good!" Arbuckle returned the dagger to his bodyguard, then called down to Otar again. "Captain! Have your people take her to her husband. Release the rest of the prisoners to their families. Use your cloaks to wrap the dead."

"Milord, this sets a bad precedent."

"Carry out my orders, Captain!" Arbuckle warned.

Otar shook his head. "I cannot countenance this action. It's foolhardy and dangerous!"

Arbuckle bristled. If he couldn't control his own Imperial Guard, how could he hope to govern an empire?

"Very well, Captain." The man relaxed for a moment before Arbuckle bellowed, "Commander Ithross, relieve Captain Otar of command and place him under arrest! You are acting captain of the Imperial Guard as of this moment."

Ithross moved forward with a squad of guardsmen.

"What? You can't—"

"I can and I have, Master Otar. You're under arrest. Hand over your weapons, or you'll be taken by force." To Arbuckle's immense relief, the captain unclipped his sword belt and handed it over to Ithross, though his face darkened with rage. Unclasping his cloak of office, he flung it to the ground and allowed himself to be led away.

A cheer rang out from the commoners in the fore of the crowd.

"Commander Ithross, did you hear my orders to your former captain?"

"I did, Milord Prince." Ithross saluted smartly.

"Carry them out at once." He looked around. "Sir Fineal!"

The knight rode his charger forward. "Milord Prince."

Chris A. Jackson and Anne L. McMillen-Jackson

"I want the knights to assist in the release of the prisoners."

"At once, Milord Prince!" Fineal snapped orders, and soon the knights and their squires dismounted to join the Imperial Guard.

Sparks flew as steel cleaved chains and struck locks from stocks, but the soldiers took the greatest care with the prisoners, helping them to the waiting arms of their grateful families. The effect on the crowd was gradual but profound. Murmurs of disbelief swelled to shouts of elation and cheers. Those receiving bodies wailed, but many more wept tears of joy.

Arbuckle raised his hands. "People of Tsing!"

Silence fell. Arbuckle's heart raced at the sight of their upturned faces, no longer fearful and despairing, but hopeful. A new eagerness and spirit shone in their eyes.

"I know you have suffered long under my father's rule, but I'm here to tell you that I will *not* perpetuate his policies. As a pledge upon my word, I grant full pardons to all those who were being punished here in the plaza, and vow to personally review the case of every prisoner currently being held in this city. Those cases found unjust by me will be dismissed."

A murmur of disbelief swept through the crowd, and a voice called out, "What of our dead?"

"I can't make up for your losses, but every family who brings to the palace the cloak we have wrapped your dead in will receive compensation."

"Blood money!" someone cried, and a dangerous murmur began.

"No!" Arbuckle shook his head. "This is not blood money, but compensation for wrongs perpetrated by your emperor. Gold can't bring back the dead or pay for your sorrow, but it can feed your children."

"How do we know we can trust you?"

Arbuckle almost smiled at the question. Already they were more emboldened than they had been in years. *Trust is earned...* But how to convince them? He clenched his fists, and the pain from the torn blisters on his palms ignited his memory of that morning, of the satisfaction at destroying his father's implements of torture. *Of course!*

"Commander Ithross, get me an axe!"

Within moments, Ithross hurried up the gallows steps, a battle

50

axe in hand, and the hint of a grin on his face. "I'm afraid it's not quite a woodsman's tool, milord."

"It'll do, Commander." He nodded at the tall square frame of the gallows. "Care to join me in an encore of our morning's work in the interrogation room, Commander?"

"With pleasure!"

Arbuckle hefted the battle axe in his aching palms. It felt good despite the pain. Hauling back, he swung with all his might, and the blade bit deep into the soft pine. A cheer went up from the crowd. Wrenching the blade free, he swung again while Ithross attacked the other support. Blood dripped from his torn palm. After several more strokes, the gallows framework lurched.

"Ware below!" called Ithross, and the nearby guards backed away. With one final blow, Arbuckle smashed through the remaining support and the frame crashed down onto the cobblestones.

Another ragged cheer rose from the crowd.

Arbuckle turned to Ithross. "Commander, have your guardsmen tear down every single post, pillory, and gallows. Pile it all right here!" He pointed down to the space beneath the gallows.

"Yes, Milord Prince!" Ithross fired off orders, and the Imperial Guard hurried to comply.

For nearly an hour they toiled, and the crowd watched in amazement. An enormous mound of broken timber rose beneath the platform upon which Arbuckle stood. He called for a skin of oil, and emptied it down through the trap door, then raised his hands for silence.

"Today is a new beginning!" he bellowed. "Today we begin to right the wrongs! Today I show you my commitment to bring justice to this empire! One justice for all people, rich and poor, noble and commoner alike!"

The cheers echoed off the buildings around the plaza, so loud that they reverberated against Arbuckle's chest. He held high the torch that Ithross had fetched. "You, the common people of Tsing, are the life and blood of this empire. This realm was built by your hands, your sweat, your labor! With this flame, I ignite a fire to burn away the injustice of the past and temper a pledge for justice in the future."

Arbuckle dropped the torch down through the hatch in the platform. Fames immediately flickered amidst the well-oiled wood, and the fire quickly spread. The crown prince descended the platform's steps amidst a flurry of sparks and raucous cheers from the crowd. By the time he reached his carriage, the bonfire raged, flames soaring into the sky. The crowd cheered, and he even saw some delighted folks dancing and clapping. Many Imperial Guard and knights grinned, while several of the younger squires hooted with relish.

"Chief Constable Dreyfus, pull your constables back. Protect the surrounding buildings and keep order, but let the people gather to enjoy the bonfire. It'll do them good."

"Yes, Milord Prince." Dreyfus didn't look happy, but immediately began relaying Arbuckle's orders.

"Commander Ithross, back to the palace!"

Arbuckle climbed into his carriage and fell against the cushions with a hearty sigh. "A good afternoon's work, if I may say so myself."

"Yes, Milord Prince."

Arbuckle started at the voice. The imperial scribe sat tucked once again into his corner. Suddenly the crown prince realized that the man had been nearby throughout the entire foray, constantly scratching on his ledger, as quiet and unobtrusive as a shadow. In fact, as far as he could remember, this was the first time Arbuckle had ever heard him speak.

"Do you know, I don't believe I've ever learned your name."

"It's Verul, Milord Prince."

"Well, Verul, how did you like my little speech?"

The scribe looked sheepish. "I…I don't know, Milord Prince. I'm so busy writing the words that I don't have time to listen."

"I know what you mean. I was so busy speaking, I don't remember exactly what I said. May I re-live it by reading?" He gestured to the thick book in the man's lap.

"I'm afraid it's not legible yet, milord." Verul turned the volume around to show a page full of incomprehensible markings. "It's just shorthand now. It's transcribed every night by the archivists."

"I wondered how you wrote so quickly to get it all down. Would you bring the archive to me once it's been transcribed?"

"Of course, Milord Prince."

Arbuckle leaned his head back and closed his eyes, tired but happy. His first action had been a resounding success. He hoped it was good portent of his upcoming reign.

Mya watched the imperial carriage pull away, Crown Prince Arbuckle tucked safely inside. The spectacle had fairly dumbfounded her. *This* was Tynean Tsing's son?

The Grandmaster had considered his heir inept and unfit to rule his empire. He was right. But then, Arbuckle didn't intend to rule *this* empire, but one of his own making. *Lad would like that.*

As the constables' line dissolved into squads, the crowd surged forward. She allowed herself to be taken with them until she felt the heat of the bonfire on her cheek. She felt a trickle of sweat on her neck, not due to the sweltering temperature—her enchanted wrappings kept perfectly comfortable, regardless of heat or cold—but the crowd was getting overly rambunctious for her comfort.

She dabbed her neck and examined her fingers. *I hope my hair dye doesn't run.*

Certain that a hunt would be underway for the emperor's murderer, she'd made a quick purchase from a cosmetic shop that morning. A hasty application had colored her distinctive red hair black. Not that it mattered much, tucked up under a cap. She had disguised herself as a boy to venture out today. She'd been right to assume there'd be no nobles in the crowd. Her fine traveling dresses would make her stand out in a crowd like this.

Pushing her way back through the crowd to the edge of the plaza, she swung up onto a street lamp with a few other cavorting boys, and gazed out across the sea of people. Everywhere, they celebrated—dancing, laughing, singing—drunk on the freedom that their new ruler promised. Here and there, however, small pockets of people huddled close, talking low, their faces showing not elation, but anger or malice. She hopped down and moved near one group, cocking an ear to hear them over the hoots and howls of the crowd.

"...don't believe a word of it..."

"A trick!"

"Just wait…"

The squads of constables that hung around the edge of the plaza watched everyone closely, especially those who seemed less than elated. They stood, facing the crowd with shields at the ready, as if they expected to be bowled over by an angry mob at any moment.

She examined the crowd: shopkeepers in worn suits and long aprons, charwomen with dingy skirts and rough hands, mothers carrying pink-faced babies, shipyard workers with wood chips in their hair, ne'er-do-wells missing hands, eyes, or legs and smelling of the foulest gutter. The entire spectrum of the city's working and lower-class citizens had attended the assembly.

A dangerous crowd, even if most of them are happy.

An uproar caught her ear, and she looked to where a small troupe of rowdies jeered and laughed at a squad of constables. Only yesterday, the officers would have immediately set about bludgeoning the young men into submission. But Arbuckle had said there would be justice, and he evidently meant it. The squad held themselves in check, ignoring the unruly youths, though Mya could see hands on swords. The rowdies took full advantage of their new-found freedom, cat calling and making rude gestures. They traded around a rum bottle, drinking and laughing at the grim constables.

Mya sighed, recognizing the type. There were always those few who just wanted to stir up trouble. Raucous laughter erupted, and one of the youths threw the empty bottle at the constables, where it shattered against a shield.

And there it goes.

The squad leader drew her sword, and the rest of her squad followed suit, stepping into a tight formation of shield-sword-shield. They took a menacing step forward. The ruffians scattered, but a couple snatched brands from the bonfire. As they ran from the plaza, they yelled back a bastardized version of Crown Prince Arbuckle's words. "Light a fire for justice!"

"Uh oh." Mya moved toward the nearest alley.

Drunk idiots with torches was a bad combination in a city this tightly packed with flammable structures. The constables intercepted one of the torch-wielding morons, dropping him to the cobbles with a shield to the face. Several others cried out in alarm, however, and cat calls started flying.

Protests of "Damned caps!" and "Fires for justice!" ripped through the crowd like rolling thunder warned of an approaching storm.

Mya turned and walked away. She had the distinct feeling that the celebrations were about to take a turn for the worse.

CHAPTER IV

Mya snapped awake, her eyes gritty and her left leg completely asleep, but relieved that she had survived another night. She'd barely slept at all with the noise of commoners celebrating in the streets until the small hours, worried that every bump in the night might be Hoseph coming to kill her. She lurched up from her corner and shook the pins and needles out of her leg, wondering if the city had also survived the night.

After leaving the Imperial Plaza yesterday, she had collected her belongings from *The Prickly Pair* and moved into a new inn, the *Tin Dulcimer*. From her window on the third floor, Mya could see the entire northern half of the city. The view from the roof was even better. She had spent much of the evening watching as fires flared and were quenched, waiting for the Docks District, with its tightly packed wooden houses, inns, taverns, and warehouses to ignite into a conflagration. Her plans for the Assassins Guild would depend on how much of the city survived.

Pulling aside the curtain, she squinted into the morning sunlight. Thin streams of smoke trailed skyward across the river, but most of the city appeared intact. She would wager that the entire constabulary had spent a sleepless night rounding up arsonists and putting out fires, however.

Nice to know someone else isn't sleeping, Mya thought with a great yawn.

Once again she had spent all night with her back in the corner of the room, daggers ready, dreaming in snippets of vengeful priests appearing out of nowhere to murder her. She glanced wistfully at the bed, then away. She had work to do.

Opening the window and leaning out, she caught sight of the

56

nearest bridge. Traffic was brisk, though constables were questioning everyone who wanted to cross. She was surprised they were letting anyone across, but supposed someone had to serve the rich their morning tea and polish their boots.

The streets were undoubtedly being heavily patrolled, so dressing like a commoner might be an invitation to be stopped by the authorities. Dressing as gentry, however, might get her accosted by troublemakers looking for an easy target. Not that she couldn't defend herself, but causing a disturbance would draw unwanted attention. She planned to visit Lady T, and considering the woman's distain for the lower classes, decided to dress as a moderately successful business woman. She donned one of her better travel dresses, but no jewelry or frippery, grabbed her simplest hat, and went down to breakfast.

"Miss Ingrid, how are you this morning?" The innkeeper met her at the bottom of the stairs with a smile.

Mya was still getting used to answering to her newly assumed name, but deception came easily. "I'm fine, Master Felche. And yourself?"

The innkeeper tucked his thumbs in his belt and bounced on the balls of his feet. "Oh, very good indeed. You were lucky you checked in so early yesterday. We were full up by evening with those coming over from the north side." The plump man lowered his voice and in a conspiratorial tone. "I don't suppose you'd consider sharing your room?"

"No, Master Felche, and I hope that my paying you for a week in advance was enough to ensure my privacy." Mya smiled as she spoke, polite but firm.

The innkeeper wilted just a little, then chuckled. "Of course, Miss Ingrid. You'll have privacy, clean towels, two meals a day, and use of the washroom, just as we agreed. I'll not have you saying that I cheat my guests."

"You run a fine establishment, Master Felche. I'm sure I'll enjoy my stay." Stepping around Rufus, the old tomcat the size of a mountain lynx who kept the place free of rats, Mya strode into a common room buzzing with chatter. She picked a corner table, sat with her back to the wall, and trained her ear on a promising conversation.

"Prince Arbuckle started the first fires his own self, he did! I swear it by my right thumb!" An old man sitting at the bar held up his thumb for emphasis as he sipped a pint of stout. "He yammered on about justice for all, commoner and noble alike!"

"That'll be the day!" The morning maid laughed as she put a plate mounded with fried potatoes, onions, and sausage before Mya, along with a steaming cup of blackbrew and a small pitcher of cream. "Ain't never gonna be the same justice for us as there is for the high-born."

Mya's mouth watered with the heavenly aroma, and her stomach growled. Despite her healing magic, it took a lot of energy to replace all the blood she had lost. She sliced a piece of sausage and popped it in her mouth, reveling in the spicy, greasy, wonderful flavor. Adding a hearty dollop of cream to the blackbrew, she washed the bite down with a big swallow.

"Come now, Dorid, don't you believe Old Rhubarb." A bargeman also seated at the bar gave the oldster a nudge. "Next he'll have you believin' that the milk he brings is from a cow and not from Madam Brixol down the way."

"Hey, a wet nurse has gotta keep the flow goin' between jobs!" Old Rhubarb laughed and finished his pint.

"You two stop that! You'll put off the payin' customers!" Dorid swatted Rhubarb with her dish towel and scowled.

"No humor in you at all!" Rhubarb stood, his bones popping and cracking. "I'm off to business, Dorid. See you tonight."

Mya looked dubiously at her blackbrew and sniffed the pitcher of cream. Pushing aside the pitcher, she shifted her attention from one conversation to the next as she ate. The gossip ranged from reasonable to ridiculous, but she resolved to check the details for herself. She finished her meal, even risking the blackbrew, though she had her second and third cups without cream, and headed for the door.

As she left the inn, Master Felche waved her over. "Goin' out then, are you, Miss Ingrid?"

"Yes. I have business to conduct."

"Best have a care if you're crossing the river. Not safe on the streets, I'm thinkin'. Would you like one of my boys to go along with you?"

"I'll be fine, thank you."

"Very well then." He frowned at her lack of caution. "You'll be back for supper?"

"I wouldn't miss it, Master Felche." She donned her hat and left the inn.

A few people still celebrated in the streets, some looking like they'd been at it all night. Even those waiting in line for the bridge were smiling and chatting. Many of the smiles turned to scowls, however, as people were confronted by the squad of eight constables manning the bridge. The constables were questioning all who wanted to pass, turning many back.

Of course, she reasoned. *The violence is happening north of the river, and most of the people perpetrating it live south of the river.*

Joining the queue, Mya listened to the constables questioning and passing judgement on those ahead of her. Only those with legitimate business across the river were being allowed to through. Mya put on her best "gentle lady" persona and waited her turn.

"Your name, Miss?" A disheveled sergeant squinted at her, his eyes red and rimmed with dark circles. The entire squad looked tired, and the tall corporal at the sergeant's elbow sported a burn across his cheek.

"Ingrid Johens."

"Out alone this mornin'?"

"Yes. I have an appointment across the river, but with the current unrest I chose to stay last night at an inn on the south side."

"Smart of you, that." He looked her up and down. "Where you stayin'?"

"The *Tin Dulcimer*."

"Is old Fenwick still runnin' that place?"

Mya adopted a confused air. "The innkeeper's name is Master Felche, unless there are two *Tin Dulcimers*?"

The sergeant quirked a smile. "Just checking your story, Miss. You understand, I'm sure."

"Oh! Well, yes, I understand perfectly, Sergeant. Thank you for the work you do. I *do* appreciate it."

"Very well, then." He touched the rim of his iron cap and waved her on. "Perhaps we'll see you on your way back this afternoon."

"Perhaps you will." Mya concentrating on walking like a lady and started across. From behind, she heard the sergeant's gruff whisper to one of his men.

"There's a cutie for ya, Jorren. She comes back this way, you should ask her if she needs an escort back to the *Dulcimer*, just to check her story, ya know."

"Not my type, Sergeant."

"They come in types?" The sergeant chuckled. "I'd settle for any type that says yes!"

They hadn't spoken loud enough for someone without her preternatural hearing to pick up, but Mya risked a glance back to see how much attention they were paying her. The sergeant was watching her, but his corporal had already turned back to his job. She hurried on her way, wondering if she should cross at a different bridge.

Mya had thought long and hard about how to find Lady T's home, and decided to simply ask one of the people who knew the city best. Other than constables—a bad idea—that meant a hackney driver. The previous night's riots, however, meant that hackneys were few and far between. Finally she managed to hail a passing carriage.

"Where to, Miss?"

"Do you know of Lady Tara Monjhi?"

"Oh, aye! Her coach is somethin' to see! Perfect matched team of four Leonarian purebreds, she has, too!"

"Yes, those beautiful black and white horses! Could you take me to her home, please?"

"Of course, Miss. Half a silver crown with all the troubles on the street, I'm afraid. Takin' my life into my hands out today, I am."

"Very well." Mya climbed aboard and settled back, one hand on the door latch. If Hoseph popped into the moving carriage, she could only hope to be out the door before he could kill her.

If she was to have any chance of recruiting him, she would have to control their first meeting. She thought about Hoseph as the carriage rumbled along, a high priest of Demia, the Grandmaster had said. She doubted he would be easy to find. She peered out the carriage window. Between the stout buildings of Midtown she caught glimpses of the towers and minarets of Temple Hill soaring into the sky. She and Lad had ventured there to deposit the injured Captain Norwood at the Temple of the Earth Mother. She shouldn't have trouble finding Demia's temple. Hoseph probably wouldn't be there, however; she'd seen on a posterboard that he was wanted for questioning. She might ask some questions of her own, though, if the place wasn't crawling with imperial guards.

Smoke tinged the air, not enough to make her cough, but sufficient to mask the rancid smell of the river. Mya kept track of their route. The streets seemed deserted compared to the bustling crowds she'd seen previously. Many of the shops and businesses they passed were shuttered, and guards patrolled outside warehouses. The celebratory atmosphere of the Dreggars Quarters was absent. Here, constables and mounted lancers made up more than half the traffic, and those few citizens out and about walked with hurried steps and furtive glances.

At each corner and turn she scratched a note in a small notebook. Mya would mark the maps in her book about Tsing later. She had no hope of learning Tsing as she knew her home city of Twailin, but she needed to know her way around.

Twailin... She felt a pang of homesickness for the *Golden Cockerel*, Paxal the innkeeper, Dee, Sereth... *Lad.* Her mind drifted. *Stop it, Mya. Pay attention!*

The carriage labored uphill, the staid buildings of Midtown giving way to the mansions of the Heights, as if social class rose naturally with elevation. They passed a smoldering building, the target of vengeful commoners. Though wholesale catastrophe seemed to have been averted, a few homes and businesses had been gutted by fire.

Finally, the carriage stopped before a lofty townhouse. Roughly twice the size of the Lad's home in Twailin, it soared four floors above the street. Tall windows, a pillared entrance, and ornate sculptures adorned the façade. If Lady T's home was any indication, business was good for the Tsing Assassins Guild.

Two men stood in front of the tall red-and-gold-painted door, thick arms crossed over their broad chests. *Enforcers, no doubt.* They watched with narrowed eyes as Mya exited the carriage.

Here we go! Mya took a deep, calming breath while she paid the driver, then turned and approached the house with a smile and confident expression. She didn't know what to expect here, and had to be on her toes. Hoseph had undoubtedly told Lady T what had happened, and might even be inside. The man had to be hiding somewhere.

"I'm here to see Lady T."

"The lady's not taking visitors today. If you leave your name and address, her secretary will make an appointment for you."

Straightforward without being blunt or rude, obviously well-enough trained to pass as an employee of a noble house. Mya was impressed. Enforcers weren't usually so subtle.

"She'll see me." Mya gestured with her hand so the sun glinted off the gold-laced obsidian ring.

The two men stared at her finger, then glanced at one another. Mya wondered if they knew the import of what they saw, and if they even knew the Grandmaster was dead. She doubted they'd recognize the Grandmaster's ring; only the guildmasters had known his identity. They might assume she was a guildmaster from another city. Mya didn't really care, as long as she got in to see Lady T.

"Your name?"

"Mya."

"Come with me." One Enforcer stepped back while the other opened the door and ushered her inside.

"Thank you."

Mya refrained from gaping in awe as she stepped inside. The resplendent foyer soared three stories high, all white marble and gold leaf. Sunlight through the tall windows glinted off an enormous crystal chandelier. Across the broad expanse of floor a grandiose staircase arched and twisted like a great white serpent to the upper landings, edged by balustrades of white marble.

Two more Enforcers manned the hall. Mya's escort muttered to one, "Tell her she's got a visitor. She wears a guildmaster's ring, but I don't recognize her or her name." The woman turned and strode up the stairs without a word.

So the enforcer had misinterpreted the ring's significance, and didn't know her name. Mya didn't know if that was good or bad, but it was interesting.

"Nice place," Mya said casually. The men just stared at her, so she resigned herself to wait in silence. She didn't have to wait long before the messenger returned.

"Lady T will see you. This way."

"Thank you." Mya followed the woman's broad, straight back up two flights of stairs, then down a short hall to a pair of double doors, and stopped while her escort rapped on the door.

This is it.

"Enter," called a lady's voice from within. The Enforcer pushed both doors open and stepped back, waving Mya in with a smile.

Mya hesitated, her well-developed sense of paranoia staying her progress. For five years she had relied on Lad to warn her of danger, but Lad was gone; she had to rely on herself now. Heightening her senses, she heard the scuff of boots behind the doors, then the whisper of metal on leather as blades were drawn. That didn't worry Mya; no assassin could harm her. But if Hoseph lurked behind one of those doors, ready to kill her with a touch... She'd have to rely on her speed. Steeling her nerves, Mya took one step forward, stopping in the doorway. "Good morning, milady."

Lady T stood behind an ornate desk, garbed only in a simple dressing gown. Smiling, she raised a small crossbow and aimed it at Mya's heart. "Goodbye, Mrs. Addington."

To any normal person, the guildmaster would seem to be standing stock still, but Mya saw her finger twitch as she tried and failed to pull the trigger. The woman's jaw clenched, the tension deforming the smug curve of her lips. In the silence, Mya heard the steady cadence of the woman's heart begin to race. Four more heartbeats pounded from behind the two open doors.

"That's not a very polite way to greet a guest." Mya held up her hand and wiggled her ring finger, then glanced left and right. "How about some privacy so we can talk?"

Lady T dropped the crossbow onto her desk and waved a hand. "Everyone out! Now!"

Two assassins emerged from behind each door, three sheathing swords and daggers, one hefting a crossbow. *No Hoseph.* Stepping past them without concern, Mya scanned the rest of the room. *Still no Hoseph.* She breathed easier. The assassins hurried out, and the doors closed.

Lady T stared at her. "How did you do it?"

"By *it*, I assume you mean kill the Grandmaster, and the answer is, I didn't. Lad did." She smiled. "I just killed four of His Majesty's blademasters."

"Which again begs the question: *how?* Lad was constrained by his guildmaster's ring." Lady T sat down at her desk, scrutinizing Mya with a raised eyebrow. "And I simply can't believe that *you* killed four blademasters."

"Then don't. That doesn't make them any less dead, but," she wiggled her finger again, the ring glinting in the sunlight streaming through the window, "to the victor go the spoils."

"I thought you said that *Lad* killed the Grandmaster."

Mya shrugged. "He did. Then I killed him. I deserved this promotion more than he did." This was the story they had agreed on this before Lad left Tsing. It was Mya's gift to him: only if the guild thought him dead could he hope to live a normal life.

"You can't be serious." Lady T looked incredulous. "You honestly think putting that ring on your finger makes you *Grandmaster?*"

Mya smiled wryly and dropped into the chair in front of the desk. "I *am* serious, but I'm not so naïve that I think I can do it alone. That's why I need your help."

"Yes, you *would* need my help." Lady T settled back, still wary but her belligerence waning. "But what makes you think I'll give it?"

"Simple. You'll help me or you'll die."

Mya heard Lady T's heart skip a beat, though the guildmaster's face remained composed. Not for the first time Mya felt the loss of Lad. He was much better at interpreting people's tells, those unconscious tics and reactions that revealed a person's true thoughts and feelings. He had read Mya's for years without her knowing.

Lady T shifted in her seat. "You just admitted that you need me. I'm too valuable to you to just throw away."

"You're valuable *if* you help me. With your backing, assuming control of the guild will be straightforward. Without it…" Mya shrugged, "…it will be more difficult. I'm sure one of your faction masters has sufficient ambition to step up and cooperate. If they're so loyal as to rebel at your side, well, the guild exists in many other cities. Who says the Grandmaster has to rule from Tsing? The point is: if you're not an asset, you're a liability. Eliminating liabilities is just good business."

Muscles knotted beneath the satin skin of Lady T's jaw. "What kind of business do you expect to run? Without the emperor—"

"We'll all be better off!" Mya slapped her hand on the desk, and Lady T jerked. "Admit it! You were terrified of the Grandmaster." She leaned back. "You'll find me a much more lenient boss than that sadistic pig. Besides, he was just using the guild to further his own cause."

"The system worked for forty years."

"It worked well for the emperor, but not so well for the guild."

Lady T's eyes widened as she spread her hands, encompassing the luxurious surroundings. "Not so well? I beg to differ."

"Under your *imperial* Grandmaster, the guild stagnated. When was the last time you exploited new territory or started a new operation? You don't know what to do beyond what you've always done! As it is, you're scraping the bottom of the barrel by only operating south of the river. The *real* wealth of Tsing is *north* of the river, but the emperor forbade fleecing his precious aristocracy because he wanted them fat, dumb, and happy."

Lady T recoiled as if she'd been slapped.

"Don't take that title of yours too seriously, *Lady*!" Mya laughed. "It's a bought thing, no more part of you than a pair of shoes or a fancy gown."

"Not that I'd expect a commoner from Twailin to understand, but the Assassins Guild isn't just about profit. We have power. We control the empire."

Mya shook her head. "You're just parroting the Grandmaster's lie. Power doesn't come from flogging the mule. Eventually the mule is going to balk. True power is coaxing the mule so skillfully that it doesn't even realize it's the one doing all the work. Are you familiar with what we've done in Twailin?"

"Vaguely." The noblewoman's lip curled in derision. "A *beneficent* guild."

"Not quite, but we treat the common people as our customers, not our chattel, and we're hiring out blades and enforcers as security services to the likes of you, rich nobles and aristocrats who fear for their safety…from the likes of *us*." Mya smirked at the glimmer of interest in Lady T's eyes. "You've been milking the poor and letting the rich off the hook at the behest of your Imperial Grandmaster, not because it was good for the guild, but because it was good for his regime! In Twailin, we're making far more gold milking the rich and charging the poor fair rates for honest services."

"*Honest?*" Lady T laughed a single sharp note. "We're the *Assassins* Guild, my dear."

"And what makes you think we should be dishonest assassins? We perform numerous services, one of which is killing people. It works better than the system you've got."

"So you came here to kill the Grandmaster and usurp his position so you can put your *better* system into place?"

"Is that *really* what you think?" Mya knew that Lady T was no fool; one didn't get to be guildmaster by being stupid. *So why is she fighting me on this? Does she want the Grandmaster position for herself?* But Mya knew that every negotiation required give as well as take. "We didn't come here intending to kill anyone, but we also weren't going to just lie down and die at the Grandmaster's command. When push came to shove…we shoved back."

"Then you shoved Lad."

"That relationship was…complicated." Mya wasn't about to give the woman details. "Lad was never truly a part of the Assassins Guild. He had signed no blood contract. He was too dangerous. It was best to get rid of him. But none of that matters. Are you with me, or do I stick that crossbow bolt through your heart?"

Lady T considered for a moment. "You give me little choice, and you make it sound…almost interesting."

"Then you'll work with me?" Mya took care to say 'with', not 'for.'

"It's not that simple." Lady T drummed her fingers on the desk. "There's still Hoseph to consider. If I oppose him, I'm just as dead as if you kill me right here and now."

I wondered when he would enter the conversation. "Yes, there is Hoseph. I need to talk with him about all this, too. I don't suppose you know where he is, do you?"

"No, but he's not likely to listen to anything you have to say." Lady T's lips pursed, as if she was considering how much to say, or how to lie. "He came by briefly to inform me of what happened, then left to contact the provincial guildmasters. He's martialing the guild to hunt you down."

So much for recruiting him. Now I've got to kill him before he kills me. Mya hid her disappointment with a cold smile. "*He's* martialing the guild? The Grandmaster said that Hoseph wasn't a member of the Assassins Guild. How does he come out on top of this? Is he giving you orders now?"

Lady T's nostrils flared and her tone became indignant. "He *doesn't* give me orders! He's…making suggestions."

"He's been the emperor's weapon too long. He thinks he's in charge." Mya leaned on the desk, riveting the woman with her gaze. "Set him up so I can kill him, and he'll never give you another order."

"No, but you will."

"The difference is, *I'm* actually a blood-contracted member of the Assassins Guild, *and* I wear the Grandmaster's ring. That brings us back to your two options. You can profit by our arrangement, or die. Your choice." Mya stood, pulled a folded parchment out of a pocket, and dropped it on the desk. "These are the changes I want made to guild operations. See that you implement them. I'll be in touch."

Ignoring the lady's glare, Mya left the office without another word. The meeting could have gone more smoothly, but all in all, she was pleased with her first encounter. *One assassin down, only about another thousand to win over.*

CHAPTER V

"Milord, Tennison is here to see you." Baris' tentative announcement stirred Arbuckle from his worried musing, but he couldn't answer, couldn't tear his gaze from the smoke trailing up into the sky.

"I don't want to talk to anyone." *My fault...my city...why...I don't understand...*

Captain Ithross had informed him of the unrest shortly after dinner. Arbuckle had watched from his balcony throughout most of the night and into the morning, his astonishment transforming to horror as fire after fire—eighteen so far—blossomed in the Midtown and Heights districts. He felt sick. Though all had been contained, there was no denying that the impetus for the riots had been his fault. *Why would the promise of justice precipitate such acts of destruction?*

"He's insistent, milord." Baris sounded miserable. "And your breakfast has gone cold."

"I'm not hungry." Arbuckle signed and rubbed his aching eyes. *I've got to face this.* "All right, Baris. Let him in." He strode into his sitting room, the cold breakfast on the table roiling his stomach.

"Milord Prince." Tennison entered the room looking nervous and bowed. "I apologize for disturbing you so early, but several of the senior nobles and magistrates insist on meeting with you as soon as possible."

"No doubt." *They probably want to lynch me.* He dreaded facing them, but there was no putting them off. They deserved to know what was being done. "Tennison, tell the nobles I'll meet with them immediately. Baris, my clothes."

"Milord Prince, if I may be so bold to suggest..." Tennison took a hesitant step forward, urgency transforming his face.

"Yes, of course. I need *someone* to tell me when I'm making mistakes."

"Milord, this meeting is crucial. You mustn't rush into it without forethought." Tennison gestured toward the uneaten breakfast. "Gather your thoughts. Eat something."

"If as you say this meeting is crucial, keeping the nobles waiting will only..." Tennison was already shaking his head. "What?"

"If you indulge them by rushing to their demand for an audience, you set a bad precedent. You show that you can be manipulated. Make them wait an hour, collect your thoughts, and arrive looking rested and alert. Thus, you show them that you're in control. An emperor must demand respect."

"I'm not emperor yet."

"No, but in time, milord. Your father was feared, but you are...kinder. The nobles will try to take advantage of that."

Arbuckle looked at Tennison with a new appreciation. The man had a point. He knew the deadly dance of court politics far better than his prince. "An hour it is. And Tennison, never hesitate to give me your opinion."

"Milord Prince." The secretary smiled, bowed, and left.

"Clothes and a quick shave, Baris. I'll eat and review Captain Ithross' reports." He sat at the table and a hovering footman poured blackbrew into a dainty porcelain cup.

An hour later, Arbuckle strode into the audience chamber, dressed, groomed, and reasonably alert. A score of nobles clustered there, looking impatient and a not a little disheveled. *Damned if Tennison wasn't right.* Just by appearing calm and in control, Arbuckle gained the upper hand.

He spotted Duke Tessifus, his nearest cousin and next in line for the throne. If rule went to the most qualified, Tessifus would win hands down. He was twenty years Arbuckle's senior and much better versed in government. Arbuckle, however, was crown prince. The line of inheritance was clear.

To one side stood a cluster of black-robed magistrates, Arbuckle's judges and legal advisors. Somber men and women all, they didn't mingle with the nobles. For forty years they'd been meting out Tynean Tsing II's justice. *No wonder they're grim.*

At the herald's announcement, the room fell silent and everyone bowed. Mounting the low dais, Arbuckle lowered himself onto the cushioned chair. He'd never sat there before, and found it less comfortable than it looked. *I had better get used to it.*

"Lords and ladies, we have much to discuss." He gestured to the nobles. "Please, proceed."

Duke Tessifus stepped forward. "Milord Prince Arbuckle. On behalf of the nobles of Tsing, I offer you our sincere condolences on the death of your father. His loss is a grave blow to us all."

Arbuckle now noticed that black mourning bands encircled every right arm but his own. Baris had offered him one, but he had refused. He would not mourn a monster. "Thank you for your condolences. Now, we have serious matters to discuss, namely this city's safety and security."

Several of the nobles looked concerned, others shocked at his abrupt dismissal of the emperor's demise, but Tessifus merely nodded respectfully and took a short step forward.

"Milord, we request that you implement martial law immediately. This uprising must be put down by force."

"The incidents of last night were isolated and have been contained, cousin. Martial law is not necessary and would only escalate the unrest."

"Witnesses say that the violence originated at the Imperial Plaza. The perpetrators were shouting 'Down with the nobles,' and 'Justice for all'. They seem to be referring to your…um…speech."

"You think that *I* incited these acts of violence?" Arbuckle asked incredulously.

"Not deliberately, milord, but it's rumored that you suggested equality between nobles and commoners." Tessifus glowered. "How can that *be*?"

Arbuckle leaned forward. "Equal *justice*, cousin. The law must apply to everyone alike or you risk rebellion. Not a single kingdom or empire that ruled through oppression and fear has survived. Revolt is inevitable. An empire is built not only on the blood and sweat of the common people, but on their loyalty. Loyalty can't be beaten into them with a lash, it must be encouraged with hope, and peace, and *justice*. My ancestors knew that, all the way down to my father's father. It was Tynean Tsing II who perverted the relationship between commoner and noble. I intend to rectify that!"

"You suggest that we kowtow to the unwashed mobs of the Downwind Quarter?" Tessifus asked incredulously. The nobles flanking him looked disgusted. "Perhaps hand over the treasury so that a charwoman can dress in silk and satin?"

"Of *course* not." Arbuckle clenched his teeth at the sarcastic question. "But the same charwoman should not be flogged for dropping a lump of coal on a noble's carpet."

"Milord Prince, our *safety* is at risk!" Count Vetres lurched forward, his jowls jiggling with the emotion of his outburst. "All it takes is a single commoner with a torch and a skin of oil to set a fire. There are nearly a quarter of a *million* of them in this city. We must have martial law!"

"Force is not the answer, Count Vetres." Arbuckle compelled his voice to remain calm. "Our resident forces include twenty-thousand constables, knights, squires, imperial guards, and soldiers within the walls of the city. Another ten thousand may be summoned within the span of a few days. They will be used *only* to maintain order and round up troublemakers, not to institute widespread oppression."

"Pardon me, Milord Prince." Duchess Vainbridge stepped forward, a lace handkerchief pressed to her powdered brow. "Is there a shortage of *rope* in the empire that we cannot hang the perpetrators of this violence?"

"That's right, put the rabble down!" another noble demanded.

"Stick a few heads on pikes, and the rest will fall in line!"

"I'll secure my own safety with hired guards!"

"That kind of thinking is what *put* us in this situation!" Standing, Arbuckle spread his hands for calm. "Lords and ladies, we have control of this situation. Treating disgruntled people like rabid animals is *not* the answer. Of course you have the right to hire whatever security you deem necessary, but the common folk must have rights, too. I will not condone acts of brutality. They deserve the right to fair judgment and freedom from summary abuse."

Vetres huffed, "Rights? How can I maintain discipline among my servants if I have to consider their rights?"

"By treating them like human beings, not animals!" Arbuckle sat back down, trying to forcibly slow his pounding heart. "If I had you flogged daily for impudence, how would *you* react?"

Vetres turned red.

Arbuckle held up a hand to stave off any further protests, and looked gravely at the assemblage. "My father ruled through fear and oppression. I will not. I will rule through justice for *everyone*. The empire is mine to govern, and I will change the laws that have brought us to the brink of rebellion."

The nobles stared at him as if he'd said the sky was falling. Arbuckle saw fear in the eyes of some, anger in many more, but there were a few who looked hopeful, and the crown prince dared to imagine that some shared his beliefs.

"Actually, Milord Prince, with all due respect…you can't." Chief Magistrate Graving stepped forward, his long black robes rustling. A confident smile crooked his lips, but his sharp blue eyes shone cold. "At least, not until you're emperor. As crown prince, you have no power to institute new laws or dispel existing laws without the support of two-thirds of the senior nobles within the walls of the city." Graving swept his arm to indicate the attending nobles.

Arbuckle sat stunned for a moment, struggling to keep his temper in check. *Is that right?* He tried to remember the law—never his favorite subject—and failed. Graving undoubtedly knew the law to the letter. A glance at the nobles' smug smiles told him he would never get the support he needed from them. He hadn't thought this through before announcing his intentions. His negligence was now coming back to smite him.

He could think of only one rebuttal. "I *will* be emperor of this realm."

"I *know* that, Milord Prince, but until you are, the laws must be upheld and enforced as they're written. Simply telling the commoners that they suddenly have rights doesn't make it so. Nobles may still discipline their servants as they see fit, and exact retribution from any commoner for impugnment as was decreed by your father. It is the *law*."

"The law will change," Arbuckle fumed.

"Not *yet*, I'm afraid, Milord Prince." Graving folded his thick arms over his thicker torso.

If I could wring a concession from him… Arbuckle swallowed his pride. "Of course you're right, Chief Magistrate Graving, but our current situation is dire. I *cannot* renege upon my pledge to the commoners. The result would be disastrous. Until my coronation, if you and the other magistrates would take into account that circumstances *will* change, and compensate in your judgements…"

The chief magistrate was already shaking his head. "Milord Prince, how would it look if we, the magistrates charged with *upholding* the law, bypassed its tenets in favor of one noble's whim. I'm afraid that, for the time being, things *must* remain as they are."

Arbuckle managed a tight smile as he rose to his feet. "We will speak of this again, Chief Magistrate Graving."

"As your lordship commands." Graving bowed formally, and smiles spread through the crowd of nobles.

Arbuckle had been outmaneuvered in his first battle for a more-just empire. Despondent, he returned to his sitting room. Pushing aside the paperwork that awaited him, he went to his bookshelf and searched the titles for those he needed.

"Milord Prince, may I be of assistance?"

Arbuckle turned to see Tennison standing with his appointment book. "What's my schedule for today? I need to study."

"You have several hours free, milord." He tapped the book in his arms. "More if you wish it."

"Good. I need several volumes from the library. Books detailing every statute my father instituted, interregnal jurisprudence, anything you can think of.

"I'll summon the palace librarian, milord." Tennison left, and Arbuckle got to work.

Two hours later, with a pile of open volumes covering his desk and a sheaf of notes, the crown prince felt like he was drowning in quicksand. *I tipped my hand before I knew all the cards… They're going to force me to renege, and the commoners will revolt. I'll be forced to institute martial law and call in the military…just as they want me to do.*

"Blast it!" He slammed a book closed and leaned back in his chair, rubbing his burning eyes.

A scratch to his right caught his ear, and he opened his eyes to see his scribe, Verul, sitting with his leger on his lap. The notion of his petulant outburst being recorded for posterity almost made him laugh.

"Gods of Light, Verul, tell me you didn't record that!"

The scribe looked up startled, but Arbuckle's smile took the sting out of the outburst. "Yes, milord, I did." His lips twitched, and his pen scratched. "Every word. Even that."

The notion brought a memory of their conversation after his speech in the plaza. "Verul, did you get that transcription of your notes from yesterday? I could use a reminder of what I'm working for."

"Of course, Milord Prince." Verul hurried out and returned in moments bearing a massive leather-bound tome. "Here you are." He opened it on the desk and turned to the proper page.

Arbuckle read, reliving his words to the crowd in the plaza, annotated with their delighted reactions. When he'd finished, however, he felt vaguely discomforted. The archive didn't read quite as he remembered. Of course, he'd been caught up in the excitement, so perhaps his memories weren't to be trusted.

He flipped back a few pages and read. Still, he felt something wasn't quite right. Back again, until once more, he was in his father's torture chamber. Arbuckle hadn't even realized that Verul had accompanied him into that hell hole, yet there it was, recorded in precise horrifying detail. *But...*

"Verul!"

"Yes, Milord Prince?" The scribe was at his side in a moment, book and pen at the ready.

"You recorded the night in the dungeons, right?"

"Yes, milord."

"And you still have your original shorthand notes there?" He pointed to the ledger in the scribe's hands.

"Yes."

"Read me what you have after I..."—Arbuckle swallowed hard—"after I was ill."

The scribe flipped back several pages of his book and began reading. "Commander Ithross: Milord Prince, you must go. Crown Prince Arbuckle: No. Your cloak, Sir Fineal. Aside: Crown prince lays Fineal's cloak over the body of the dead woman. Crown Prince Arbuckle: Master Corvecosi, take care of her. Master Corvecosi: As you wish, Milord Prince. I'll also see that your father's body is properly attend—. Crown Prince Arbuckle: No. Divest him of any accoutrements of his former office, then burn his corpse and cast the ashes down the nearest cesspit."

"Enough!" Arbuckle bit back his temper. "Now, this is how the archive reads. Ithross: Milord Prince, you must go. Crown Prince Arbuckle: No. Your cloak, Sir Fineal. Aside: Crown prince lays cloak over the body of the *emperor*. Crown Prince Arbuckle: Master Corvecosi, take care of him. Master Corvecosi: As you wish, Milord Prince. I'll also see that the spy's body is properly attended to. Crown Prince Arbuckle: No. Burn the corpse and cast the ashes down the nearest cesspit."

"I...I don't understand." Verul looked panicked.

"Your version rings truer than the archived version." Arbuckle gritted his teeth. "Who is in charge of transcribing your notes?"

"Imperial Archivist Kelnik oversees all the archives. Not only the transcripts, but all governmental papers, court documents, and legal proceedings."

"Tennison, send for the imperial archivist."

While he waited, Arbuckle and compared several more transcribed sections with the originals. Many matched word for word, but some transcripts had been altered to show the emperor— or Arbuckle, in the newer transcripts—in a favorable light.

Soon enough, Tennison opened the door to admit a robed figure, a pale face beneath a shock of white hair, spectacles perched on a long, thin nose. The man's back was bent from years hunched over a desk, but he looked no older than sixty.

"Master Kelnik, I don't believe we've ever met."

"No, Milord Prince, we have not, though I have documented your life upon many occasions." Kelnik smiled and bowed.

The notion chilled Arbuckle's bones. *My life...* "How long have you been Imperial Archivist, and what exactly are your duties?"

"It's been thirty years since your father appointed me. All the records of the realm are my responsibility: making fair copies, cataloging, that sort of thing."

Arbuckle raised his eyebrows. "That's a lot of paperwork. Surely you have help."

Kelnik chuckled. "I do, milord, four junior archivists, but the ultimate responsibility is mine."

"And part of that responsibility is to ensure that the daily transcriptions are accurate?"

"Of course, milord."

"And if I were to tell you that they are not, in fact, accurate?"

For the first time, Kelnik's smile faltered. "I would beg to differ, milord. They are accurate."

"Are they now?" Arbuckle frowned and pointed to the two books, Verul's ledger and the archival volume. "Master Kelnik, do you know how to read shorthand?"

"Of course."

"Good. Please read and compare the open pages."

Kelnik peered intently at the books. After a couple of minutes, he stood and smiled proudly. "Excellent work, that. Transcribed by TSU,"—he pointed a crooked finger at a tiny notation in the lower right-hand corner of the archive page—"Tamira Soveal Ursin. I trained her myself."

Arbuckle stared in shock at the man's curious attitude. "Explain to me why there's a discrepancy between the two versions."

"Oh, we don't consider that a *discrepancy*, Milord Prince. We merely *clean up* the transcript. As you well know, the archive is the *official* record of an emperor's reign maintained for posterity. You'll find no disparagement to His Majesty within. And be assured, we'll take the same care of the records for *your* reign!"

"Why in the names of all the *gods* would you do that?" Arbuckle couldn't hold his temper in check.

Now it was Kelnik's turn to look bewildered and clearly frightened. "But...but...that's the way we've *always* done it! I was *trained* thus. Your father himself commended me on a job well done!"

"And the original notes?"

"Destroyed once they're fully transcribed, milord. Why would we keep them?"

Arbuckle fumed, remembering an old adage: *History is written by the winners.* Those words rang horrifyingly true. *Not during my reign!*

"Master Kelnik, I'm afraid you are unwittingly complicit in something that is tantamount to treason."

"Treason?" The man stumbled back a step. "Milord, I *never*—"

Arbuckle raised a hand for silence, though Verul's pen continued to scratch along. At least those words would be archived accurately.

"You were instructed by my father to alter records, and you did as you were ordered. I hold no fault on you for this, and absolve you of any wrongdoing, but this practice must *stop!*" He stood and went to his wall of bookshelves, fingering the leather-bound spines. "If we don't record every word accurately and honestly, no future historian can learn from our mistakes." He picked out a volume of recent lore, barely thirty years old, and held it out for the archivist to see. "Your actions, on the orders of my father, have made this a lie." He dropped the book to the floor.

Kelnik stared down at the book in horror. "Milord, I…" He dropped to his knees, reaching out to touch the fallen tome, and looked up, his eyes swimming with tears. "My life's work, milord! It cannot be *all* lies."

"Perhaps not, but without the original notes, we can't discern truth from fiction."

"I'm…sorry, milord." He bowed his head, tears darkening the leather cover of the book he held.

"I can't hold you responsible, but I also can't hold you in my service any longer. I'm afraid I can't trust you to truthfully record my reign, Master Kelnik." Arbuckle felt horrible, but knew he was right. A lifetime of training could not be broken.

"Let me fix it!" Kelnik looked up, his face streaked with misery. "Let me *correct* it!"

"Trade one fiction for another?" Arbuckle shook his head. "No. No, we'll append the records with notes indicating their questionable accuracy. When that's done, you will be dismissed from imperial service with your full pension. I'm sorry, Master Kelnik, but I can't trust you."

"I understand, milord." Kelnik struggled to his feet and bowed.

Once Tennison had shuffled the wretched archivist from the room, Arbuckle turned to his scribe. "Verul, would you be interested in his position?"

"I… " Verul stared at him, his eyes as round as eggs. "With all due respect, Milord Prince, I'd rather stay at your side. Someone's got to make sure your words are recorded accurately."

Arbuckle smiled. He liked this man. "I'll hold you to that, Verul. Mine with be an open, honest reign. See to Master Kelnik's replacement, and the notations I mentioned." He pointed to the shorthand ledger in Verul's hand. "And the original notes are to be kept from now on. Nothing is to be destroyed. Make sure the junior archivists are retrained properly. I'm just going to be reading for the next few hours, so why don't you go and do that now, before there's something important to record. You can send up an assistant if you're going to be very long."

"At once, milord!" Verul hurried out.

The crown prince turned back to his books, looking on the volumes littering his desk in a new light. *Truth or fiction?* he wondered. The law, at least, was clear, though it seemed to be against him. He had promised the common people of Tsing justice.

I'll be damned before I let the law make me a liar.

Hoseph materialized in Lady T's sitting room and found himself staring down the shaft of a crossbow bolt once again. He felt a brief wave of dizziness, and passed it off as eye strain from focusing on the bolt's needle-sharp head quivering mere inches from his face.

"Put that down!"

The lady of the house clenched her jaw and lowered the crossbow. ""Damn it, Hoseph! You need to stop appearing unannounced. I've already had one heart-stopping surprise visitor today."

Her obvious discomfort ignited his curiosity. "Who might that have been?"

"Mya." She put down the crossbow and headed for her dressing room.

He followed her, his mind reeling. "And you let her leave alive?"

"I didn't have a choice. She wears the Grandmaster's ring. She told me she was taking over the guild." She pulled a dress down from the rack and glared at it.

"She took it for herself?" That surprised him. He would have thought Lad would claim the ring as he had the Twailin guildmaster's. "What about Lad?"

"She told me that she killed him." Lady T put the dress back and picked another, turning to hold it up before her as she looked into the full-length mirror. "She said she deserved it more than he did."

"That doesn't make sense. She stepped between Lad and the Grandmaster's blade, risked her *life* for him. Why would she kill him?"

"With the Grandmaster's *ring* up for grabs?" She looked at him in the mirror, one eyebrow arched.

Mya was certainly ambitious, of that there was no doubt. Hoseph had originally suggested appointing Mya as Twailin guildmaster based on reports of her quick mind and leadership qualities. Still, something didn't make sense. If Mya killed Lad before he had a chance to don the ring, why not simply leave the body there? She might be strong, but Norwood was in no condition to walk, and she couldn't have carried the bodies of two grown men—one dead, one incapacitated—out the passage. *Unless she didn't.*

"Have you checked the passage into the palace dungeons?" Only someone with a guildmaster's ring could access the tunnel leading from the guild-owned wine shop into the dungeon.

Lady T wrinkled her brow. "No. Why?"

"I don't know if I believe Mya. She might be hiding Lad somewhere." There were still too many unanswered questions. "You should check the passage for any sign of them. Now, why did she come here?"

"I told you: to tell me she was taking over as Grandmaster." Picking out a green gown, she held it up before her and looked in the mirror.

"How does she propose to manage a takeover without—" He looked at Lady T anew. "She tried to recruit you."

"She gave me two options: help her or die." Lady T returned the green gown to the rack and picked out a red one.

"And what was your answer?" Hoseph surreptitiously shifted his gaze. Lady T's crossbow lay several paces away. He didn't doubt that he could send her soul to Demia before she could reach the weapon, but she was an assassin. She might have a half-dozen lethal implements hidden within reach.

"Do I *look* dead?" Lady T stood in front of the mirror, but she watched him in the reflection. "If I had denied her, she would have killed me and recruited one of my masters, and there goes your only ally. I think the question rightfully is: what are *you* going to do about her?"

"Kill her, of course, but I have to find her first. Did you have her followed?"

Lady T barked a sardonic laugh. "Send assassins to follow a Master Hunter wearing the Grandmaster's ring? I may as well slit their throats and dump them in the river myself."

She had a point. He'd seen Mya fight. "Play along with her for now and we'll set her up for the kill. We've got bigger problems to deal with first. What in the Nine Hells happened yesterday? I came out this morning to smoke thick enough to choke on, rumors of uprisings, and commoners strutting the streets as if they owned them."

Eyes narrowing, Lady T said curiously, "You must sleep in a tomb to not have heard the ruckus. They're calling it the Night of Flame. All instigated on by dear Crown Prince Arbuckle."

"What?"

Hoseph listened with growing astonishment as the guildmaster related the tale of the heir's speech to the unwashed masses, and the bonfire in the Imperial Plaza that started a night of riots. Evidently, Arbuckle was not as weak-willed as they'd thought.

"And just before you arrived, I received word that Arbuckle reprimanded the senior nobles when they insisted he institute martial law to control the violence. He told them he intends to *change* the laws to implement equal justice for all, nobles and commoners alike!"

"He *is* a fool!"

"Well, he got put in his place by Magistrate Graving. He can't change any laws until he wears the crown." She shrugged out of her night dress and started donning the red gown. "Not without backing from two thirds of the nobility."

Hoseph's anger warmed his face. "We have to make sure he doesn't get it."

"It's not likely he will. Not with Graving waving the law in his face." She began lacing the gown, her arms bent behind her back like a contortionist.

"We have to make sure." Hoseph paced the small space, deep in thought. On the third turn, the seed of a plan began to germinate in his mind. By the fifth, details were emerging like budding spring blossoms. "We can't let the coronation proceed. We've got to have him killed before he's emperor."

"Duke Tessifus is next in line for the throne."

"Yes, and he's got a family." Hoseph's plan burst into full bloom. "He can be pressured. Take his sons and we'll have him in the palm of our hand. He'll jump exactly as high as we want him to."

"I suggest we wait until after Arbuckle is dead." Finally dressed, Lady T sat and picked out a pair of shoes. She pressed a tab in the side of one, and a thin blade popped out from the toe, proving Hoseph right in his assessment of weapon accessibility. "First things first."

"I disagree. We need to know that Tessifus will be our pawn *before* we eliminate Arbuckle. If we don't, we'll be right back where we started. As presumptive heir, he'll be harder to get to, his sons protected by blademasters and imperial guards. Take them today."

"All right, I'll arrange the abductions." The lady pressed the tip of the blade against the edge of her vanity until it clicked back into hiding, then slipped the shoe onto her foot. "Do we send him one of them in pieces to make our point?"

"I don't think so. At least, not yet, but warn the duke not to go to the authorities." He continued pacing, his mind racing ahead. "Separate them and treat them well; one of them will be our next Grandmaster. We have to choose the right one, but that can wait until after we remove Arbuckle."

"Killing the crown prince isn't as easy as that." Lady T pursed her lips and applied lip rouge. "Setting it up properly will take time, and Arbuckle can do a lot of damage before he dies. If he gets enough nobles to back him—"

"He won't. I'll see to that. Contact your operative inside the palace and start the ball rolling."

"If the prince dies there'll be unrest." She reached for a dark eye pencil. "The commoners won't be easily subdued, now that they think they've got *rights*."

"You worry too much about that, Tara. With the military on one side of the river and the Assassin's Guild on the other, they'll have no safe haven. I'll work on making sure the provincial dukes will oppose Arbuckle, and you work on killing him."

"Have you contacted the other guildmasters yet?"

"Yes. Everyone's on board except Twailin. I'm meeting with their interim guildmaster today."

"And they have no problem with you presuming to order them around?"

Hoseph smiled at her sarcasm. "They're not as obstinate as you." He clutched Demia's talisman and concentrated on Lad's townhouse in Twailin. He had a feeling this was all going to work out perfectly.

CHAPTER VI

Dee peered out the parlor window onto the busy street. Carriages trundled down the cobblestoned street, and gentry strolled the sidewalks. No robed acolytes in sight. No Hoseph.

"Stop fidgeting, Dee." Sereth leaned against the fireplace mantel as if he hadn't a care in the world, arms folded, his head tilted as if listening to a quiet strain of music.

"I'm not fidgeting. I'm watching." In truth, Dee was nervous, and resented the ease with which the Master Blade perceived his apprehension. Though Hoseph *was* late, more troubling to Dee was that he had no idea what Sereth was going to do. The Blade had been tight-lipped since his arrival, his face passive. He had even sent Dee to fetch a pot of blackbrew and pastries, as if they awaited a friend and not some killer priest who lusted for their master's blood.

What if Hoseph offers Sereth the guildmaster position, and he accepts? Dee's stomach roiled as he unobtrusively checked the dagger inside his jacket. He wasn't much of a killer, but anyone who could appear from nowhere and kill with a touch made him nervous. *Why isn't Sereth nervous?*

"Dee." Sereth nodded toward the open parlor door.

Dee turned to see a darkening of the air in the foyer. The shadow thickened into a black cloud that coalesced into a man. He'd already seen Hoseph's vaporous departure once, but gaped no less at his arrival. Could he pop in anywhere? Dee glanced at Sereth, but the Blade still leaned casually with arms folded.

Hoseph looked around with a flash of annoyance before he caught sight of them. He strode into the parlor, eyes on Sereth. "You must be Master Blade Sereth."

Sereth nodded once in acknowledgement. "And you're Hoseph,

I presume."

"Yes." Hoseph flicked a glance in Dee's direction. "Has he told you why I've come?"

"He told me *some*, but frankly it's pretty unbelievable." Sereth waved Hoseph to a seat on one side of the low table and took the opposite chair. "I'd like to hear from you exactly what happened and what you expect of me."

Hoseph smiled without humor. "What *happened* is that Guildmaster Lad and Master Hunter Mya murdered the Grandmaster."

Sereth's brow knitted. "Dee gave me that much, but I'm afraid I don't see how it could be true. Both Lad and Mya wore rings." He raised his left hand, where a band of obsidian encircled his smallest finger. "They could no sooner attack the Grandmaster, than I could."

"Nevertheless, they killed the Grandmaster and five of his bodyguards."

"Only *five* bodyguards?" The Master Blade looked surprised. "Didn't you know about Lad?"

Hoseph waved dismissively. "Of *course* we knew about Lad. Mya, however, was a surprise. What can you tell me about her? She's obviously enhanced in some way. Does she possess some talisman? What's her weakness?"

"She's fond of sweet rolls." Dee said it before he could stop himself.

Hoseph cast Dee a scathing glance.

"Don't mind him." Sereth chuckled and waved dismissively, setting off another alarm in Dee's head. He'd never seen Sereth laugh. "Dee's not very bright, but he does know everyone's favorite noshes, and makes great blackbrew."

Dee's face burned. Something wasn't right with the way Sereth was pandering to this priest. Dee left the window and approached Sereth and Hoseph, bending to pour them each a cup of blackbrew. The steamy aroma gave him an idea. *If I throw hot blackbrew in Hoseph's face...*

"Tell me about Mya," Hoseph insisted. "What's her background and training? Where might she go to ground if she were on the run?"

Sereth barked a laugh. "She looks great in a tight pair of pants, but that's really all I know about her. Hunters aren't like *real* assassins. They're better at looking up addresses than doing the actual dirty work that's the lifeblood of this guild. I tell you what. I'll ask around and see what her people can tell me about her."

Dee hesitated, the pot of blackbrew heavy in his hand. *What the hells is he talking about?* Sereth knew that the Hunters were intrinsic to the success of the guild. And as for information about Mya, Dee knew more about her than anyone. *So why would he...*

You idiot! Realization struck, and he put the pot down. *He's plying Hoseph for information.*

Ashamed that he had mistrusted the Master Blade, Dee proffered the tray of pastries to the priest with an insipid smile.

Hoseph ignored him and focused on Sereth. "Good! We've got to hunt these traitors down and eliminate them."

"So...you don't know where they are now?"

"If I knew that, they'd already be dead!" The priest looked annoyed.

Sereth shrugged as he picked up his cup of blackbrew. "Anything you can tell me will help in my search."

"Mya is still in Tsing, but Lad may already be dead. If true, that's half of our problem solved, but I think it's safer to assume that he's still alive. If he returns to Twailin, kill him."

Dee struggled to hold the tray steady at the news. *Lad dead?* Sereth lowered his eyes to his steaming cup and sipped. When the Master Blade spoke again, his tone was no longer deferential, but sharp.

"Let me get this straight. Lad and Mya *allegedly* killed the Grandmaster—"

"There's nothing alleged about it. They killed him."

"So you say."

Hoseph's eyes narrowed. "No, I know it to be fact. I was there!"

"Then you should have no problem telling me *how* they managed it."

"I didn't witness the actual killing. I left to get help. That's not important!" Hoseph's face flushed. "All you need to know is what I've already told you. Lad and Mya killed the Grandmaster, which makes them traitors to this guild! The sentence for treason is death."

Sereth leaned back in his chair and crossed his arms as he stared at the priest. "You keep saying that, but you have no proof. Let me tell you what I think happened. For some reason, you didn't want Lad to discover the truth behind his wife's murder, so you killed Baron Patino, then tried to kill Lad's informant. Now you're trying to pin blame for the Grandmaster's death on Lad and Mya. Maybe *you* killed your master. I notice you don't wear a ring..."

"You've been digging into matters beyond your ken, Master Blade Sereth." Hoseph's sneer belied his seeming sincerity. "You asked what I expect from you. I expect you to follow orders. I expect you to kill Lad."

"On whose authority?"

"*What?*" The priest's eyes bulged, his jaw trembling at Sereth's simple question.

"On whose authority are you ordering me to hunt down my own guildmaster?"

"As the Grandmaster's representative I—"

"You are *nothing*." Sereth's interruption dropped Hoseph's jaw. "You're a dead man's *assistant*! You giving me orders is no different from Dee giving me orders if Lad was indeed dead. I don't take orders from *assistants*!"

"The Grandmaster—"

"—is dead. Which makes you the right hand of no one." Sereth smiled, but there was no humor in it. "I owe allegiance to only two people: my guildmaster and the Grandmaster. According to you, the Grandmaster is dead, so until there's a new one appointed, I take orders *only* from Lad."

Dee watched Hoseph closely, shifting his grip on the pastry tray to use it as a shield. According to Lad, the priest could kill with a touch.

"You...*traitor*!" Hoseph bolted up from his seat, one clenched fist glowing with a pearly light.

Sereth's piercing whistle startled both Dee and the priest. Before Hoseph could move, assassins appeared from behind draperies, cabinets and closed doors, crossbows leveled at the priest's chest. Closer at hand, two daggers slipped from Sereth's sleeves, ready to fly into the priest's throat. Dee stepped back from the field of fire in case Sereth gave the order.

Hoseph seethed with impotent rage. "You've betrayed your guild, all of you! Your lives are forfeit!"

"Our lives are our *guildmaster's* to spend, not yours! You're not even an assassin! Go back to wherever you came from and try to sell your story, but you have no authority here."

"You will die for this!" With the same flick of the hand and flash of silver Dee had noticed before, Hoseph dissolved in a cloud of swirling black smoke.

Dee dropped the tray with a clatter and leaned back against the sideboard, heaving a deep breath to steady his knees. Assistants didn't often have to deal with killer priests.

"I guess I just kicked the hornet's nest, didn't I?" Sereth slid his daggers back into the sheaths hidden in his sleeves. "That's one way to—"

A shadow coalesced behind Sereth, and from it emerged an enraged Hoseph, glowing hand extended. As he reached for the back of the unsuspecting Blade's neck, Dee lunged. "Sereth!"

The Master Blade twisted, but Dee slammed into Hoseph before he could bestow the lethal touch. They landed hard, and Dee rolled away from priest's deadly grasp. Crossbows fired, but the dark mist had already writhed forth. Bolts pierced the dissipating cloud, but only thudded into the floor where Hoseph had been.

"Dee!" Sereth grabbed him by the arm and heaved him up. "You all right?"

"Well, I'm not dead, anyway." He winced at the pain in his shoulder where he'd hit the floor.

"Thanks for keeping him off of me." Sereth patted Dee's jacket right where the assistant's blade was concealed. "You might try a dagger next time."

"I'd have missed." Dee straightened his coat.

Sereth snapped his fingers, and his Blades fanned out. "Stay sharp. He could appear anywhere. If he does, don't wait for an order, just skewer him."

"You sent me for blackbrew to place your Blades, didn't you?"

The corner of the Master Blade's mouth twitched. "I couldn't afford to have you give them away. You're not as good at hiding your emotions as you think you are. But forget that. Send runners to the other masters. Tell them everything. I'm putting the whole guild on alert. Anyone with families should see to their safety."

"Your wife?"

"Jinny's already in a safe house." Sereth looked grim. "I thought this might go badly."

"What about Lad and Mya? Do you think Lad's really dead?"

Sereth shook his head. "I don't know what or who could kill Lad, but we'll assume he's alive until we learn otherwise. The problem is, Hoseph has the rest of the guild hunting them, so they'll be on the run. How do we find them?"

"Lad will go to his family." Dee knew that as well as he knew anything. He'd watched Lad stare out from his balcony toward the Westmarket district where the *Tap and Kettle* stood, where his daughter, Lissa, lived with her grandparents and uncles. "He'll want to protect them."

Sereth nodded. "Jingles has standing orders to watch over them. I'll have him double the guard and they can warn Lad if he shows up. The problem will be getting get word to Mya. Hoseph said she was in Tsing. It's a big city."

"You want to help Mya?"

Sereth looked surprised. "Of course. Why would you think I wouldn't?"

"The guild factions have been...estranged for years. It wasn't too long ago that your master was trying to kill Mya."

Sereth shook his head firmly. "Horice was an idiot. Lad was right about one thing; working together is the only way to get things done. So if Mya has a problem, we all have a problem. I think Hoseph made that abundantly clear."

Dee smiled, grateful that Mya wasn't to be tossed to the wolves, then sobered when he considered the situation. "Why would she stay in Tsing?"

"I don't know." Sereth chewed his lip, then his eyes widened. "If they *did* kill the Grandmaster...you don't suppose she took the ring, do you?"

"I...don't know." Dee's mind spun anew.

"Well, we've got to send someone to find her, if for no other reason than to find out what really happened. I still don't understand how they could kill the Grandmaster. Get a good horse and pack light; you'll want to travel fast."

"*Me?*" Dee swallowed hard. "I'm...not much of an assassin."

"You signed a blood contract, so you're an assassin. What's more, you're a Hunter, so you know how to find information and people. You also worked for Mya for years, and know her better than anyone. Besides, did you think I was *asking?* Until Lad's back, I'm Twailin's guildmaster, and I'm ordering you to go."

"Um...of course, sir."

"Good. Now send those runners, then make arrangements for your trip. I want you on the road tomorrow morning." Sereth whirled away, barking out commands to his Blades.

Dee hurried out of the parlor, his mind flicking through the tasks he needed to accomplish before his trip. If he was to have any chance of finding Mya in Tsing, there was one person he needed to talk to.

"Milord! This is unprecedented!"

"No it's not, Chief Magistrate. Read your history." Arbuckle scrawled his signature on the last of the edicts he'd had drawn up. Pressing the imperial signet ring to the bottom of the parchment, he felt a slight tingle as its weak magic impressed an indelible seal on the paper, ratifying its authenticity. This ring was the only one of his father's that he consented to wear. "The Articles of the Foundation grant the senior noble final judgment in all cases and the right to pardon those convicted of crimes. Effective immediately, I'll review all judgments and sentences."

"That makes a *mockery* of the judiciary!" Graving clenched his hands at his sides, quivering in rage.

"The *mockery* is what currently passes as justice in this realm!" Arbuckle stifled his temper. "I may not be able to *change* the laws yet, but I can nullify unfair judgments on a case-by-case basis."

The chief magistrate rocked back on his heels, seeming to gather his resolve and gird his temper. "Milord Prince, I'm sure you have more important things to do with your time than review *commoner* court cases. With the recent unrest, there are hundreds!"

"Only hundreds?" Arbuckle handed the signed edict to

Tennison with a wry smile. "Then it's not as bad as I feared. And what better use of my *time* than assuring that justice is served for *all* my subjects?"

"But the *law*—"

"The law is draconian and abusive!" He bit back his tirade. There was no point in it. "But as you pointed out, I can't change it yet. The Articles of the Foundation do, however, allow me to pass final judgment."

"I *know* the Articles, milord!" Graving's face flushed from crimson to almost purple.

"Good! Perhaps you'll start instituting them." Arbuckle clenched his teeth to avoid saying something he would later regret. "I won't argue about this. You're dismissed, Chief Magistrate Graving."

"You *can't* dismiss me!" Graving sputtered. "Only the emperor can appoint or dismiss magistrates!"

"I didn't mean *permanently*." Arbuckle smiled with an utter lack of amity. "Not *yet*, anyway. I meant that I have much to do, so you may leave now."

Quivering with rage, the chief magistrate whirled and stalked out of the audience chamber. The crown prince ignored the insult; no commoner would dare present their back to a monarch. *No matter. I'm not emperor yet.* As the tension of the encounter waned, Arbuckle longed to close his eyes and lay his head to the table. He had spent half the night poring through tomes of law and history, rooting out precedents for the changes he wanted to make. Unfortunately, there was still work to be done.

"What next, Tennison?"

"Your missive to the provincial dukes, Milord Prince." The secretary handed over another sheet of parchment.

"Good. I'd like this to get out right away. Please summon Archmage Duveau while I read it through."

"Yes, Milord Prince."

Arbuckle had drafted the missive that morning, then given it to Tennison to be copied fair and embellished with the requisite official flourishes. It laid out the essence of his edicts and instructed the dukes to review all judgments levied by their magistrates to ensure evenhanded justice. It also required them to submit to Arbuckle reports enumerating the number of cases, the judgements, and sentences. His orders wouldn't be popular, but they were necessary. He read it through twice and was approving it with his signet ring when Tennison returned.

"Milord Prince, Archmage Duveau."

Arbuckle looked up from the page into the red-rimmed eyes and sallow features of his archmage. "Gods of Light, man, are you ill?"

"I am fatigued, Milord Prince." Duveau nodded respectfully, his lips a thin white line. "Do you not recall commanding me to re-cast the magical wards upon the palace with no delay?"

"I recall ordering the dungeons be protected along with the rest of the palace. I had no idea it would be so taxing...or take so long."

Archmage Duveau sniffed. "The wards are complicated and intricate, milord. To protect the lower levels, the entire lattice had to be replaced. I have only just completed the final spell. The barrier is impenetrable and seamless. No one may use magic to enter or leave the palace grounds."

"And that includes the dungeons?"

Though the mage's face seemed set in stone, he fairly radiated indignation. "Of course, Milord Prince."

"Thank you. I'll sleep better knowing that I'm protected by your skill."

The mage bowed, though not deeply. "I'm at your service, Milord Prince. Now I must rest before—"

"Just one more thing." Arbuckle held out the parchment. "I need you to send this to all the provincial dukes by magical messaging."

Duveau's bushy eyebrows raised even as the corners of his mouth turned down. "Now?"

"Immediately, Archmage." Arbuckle could brook no delay on this. The longer the missive took to reach the dukes, the more commoners would be unfairly beaten or killed.

Plucking the missive from Arbuckle's hand and holding it with his fingertips, Duveau scrutinized the page. "The *entire* message, milord?"

"Yes. Word for word." Arbuckle wondered at the mage's reticence.

"To *every* provincial duke?"

"Yes. Is there a problem?"

"It is…labor intensive, Milord Prince, and I'm the only one of the Imperial Retinue of Wizards privy to the secret of the messaging device."

Arbuckle flushed with irritation, his lack of sleep undoubtedly curtailing his patience. He strove to calm himself before continuing. "I'm sorry, but there's really no way around it unless you want to teach one of the other members of the retinue to use the device. The new edicts must be implemented immediately."

"Of course, Milord Prince." Duveau bowed again, his face clouded in a mask of discontent. "Anything else?"

"Nothing right now. Thank you."

When the door closed behind the archmage, Arbuckle slumped back in his seat. "Why does it feel like scaling a battlement just to get anyone to *do* anything around here?"

"They're testing you, Milord Prince," Tennison explained. "The chief magistrate and archmage served your father without question for decades. Through his favor, they rose to high offices and became accustomed to doing as they pleased. That privilege has ended."

Arbuckle shook his head. "They better get used to it. What's next?"

"Commander…ah, *Captain* Ithross and Chief Constable Dreyfus await an audience, Milord Prince. They arrived just as Archmage Duveau did, and are eager to speak with you."

"Very good. Show them in." Arbuckle's heart beat a bit faster, sweeping away his drowsiness. *Perhaps they have news about the unrest in the city.*

The two officers stepped through the door with a broad-shouldered man leaning heavily on a cane between them. Despite the drastic change in the man's appearance—his resplendent uniform replaced by simple rough-spun clothing, his healthy complexion now sallow—Arbuckle recognized the man instantly.

"Captain Norwood!" The crown prince stood. A curious thought popped into his head: *If this is the man who murdered my father, should I kill him or thank him?* "Chief Dreyfus, where did you find him?"

"At the Temple of the Earth Mother, Milord Prince." Dreyfus

bowed low. "I brought him immediately to Captain Ithross."

"Milord Prince." Ithross bowed. "I tried to question the captain, but he refused to answer, insisting that he speak with you personally. I was suspicious, but...this situation is unusual. I thought it best if we—"

A knock at the door interrupted Ithross, and Tennison admitted Master Keyfur, member of the Imperial Retinue and second only to the archmage. His flamboyant dress—a wild mix of lavender, yellow, and green that highlight his ebony skin—seemed to brighten the entire room.

The mage bowed low, the peacock feather stuck behind his ear sweeping nearly to the floor. "Milord Prince."

"I sent for Master Keyfur, Milord Prince, to determine the truth of the captain's statements," Ithross explained.

Arbuckle noticed that Norwood was shaking, leaning heavily on his cane. "Guards." He waved his blademasters forward. "Bring the captain—"

Captain Norwood's cane clattered to the floor. He stumbled back and collapsed to his knees, his face blanched white and his eyes wide. "Please, Milord! I had no part in the emperor's death! I beg you! Don't—"

"What?" Arbuckle held out a hand to forestall his guards, dumbfounded by the captain's distress.

What could have turned such a strong man into this quivering wreck? Looking closely, he spied pin-point bruises on the captain's hands and face, saw how he flinched as Ithross and Dreyfus reached down to grasp his arms. *Dear Gods of Light...* He remembered Norwood's arrival, how the emperor had ordered Arbuckle, Tennison, and the scribe from the room. *No witnesses...* Then he recalled blood-tipped spikes in an iron cage.

"It was you, wasn't it? You were held in the dungeon. Tortured by my father."

"Yes, Milord Prince." Norwood struggled to his feet with the officers' help, still trembling, his eyes darting to the blademasters at Arbuckle's sides. "I was...taken, and Sergeant Tamir was... murdered by the emperor's bodyguards."

"Murdered..." Arbuckle glanced at his contingent of stone-faced blademasters. They would follow any order he gave them, oath-bound to obey. *No wonder he's so frightened of them.* "Blademasters, take position behind me. You will only intervene to protect me. Tennison, fetch some chairs, and cancel the rest of my appointments for this afternoon. I'm going to have a chat with Captain Norwood, and I don't want any interruptions."

Norwood seemed to relax a trifle as the guards and secretary obeyed.

Ithross, however, looked distinctly nervous. "Milord Prince, before we relax our guard, may I establish that this man is no danger to you?" He gestured to Keyfur

"Of course, Captain. Chief Constable Dreyfus, I'll let you get back to your duties. Good work finding Captain Norwood here. Oh, and please see Tennison later for a copy of the edicts I just authorized. They'll affect the way your constables conduct their duties."

"Milord." Dreyfus bowed and left the room, for once looking disappointed at being dismissed.

"Captain Norwood, Master Keyfur here is going to cast a spell to ensure that what you say is accurate."

"I would have insisted upon it myself, Milord Prince." Norwood's voice sounded firmer now, and some color had returned to his face. "What I have to say may be difficult for you to believe, and I want no doubt that I'm telling the truth."

"Very good. Master Keyfur, please proceed."

The wizard plucked the feather from behind his ear and waved it in a circle before the captain's face. "Captain Norwood, do you intend any harm to Crown Prince Arbuckle?" The mage's voice rumbled low and melodious, almost hypnotic.

"No, sir, I do not."

"Did you have anything to do with the death of Emperor Tynean Tsing II?"

"No, sir, I did not."

"Do you know who killed my father?" Arbuckle interrupted, catching Norwood's eyes in his gaze. The captain stared back without flinching.

"No, Milord Prince, I don't."

"He speaks the truth," confirmed Keyfur.

Tennison returned then, along with several servants carrying chairs, and two more bearing a full blackbrew and tea service and platters of neatly prepared sandwiches.

"Ah, Tennison, you read my mind. Perhaps something stronger than tea would be welcome as well." Arbuckle motioned toward a sideboard by the window. "Captains, Master Keyfur, please sit down and help yourselves. I'm sure getting the entire truth laid out is going to be a long, difficult process. Verul, make sure you don't miss anything."

"Yes, Milord Prince."

"Now, Captain Norwood, what brought you halfway across the kingdom to warn my father of a threat to his life?"

"An investigation into a noble's death in Twailin led me to believe that there was a spy in the palace." Norwood swallowed audibly. "I was wrong, milord."

"What do you mean? There was no spy?"

"Not exactly, milord. When I told the emperor of my suspicions, he…told me that he was the master of the Assassins Guild."

"What?" Arbuckle lowered his cup, the porcelain clacking against the saucer as his hand shook. He looked to Keyfur for confirmation.

The mage nodded, his eyes wide. "He speaks the truth, milord."

Arbuckle had thought that no revelation about his father could be worse than what he had already learned, but this…the emperor of Tsing as master of a guild of murderers?

"It seems impossible." Arbuckle motioned Tennison forward, and his secretary dutifully topped up his and Norwood's cups with fine single-malt whiskey. Arbuckle sipped, taking strength from the heady concoction. "Go on, Captain Norwood. Please start at the beginning and spare no detail."

Two hours later, Arbuckle knew the truth, or at least, as much as Captain Norwood could provide. The crown prince didn't know what sickened him more, hearing what the captain had endured, or what his father had revealed to his captive about his empire-wide syndicate of organized assassination and terror. Norwood had obviously not been meant to leave the dungeons alive. What was more, the priest Hoseph had been transformed from suspect to full-blown accomplice as the emperor's right-hand man in this society of death. But still unanswered was the question: who killed Tynean Tsing and his five blademasters?

Norwood rubbed his eyes and shook his head, downing the last of his cup of whisky-laced blackbrew. "I wish I could tell you more, Milord Prince, but I can't. I passed out, and woke in the care of the priests."

Arbuckle glanced once more to Keyfur, and received a nod in reply. The captain was telling the truth.

"Well, that's it then. Tennison, provide Captain Norwood with a room in the palace and see that he has every comfort. Also, post a guard at his door for his protection. Master Keyfur, if you would be so good as to tell Archmage Duveau to send a fast message to Duke Mir in Twailin informing him that his Royal Guard Captain is here." Turning to Norwood, he asked, "Will you need transportation home?"

"I came in a carriage, and...there was a dog inside, a mastiff that I'm quite fond of." Norwood looked beseechingly at the crown prince. "I'd like to know if he's all right."

Ithross surprised them all with a wry laugh. "The dog's quite well, Captain, but I'm glad you've shown up to claim him. He nearly bit off the stableman's hand when they tried to remove him from the carriage, so they decided to let him stay inside. They've been feeding him from the kitchens. I'm afraid the carriage is a bit of a mess."

"There you are, Captain, everything safe and sound. Why don't you go down to the stables and see to your dog while a room is readied for you."

"Thank you, milord. Thank you!"

"My pleasure, Captain." Arbuckle stood and extended a hand. "I'm sorry for what you endured at my father's hand. Anything I can provide to make your rest here easier, just ask."

"Milord, I..." Norwood took his hand tentatively and shook it. "You've already done more than enough. I'm sorry for...what happened."

"No more than I, Captain. No more than I."

CHAPTER VII

Lad was right. It'll take years to learn this city! Mya paused at yet another corner and checked the street name on the lamp post. *Archer Street, which means I'm back in Midtown, I think.* Checking the map in the guidebook, she frowned. Midtown, yes, but not where she had thought she was. Looking around, she noted several distinctive landmarks—Landstead's Fabric Warehouse, Redeye Tavern, Teeny Weenie Sausages—and committed them to memory. She had spent most of yesterday, after her meeting with Lady T, exploring the Heights District, and had continued her rambles this morning. Though it was tedious, she was making progress.

She was having better luck assessing the mood of the citizens. Mya stopped at blackbrew cafés and pubs every hour or so. It surprised her how many were open, since most of the larger businesses had boarded their doors and windows against looters. Sustenance aside, the cafés and pubs served her well. They buzzed with all kinds of conversation and rumors.

Observations of other pedestrians also offered perspective. There were few nobles about, and those who were out surrounded themselves with well-armed muscle. She hoped Lady T took note. Hiring out Enforcers as bodyguards would be lucrative.

As for the commoners out and about, she had grouped them into three broad categories: troublemakers, quiet hopefuls, and nutters. The first were the most dangerous. They wandered the streets in gangs, sometimes drinking, loud and scornful, inciting revenge or even random violence against the nobility, constabulary, and military. She'd even seen them accosting those who merely looked affluent.

Most abundant were the quiet hopefuls. They crowded the

cafés, sipping tea and blackbrew and discussing the future. They seemed to be as frightened of the troublemakers as they were of the nobility and constables. They knew that violence only led to more violence, and they'd already seen enough. They spoke of rights and justice. Mya didn't know whether to laugh at them or cheer them on.

The nutters were a small but vocal minority, throwing out cockeyed theories as to who killed the emperor and what was to come. Some preached pathetically alone on street corners, while others gathered with their oddball peers at corner tables in cafés and pubs, eyeing other patrons suspiciously and whispering their convoluted conspiracies. Mya just smiled and shook her head. Even the most farfetched seemed saner than the truth.

Turning onto Archer Street and starting down the hill, Mya spotted yet another imminent confrontation between a gang of troublemakers and a squad of constables. This was the fifth she'd witnessed this morning. She stopped and leaned against a building to watch.

"On your way!" said the middle-aged corporal in charge. His people wielded truncheons, but wore swords at the ready. "We don't want any trouble from you lot."

"Trouble from *us*?" A motley young man in the fore of the throng stabbed a finger at the closed shoe factory behind the constables. His other hand held a stout stick. "What about the trouble we had from that son-of-a-bitch Count Renley who owns this place. He hires young-uns and beats 'em when they don't work fast enough!"

"An' he's sold others into slavery!" shouted a girl in a ragged skirt. "My little sister just disappeared outta there, an' I never heard from her again!"

"There'll soon be legal ways of dealing with these problems," the corporal promised. "If you've got a charge to make, you need to—"

"Legal this!" A cobblestone flew from the midst of the troublemakers and shattered a second-story window.

That's it, Mya thought.

The troublemakers surged forward, met with shields and truncheons. Four went down in a flash, but one constable fell when a stone met with his nose. The corporal blew a shrill note on a whistle. Mya had heard many of those the past two days, and knew it meant more constables would arrive soon.

Most of the troublemakers scattered, but others fought on. Still, the constables hadn't drawn swords. During previous altercations, Mya had seen constables holding back on lethal force, but making a lot of arrests. She had overheard more than one assertion of detainees being released with only a warning.

Either this is the new justice, or they don't have enough jail cells enough to hold them all.

Judging it time to leave, Mya turned down a side street and hurried down the hill. She was in no danger, but didn't want to be detained as a witness. She tried to look inconspicuous as another squad of constables rounded the corner ahead and trotted toward the conflict, but they barely spared her a glance.

Enough aimless wandering for today. Learning the streets was one thing, but learning the *city* was a more complex challenge. She needed to find a local willing to help her. She also needed to find out if Lady T was following her orders. Setting her mind on a new goal, Mya headed down toward the river and Fivestone Bridge.

"Miss Johens." The same slovenly sergeant she'd met before touched the rim of his iron cap and grinned with tobacco-stained teeth. "Done with your business so early?"

"For now, Sergeant. Thank you for asking."

"If you need an escort back to the *Dulcimer*, I can assign my corporal to see you there safe."

Mya considered the offer. Constables *did* know the city like few others, and this corporal was tall and admittedly good looking. She might learn a lot...and even teach him a thing or two.

Cozy up to a constable? Reality dashed her slim hopes of alleviating her loneliness. *Don't kid yourself, Mya. You're a monster, and there would be questions you couldn't answer.*

The last thing she needed was a constable dogging her steps. With a pained smile, she said, "Thank you, but there's no need, Sergeant. It's only a few blocks, and I'm quite safe at this time of day."

"I wish you wouldn't do that, Benj," she heard the corporal mutter in a tone intended not to be overheard.

"And I wish you'd get loosen up and get laid." The sergeant

hawked and spat into the river. "You don't get some female company soon, you're gonna end up a bitter old man like me."

"You're not that old," the corporal countered, and the other constables snorted in laughter.

Though their attention grated on her nerves, their familiarity had an advantage. This morning the constables had simply waved her past, having seen her twice yesterday going back and forth.

Mya stopped in at the *Tin Dulcimer* to use the chamber pot—she'd imbibed far too many cups of blackbrew during her morning café hopping—and change clothes. She'd spent half the night altering her drabbest travelling dress into a working woman's outfit to better fit in with the less-affluent neighborhoods of the Dreggars Quarter. The rest of the night she'd once again spent with her back in the corner, her daggers at the ready.

It took her some time to find the pub where she and Lad had been waylaid by a team of Enforcers their first night in Tsing. *Only four days ago?* It seemed like years. The poor thugs were probably still tending their wounds. Mya stood at the corner across from the pub watching passersby: working people, mothers with children, and the occasional vagrant. Half a lifetime in the Assassins Guild had taught her exactly what to look for, and eventually she spotted it.

Two Enforcers strolled down the street, too burly and cocky to be simple laborers or dock workers. Swords were illegal for commoners in the city, but they sported daggers and short clubs. Having decided on a straightforward approach, Mya walked up to the pair without pause, which was enough to take them off guard.

"You work for Borlic?"

"Who wants to know?" One man's hand drifted toward the dagger at his waist.

"Mya from Twailin."

The Enforcers' eyes widened and they subtly shifted their stances. The hand moved away from the dagger.

At least they seem to know who I am now.

Mya raised her hands palms out in a gesture of harmlessness, and to make sure they got a good look at the ring on her finger. "I'm not here for trouble. I just need to speak with Borlic. If you would be so kind as to point me in the right direction…"

The Enforcers shared a dubious glance, and the one who had

spoken pointed up the street. "Two blocks up, there's a cobbler's shop. Bull-Leather Soles. Ask for him there."

"Thanks." As Mya walked away, she cocked an ear to listen.

"If she kills Borlic, it's on your head."

"What was I supposed to do? They said if we see her to just report. If she's going to Borlic, then he'll report, too."

Their words told her little, but she might get more from Borlic. Mya pushed through the door to the cobbler's shop and told the woman behind the work table, "I'm here to see Borlic."

The cobbler glanced up with a frown from the boot she was repairing. "Who's that?"

"I'm sure you know him." Mya wasn't about to blurt out guild business. Most likely the woman knew what was going on in her shop, but one never knew. "He's probably wearing a sling on his arm."

The woman's frown deepened. "Up the stairs there. First door on the left."

"Thank you."

"You'd best knock. He's been in a mood lately."

Mya climbed the steps, wondering if Borlic's mood had to do with more than the shoulder Lad had dislocated. *Something like being told he had a new Grandmaster, maybe?* Heeding the cobbler's advice, she knocked on the door and waited. The door opened, and a huge figure filled it.

"What do you want?" The woman in the doorway showed some interesting heritage, with shoulders barely narrower than the portal, a flat face, jutting jaw, and pronounced lower canines that flashed when she spoke.

"I'm Mya. I need to speak with Borlic."

Again, subtle recognition and caution. The mountainous woman stepped aside and waved her in.

Mya immediately felt claustrophobic. The room wasn't large, which was no surprise, since Borlic was only a journeyman. Aside from the small desk, there was barely enough room to accommodate the three Enforcers already there. They gazed at her as if deciding whether she'd would taste better roasted or raw. Mya would have felt threatened if any of them could have harmed her in the slightest.

"What can I..." Borlic's question trailed off as he recognized her. He stood from behind his desk, his good hand near the dagger at his belt. The other arm, as Mya had suspected, hung in a sling. "What do you want?"

"How's the arm?"

"It hurts. Now what do you want?"

"Information. Where do I find the Master Enforcer?"

"Why should I tell you? You're not my boss."

So that's how it is. Lady T had obviously not told the rank and file that Mya was Grandmaster. She raised her hand to show him the ring girding her finger. "Actually, I'm your boss' boss' boss."

His eyes widened, then narrowed. "That's not what I've been told."

"What *have* you been told?" she asked with a cold smile.

"That you're not my boss." The muscles at Borlic's jaw bunched and relaxed rhythmically. "Look, I'm not giving you an excuse to break my other arm. You got a beef with the guild, you talk to the masters. The Master Enforcer's name is Clemson. She's got an office on the bluff overlooking the shipyards." Borlic sat back down. "You want someone to take you there?"

"That would be perfect."

"Jolee, take her to Clemson."

"Thank you, Borlic. You've been very helpful." Mya thought that Borlic would have agreed to anything to get her out of his office.

The walk across the Dreggars Quarter took about a quarter hour. Hackneys didn't venture this far south of the river, and Mya doubted that her escort would have fit into one even if she'd chosen to ride. Mya pondered the huge woman's heritage as she hurried to keep up. She'd seen crossbreeds before, but the offspring of humans and other distantly related cousin-races were rare in Twailin. They seemed a bit more common in Tsing, though treated as second-class citizens even by the commoners. *Though they certainly make good Enforcers...*

Clemson's headquarters were housed in a chandlery. The scents of wax, oil, and herbs smelled like a perfumery compared to vile industrial odors that smothered the rest of the quarter, and, indeed, most of the city. It discomforted Mya to realize that the stench of tannery sludge, offal, and open sewage hadn't bothered her as much the past couple of days.

Jolee escorted her through the main work room. Workers stirred huge bubbling vats of beeswax, tallow, and whale oil, dipped lengths of cotton twine into the molten wax, and hung the drying candles by their wicks on multi-tiered racks. Men and women alike were stripped down to near indecency against the stifling heat, but Mya's enchanted wrappings kept her cool.

At the top of a long stair in the back of the building, Jolee knocked on a door with surprising gentleness. The door opened, and an Enforcer equal to Jolee in height and girth met them with a narrow-eyed stare.

"What?"

"Borlic sent her to see Clemson." Jolee hooked a thick thumb at Mya.

The new Enforcer frowned, looked Mya over, and nodded, beckoning them inside.

This is too easy, Mya considered. She hoped she wasn't being set up. She listened, but detected no scuffling or sounds of weapons being drawn.

A far cry from Borlic's office, this room was positively palatial. The red-leather upholstery, wood-paneled walls, gleaming brass lanterns and fixtures, and a rug woven in the pattern of a compass rose all gave the place a nautical motif. The west wall sported large windows of leaded glass that commanded an impressive view of the shipyard below the bluff, the bay, and the sea beyond. The afternoon sun haloed a tall, slim woman looking out the window, a single long braid of blonde hair hanging down her back to well below her waist.

"Who is it?" The woman turned, and Mya stifled her surprise. She was truly beautiful, with high cheekbones and exotic almond-shaped eyes, and upturned ears attesting to some degree of elven blood. Her blousy white shirt, in which she could have hidden a half-dozen daggers, was tucked into a low-slung pair of snug black pants that could have hidden none. Her soft leather boots with turned-down cuffs definitely hid steel. She was, to Mya's mind, the very image of a pirate captain of tall tales.

"Borlic sent her to see you, Master Clemson." Jolee stepped aside, indicating Mya with a wave of one massive hand. "He called her *Mya*."

One of Clemson's incongruously dark eyebrows twitched. "Very well." Waving her Enforcers out of the room, Clemson stepped closer, eyes the color of honey raking Mya from head to toe. "Master Hunter Mya... You and your guildmaster beat up several of my people a few nights ago. I'm surprised that you'd show your face here again."

"I *was* Master Hunter Mya. Now it's Grandmaster Mya." Mya wiggled her ring finger.

"So I had heard." Clemson leaned on the corner of her broad desk. "A little young to be Grandmaster, aren't you?"

Mya smiled thinly. "I didn't realize that there was an age requirement." She looked Clemson up and down again. "A little skinny to be a Master Enforcer, aren't you?"

Clemson's flawless lips twitched, her long fingers brushing nonexistent wrinkles from her trousers. "I prefer the term 'slim'. You'll forgive me, I'm sure, if I test your claim."

"Feel free."

The woman drew a throwing dagger from her blousy sleeve and raised it. Her hand hung in the air, trembling with the effort to throw the blade into Mya's eye. Finally she relented and tucked the dagger away. "Well, it seems that is the Grandmaster's ring after all."

"I'm not likely to lie about it." Mya considered how to phrase her first question. "Borlic said he'd been told I wasn't his boss. What have you been told?"

"Lady T sent word that the Grandmaster had been killed. She failed to mention that his successor had been selected." Turning to a broad sideboard, the Master Enforcer pulled a stopper from a crystal decanter. "Thirsty?"

"Yes, thank you."

Clemson poured into two tumblers and offered one to Mya.

"I wasn't selected, but I'm *taking* his position." Mya accepted it and inhaled the fragrant aroma of spiced rum. She sipped, and the liquor caressed her throat like velvet fire, stoking her resolve. "I need to ask you a few questions."

"Ask all you wish, but you must understand my position." Clemson downed her drink in one long swallow and set her tumbler down on her desk. "The guild has a strict hierarchy, and I can't accept you as my Grandmaster until my guildmaster tells me you are."

"And you must understand my position." Mya finished her rum and tossed the tumbler to the Master Enforcer, who snatched it deftly out of the air. "I'll get my answers, or I'll have a new Master Enforcer by tomorrow morning."

The Enforcer stared at her for a time, her face expressionless. Mya simply stared back. No one could hurt her here. She held all the cards in this game, and Clemson knew it. Finally, the Enforcer put Mya's glass beside hers and waved at one of the velvet-upholstered chairs.

"Have a seat and ask your questions." She took a seat behind the desk.

"First, I'd like to know what orders you've received recently from Lady T." She sat and crossed her legs, trying to appear casual and confident, though she didn't feel either.

"You're asking me to betray my master."

"No, I'm asking you to tell me if my orders to your master have been passed on to you. If they haven't, I need to make my orders clearer."

Clemson considered this for a while, then shrugged and answered. "I've been told to expand our operations to north of the river once the unrest settles down."

That's encouraging. "What kind of operations?"

"Everything. Protection and extortion rackets, prostitution...everything."

"What about new strategies? Anything different?"

Clemson wrinkled her brow. "No. New...like what?"

Mya's brow furrowed in confusion. Was Lady T following her instructions or not? *I need more information.* "Never mind. Give me the names and addresses of the other masters. I'll be paying them visits, too."

"Nice to know I'm not special." Clemson's lip curled, but she broke away from Mya's stare. "The nearest is Master Blade Noncey. His office is here in the Dreggars Quarter, in the back of a gambling house in the basement of the Yellow Briar pub on Tannery Row. Next is 'Twist' Umberlin, the Master Hunter..."

Mya committed the names and addresses to memory and bid the Master Enforcer good day. Curious stares followed her through the chandlery on her way out, but no one tailed her. She checked her map and headed to meet Master Noncey. She hoped interviewing the masters would shed some more light on what was going on in the guild, but wouldn't bet her life on it.

Hoseph scuffed along the quiet street, the throb of a swelling blister on his heel plaguing his concentration. He wasn't familiar enough with this particular Heights neighborhood to travel using his talisman, and though high priests might ride in carriages, acolytes walked. He cursed the necessity for this charade. The disastrous trip to Twailin hadn't improved his mood, but he would deal with those traitors later. He had bigger fish to fry.

He approached an imposing house—great stone blocks girded by a high wrought-iron fence—that seemed more like a fortress than a private residence. Of course, when you were the official responsible for the punishment and imprisonment of a significant portion of the populace, safeguards were essential. Meting out the emperor's justice had not endeared Chief Magistrate Graving to the common folk.

Hoseph recited his calming mantra as he approached the constables manning the gate. He knew the constabulary was searching for him, but doubted he would be recognized. The stern-faced, richly dressed high priest whose likeness adorned wanted posters throughout the city bore little likeness to the lowly, contrite acolyte who stood before them. He drew back the cowl of his robe and painted on a bright, oblivious smile.

"Good constables, I hope the day finds you well. I am Brother Tomari, acolyte of our most beneficent goddess Demia, Keeper of The Slain." He bowed deeply. "I beg an audience with Chief Magistrate Graving in a matter of vital importance to my order."

The two constables shared a glance, and Hoseph tried to maintain a pleasant expression. Did they recognize him, or did they think he was bluffing his way in to ask for a donation?

"And what might this matter be?" the older constable asked, his tone as hard as the iron cap that crowned his head.

"I was charged with delivering a message to Chief Magistrate

Graving personally. All I can tell you that it has to do with a wayward member of our order—High Priest Hoseph."

"If this is information about the investigation, why not take it to the Chief Constable?"

Hoseph shrugged. "I'm simply following orders, sir. I was sent here. I would hate to have to report that I was rejected before delivering the message..."

"Very well." The constable opened the gate. "Take the brother in, Maris."

"Yes, sir." Maris ushered Hoseph through the gate to the door, past two more constables stationed there, and rapped the brass clapper three times. Yet another constable answered the door. "Visitor for the magistrate. Brother Tomari from Demia's temple with news about the traitor priest."

Traitor? Incongruously, it bothered Hoseph more to be named a traitor than a murderer. He hid his displeasure and stepped into the magistrate's lavish home. Hoseph's feet sank deep into the plush rug, and he regarded the luxurious décor. The chief magistrate had done well for himself. If only half of what Hoseph had heard about the tension between Arbuckle and Graving was true, the man must certainly fear losing the position that had bestowed upon him such an abundance of power and riches. That boded well for their meeting.

"This way." A butler motioned for Hoseph to follow, leading him down a long corridor toward the back of the house.

The butler's rap on the thick oaken door at the end of the hall heralded an impatient call from within. "Yes! What now?"

The butler opened the door and bowed low. "Brother Tomari, acolyte of Demia, to see you, Chief Magistrate. He bears news about the traitor priest."

"What?" The magistrate looked up from a desk littered with papers.

Hoseph tensed as Graving's eyes fixed upon him, but he saw no recognition. Though both had attended palace functions, they'd never been formally introduced.

Graving looked annoyed. "Why bring it to me? If you know where he is, tell the chief constable to have him arrested."

"Chief Magistrate, I was instructed to relate this information to your ear only." Hoseph cast a sidelong glance at the butler.

"Oh, very well. Come in. Bentley, get out."

"Yes, Chief Magistrate." The butler bowed and left.

Two leather-upholstered chairs fronted the magistrate's desk, but Graving made no offer. Instead, he jammed his pen in his inkwell and leaned back in his chair, ink-stained fingers nesting upon his formidable belly. "Well, what's so important that it couldn't wait until I was in my office tomorrow?"

Hoseph took a steadying breath before speaking. He would have to play this carefully until he was sure of Graving's allegiance. "There are those, Chief Magistrate, who are concerned about the direction in which Crown Prince Arbuckle is taking this empire."

"Direction! There *is* no direction! It's utter chaos! He'll be serving the bloody commoners our heads on silver platters if he keeps it up!" Graving narrowed his eyes. "What does this have to do with the traitor priest?"

Hoseph struggled not to smile. Now that he knew Graving and he were of the same mind, he made his opening move. "First, let me assure you that High Priest Hoseph is no traitor to the empire. He served our emperor dutifully, though his tasks were necessarily not as publically acclaimed as your own. He had nothing to do with the emperor's death, but was privy to many of Tynean Tsing's confidences. He was forced to flee rather than be compelled to divulge the emperor's secrets."

"How do you know this? If—" Graving's piggish eyes widened. "Good gods, it's you!" His hand reached behind the desk.

"Please, Chief Magistrate, don't do anything rash! If you betray my trust, I'll simply vanish. I'm sure you've heard the story of how I escaped the dungeons, so you know I can do it." Hoseph fingered the tiny silver skull, ready to flee, but praying to Demia that he wouldn't have to. "Do you want rumors to spread that you met with a traitor? And do you truly want Arbuckle to be your next emperor?"

"Of course not! The man's a disaster!" The magistrate pulled a small silver flask from one of the desk drawers. Unscrewing the cap, he tilted it into his mouth with a quivering hand. "Your question implies that Arbuckle's ascension to the throne isn't assured."

Hoseph spread his hands and smiled. "You know the saying, 'The only sure things in life are taxes…'"

"…and death." Graving glanced warily around the office as if he expected someone to hear his whisper. He tilted the flask again. "What does this have to do with me?"

The interest in Graving's eyes warmed Hoseph's heart. He was in. The priest settled into one of the leather chairs. "It takes time to arrange such matters, but that's my job. Your job will be to organize a network of nobles and magistrates who think the way we do. Their jobs will be to prevent Crown Prince Arbuckle from getting the support he needs to make significant changes in the interim."

"He's making trouble enough with his blasted *edicts*, and he won't need the nobles' support after he's crowned."

"He'll never be crowned."

Graving digested this information and his thick lips twitched. "All right. I'll draw up a list of potential—"

"No, Chief Magistrate. This is too sensitive an undertaking to put names to parchment. Besides, I can't just go around visiting nobles. Not only would it draw attention, but each encounter with the constabulary increases the chance that someone will recognize me. *You* will visit our prospective allies. If you decide that they're worthy of our cause, and our *trust*, have them pen a mundane invitation that will allow me to visit them without suspicion or undue scrutiny."

"You're very devious."

"I'm very *careful*." Hoseph nodded respectfully. "When I talk with them, I'll invite them all to a meeting to discuss the situation."

"When do you want to have this meeting?"

"Tomorrow evening."

Graving pursed his pudgy lips. "That will take some doing, but the sooner the better, I suppose. Arbuckle's already causing *riots*. The way things are going, we'll have people begging to join our conspiracy."

Hoseph frowned. "Conspiracy is an ugly word. We'll be the saviors of this empire, nothing less."

"Saviors…" Graving considered for a moment. "Yes. I like that better. Now, Duke Tessifus is next in line for the throne, but he doesn't seem the type to join this sort of…endeavor. Should I—"

Hoseph was already shaking his head. "Tessifus has already been taken care of." *At least, if Lady T has done her job.* "He'll cooperate when the time comes."

"I see. Very well, I'd best get moving." Graving heaved up from his chair.

"Be discreet, Chief Magistrate. Tell them only enough to enlist their cooperation. We must keep this group small and be absolutely sure of those we recruit. There can be no chance of betrayal."

"Do give me *some* credit." Graving sniffed, then looked suspiciously at Hoseph. "What do you intend to do if someone declines?"

Hoseph met the man's gaze calmly. "Don't worry. People won't be dropping dead immediately after you've visited them. That would be noticed. Just let me know if you suspect a problem, and I'll deal with it."

"All right. But how discreet will a meeting of nobles and magistrates be? Hardly anyone is leaving their houses with the current unrest. Where in the Nine Hells will we meet?"

"Leave that to me. I'll transport everyone magically so there'll be no chance of someone seeing us come and go."

Graving blanched. "I'd...rather not."

"I didn't ask you what you would *rather*, Chief Magistrate." Hoseph surveyed the room, memorizing it for later use. "The only other option is to risk discovery. Now, on with your task. I'll come for the invitations at precisely nine o'clock tomorrow morning. Be here in this room...alone."

Mya clenched her jaw as she stepped out of the dry-goods store into the darkening street. Ten strides took her to a narrow alley and she ducked inside, stepping around the piles of trash. Loosing the reins on her frustration, she smashed her fist against the wall. Mortar crumbled and two bricks cracked under the blow. The bones of her fist also undoubtedly fractured, but she felt no pain, and the injury healed instantly. Leaning her forehead against the cool bricks, she sighed. Her day had not gone well.

Clemson's directions had been good, and Mya had no problem

finding the other masters' offices. That was where her luck ended.

She'd visited Master Blade Noncey first. Tall, broad-shouldered without looking brawny, and good looking, he reminded her of Sereth. Despite the city-wide law banning swords to all except constables and nobles—or perhaps because of it—he did a good business supplying ne'er-do-wells with all manner of dangerous implements, some of which she'd never even heard of before.

Master Hunter Umberlin proved as slimy as Noncey had been suave. An obsequious little man with a bald pate and a smarmy smile, he made her skin crawl. He seemed less like a Hunter than an Inquisitor.

Or a solicitor, she thought.

The two men had one thing in common; like Clemson, neither would acknowledge her without Lady T's endorsement. She doubted the last two masters would prove more amenable.

Squeezing her eyes shut, Mya forced down despair. *Why did I ever think that I could pull this off? Lady T's right—just because I wear the Grandmaster's ring doesn't mean I'm in control of the guild.*

Scuffling footsteps at the mouth of the alley drew Mya's attention.

Five figures advanced, fanning out to block her exit. *Did Umberlin send people after me?* That seemed foolish, but then she saw that none of the figures was very large or very old. *Not yet teens,* she estimated, relaxing. *Street urchins?*

"Good evenin', *lady*." The boy in the fore looked to be the eldest, wiry, in torn britches and a canvas shirt, a rusty kitchen knife in one grimy hand. "Out for a stroll?"

I do not *need this right now.* Mya was exhausted from her lack of sleep, frustrated by her lack of progress, and had an hour-long walk back to her inn. To add insult to injury, her stomach growled loudly.

"What I'm doing is none of your business. And you're in my way, so move." She stepped forward.

As if on some silent command, the other youths all pulled out weapons, though more pitiful than fearsome. One boy wielded a broken bottle, while another brandished a board with a protruding nail. A third boy held two stout sticks, and beside him a girl with a twisted leg twirled a makeshift sling. Stopping, Mya looked behind her, but the alley was a dead end, strewn with rotting crates and refuse.

The leader stood his ground, the knife steady. "I don't think so, *lady*. Now cough up your purse or you'll be coughing up blood. It's both the same to us."

Mya regarded them critically. The boy's eyes glinted with desperation, and the rest were no better. They were all malnourished, with prominent collar bones and wiry ropes of muscle under grimy skin. They were on the edge—rejected, abandoned, fighting to survive.

She'd been there once.

Years ago, living on the streets of Twailin, not quite a child but not yet a woman, her belly tight with hunger, Mya had known that desperation. They would take everything she had, or die trying. They didn't know the monster they faced.

But even a monster doesn't kill children.

"I tell you what." Mya fished a gold crown from the pouch at her belt and held it up. "Take this and—"

The blow to the back of Mya's head came without warning, hard enough to send her sprawling. Stars exploded in her vision, and the cobblestone street came up to smash her in the face. Blinking hard, she shook the ringing from her ears.

"Finish her, Knock."

Instinct took over. Mya thrust her palms hard against the cobbles, kicking out in the direction the blow had come from. Her shoe struck something solid. As she landed on her feet, she caught a glimpse of a squat girl wearing only short breeches and a rag tied around her chest tumbling backward into the refuse in which they had apparently been hiding.

The girl landed with a crash, and lay there for a moment staring at Mya. An ugly little thing, the girl peered out from beneath a jutting brow, her gaping mouth full of crooked teeth, with one prominent tusk jutting up from the left side of her lower jaw. She looked strong, and clutched an axe handle in one broad fist. Thankfully the axe head was missing, or Mya's brains would have been dashed across the side of the building.

How the hell did she get close without me hearing her? Mya didn't have time to ponder the question.

The rest of the urchins attacked.

112

As the lead boy slashed with his rusty knife, Mya caught his wrist and wrenched the weapon away, then planted a foot on his chest and sent him flying. With a twist of her wrist, she used the flat of the blade to deflect a sling stone aimed at her head. She batted away the nail-studded board an inch before it pierced her skull, and dropped that boy to his knees with a kick to the gut. She'd pulled most of the force from her blows, unwilling to kill.

These little ruffians are playing for keeps!

A stick cracked her shoulder as the boy with two clubs flailed at her. Mya smacked his knuckles with the back of the rusty knife hard enough to send one of the sticks flying from his grasp. Snatching it, she shattered the last boy's broken bottle in his hand, eliciting a startled yelp. Stick boy struck again. Mya parried with the knife and slapped aside another stone slung by the crippled girl. The board came down at her head again as the boy she'd kicked in the gut recovered. She dropped the knife and flung up a hand to catch the blow. The nail pierced her palm.

Enough is enough!

Mya jerked the board from the boy's hand and cracked it across the lead boy's wrist as he tried to recover his fallen knife. She batted another slung stone away with her stolen stick, then flung the club at the girl, striking her square in the forehead. Bending under the next stroke of the stick wielder, she swept his feet out from under him. Sling girl and stick boy both hit the ground hard.

"Knock!"

Mya whirled to see the axe handle coming at her. She braced the board stuck to her hand to intercept the blow, but it snapped under the impact. The hardwood shaft smashed into Mya's face, and she felt her cheekbone shatter.

The kids fell back, panting with their efforts, wide-eyed to see their foe still standing.

Mya bit back ice-cold rage and spat blood. She might have just walked away, but for some unfathomable reason, she couldn't. Instead, she shook her head, felt the bones of her face click back into place as she pulled the nail from her hand and flung the broken board away. Grinning at their surprise, she spat another mouthful of blood at the feet of the stocky girl who had twice hammered her.

"You're good with that stick."

"Knock!" The girl's lip curled back from her crooked teeth in either a snarl or a grin, Mya couldn't tell. "Knock knock!"

She swung again, lightning quick, but Mya wouldn't underestimate her again. Leaning back, she let the axe handle miss her head by a hair's breadth.

"But not that good." Mya reached out and slapped the girl on both cheeks.

The girl blinked in surprise, then grimaced. "Knock!" She swung again.

Mya ducked the blow, reached out to slap her twice more, harder this time. The girl stumbled back, blinked. Amazingly, tears rolled down her cheeks. "Knock!"

"Stop it!" The lead boy stepped between them and glared at Mya. "Don't you hit her like that!"

They all glared at her, murder in their eyes.

Mya couldn't believe this. "She was trying to *kill* me, and you're mad because I *slapped* her?"

"Killin's part of livin'," the boy said. "But there ain't no call for slappin' her like she was some bratty kid!"

"*What?*"

"She ain't your kin. You got no right to slap her like she was your blood."

A memory rushed through Mya's mind, so real that she felt the sting of her mother's open hand on her cheek, her ears ringing with the blow. She remembered the gut-wrenching anguish of being abused and humiliated. These urchins may have attacked her, but they were still children. *She* was the one who should know better. Killing was survival. Torment was just wanton cruelty.

"I'm...sorry."

Again they stared at her. Perhaps they'd never heard an apology from an adult before.

"What *are* you, lady?" The boy took a step back and the others with him. "Knock put you down. Nobody gets up when Knock puts 'em down."

Monster... "You don't want to know what I am."

She watched as the lead boy pulled the crippled girl to her feet and tried to wipe her bloody forehead clean with his filthy shirt tail. Stick boy helped pluck glass splinters from the hand of the boy who had wielded the broken bottle, while the crossbreed girl watched over her companions protectively. They might be homeless urchins, but they were tough and they were loyal.

And they were leaving. Slowly, they slunk back into the shadows.

"Wait!" Mya surprised herself with the outburst. *Loyalty...desperation...street smart...hungry!* "I have a proposal for you!"

They stopped but didn't come back. Mya pulled another coin out of her pouch and held it up. She had to be frugal if she wanted her money to last until she had won over the guild, but this seemed a smart investment.

"You already have one crown. That should feed you well enough for a while, but if you want to eat every day, come work for me."

The urchins inched forward.

"What kind of work?" asked the lead boy.

"Knock!" The girl who had nearly spattered Mya's brains across the street grinned and smacked her stick into her palm.

Mya held up a forestalling hand. "Not exactly that kind of work. I need someone I can trust to watch while I sleep. Someone's trying to kill me."

"Kill *you?*" The boy shook his head. "Dunno if I want to fight nobody who could kill you. Knock put you down, and you popped up like you was some spring toy!"

"You wouldn't have to fight, just watch and warn me." Mya's mind spun as she considered other ways in which she might use the urchins. Street kids like these were ubiquitous in a city like Tsing, utterly ignored as long as they weren't making trouble. "And maybe do a little spying. You can fight, and you're tough, but I need smart, too. I need you to be quiet and sneaky and watch people for me. Do you think you can do that in exchange for food? If it works out, I'll see about getting you a dry place to sleep and better clothes, too."

The children looked at one another, more communication passing in their glances than most people accomplished with whole sentences. Each nodded in turn.

"Okay." The lead boy hooked a thumb at himself. "I'm Digger." He pointed to the others in turn. Nestor was the boy with the broken glass in his hand, and Gimp the girl with the twisted leg.

The boy with the two sticks they called Twigs, and the boy who had nearly put a nail through Mya's skull was called, appropriately, Nails. The crossbreed girl, of course, was Knock.

"I'm Mya." She looked them over and grimaced at their injuries. "I hope I didn't do any permanent damage."

"Nah." Digger flexed his injured wrist. "Nothin' broke. A few scratches."

"Good." She considered them. "Don't the rest of you speak?"

"Not to strangers." Digger tapped himself on the chest. "I'm oldest. I do the talkin'."

"Right." She bit her lip, wondering how she could manage to get them all where she needed them. If anyone saw her walking with a gaggle of urchins in tow like a row of ducklings, there would be too many questions. "You know where the *Tin Dulcimer* is?"

"Sure. Big fancy inn near the river."

No one Mya knew would have called the *Dulcimer* fancy. "Meet me in the alley behind the inn. I'll bring food and we'll talk."

"Okay." Digger nodded and the urchins followed him out of the alley.

Mya grinned to herself as she trudged back to the inn, fingering the blood-stiff hair on the back of her head and wondering if she'd been knocked silly. Most people wouldn't give a bunch of street urchins very good odds against the Assassins Guild, but they were street savvy and as tough as nails. When she was done training them, they'd be invisible and everywhere. Six more pairs of eyes for the cost of a few meals seemed like a solid investment.

"I *must* be crazy."

CHAPTER VIII

Leather creaked as Paxal lurched up into the saddle. At least Dee thought it was the saddle creaking, and not the old innkeeper's bones.

Dee had visited the *Golden Cockerel* to tell Paxal that Lad and Mya were in trouble, and ask him some questions. He hadn't expected the man to insist on coming along. He knew that the innkeeper cared deeply for Mya, but he seemed a bit old to go running off on the spur of the moment.

"Are you sure you're up for this, Pax? I'm going to be riding hard, changing horses at the way inns for speed."

"Horse does most the work." Paxal didn't even look up as he checked his saddlebags. "All I gotta do is stay in the saddle."

"Right." Dee mounted his own horse, gritting his teeth. *This is going to be a long trip with him giving me the cold shoulder for a thousand miles.*

Paxal had never actually shown a dislike for Dee, but didn't really consider him much more than a secretary. Then Dee's dalliance with Moira, the Thieves Guild spy who had used their affair to snoop on Mya, had soured his reputation even more.

"Dee!" Sereth strode into the stable carrying a pair of saddlebags. "Don't forget this."

"Thanks, sir." Dee took the bags, and the weight threatened to drag him out of the saddle. "Gods, did you rob Duke Mir's treasury?"

"Not at all." Sereth shrugged, as stone-faced as ever. "Just what was in the guild coffers and the quarterly profits that we'd normally send to the Grandmaster. Since we don't *have* a Grandmaster anymore, and I'm not about to hand anything over to that bastard Hoseph, I thought I'd put it to good use. If you need more, send a

117

courier."

"I'll send one anyway, as soon as we know something." Dee secured the heavy bags to the saddle, then tugged the reins to bring his spirited mount under control. The gelding didn't appreciate the additional weight.

"Do that." Sereth held out a hand. "Good luck, and be careful."

"We will." Dee shook the proffered hand, trying not to wince at Sereth's iron grip.

He had hoped to take some muscle on the trip, an Enforcer or two to make up for his lack of bulk or skill with a blade, but speed was more important than prowess. Also, the guild was shorthanded on Blades and Enforcers since Lad and Mya killed so many in the recent war between the factions. The rest were needed here in case Hoseph returned with reinforcements. *So all I've got is a crotchety old fart who probably hasn't been on a horse in twenty years.* He sighed, resigned to his fate.

"Ready, Pax?"

"I was ready an hour ago. Let's get this floor show on the stage." Paxal kicked his gelding, and the horse fairly leapt forward.

"So long, Master Sereth. I'll send word."

"Take care, Dee." Sereth slapped Dee's gelding on the flank. "And don't get robbed on the road."

"Right!" Dee kept his mount to a canter until they were through Twailin's west gate. Once the cobbles gave way to hard-packed earth, he and Paxal let their horses have their heads. Dee leaned over the gelding's neck and relaxed into the rhythm, the morning sun warming his back.

Six or seven days to Tsing, unless we find them on the road. Dee kicked his horse harder. He'd be happy if they found Lad and Mya alive, considering that the entire guild would also be looking for them.

At the approaching clatter of hooves and wheels on cobbles, Hoseph looked up from under the raised cowl of his robe. He'd positioned himself on the primary avenue about a block from the palace, close enough to watch all the traffic coming and going, but not so close as to draw the attention of the imperial guard. Like so many others coming and going from the palace, this carriage bore an elaborate coat of arms upon its door. Unlike the others, however, this was the one the priest had been waiting for. Hoseph peered from his shadowed hiding place into the carriage as it passed, fixing the interior in his mind. Duke Tessifus rode alone, his gaze straight ahead, ignorant that he was being observed.

Hoseph smiled. "Perfect." Clutching the silver skull in his sleeve, he vanished in a swirl of ebony mists, already visualizing his destination.

Arriving within a moving target was tricky, but the astonishment on Duke Tessifus' face was quite delicious. Hoseph forestalled the duke's imminent shout with a raised hand and a cold threat.

"If you want to see your sons again, you'll remain absolutely quiet, Milord Duke."

"My *sons*!" Tessifus jerked a jeweled dagger from his belt. "Tell me what you've done with them or I'll make you wish you'd never been born."

"What did I say about being quiet? Are you so eager to put your sons in danger?" Hoseph drew back his cowl and favored the duke with a dangerous scowl.

Recognition slowly spread across the duke's face, and the dagger sagged in his grasp. "You're the priest! Hoseph! The traitor..."

Hoseph's pique flared, but he held his tongue. After all, the duke was under a lot of stress. *Stressed, but not* stupid. According to guild spies, Tessifus was following the instructions left by Lady T's Blades when they kidnapped the boys: "Do not contact the authorities. Do not conduct your own search. Do not make us hurt your sons."

"Milord Duke, for the sake of your sons, put away that dagger and listen to me. First, I am no traitor and had nothing to do with the emperor's death. In fact, I'm trying to salvage something from this catastrophe. But we need your help. We need you to do your duty."

Tessifus reared back. "Don't insult me! I've *always* done my duty."

Hoseph nodded in acknowledgement. "And that includes your protests against Crown Prince Arbuckle's edicts. Am I right?"

"Of course. They risk economic collapse and rebellion."

"Exactly!" The conversation was going perfectly so far. Perhaps Tessifus would prove to be even more compliant than Hoseph had suspected. "Arbuckle is a weak fool. Tsing deserves better."

"I'll petition—"

"Petitions will do nothing! You've seen what a fanatic the prince is. He gives a speech, and riots follow. He can't even wait until he's on the throne to institute his changes. We need someone with the will to maintain Tynean Tsing's legacy and the devotion to assure this empire's rightful place in the world. We need *you* on the throne."

Tessifus shook his head. "Arbuckle will never abdicate."

"No," Hoseph agreed, a complacent smile on his face. "He *won't* abdicate."

The duke's eyes widened. "I'll not be a party to regicide,"

"Arbuckle's not emperor, Milord Duke, so his untimely death will not, in fact, *be* regicide."

"Don't bandy words with me! I'll not betray my oath to the empire." The muscles in the duke's jaw writhed, his teeth clenched so tight that Hoseph thought they might crack.

"I'm not asking you to. I'm simply asking you to allow the crown to rest upon your own head rather than a witless fool's. You'll take no part in Arbuckle's death, and there'll be no subversion in your assumption of the throne since you're the rightful heir. I'll make you the most powerful man in the empire, Milord Duke."

Tessifus considered that for a moment. "Then why take my sons?"

"To assure that you do as *we* wish once the crown rests on your brow."

"I demand that you return them to me immediately. My wife is frantic with worry."

Hoseph sighed. He had hoped too high. It was one thing to play to the duke's ego, but now Tessifus seemed to think that he actually had a say in the matter.

"Milord Duke, let me tell you about a lady I know. She's an artist who creates masterpieces of pain. It takes her days to complete each individual work. Do you really want me to introduce your sons to her?"

The duke just stared at him, shaking with rage.

"If you continue to *demand* things, your duchess will begin to receive packages. A finger, a toe, a tongue… When she receives them all, your sons will have been returned in full."

The duke's face blanched.

"Your sons are quite safe for the time being, and will remain so as long as you do as instructed. The day you assume the throne, two of them will stand by your side."

"Two! Don't you think people will be suspicious if all my heirs don't reside in the palace with me?"

"Not at all. The preservation of the royal bloodline is paramount. In troubled times, it's commonplace for a younger heir to be raised in seclusion to ensure their safety. You can't be too careful, you know. There are assassins everywhere." Hoseph smiled at his little joke, though he knew the duke wouldn't understand.

"You really are a *bastard*," Tessifus seethed.

"No, Milord Duke." Hoseph flipped Demia's talisman into his hand. "I was the right hand of the emperor…and will be again."

Mya opened her eyes to bright sunlight streaming in the window…and smiled. She had slept through the night, *really* slept for the first time in days. Sitting up, she glanced over the foot of the bed. Gimp sat on the rug wrapped in a blanket. Beside her, Nestor huddled in another fast asleep. Her little guardians.

"Good morning, Gimp."

"Morning Miss Mya." The girl nudged her partner and Nestor bolted up, the blanket falling away from his skinny chest.

"What?" Blinking and rubbing his eyes, he looked around. "Oh."

Mya got out of bed. "You two get dressed, and we'll slip you out the back door. Your clothes should be dry by now."

Mya had insisted that her clandestine guests bathe to avoid giving themselves away with their odor. They'd been embarrassed at the suggestion, but complied readily enough if it meant a night spent in a real inn. They'd been enthralled by the *Tin Dulcimer*, looking around in amazement as she snuck them up the back stairs to her room.

If they think this inn is fancy, what would they make of the Drake and Lion? She remembered the marble columns and crystal chandeliers of the Heights inn where she had stayed with Lad with a twinge of heartache. She wished once again that things had turned out differently between them. *Maybe it was just too soon. Maybe one day he'll want someone...*

Gimp and Nestor scrambled up and pulled on their now-clean clothes, their dreadfully skinny bodies reminding her what real hunger looked like. Mya pulled a dress on over her wrappings—the urchins had been startled when she stripped down to sleep, unfamiliar with the concept of night clothes—pushed her feet into shoes, and ran her fingers through her hair.

Love is a weakness...

"Ready?"

They nodded and grinned. She had promised them breakfast.

Mya opened the door and surveyed the hallway before motioning for the children to follow. They scampered down the back stairs after her, waiting at the bottom as she checked the kitchen hallway.

"All's clear. I'll meet you at the stable." They crept out the door onto the side street and dashed away.

Mya continued on to the common room and settled herself at a table. "Good morning, Dorid."

"Morning, Miss Ingrid." The morning maid put a pot of blackbrew on the table. "I'll just get your breakfast."

"Thank you. After breakfast, would you please wrap some sausage, cheese, and a loaf of bread for me? I'm meeting a couple of friends and aren't sure if they'll have eaten." She couldn't do this every day, but this once wouldn't draw suspicion. She had a big day planned for her urchins.

"No problem at all, Miss Ingrid."

A half hour later, the savory bundle tucked under her arm, Mya strolled down the street, glancing casually about. So far, no assassins had shadowed her, or if they had, she hadn't spotted them. Two blocks from the inn, she ducked into an abandoned stable that smelled of moldy hay, pigeon droppings, and worse. The place looked empty, but she knew better.

"Hello?"

The urchins emerged from hiding. That was one thing she wouldn't have to teach them. They'd probably been hiding all their lives.

"I'm impressed! Are you always so stealthy?"

"Never can tell who might be comin', so we hide 'til we know it's safe." Digger motioned the younger children forward.

All eyes were fixed on the bundle under Mya's arm. When she laid it out, Digger carefully proportioned it out equally, and they ate like ravenous wolves. Knowing they wouldn't pay proper attention until they were finished, she waited, reviewing in her mind what she needed to teach them. When the last crumb vanished, she settled them down to begin.

"All right, everyone take a seat. As I said, I need some help. I can't be everyplace at once, and extra eyes might mean the difference between me succeeding at my job and being able to keep feeding you...or not."

"You keep feedin' us, and we're your own private army, Miss Mya." Nails picked up his new nail-studded board and brandished it. "Just tell us what to do."

"First, you need to learn a few things. I'm a Hunter." Mya smiled thinly. "So I'm going to teach you to hunt. Hunting is all about seeing things that other people miss..."

Hours later, Mya had talked herself hoarse, but was pleased with the progress they'd made.

"I'm going to test you now. Let's say that I ask you to keep watch on the *Tin Dulcimer* in case someone is spying on my. Digger, what do you do first?"

The boy rolled his eyes up and thought for a moment before answering. "I find someplace that has a good view of the street, settle down comfortable like I'm begging cause I'll probably be there for a while, then watch for what's not moving. That's cause people just passin' by are goin' somewhere, but if someone's watching the inn, then they're not moving."

"Excellent! Gimp, what if someone approaches you when you're keeping watch?"

"I stick my cup out and beg for money!" She grinned. "That's easy, 'cause that's what I do anyway."

"Good. Nails, what if the constables tell you to move along?"

"Caps."

Mya furrowed her brow. "Caps?"

Nails nodded. "Caps is what we call constables. If you don't call 'em caps, people'll know you're not from around here."

"Okay. That's a great thing to know. Now, what do you do—"

"I move along, circle round and come right back."

"Good. Twigs, what if someone looks at you suspiciously?"

"Pick my nose or scratch my bum!" he replied. The others chuckled and grinned.

"Okaaay. That ought to get someone to ignore you. Basically, anything you can do to look like an innocent kid on the street is good. And Knock..." Mya was stumped. The girl looked as eager to help as the others, but her unusual looks—was a cross between a dwarf and an ogre even possible?—made her conspicuous. Besides, how could she ever give a report with her one-word vocabulary? "Knock, I'm going to find a special job for you."

"Knock knock!"

"Nestor, what do you do once your watch is over?"

"Come back here and report." The answer was prompt, but the boy hung his head.

"That's right, Nestor, so what's wrong?"

"You said we had to tell you how many people we see, but...I don't know my numbers. Never had no teachin'."

"Ah." Mya's heart sank. She had more to teach them than she thought. She smoothed over the dirt in front of her and drew a single line. "This is one..."

After spending much of the afternoon learning their numbers, most could count to ten using their fingers. Judging them ready for some exercise, they hit the streets.

"Okay, I want you to all follow me, but I don't want anyone to know you're doing it, including me. If you can keep track of me for two hours, we'll get sweet rolls." She stood up and brushed the straw from her dress. "Go."

Mya was amazed.

The urchins knew the Dreggars and Downwind Quarters like the backs of their hands. They paced her, leapfrogging ahead and hiding in all manner of ways. She rarely caught a glimpse of them, and thought she'd lost them twice. They would separate and converge and separate again, as if they could read each other's minds. An hour into their game of cat and mice, Mya saw Nestor cup his hands over his mouth as he turned to dash down a side street. A whistle like a chickadee rang out from there, and she realized how they were signaling one another, their messages twittering through the air with no one else on the streets the wiser.

Wily little rats...I'll have to get them to teach me their signals. She hid her smile and stopped in a bakery for sweet rolls. The sun was setting when she and her wards straggled back to the stable. Weary but heartened, Mya watched as they feasted on the treats. She had intended to visit the remaining two Assassins Guild masters this afternoon, but didn't regret putting it off. The work she had done here might make all the difference.

"Tomorrow I want to take you across the river, but I'm worried about getting you across the bridge."

Digger grinned. "Never you mind, Miss Mya. We know how to get over the bridges. Plenty of kids work over in the Midtown factories makin' rich folks shoes and such. We just go along with the rest. Nobody pays no attention to us. 'Cept for Knock. They...uh...don't like her over there."

All the kids cast commiserating looks at the girl, but Knock just grinned and slapped her axe handle against her palm.

Mya laughed. "All right! I'll meet you here with breakfast, then we'll head out. Knock, you'll watch the inn while we're gone. Remember, one of you is always watching the inn during the night. When you're off watch, sleep. Who's got bed-watch duty tonight?"

Twigs and Nails raised their hands.

"Watch my room window. When you see me open it, come to the back door."

"We'll be there, Miss Mya. Do we have to have a bath, too?" Twigs frowned.

"Yes." Sleeping in the filthy stable left a thick reek. "And I want you to start teaching me your whistles. I know you're sending signals, and I need to be able to understand them."

"Oh, sure!" Twigs grinned and nudged Nails, obviously elated that they would be actually teaching her something.

Mya bid them goodbye and left the stable. As always, she

watched for stalkers on her way back to the inn. She hadn't spotted any yet, but that didn't mean they weren't there. Mya was putting a lot of faith in these kids to keep her safe, but they had accomplished so much today. For the first time since Lad had slid the Grandmaster's ring onto her finger, she felt a bit of hope. She wasn't alone anymore.

CHAPTER IX

Mya stomped down the street of the Heights District, not caring that her aggressive stride belied her genteel appearance. Her visits to the last two masters had put her in a foul mood.

The Master Alchemist, a skeletally thin man named Kittal, had stonewalled her completely. Rude and inhospitable, he had refused to give her even the time of day until Lady T informed him that Mya was the new Grandmaster.

From Kittal's Midtown apothecary, she had taken a carriage to the Heights where the Master Inquisitor posed as the proprietress of an elegant bath house. Inhaling the heady aromas of exotic oils as she followed an attendant through the establishment, Mya had wished she could slip into one of the baths and float among the lotus blossoms, or have a massage to loosen her tense muscles. One of the disadvantages of being covered neck to wrist to ankle in magical runic tattoos, however, was that she could never bare her skin to anyone.

Master Inquisitor Lakshmi surprised her. A gracious older woman with a maternal air, she had received Mya with seemingly genuine hospitality, the golden sequins on her sari swaying gently as she personally poured tea into shallow ceramic bowls and offered Mya sweet cakes on a silver platter.

The hospitality had shattered when she said, "I wish you the best of luck, but I'm afraid that until Lady T identifies you as our new Grandmaster, I can't even consider helping you."

It all boils down to Lady T. Mya had given the woman three days to get the word out, and she had apparently done nothing. Mya couldn't tolerate that degree of insolence. It was time to confront this problem.

By the time she reached Lady T's neighborhood, the late-afternoon sun tinted the buildings a golden hue, casting deep shadows between them. She strolled by the house, stopping some way beyond to drop a copper into the outstretched cup of a young beggar.

"Anything to report, Digger?"

"The lady went out this afternoon in a carriage. Hasn't come back yet."

"Black-and-white horses pulling it?"

"Yeah."

Mya fumed. She wanted to get this over with. "All right. When she returns, fetch me at the café two blocks down the hill. Where's Gimp?"

"Out back. Look under the bushes."

"Got it." Mya continued on, turning at the corner to go around the house.

The entire back of the mansion was lined with manicured bougainvillea, their inch-long thorns a formidable barrier against prowlers. Surely the girl wouldn't try to hide beneath those; she'd be torn to shreds. Mya strolled on, scanning the shadows. At the end of the block, across the street from the back of Lady T's house, she spied a short wrought-iron gate that opened into a courtyard garden. Beneath one of the two lush shrubberies that flanked the gate hunkered the girl with a twisted leg. Mya would have missed her if she hadn't known what to look for.

Stopping to lace her shoe, she winked at the girl. "See anything good, Gimp?"

"Aye, miss," the girl whispered. "I seen the lady at them windows there earlier, and then a carriage leavin'. Careful, there's two watchmen inside the carriage gate."

Mya glanced to the wide, wrought-iron gate that undoubtedly led to Lady T's inner courtyard and stable. Two thick figures lounged against the sides of the arch, one smoking a pipe. *Sloppy, but good for me.* She gave Gimp directions to the café, finished with her shoe, and headed for a well-deserved cup of blackbrew and a sweet roll.

As the day settled into evening, Mya's head buzzed with blackbrew, and her teeth felt sticky from the sweet pastries. She wished she'd brought something to read, but she hadn't expected to have so much free time to sit and stew in the juices of her frustration. Finally the bang of the door and the plaintive voice of a street urchin announced her deliverance.

"Got any stale buns?" Digger caught her eye.

"Get out of here!" The shopkeeper rounded the counter, but Digger was already out the door.

Leaving a coin on the table, Mya went out into the darkening street. Digger shuffled away, then turned into an alley. Mya followed and pretended to twist an ankle at the corner of the alley.

"She's home." he announced.

"Alone?"

"Yep."

"Good."

Mya headed toward Lady T's house. Crossing the last street, she heard the twitter of a bird—Gimp—though she couldn't remember what the particular call meant. Circling to the adjacent block, she hopped a low gate on the opposite side of the courtyard garden and flitted through the shadows to where Gimp crouched.

"Gimp, what did you see?"

The girl blinked at Mya's surprise arrival, and whispered through the gate. "The carriage came back, then the lights in that room started actin' funny." She pointed a grimy finger to a third-floor window at the back of Lady T's house. "Them ones, where I seen the lady before."

"Funny how?"

"Watch… There!"

The light behind the gauzy curtains faded, then brightened, as if someone inside turned the lamp down, then up again.

"That *is* odd. How many times has that happened?"

Gimp looked down at her fingers, folded three down. "Maybe that many. Seven."

Mya patted the girl on the shoulder. "I'm going up there. You keep watching, and do your bird whistle if you see anyone coming around."

"But how are you—"

"No questions, Gimp. Just watch."

"Yes, miss. Careful. Them two are still watchin'." Gimp pointed to the carriage gate.

"Thanks."

Mya was no burglar, but she knew how to case targets. Looking up at the illuminated windows, she gauged the angle to the carriage gate. The watchers inside the gate wouldn't be able to see the back of the building, but they could certainly see the street, so she couldn't just dash across from here. If she approached along the thorny hedge, the angle and the shadows should conceal her.

The first-floor windows were dark and barred, but the second- and third-floor weren't, with jutting stone sills and lintels. Mya plotted her path up the side of the building, thanking Lad once again for showing her exactly what her magically enhance strength and coordination could accomplish. She felt another pang at the memory of their brief time together; platonic though it had been, she had felt a synergy with him that she had felt with no other human being.

Stop it! Focus!

Mya backed into the deep shadows of the garden, stripped down to her wrappings, and hid her clothing and shoes beneath a bush. Her pale face and hands might be a problem, but she had no way to darken them. Leaving the garden by the opposite end, she dashed around the block and across the street behind Lady T's house. Thankfully, it was late enough that she could avoid the occasional pedestrian by keeping to the shadows. Mya eased down the street close to the thorn hedge, listening for any sign that the watchers had spotted her. Nothing.

Beneath the illuminated window, she leapt up and over the bougainvillea to the first-floor window. The thick bars offered a perfect perch for her to listen for a moment. Hearing nothing, she launched herself up to the second-story, catching the windowsill. One hard jerk brought her up to stand on the sill, her palms braced on the stone frame. Leaning back as far as she could without falling, she looked overhead to the lit window. People inside probably wouldn't see her peering in through the drapes if she didn't make herself obvious.

Careful now.

Thrusting with her legs, she leapt and clamped onto the sill of the third-story window. Mya hung there a moment to listen. No shouts of alarm from the watchers or whistle from Gimp meant she hadn't been seen yet. She felt horribly exposed hanging in the open, but, a glance left and right confirmed that there were no passersby.

Pulling herself up, Mya peered through the casement. The gauzy drapes hazed her view, but she recognized the sitting room where she'd spoken with Lady T. The scene within, however, furrowed her brow.

A party?

A handful of well-dressed people sipped drinks out of crystal glasses and ate tidbits off of silver trays. Digger had said that Lady T arrived home alone.

So where did they come from?

Cocking her head, she could just make out their muffled voices through the glass.

"Really, Lady T, don't you have *servants* to attend us?" A short man in a silk brocade jacket picked a dainty off a tray held by his hostess. "Perhaps after spending all of your money on your *title* and this *lovely* home, you can't afford any?"

Lady T inclined her head graciously despite the man's snide comment. "Security demands sacrifices, Duke Seoli. This is not the type of meeting one wants discussed in the kitchen."

"What's the world coming to when one can't trust one's own servants?" complained a stately older woman as she ineptly poured wine from a decanter. "All this cloak-and-dagger nonsense is silly. I don't know why you insisted upon it, Graving."

"In this, Duchess Ingstrom, I wouldn't trust my own mother." A portly man whom Mya assumed to be Graving plucked a tidbit from the tray, popped it into his mouth, and reached for another.

The duchess sniffed. "It's a wonder you magistrates trust anyone, dealing with *commoners* every day. But such secrecy for mere politics is—"

The conversation ceased as the light suddenly dimmed. Mya's eyes locked onto one corner of the room where a whirl of shadow obscured the glow of the nearby lamps. The shadows cleared, and the radiance was restored, illuminating a man in gray robes and woman in a severe black dress, neither of whom had been there a moment ago.

Remembering the swirling black mists during their fight in the imperial dungeons, Mya immediately thought of Hoseph, but she didn't recognize this bald man. *Another priest?*

Her attention followed the woman in black as she jerked her hand from the man's grasp and hurried to the sideboard, her face white with horror. Grabbing a decanter, she splashed a measure of liquor into a tumbler and knocked it back.

"Hells below, what a *horrid* way to travel!"

"The *gall!*" Duke Seoli glared at the woman. "Have you no manners at all? You're in the house of a noble of the realm!"

"I take no offense, Duke." Lady T nodded and gestured graciously to the woman. "All are welcome in my home, noble and magistrate alike. And since you so accurately pointed out my lack of servants to attend us, I encourage everyone to feel free to help themselves. Let's not quibble about propriety."

"Thank you, Lady." The woman's hand shook as she poured another stout drink. "I certainly meant no offence."

Mya ignored the sniping nobles, her eyes drawn back to the man in gray robes. Squinting through the drapes, she studied his angular features and realized that she'd been fooled by a thin disguise. *It is Hoseph!* Lowering herself until only her eyes and dark hair edged above the sill, she examined her nemesis. She'd given her urchins an inaccurate description of the priest, and wondered now if he'd been lurking around her inn under their noses in this new disguise. *Probably not. I'm still alive.*

"Lords and ladies, distinguished magistrates, we can ill afford dissension amongst ourselves. The future of the empire depends on us." Hoseph nodded toward the portly man chewing yet another savory. "Chief Magistrate Graving has identified each and every one of you as loyalists who esteem the great empire of Tsing. We share a common goal here tonight: to oppose the dangerous policies of that weakling upstart Arbuckle. We must set aside our differences for the common good!"

What a crock of bullshit, Mya thought.

"What's *your* role in this?" demanded a thin-nosed man in satin breeches and jacket. "Other than whisking us all around the city, I mean. Being seen with a wanted fugitive would ruin me."

Despite Hoseph's static smile, Mya could see the twitch of his jaw muscles as he clenched his teeth.

"You know me only as the emperor's spiritual advisor. His

Majesty also entrusted me with deeper responsibilities." He made a grandiose gesture. "One cannot maintain control over the unruly masses wielding only an iron fist. The emperor also had a...more subtle organization to root out subversion and apply pressure when and where necessary. You might consider us as the emperor's secret constabulary."

That's my Assassins Guild you're talking about, buddy!

"Spies?" someone asked.

"Spies...and more."

"You say the *emperor's* private constabulary. Doesn't that mean you're working *for* Arbuckle?" Duke Seoli's question startled several of the guests.

Hoseph smiled. "Arbuckle is not yet emperor, and we intend that he never will be."

So that explains all the secrecy. They're planning to assassinate the crown prince.

Over the ensuing barrage of questions, Mya heard the twitter of a bird, recognizing the signal for danger. Glancing down the street, she spied a troop of constables rounding the corner, still a block away, but approaching. They might pass without seeing her, but she couldn't take the chance.

With a surge of panic, she sought a way out. She'd made a foolish mistake by not planning an escape route. Climbing up to the would risk being seen from inside the window, and noise if any shingles happened to be loose. The only other direction to go was down. Mya peered into the thorny foliage beneath her and chose a gap to her left. If she landed just right, she could hunker in the shadows beneath the colorful leaves, invisible in her dark clothing. Mya winced as she remembered the shrub's long thorns.

No pain...

Mya swung her legs and released the window sill, plummeting like a stone. Only a light rustle of leaves marked her passage into the shrubbery. She flexed her knees as she hit the ground and remained crouched, lowering her face and holding her breath, listening. Slowly, she withdrew a long thorn from the back of her hand and felt warm blood trickle down to her wrist. She wondered how many pierced her elsewhere.

The constables talked quietly as they passed by, but none spied anything amiss. With the recent violence, they were probably looking for mobs of troublemakers, not burglars.

Mya considered climbing back up to listen some more, but reconsidered. She had gleaned the most important implication of the meeting: Lady T was working with Hoseph. Their plan to assassinate the heir to the throne didn't concern Mya. That wasn't her fight. She had enough on her hands trying to gain control the guild. Easing from the prickly embrace of the hedge, she made her way back around the block and through the courtyard garden.

Kneeling down by the gate, she whispered to Gimp, "Thanks for the warning. That's enough for tonight. Go get some rest. Tell tonight's night watch to meet me behind the inn, but it's going to be a while. I'm going to have a little chat with Lady T after her party's over."

"Aye, miss." Gimp hobbled off into the night, surprisingly stealthy despite her uneven gait.

Mya recovered her clothes and settled down to wait, considering what she'd heard. It sounded like Hoseph was making all the plans, but she couldn't imagine the guildmaster playing second fiddle to the non-guild priest. Patiently, she watched the window and planned her approach.

Tonight I find out what game Lady T is playing.

Dee blinked at the light looming out of the darkening gloom. His gelding snorted and lunged from a canter into a gallop despite the mist and dark. This was the third mount Dee had ridden today, and he recognized that behavior. The horse knew that a way inn was close, and Dee was more than ready to stop for the night.

If I'm this sore, how must Pax feel? He glanced over, but shadows rendered the innkeeper's face unreadable, and Paxal wasn't talking much, at least not to him.

The geldings bolted through the open gate, across the turning court, and straight for the stable where they stopped and blew noisily. The way-inn stableman stepped out and took the reins as they dismounted.

"Room for the night, sirs?"

"Room, food, and somethin' to soak my achin' arse in, if you don't mind." Paxal stumbled as his feet hit the ground, his back popping audibly.

"And fresh mounts an hour before sunrise, if you please." Dee dug a silver crown from his pocket and handed it to the man. He pulled the precious saddlebags off the horse and slung them over his shoulder, trying to look as if they weren't heavy with tightly packed gold crowns.

"Happy to oblige. Just see the missus about supper and a room." The stableman tipped his cap and led the two horses into the stable.

Dee followed Paxal into the inn, his mouth flooding with saliva at the aromas of savory cooking. Jerky and bread on horseback hadn't made for a satisfying lunch.

A man and woman in merchants' garb were the only other guests in the common room. That wasn't surprising, considering the late hour and the inn's location, far from any town or village. They'd be getting no locals in for an evening drink, which was fine with Dee.

"Good evening, sirs." A matronly woman bustled forward. "You two look done in."

"Whipped like a rented mule, ma'am." Paxal doffed his hat and jacket, and Dee followed suit.

"We need a room for the night, and a meal if it's not too late for supper, please." Dee kept the saddlebags in hand.

"Of course. Would you like to put your bags in your room before supper?"

"There's no sense in climbing stairs twice, is there?" Dee wasn't about to let the saddlebags full of gold out of his sight.

"Not at all. What will you be wantin' to drink?" She gestured them to a table.

"Wine please."

"Ale for me." Paxal winced as he sat down. "A large tankard if you please, ma'am. I gotta kill the pain in my...um..."

"No need to explain. We get couriers all the time. I'll be back in a trice!" She bustled off.

"Rethinking your decision to come along, Pax?"

Paxal shot Dee a cold glance. "No."

They sat in uneasy silence until the kitchen door banged open, and the woman hurried back with a large tray.

"Here you are, sirs." She set out laden plates and brimming cups, then placed a key on the table. "You're in room number three, just left at the top of the stairs."

"And would a bath be available?" Paxal looked up hopefully.

"Of course! I'll heat the water. When you're done eatin', the washroom's just through there." She pointed to a door leading off the common room.

"You're an angel of mercy, milady." Paxal lifted his tankard to her and drank deeply. "Gods of Light, I may survive after all."

Laughing, she bustled off again.

Dee dug into his dinner. His tongue tingled at his first bite of the spicy potato soup, but cool wine quenched it nicely. Thick gravy drenched tender mutton and a mound of stewed greens. He sopped up the excess with slices of crusty warm bread, and only slowed when his plate looked like it was ready to put back in the cupboard. Picking a tart from the desert plate, he nibbled, but his belly was already too full. Looking around, he saw that the merchants had apparently gone to bed. Aside from the stableman, who busied himself tidying up, the place was empty.

"I know these way inns get an imperial charter to get started, but how do they make a living out in the middle of nowhere?"

"Likely family run. No mortgage, no rent, and no employees to pay. Ain't bad land hereabouts, so they probably have a plot to farm, a few sheep and chickens." Paxal stuffed a huge piece of mutton into his mouth and chewed. He didn't seem inclined to more conversation, but those had been more words than he had said to Dee since they started. The old man had no problem chatting with innkeepers or stablemen, and Dee had seen him carry on a half dozen simultaneous conversations tending bar at the *Golden Cockerel*.

Dee sighed. They couldn't go on like this all the way to Tsing. "Paxal, we've got to talk. I know you don't like me, but—"

"Don't dis*like* you, just don't trust you much!" the innkeeper barked.

"What do you mean by that?" Dee bristled. "If you think I intentionally—"

"Doesn't matter what you *intended*. You were set up and fell for it hook, line, and sinker."

Dee gritted his teeth. He didn't like to remember the way he'd failed Mya. "You're right. I screwed up. But Morin's dead, and Mya kept me on."

"Mya's the forgiven' sort. Always been that way." Paxal frowned. "If I thought you'd learned something from it, I might—"

"You think I *didn't*?" Mya had trusted Dee with her most private correspondence, and he had failed her. She could have killed him, but instead, she had given him a second chance.

The old man looked up with a curious expression, then back down at his plate. "Maybe you did at that."

"You've known Mya longer than anyone, haven't you?"

The innkeeper slathered butter on a slab of bread and took a bite, a faraway look in his eyes. "She was just a skinny girl when I first caught sight of her hanging 'round the alley behind the *Cockerel*. Skittish as a stray cat she was." A smile twitched his lips, then disappeared. "She reminded me of…someone, so I let her work for scraps and a cot."

"The word is you sent her to the guild."

Paxal shot him a glare from under bushy eyebrows. "Word from who?"

"Come on, Pax." Dee spread his hands. "Mya's the youngest Master the guild's ever had, and you think people don't gossip about her? They gossip about you, too. The *Golden Cockerel*'s more than just an inn, after all. It's been Mya's headquarters for years."

"That's just good business." Paxal quaffed his ale. "She pays more rent than she ought for what I do."

"She owes you." Dee chuckled at Paxal's glare. "She cares for you. It's obvious. And everyone knows you care about her. You wouldn't be here if you didn't."

"You think I'd leave her fate in *your* hands?" Paxal's sarcastic snort took the sting out of the sarcastic comment. He pushed his plate away and sighed. "Look, I know you care about Mya, too. I think you're just a little…green is all. Maybe you think you'd do better if you was out here alone instead of having an old man slowing you down."

"Don't be ridiculous!" Dee shook his head. "You're not holding me back, Pax."

Paxal met Dee's eyes and nodded. "All right. I know Mya, and I know Tsing, if we don't find them on the road. You know guild business and how she operates."

Dee nodded. "And I know Lad, too, to a certain degree. Between the two of us, we've got a better chance than anyone of finding them."

"And we *will*."

Heartened, Dee picked his tart back up and took a bite. The flaky crust melted in his mouth, the flavor of apple and cinnamon burst delightfully on his tongue. He wiped away the sweet juice dribbling down his chin with a napkin.

"How well do you know Tsing?"

"Born and raised there." Paxal sat silently for a moment before continuing. "It was a good place once. Good and bad, like any city, I guess, but you could make your way. I had the hopes and dreams of a young man. Opened an inn, got married, had a daughter…then things went bad."

"What happened?"

"The emperor died, and the new one took over. There was trouble and… Someone broke into my inn, and…my wife and little daughter were killed." Paxal hung his head.

"I'm sorry, Pax. I ask too many questions."

"No, it's all right." Paxal rubbed his face, then sipped his ale and sighed. "Just been a long time since I thought of it, is all. That's who Mya reminded me of at first, my little Nance. But Tsing's rotten through now. It's no place for Mya. She's too afraid."

Dee stared slack-jawed at the older man. "Mya? Afraid? That's the last thing I'd think of her."

"Shows you don't know her like I do." Paxal finished his ale and picked up his apple tart. "She was so scared when she was little, you could see it in her eyes. You'd twitch, and she'd shrink back like she expected you to backhand her. Don't think she had much of a childhood."

Dee tried to reconcile Paxal's description with the strong, vital woman he knew. They didn't mesh. "She certainly doesn't show it."

"I gave her some advice, but not what your *rumors* say. She needed to feel safe, and I told her to be safe you had to be strong. That if somethin' scared her, she had to learn to fight it." Pax chuckled wryly. "She disappeared, came back a few days later with a pocket full of silver and a dagger on her hip. She'd joined the guild. Not quite what I had in mind, but it worked out okay."

"How was dinner?" The landlady approached, smiling down at their polished plates.

"Delicious," Dee said, and Paxal patted his belly contentedly.

"Good! Docey's told me that you're leavin' before dawn. I'll have porridge and hot scones for your breakfast, and pack you a cold lunch. Docey'll have fresh horses ready." She picked up the plates and nodded to the washroom. "Your bath's drawn, and there's soap and towels laid out for you."

"Did I say you were an *angel* of mercy?" Pax pushed himself up from his chair. "Make that a *goddess*. Thank you, ma'am."

Dee grabbed the room key and his saddlebags, pleased with the way the evening had turned out. "Don't take too long, Pax. I'd like to wash up before bed."

"Can't promise to hurry. These old bones need a good soak."

"Well, soak them fast. We're on the road before daylight."

An hour or more must have passed before the light beaming from Lady T's sitting room dimmed and brightened, dimmed and brightened, again and again. At last, all the lights were doused.

Mya retrieved and donned her clothing, then made her way to the front of the house. She'd thought long and hard about the best approach. Smashing through Lady T's bedroom window would be satisfying, but might also get her killed. The guildmaster of the Tsing Assassins Guild surely protected her doors and windows with traps. She'd settled on a more direct approach. It had worked once, why not again?

As Mya strode up to the front door, the two guards there pulled heavy cudgels from their belts.

She stopped a step away, well within reach. "Mya here to see Lady T."

"The lady's not home." The Enforcer's face remained admirably blank.

"Oh?" Mya considered for a moment that he might be telling

the truth. Hoseph could have whisked her off to who knew where. "Then I'll wait for her to come back. Open the door."

"She won't be back until morning." He blinked and his eyes flicked away from hers.

Nope, he's lying. "Then I'll wait until morning. Open...the...door."

"I...can't let you in. Orders."

"Ah, now at least you're telling me the truth." Mya put her hands on her hips. "I'm giving you new orders. Open the door. *Now!*"

The speaker glanced to the second guard, but his companion seemed quite content to let his partner call the shots. The guard licked his lips, a fine sweat breaking out on his brow. "If you come back in the morn—"

"Do you *like* your testicles?"

"What?" The man's eyes narrowed, the cudgel twitching at his side.

"I asked if you like your testicles, because if you continue to stand there being stupid instead of doing what I tell you to do, I'm going to tear them off and stuff them up your nose. Now, *open* the *door*."

"Cocky bitch," the man muttered beneath his breath as he turned to unlock the door. He'd probably intended it to be inaudible, but Mya heard it.

"Yes, I am. Remember that next time."

The muscles of his face tensed as he turned his key in the lock. Pushing open the door, he stepped out of her way without another word.

Mya strode through and found herself staring down two loaded crossbows. If the man and woman holding the weapons were guild members, they couldn't shoot her, but Lady T might have hired some non-guild killers. She wasn't going to take any chances. Mya raised her hands in surrender, but kept walking forward.

"Now just be careful with those—" When she came within reach, Mya lunged and snatched the two crossbow bolts from the weapons. By the time either of them could even blink, she had the bolts reversed and the tips under their chins. "Where's Lady T?"

The two stared in shock down at their impotent weapons and

the deadly shafts that could end their lives. The man swallowed hard and lowered his crossbow. Mya smelled the telltale scent of urine. Evidently, she'd startled him rather badly.

"Relax! I'm not going to kill you unless you don't tell me where your mistress is."

The woman lowered her crossbow and reached for an ornate rope pull on the wall. "Lady T's gone to bed, but I can call—"

"Uh-uh!" Mya pricked woman's chin with the needle point of the crossbow bolt before she could touch the rope. "You'll call no one—either of you—and you'll answer my questions. If I ever find out that you lied to me, I'll turn you over to Master Inquisitor Lakshmi for her apprentices to practice on. Now, where's Lady T?"

After the barest hesitation, the woman said, "In bed."

"Yes, you said that. Where's her bedroom?"

"I can—"

"Just *tell* me!"

"On the third floor, down the hall to the left."

"That's her sitting room." Mya wondered if she was being led astray.

"Yes. You have to go through her sitting room. Once inside, there are two doors to your right. The first opens into her bedroom. The second goes through her dressing room."

"Is she alone?"

"I don't know." The woman looked to her partner.

"No company that I know of."

She wondered if they even knew of the well-attended meeting an hour ago in the lady's sitting room. "Is there anyone else lying in wait for me?"

"No."

"Good." Mya dropped the crossbow bolts and dashed up the stairs three at a time.

She approached the door at the end of the hall silently and stopped to listen, her senses straining for any sign of alarm or ambush. She heard nothing through the door, not the scuff of a shoe, a heartbeat, or breathing. The coast seemed clear. Thumbing the latch, Mya eased open the door. The sitting room where she had met with Lady T stood empty, though she could smell the scent of several competing perfumes. She stepped into the room and faced the two doors. Listening at the first, Mya heard the soft, steady breathing of a single person at rest.

It's time to answer for your insolence, Lady T. Mya opened the bedroom door and stepped through.

The faint click of metal on metal was her only warning. She started to turn, but too late. The door frame exploded in a shower of splinters, and the broad head of a spear plunged into Mya's side, grating between her ribs. The impact slammed her against the opposite door frame.

Mya looked down. The shaft pierced her just beneath her left breast. There was no pain, of course—the magic of her tattoos prevented that—but that didn't prevent her from feeling queasy at the sight of being impaled. The room spun, and her knees started to fold at the sudden wave of weakness. The spear had struck something vital. Not her heart, for that would have killed her outright, but certainly a major blood vessel. If she passed out from blood loss, she would die within minutes.

"Light!" Radiance blossomed from a glow crystal beside the bed, and Lady T lurched up from beneath the coverlet, a crossbow in hand. Her eyes widened at the sight of Mya pierced and bleeding, then one eyebrow lifted in a wry expression. "Perhaps that will teach you to *knock*."

Anger burned away Mya's weakness, and her lips twisted into a wolfish grin. "Perhaps not."

Mya gripped the spear and pushed the shaft out of her chest. The mechanism hidden in the wall whined in protest, but its gears and springs were no match for her strength. The bloody head of the spear grated from between her ribs, followed by a spurt of bright red blood before the wound closed. With a twist and a jerk, she snapped the hardwood shaft off at the door frame.

"Gods and devils!" Lady T stared, her useless crossbow dropping to the floor.

"You once asked me how I killed four blademasters." Mya brandished the bloody spear as she strode across the room. "Let me show you!"

"Wait!" Lady T scrambled back. "I didn't…"

"Didn't *what?*" Mya pinned her against the wall, fingers tight around her throat, the spear's bloody tip an inch from the noblewoman's eye. "Just try to kill me? It sure seemed like it!"

The guildmaster's voice came as a strained hiss. "I didn't know you were coming! Of course I have protection. I have *enemies*." She clutched Mya's wrist, but couldn't push her away or strike.

Mya hesitated. As much as she hated to admit it, the lady had a point. Mya had her own security measures back in Twailin, but mostly relied on secrecy and a building full of loyal Hunters watching her back. She could have let someone escort her up to the lady's room and knock on the bedroom door, but Mya had been angry, wanting to make a grand entrance. She'd been a fool to blunder in, and that mistake had nearly cost her life.

But I'll be damned if I let her *know that!* She loosed her grip on Lady T's neck so quickly the woman had to steady herself against the wall to keep from falling.

"I gave you two tasks: implement my changes to guild operations, and set up Hoseph so I could kill him. You've done *neither!* Instead, you expand your *own* operations and cozy up to Hoseph."

"What was I supposed to do? Declare you Grandmaster?" Lady T rubbed her throat, her eyes flicking to the bloody spear still in Mya's hand. "Hoseph would pop in here while I slept and murder me."

"Then you're in a tough spot, because *I'll* murder you if you don't!" Mya waved the tip of the spear under her nose for emphasis. "You won't cooperate with me, but you seem to be cooperating with Hoseph, plotting to murder the crown prince."

The guildmaster's eyes narrowed. "How…"

"I have my sources." *Let her stew about how I found out.* Mya knew killing Lady T wasn't the answer, but she had to convince the woman to cooperate. "First things first: why did you expand your extortion rackets north of the river?"

"The future is uncertain." Lady T shrugged, regaining a bit of her composure. "I want to build up a financial cushion to hold us over until things settle down, and extortion is what we know."

Mya began to pace. "Protection rackets take time to pay off. The upper classes are *begging* to be fleeced, and you're ignoring them. With the current unrest in the city, you could be raking in gold by selling security services to your noble friends and rich merchants.

That alone would provide the income you need to weather this storm. Think of what you could charge your rich friends for the services you use yourself. Enforcers guarding the doors of every noble house and fancy shop in the Heights will make you filthy rich."

"*You* got by my guards easily enough."

"That's because I'm *me*." Mya quirked a dangerous smile. "Back to the subject. I gave you a detailed list of the changes I wanted. We've used these kinds of operations in Twailin for five *years*. They work."

"And you think Hoseph won't notice?" Lady T donned a robe from a clothes tree beside her bed. She looked less terrified now, but her eyes still followed the bloody spear.

"Frankly, no I don't. He's too busy trying to murder the crown prince to notice what's happening on the streets!" Mya stopped and regarded the woman. Something didn't fit here. "If you fear him so much, why don't *you* kill him? You're an *assassin*!"

Lady T folded her arms and pursed her lips in annoyance. Mya wondered if the pursed lips were one of the lady's tells, and made a mental note to watch for it.

"And if I miss, I'm dead."

"Then set him up for *me*." Mya dropped the bloody spear onto the fluffy white coverlet, earning a glare from the guildmaster. "All I need to know is where and when."

"He flits around like smoke on the wind. I don't know when he'll pop in or where he sleeps. In order to set him up, I've got to make him trust me. That'll take time."

"Time…" Mya thought about her dwindling funds and wondered if Lady T was playing her. "Make it take less time."

"I can't promise anything." She folded her arms and pursed her lips again. "If I learn where he'll be, how do I let you know? Where do I send a message?"

Oh, you're good. She wasn't about to tell the guildmaster where she was staying and risk a midnight visit from the murderous priest. "Hang a handkerchief in your bedroom window, and *I'll* contact *you*."

"Fine."

"And the security service?"

"I'll start up a sham security company and start selling protection to the rich and powerful, but I have to go along with Hoseph to earn his trust." The lady's eyes narrowed. "When I tell you where to take Hoseph out, don't miss. If he traces it back to me, we're *both* dead."

"I won't miss." Mya inspected the hole in her dress and the thick bloodstain down her side. "And you owe me a dress."

CHAPTER X

"Good morning, milord." Baris entered his master's bedchamber and drew back the drapes.

"I don't know how good it is yet, Baris." Arbuckle blinked at the bright sunlight and climbed reluctantly out of bed. "I've only slept a few hours. I won't know anything until I've had a pot of blackbrew."

"Of course, milord." Baris held a silk robe for him, his face blank, though his voice might have held a hint of amusement.

Arbuckle slipped into his robe and refrained from glaring, thinking only of blackbrew and the pile of work that awaited him. "Summon Tennison. I'll dress before breakfast so we can get right to work."

"As you wish, milord."

By the time Arbuckle had finished his morning ablutions and dressed with his valet's deft aid, his desire for blackbrew had sharpened into all-out yearning. Entering his sitting room, he was pleased to see the table already set. The fine porcelain dishes and crystal goblets gleamed in the early morning sunlight streaming through the window.

"Breakfast is on the way, milord."

"Thank you, Baris." Arbuckle settled into his seat as his valet retreated to the bedchamber to tidy up, and nodded good morning to the blademasters guarding the door. He sometimes wondered why he bothered being cordial to the bodyguards; they never gave the slightest indication that they noticed, and certainly never returned the greeting.

"Good morning, Milord Prince." Tennison entered, followed by a dour young woman toting a thick ledger. "Renquis here will serve as your scribe for the next few days while Master Verul organizes the archives."

"Welcome, Renquis."

"Milord Prince." The woman's whisper barely reached his ear. After an awkward curtsey, she hurried to the chair in the corner and sat down as rigid as a mannequin with her ledger on her lap, her pen hovering over the page, ready to take down Arbuckle's every utterance.

"Your schedule is heavy today, milord." Tennison opened his appointment book and ran his finger down the page. "Four nobles have requested audiences this morning, then lunch with Duchess Ingstrom. This afternoon, Chief Constable Dreyfus wishes to see you about the lack of prison space for incarcerated malcontents."

Arbuckle cocked an eyebrow. "Did Dreyfus actually call them *malcontents*? That seems like a mild term, considering his usual attitude."

"I paraphrased his rather stronger and lengthier descriptive," Tennison admitted.

Arbuckle sighed. "Malcontents... Most of the incarcerated have good *reason* to be discontent. Do you know that most of the cases I reviewed last night were charges of failure to follow a lawful order to disperse and resisting arrest?"

"I did not, milord."

"The jails overflow with those too slow to evade the constables, and it seems I'm paying for my foolishness. I hate to admit it, but Magistrate Graving was right about one thing: there are far too many cases for me to personally review."

The scratch of the scribe's pen recording his admission unreasonably annoyed Arbuckle. It didn't help that his blackbrew craving had evolved into a headache. His stomach growled, and he wondered if Renquis would put that in the log, too.

"There may be a solution, milord." Tennison tapped the edge of his book with a finger, a habit Arbuckle had learned signified deep thought. "There are several retired knights of the Order of Paladin in the city. They're learned in law and loyal to a fault. I'm sure they'd appreciate the opportunity to once again serve the empire."

"Hmmm. Where might we find them?"

Tennison looked surprised. "There are four currently living in the palace, milord."

"There are? Why didn't I know of them?" Arbuckle's surge of annoyance dissipated when the door opened and two footmen entered. The first bore a tray with covered plates, the second, a silver blackbrew service. The crown prince inhaled the heady aroma of fresh blackbrew, anticipating his first euphoric sip.

"I didn't realize you weren't aware of the paladins' presence," said Tennison. "If you wish, I'll set up appointments for them to attend you, though it may be difficult for Lord KerBalish and Lord MalEnthal. They're not ambulatory."

Arbuckle's mouth watered as a footman swiftly laid out his breakfast: plates of kippered herrings, poached eggs, potato pancakes, toast, and a bowl of steaming porridge. The other, the blackbrew pot in one hand, plucked the porcelain cup from the table to pour.

"Not to worry," Arbuckle said, "I'll go to them. As long as their minds are keen and they understand—"

A sharp crack took everyone unawares.

The blademasters reacted instantly, hands on their swords as their eyes snapped to the source of the noise. The footman holding the blackbrew pot stared wide-eyed down at his hand. The cup he'd been holding had cracked and split so completely that only the handle remained in his grasp. The pieces lay upon the rug amidst a spatter of blackbrew.

"Your pardon, milord!" The man looked horrified, his voice trembling. "I…don't know what happened. I just… I just poured."

Arbuckle was more startled by the abject fear on the man's face than the shattered cup. *If he'd been serving my father, his head would probably already be on the floor beside the broken cup.* It would take time for the staff to learn that their new lord didn't consider a simple mishap to be a capital offence.

"Blademasters, stand down." The prince kept his tone casual. "There's been no harm done that can't be cleaned up. In fact, it looks as if there was hardly any blackbrew in the cup to spill. Just pour me another cup, good man. I'll survive."

"Yes, milord!" The footman with the blackbrew pot looked reassured as he retrieved a new cup from the sideboard. He hurried back to the table and poured steaming blackbrew.

The cup shattered, splattering the dark liquid across the table and setting off a chain reaction of detonating dinnerware. The saucer, the juice goblet, and two of the plates exploded into pieces, showering the crown prince in shards of porcelain and bits of his breakfast.

"What the hell?" Arbuckle jerked back, nearly toppling his chair.

The blademasters lunged forward, swords drawn, one to stand protectively beside the prince, the other with his blade at the terrified footman's throat.

"Milord!" Tennison gaped at the destroyed place setting.

"Good Gods of Light, what's going on?" Arbuckle edged away from the table. This wasn't a simple accident. Something was truly amiss.

"I don't know, milord." The server looked as if he didn't know which frightened him most, the blademaster's sword at his throat or the blackbrew pot in his hand. "I just...poured."

Arbuckle stared at the mess on the table, porcelain and crystal shards everywhere, and the white linen cloth stained with blackbrew. Only a few dishes on the unsoiled corner of the cloth had escaped the destruction. *That's curious...* "Blademasters, lower your weapons. Give me the pot. I want to try something."

Tennison stepped forward. "Milord, caution, if you please."

"If the pot's not hurting the footman, Tennison, I doubt it will hurt me." Retrieving the pot, Arbuckle dribbled some blackbrew onto one of the unscathed plates. The fine porcelain shattered. "Well!"

A blademaster plucked the pot from Arbuckle's hand and set it in a far corner, as if isolating a potential threat.

Arbuckle wiped his hands self-consciously on his doublet. "Well, something's not right. Fetch Master Duveau. I want him to look at this."

"At once, milord!" The second footman dashed out.

Arbuckle gazed longingly at his ruined breakfast. "Damn it, I was looking *forward* to that blackbrew."

"Milord." Tennison looked worried. "Might I suggest that you withdraw to your bed chamber until the archmage arrives? This is...well...disturbing, to say the least."

Arbuckle started to protest, but his blademasters nigh herded him into the inner room and closed the door. Baris looked horrified when Arbuckle told him of the exploding cups and plates, and had a fresh shirt and doublet for him in moments. Sighing in contrition, the prince picked up one of the case descriptions he'd been working on the previous evening, reading it as he paced the floor. His mind, however, was not on his work, but on his strange exploding breakfast. *What could cause tableware to shatter? Some kind of magic, or curse?*

Arbuckle lay the book aside when he heard voices in the outer room. Opening the door, he discovered Captain Ithross and several imperial guards entering from the corridor.

"Milord Prince, are you all right?" The captain swept his gaze around the room, focusing briefly on the soiled tablecloth and shattered porcelain before fixing on the crown prince. "A footmen said that all Nine Hells had broken loose in here."

"Not quite *all* nine, but we have had a bit of a surprise. It's something to do with the blackbrew. I've sent for Archmage Duveau to try to figure out what happened."

"Milord, we've got to get you away from here."

"I seem to be safe enough, Captain, and I want to know what Duveau discovers." Arbuckle would be damned if he'd get shunted away now.

Ithross shook his head. "I really must insist—"

The door opened again, and Archmage Duveau entered. "Milord, I really must—" The wizard stopped short at the sight of the wreck of Arbuckle's breakfast table. "Ah, so *that's* it."

"*What's* it, Master Duveau?"

"Someone has tried to poison you, milord." Duveau might have been saying that it was sunny outside for all the concern in his voice.

"Poison?" Arbuckle swallowed hard. *Someone just tried to kill me.*

"How do you know that?" Ithross demanded.

Duveau ignored the captain and bent over the table to examine the shattered cups and plates, then noticed the blademaster standing guard over the pot in the corner. "The blackbrew?"

"How do you *know?*" Ithross repeated.

"I *know* because the imperial family's tableware is enchanted to break if it is ever touched by poison." Duveau stepped past the blademaster to pick up blackbrew pot. Moving back to the table, he lifted a spoon, dipped it into the pot, and drew it out. The end of the spoon had melted away. "Yes, without a doubt, the blackbrew is poisoned."

While Arbuckle's mind spun, Ithross spoke in a whisper to one of his guards. The woman saluted and dashed from the room.

"Enchanted tableware? Why didn't I know about this?" Arbuckle was beginning to wonder just how much there was that he didn't know about his own home.

"Very few *do* know of it, milord." Duveau shrugged and put the melted spoon onto the table. "The emperor, of course, myself, and Mistress Ellis, our resident runemage, who is tasked with maintaining the magic on the service and enchanting new pieces." The archmage cast a thunderous glare around the room. "And now, everyone *here* knows of it. And let me inform you all that it is imperative that it *remain* absolutely secret. If I learn that one word of what I've said about this precaution has left this room, the loose tongue will be found out and *removed!*"

The footmen and several imperial guards paled under the archmage's wrath.

The threat tweaked Arbuckle's temper. "You needn't be so harsh about—"

"With all due respect, Milord Prince, I do! If this becomes common knowledge, it is useless as a protection and puts your life at risk. Only by remaining a secret did this enchantment save your life and offer a chance to catch the culprit before he knows his attempt has failed."

"Very well." Arbuckle swept the room with his eyes. "Everyone here is sworn to secrecy with regard to this enchantment under penalty of treason. Is that understood?"

Everyone bowed and muttered, "Yes, milord."

Arbuckle turned to Ithross. "Captain, can we catch this assassin?"

"Already working on it, milord. The palace is being locked down as we speak. No one can leave or enter until I say so. But I have to wonder," he pointed to the destroyed tableware, "how could such a thing be done?"

"It's no trivial matter." Duveau stood a little taller. "The spell is subtle, the runes hidden beneath the outer layer of glaze. It's quite beyond the skill of all but a few. I have a fascination with rune magic, but this, I must admit, is beyond even my expertise. It requires a—"

Ithross interrupted the mage by clearing his throat. "I *meant*, how could someone poison the prince's blackbrew."

Duveau scowled at the captain's interruption, and Ithross scowled right back.

"Gentlemen!" Arbuckle tried to keep the quaver from his voice. "Someone has tried to *kill* me. I want to know who and why."

"We'll question the kitchen staff and anyone who had access to this pot of blackbrew." Ithross pointed at the trembling footman. "Starting with *you*."

"I just *poured*!" the servant cried.

Arbuckle threw up his hands. "That must be a very short list of people, Captain. Aside from the cook and the footman carrying the tray, who else could have touched that pot?"

The captain and the footman both blinked, stared at the prince for a moment, then looked at each other.

"Milord, there are many servants who might have had access." Ithross glanced back to the footman. "Perhaps thirty or..."

"More like a hundred, sir." The footman looked from face to face. "The kitchens are a right madhouse this time of morning. There's fresh produce and meat bein' delivered, twenty cooks all workin' at the same time, with twice as many scullery maids and potboys scurryin' about. Not to mention the footmen, lady's maids, chambermaids, valets, and who knows who else comin' and goin'."

"Good Gods of Light." Arbuckle took an involuntary step back. So many people just to serve him and the few guests currently in the palace? How such an endeavor could go without his notice, he couldn't fathom. Who else? *Gardeners, drivers, maids, grooms...* "How many servants *do* work in the palace, Tennison?"

"I...don't know the exact number, milord." The secretary looked discomforted. "Some hundreds. More, if you count those who come and go with deliveries."

Arbuckle's mind reeled. *Hundreds...and one, at least, wants me dead.*

"Archmage Duveau, you can discern truth with your magic, can you not?" Arbuckle asked.

"Of course, milord."

Who wants me dead? There was only one way to find out. "Question everyone." Arbuckle knew he was being paranoid, but he couldn't live in fear in his own home. "While the palace is locked down, I want every single person interviewed."

"Impossible!" Duveau's face contorted into a mask of incredulity. "That would take *days*, milord!"

"Milord, we can't keep the palace locked down for days, but we can start with those who arrived this morning on errands or deliveries, letting them leave once they're proved innocent, then focus on the palace staff working in or around the kitchens." Ithross glanced from Arbuckle to the archmage. "That, perhaps, could take a day."

"I don't care how long it takes." Arbuckle glared. "You will find this assassin! Use whatever resources you must, and use your judgment, but I want everyone in the palace questioned eventually, not only to see if they had anything to do with this assassination attempt, but also to confirm their loyalty to me. Do you understand, Ithross? Duveau? You are to personally interview each and every one."

"But Milord Prince, the labor involved in interviewing so many is inordinate. I'm already exhausted from adjusting the palace wards and sending out missives to the provincial dukes. I simply can't—"

"You *can* and you *will*. My life is at stake, and I need you to do your job!" Immediately Arbuckle regretted the harsh words. He had already ruffled feathers by speaking his mind too quickly. *Think it through, Arbuckle. Always think it through.* "You'll have help. Master Kiefer is skilled at this spell, too, isn't he? Have him assist you."

Duveau's face reddened, but he nodded respectfully. "Very well, milord."

The prince turned to Captain Ithross. "Do *you* have any problem with my commands, Captain Ithross?"

"None at all, milord. I suggest we do the interviews in my office. Archmage Duveau," Ithross couldn't hide his smirk as he bowed and waved toward the door, "after you."

Renquis' pen scratched along in her ledger, the only sound in the ensuing silence. Arbuckle's shoulders slumped. *Someone tried to kill me.*

"Milord, a fresh breakfast is on the way." Baris gestured toward the bedroom. "Perhaps you'd like to eat in your bed chamber while this mess is cleared."

"No. Let's move my breakfast down to my office." Arbuckle started for the door without waiting for his retainers. "We need to make a list of people who would benefit from my death. I seem to have made some enemies."

Hoseph strode up the avenue toward the palace, panting with the uphill effort. He welcomed the exercise. The morning was cool, the blisters on his feet had healed, and he was well rested, his spirit calmed by the morning's meditation. Unlike priests of other deities, Hoseph never prayed for guidance. Demia cared little for the machinations of mortals. Only when their souls had been released from their flesh did she intervene, directing each to its appropriate resting place, be it one of the Seven Heavens, Nine Hells, or an alternate sphere of Earth or Sky. His own soul, he knew, would travel immediately to Eroe, Demia's heaven, as reward for his lifetime of service. Until then, he would toil in this world. He had no shortage of work to do.

His current task, to assassinate the crown prince, might already be completed. Lady T had assured him that her man in the palace was well positioned and skilled. Once Arbuckle was dead, Hoseph would shift his focus to ridding the guild of the usurper, Mya. Lad seemed to have vanished. Perhaps Mya had indeed killed him.

The rebellious Master Blade of Twailin concerned him also. Lad's house in Twailin had been deserted when Hoseph returned. In fact, all the Twailin assassins' homes and businesses that Hoseph knew of were also empty. No matter. Once things were settled in Tsing, the guild would hunt down those who wouldn't pledge their loyalty. Until then, Hoseph would wait and watch for signs that Arbuckle had met his end.

Topping the hill, Hoseph settled into his accustomed spot for spying on who came and went from the palace, a narrow alley between two grandiose buildings along the promenade.

A shout rang out, drawing his mind from his musing. Hoseph edged into the open to see two heavy wagons turning on the wide street, maneuvering around each other as their drivers cursed. That was odd.

He leaned out to view the palace gate. The avenue opened into a broad boulevard that girded the palace wall. The main gates had been built to impress as well as protect, a massive portcullis set in the outer curtain wall flanked by great towers. During the day, the outer gate was generally open to allow supply wagons to pass into the outer courtyard, but now the iron-bound grating was closed, guarded by four imperial guards, their halberds glinting in the sun.

Hoseph's heart skipped a beat. *The palace closed? Is it done? Is Arbuckle dead?* He emerged from the narrow alley and strolled closer, his hood drawn low to conceal his face. As the wagons departed, a noble's carriage pulled up to the gate and one of the guards strode forward.

"The palace is closed to visitors until further notice, milord. All morning audiences have been canceled."

"But I have an appointment!" The petulant whine from within the carriage garnered little sympathy from the guard.

"All appointments have been cancelled. You'll have to make another."

"This is ridiculous!"

"I'll mention your displeasure to Captain Ithross, milord. Now, please tell your driver to move along." The guard backed away from the carriage as the driver applied the whip and turned the team of four prancing horses.

Heartened, Hoseph turned and strolled back to his place of hiding, then paused to recall another narrow alley near the north wall of palace. Invoking Demia's gift, he stepped into the Sphere of Shadow, focused upon his destination, and stepped out again. Brick walls loomed above him, echoing with the sounds of a nearby commotion. Thankfully, the crowd's attention was focused not on him, but on the small postern gate in the palace wall.

This entrance allowed foot traffic for small deliveries and the passage of workers. At this time of day the flow of traffic should be brisk, but the door was closed, and four more guards barred the entrance to a small crowd of commoners carrying parcels. Hoseph cocked an ear to listen.

"I'm sorry, folks. Try back later. The gate's closed for now."

"What's this about? I've got perishables to deliver, and if they go bad, it's money out of my pocket!"

"You'll be paid for your loss, but there's nothing I can do. The gate's closed."

"For how long?"

"Until my captain tells me to open it."

"But why?"

"I'm not at liberty to say. Now please move along."

Hoseph smiled. This boded well. Something had clearly happened within the palace. The gates had also been closed when Tynean Tsing II died.

Back in the alley, Hoseph once again stepped into a mist of shadows, emerging this time in Lady T's sitting room. After blinking away momentary dizziness, he noted that the room was empty. A careful check of her dressing room and bedroom revealed the same. He pulled the bell rope in the sitting room and paced. Presently, the door opened to admit an assassin dressed as a butler, a man well-used to Hoseph's unannounced visits.

"Where is she?"

"The lady is out, Master Hoseph."

Generally, Hoseph would simply return at a more convenient time, but this was too important to wait for. "Tell me where she is."

Hoseph could see the butler weighing the wrath of Hoseph against that of his guildmaster. Finally, the more prominent threat won out.

"She's meeting with Master Lakshmi."

"Excellent!" Hoseph visualized his destination and disappeared.

He arrived in a narrow dead-end alley from which he could observe Master Inquisitor Lakshmi's bath house. He reeled with sudden dizziness and the twinge of a headache, undoubtedly from the change of lighting. Ignoring the dull ache, he settled down to wait.

Shortly, Lady T's distinctive carriage pulled up to the front door of the establishment. The driver and footmen—all assassins, of course—glared down from the grand conveyance, quelling the jealous glances of passing commoners. The ornate double doors of the bath house opened, and Lady T emerged and boarded her carriage.

Through the window, Hoseph saw her settle into her seat, and the conveyance rumbled away from the curb. Focusing on the interior, Hoseph ghosted through the shadows and materialized in the carriage.

Lady T jerked, steel flashing into her hand, but her features transformed quickly from anxiety to anger. "Hoseph! You'll get yourself *killed* someday doing that!" She tucked away the dagger. "What's so important that you have to disturb my work?"

"Work?" Hoseph wrinkled his nose at the scents of exotic bath oils and perfumes that permeated the carriage. "It seems to me that *I'm* working while you enjoy a relaxing morning bath!"

Lady T rolled her eyes. "I'm *not* relaxing. I'm conducting the day-to-day business of my guild. In fact, I'm checking on our progress with Duke Tessifus' sons. The youngest has potential. Now, what's so important?"

"I believe your man has completed his task. The palace has been closed to all traffic."

She shrugged. "That might mean something's happened, but there's no way to know until we get confirmation."

"The reins of the empire are all but back in our hands! How can you do nothing but sit and wait?"

"There is nothing to do *but* wait! You need to learn patience. If the attempt succeeded, we'll know soon enough. If not, we'll learn that, too, but we'll learn *nothing* until the news breaks through normal channels. If we start asking questions, we'll draw attention."

It galled Hoseph to admit that the woman had a point. He was used to more direct action.

"I'll visit you this evening." He flicked the silver skull into his hand. "Your people should have picked up some news by then."

"No later than sunset. I have an appointment."

Hoseph nodded. "Sunset, then." Invoking Demia's gift, he faded into his shroud of shadows.

Arbuckle contemplated the long list that he and Tennison had compiled, the names of those who might want him dead. The number of dukes, counts, barons, and magistrates was disconcerting.

He shoved the parchment across the desk. "It would be shorter if we listed the people who *didn't* want me dead."

Tennison shrugged. "You've upset a number of notable people, Milord Prince. Those accustomed to getting what they want react poorly to being told they can no longer have their way."

Arbuckle sighed and slumped in his chair. As a student of history, he knew that assassination was a time-honored method of eliminating rulers who displeased their subjects. His father had abused and berated the common folk for forty years, and finally someone had devised a plan to eliminate him. How ironic that the emperor—master of an empire-wide network of assassins—had himself been assassinated. Hopefully Ithross would have more luck tracking down whoever poisoned Arbuckle's blackbrew than he had the emperor's killer.

The list of people who would benefit from his death haunted Arbuckle's thoughts, but he resolved to refrain from thinking ill of anyone until he had proof. He was not his father to intimidate his peers into submission. Vigilance seemed the only prudent course of action.

A knock on the door interrupted Arbuckle's reverie. Tennison slipped out and immediately returned with an imperial guard officer.

"Milord Prince." The young lieutenant Rhondont bowed with a flourish. "Commander Ithross and Archmage Duveau wish to inform you that their task has borne fruit. If you would like to—"

Arbuckle was out of his chair before the woman could finish. "Take me to them immediately."

Following her down the steps to the main floor with blademasters stalking by his side and Tennison and Renquis trailing behind, servants, commoners, and guests of the palace scattered from their path like leaves before a gale. The opulent surroundings faded to utilitarian stone passages and plain wooden doors, as the officer led him into areas of the palace he had not seen in decades. Not since his boyhood had Arbuckle visited the service areas. He'd forgotten how austere they were.

The lieutenant finally stopped before a nondescript door and knocked. The door opened and a woman wearing a maid's uniformed emerged. At the sight of the crown prince she beamed and curtsied.

"Thank you, Milord Prince! Thank you very much!" With another curtsey, she flitted down the corridor.

Arbuckle watched her go, bemused by her apparent delight at seeing the man who had ordered her loyalty questioned. "What was that about?" he asked Ithross as he entered the captain's chambers. A few upholstered chairs—one occupied by a weary and frowning Archmage Duveau—were set in a circle around a low table.

"We've told everyone that the interviews are being conducted as a job evaluation, which allows us to ask about their duties, access to your food, their whereabouts this morning, and so on without raising suspicion. They are thanked in your name and given a small reward for their service." He indicated a stack of silver crowns on the table.

The archmage stood and nodded politely, but didn't bow as he should have. "With your permission, milord, I'll leave. I must rest. I'll send Master Keyfur to continue the interrogations."

"That's fine." Arbuckle let the slight pass without comment. "I was informed that you discovered something, Captain."

"In here, milord."

Arbuckle followed Ithross into an adjacent room and caught his breath when he realized there was a dead man lying on the table. He recognized the wine steward instantly. The man had served him many times, on more than one occasion politely answering questions from the crown prince on the provenance of this wine or that. The man had always seemed so knowledgeable and sophisticated. Now he was dead, white spittle riming his pale lips.

"What happened?" Arbuckle swallowed, his throat so dry the words barely scratched out.

Master Corvecosi straightened from his examination of the corpse and bowed. "Poison, Milord Prince. Self-administered."

Ithross shrugged. "He arrived for his interview and seemed calm until he saw Archmage Duveau. Then he clenched his jaw, started foaming at the mouth, and collapsed. We summoned Master Corvecosi immediately, but the man was dead in seconds."

Corvecosi indicated the man's mouth. "He had a false tooth that held the toxin."

"A false tooth?"

"He was a professional, milord." Ithross looked grave.

"He was a member of the palace staff!" The words sounded

ridiculous as soon as they left his mouth. *My father was master of an assassins guild.* Was the wine steward one of those assassins? Was the poisoned blackbrew retaliation for the death of Tynean Tsing? *I had nothing to do with it!*

"I concur with the captain." Corvecosi opened the wine steward's mouth with a finger. "Such things are rare and expensive."

Arbuckle swallowed hard. "Carry on, Master Corvecosi. Captain, we need to discover all there is to know about him, but quietly. I want the Imperial Guard to conduct the investigation, even if it leads outside the palace walls. If you have trusted guards…"

"I took the initiative to have all the imperial guards interviewed by Master Kiefer, milord. Only two didn't pass, for reasons unrelated to this situation, and they've been dismissed. I'll vouch for all the rest."

"Good!" The prince looked again at his would-be killer. "I suppose we can open the palace. What story can we make up about the lockdown?"

"Already done, milord. We were conducting security drills in preparation for your coronation."

"Excellent! I'll keep my appointments this afternoon, Tennison, else it will be assumed that something's amiss."

"Do you think that wise, Milord Prince?" The captain looked worried.

"I think it *necessary*, Captain Ithross."

Arbuckle made his way back to his office in silence, all the while considering the attempt on his life. He owed his survival to the paranoia of whichever long-dead ancestor had requisitioned the enchanted dinnerware. He or she must have had many enemies to go to such lengths.

Enemies… Arbuckle hoped his defenses were sufficient to protect him He glanced at the blademasters surrounding him. Despite the spectacular failure of his father's bodyguards, the blademasters' solid presence—silent, vigilant, and ever watchful—reassured Arbuckle. This assassination attempt wouldn't be the end of it.

Who wants me dead, and what will be their next step? He didn't dare hope that the next attempt would be so simple or so easily foiled.

"How could this happen?" Hoseph paced the sitting room, clenching and unclenching his hands.

"Operations don't always proceed as intended." Lady T's casual tone juxtaposed the wrinkles marring her brow. "Arbuckle was definitely alive this afternoon, and my operative's nowhere to be found. He was one of my best. If he was alive, he'd have reported in. I've got to conclude that he's dead, and the attempt failed."

"Such failure is unheard of! You *always* reported success to the Grandmaster."

"Of *course* I did!" Her worry transformed to indignation. "I wouldn't bother *him* with recitations of failure. If an operation doesn't succeed, we revise our approach and try again. It's called perseverance."

Hoseph glowered at her, then reigned in his temper with a deep breath. *Blessed shadows of death sooth me...* "How do you propose we *revise* our approach? What are Arbuckle's weaknesses?"

"His weakness is an absurd affection for commoners. We may consider posing someone as a peasant begging an audience." She shrugged. "His strengths are the palace itself, a company of loyal guards, and his blademasters, though after their failure to protect the emperor, I imagine their honor has been seriously besmirched. They're undoubtedly on pins and needles."

A spark ignited in Hoseph's mind. "Yes, they *have* been discredited..." The high priest glanced out the window at the darkening sky. *Yes... Tonight. First the archives, then...* "Do nothing until I contact you."

"What are you—"

The lady's question dissolved in the swirling blackness that enveloped him.

Hoseph drifted through mist and shadow, concentrating on his earthly destination, the Temple of Koss Godslayer. He'd only been inside the temple once, long ago as an acolyte on an errand for his high priest, but once was enough.

Unless they've rearranged the Great Hall. He invoked his talisman to reenter the real world, and felt no resistance. The way was clear. Though he couldn't actually *see* his intended destination, he could *feel* when an object blocked his arrival, and adjust accordingly.

The Sphere of Shadow faded away, but the lighting barely brightened as Hoseph materialized. Reaching out a hand, he felt a smooth wall and edged forward, his eyes growing accustomed to the dimness.

The Great Hall of the Temple of Koss Godslayer was long and narrow and as austere as he remembered it, empty save for row upon row of hard stone benches before the altar. Worshipers of Koss Godslayer were equally austere and strictly regimented, with specific hours designated for prayer, meals, sleep, and training the mind and body to exacting standards. Consequently, unlike the cults of more risqué deities like Thotris, the goddess of beauty, or Bofuli, the god of wine and merriment, who had more applicants than they could accept, few devoted themselves to the rigorous devotion of Koss Godslayer. Those who did were fanatic in their worship.

Hoseph walked slowly down the isle between the pews and the wall toward the towering sculpture of Koss Godslayer behind the altar. Its glow-crystal eyes illuminated the cunningly wrought bas-reliefs depicting the story of Koss' ascension. Along the right-hand wall, Koss was born of Eos All Father and a mortal woman, presented with Godslayer, the Sword of Light, and blessed by the Gods of Light. The left-hand wall depicted the coupling of Seth the Defiler and Draco Father of Dragons, the birth of their single offspring, and the unfettering of that nameless serpent onto the world to corrupt all of mortal-kind. Upon the north wall, behind the looming statue, the two stories culminated as Koss slew the serpent-god, and bonded with Godslayer, ascending to godhood as Koss Godslayer, man and weapon as one.

Such a simplistic cult...

The blessing granted to Koss by the Demia was the reason for Hoseph's visit this night. Sleep being akin to death, Demia had entered and soothed Koss' troubled dreams. It was a skill taught to her most devoted of worshipers as a final solace to the dying. Tonight, he would use that skill for a different purpose.

Hoseph looked around to get his bearings. Earlier in the

evening he had surreptitiously visited city archives and reviewed copies of the original architectural designs for the temple. Now he pictured those drawings in his mind and matched them to what he saw.

Four large doors exited the north end of the main hall of worship, leading to the wings for the Orders of the Body, Spirit, Mind, and Sword. It was the last that interested Hoseph. Somewhere behind this door slept High Priest Saepse, the master of the blademasters of Koss Godslayer in Tsing.

Hoseph tried the door's latch, but it was locked. He was no assassin, and certainly no burglar, but stealth and intrusion were redundant when one could walk the realm of shadows. He peered through the large keyhole into the corridor beyond. Touching his silver skull, he vanished and reappeared on the other side of the door. Through two more doors like a breeze through a shutter, and still no sign of guards. Unnecessary—none would dare confront blademasters.

A nagging ache pulsed behind his eyes, and Hoseph swayed, lightheaded. *Fatigue...I'm working too hard.* Recalling the diagrams once again, he assessed his position. *Left at the end of the corridor, and Saepse's quarters should be on the right.*

Finally coalescing before the thick oaken door embossed with the coat of arms of the Order of the Sword, Hoseph stumbled and steadied himself against the wall. His head throbbed and he felt dizzy. *What's wrong with me?*

Hoseph looked at the silver skull in his hand. Could Demia's divine method of travel be taking a toll? He'd never experienced any side effects before, but then, he'd never used it so much before. Prior to the emperor's death, he'd rarely travelled more than once or twice a day. Lately, he'd been flicking through the Sphere of Shadow constantly.

Nothing to be done about it. Just a few more tonight, then I can rest.

Hoseph knelt to peer through the keyhole, but his eye met only darkness. Cupping his hands to block the light from the nearby wall sconce, he closed his eyes to let them to adjust. Opening one to peer through the aperture, he divined by the starlight a small, sparse room with a wide bed, a bedside table with an unlit lamp, and the lump of a sleeping form.

Perfect. Ignoring his headache, Hoseph touched his talisman and flicked through the shadows into the room.

Slow, steady breathing greeted him. The high priest slept deeply beneath a white coverlet embroidered in silver thread with the blazing Sword of Light.

Two steps took Hoseph close enough to peer down at the sleeping priest's face. Silently invoking Demia's favor, he closed his eyes and searched his senses. *Dream... Dream, and show me your soul...* Scenes flashed into his mind, dreams of training, honor, regimen, duty. Hoseph delicately inserted his own memories of the palace dungeon: first the dead blademasters, their grievous wounds and blank, staring eyes; then their dead charge, Tynean Tsing, with his expression of stark terror, his own dagger thrust into his throat. Finally, he wove a careful suggestion.

You have failed! You have broken your oath to the emperor and to Koss Godslayer. You have failed...and failure is the ultimate sin. Royal blood wets your hands. You have failed...and there is only one atonement for failure...

CHAPTER XI

T hank you, Lord MalEnthal. Your aid in this is invaluable."

"It's the least I could do, Milord Prince." The aged paladin sat propped up in bed. He nodded toward his nurse, a surly looking man in a tabard emblazoned with the crossed scrolls of Oris the Overseer, god of knowledge and learning. "Jamis here provides me with reading material, but there's no real work for a paladin with no legs, is there?" The man smiled ruefully, his large, scarred hands patting the flat blanket below his torso.

"You can thank Tennison here for suggesting that I solicit your assistance." Don't hesitate to call on me if a particular case doesn't fit in to the parameters we've established."

"Yes, milord. No incarceration for non-violent protests, and short prison sentences without corporal punishment for damage to property. Anything involving theft or injury comes to you for review." The paladin nodded in approval. "I must say, I'm happy to see an end to the brutality. It's good to have someone with a heart in command again."

"Again? You knew my grandfather?"

"He knighted me." The grizzled old face split into a grin, but the joy faded. "No disrespect to your father, of course."

"My father deserved your disrespect, Lord MalEnthal. The empire's a better place without him."

"Yes, milord." The knight frowned deeply.

Arbuckle wondered what acts of brutality MalEnthal had committed under the orders of Tynean Tsing II, then realized he'd rather not know. That chapter in the empire's history was closed. It would take years to right the wrongs, but holding a grudge against those forced by their oaths of fealty into implementing the will of a brutal tyrant would do no good.

Arbuckle left the chamber with his entourage once again at his heels and new hope in his heart. "That should take some of the weight off my shoulders. Three extra sets of eyes to review court cases will make the work go much faster." The fourth paladin in residence had been unfit to serve, the man's mind addled with advanced years. "What next, Tennison?"

The secretary consulted his ledger. "The vote, milord. All the senior nobles of the city await you in the Great Hall. Afterward will be a discussion of the coronation plans."

"Must *all* the provincial dukes be present for the coronation?" Arbuckle chafed at the delay.

"Yes, milord." Tennison looked apologetic. "They must personally swear fealty once you're crowned emperor. The law's quite clear."

"I suppose we mustn't flout the law. Perhaps today's vote can abolish one of my father's unjust ones." Until he took the throne, trying to cajole two-thirds of his ranking nobles into supporting his changes was his only recourse.

They descended the sweeping stairway to the ground floor and turned down the long Hall of Arms. The gleaming coats of arms of each noble house hung for all to see, and beneath each stood an imperial guard, as immobile as a statue.

"I don't suppose there's any way we can hasten the coronation."

"Short of magic, none that I know of, milord."

"Magic…" Arbuckle cocked his head in thought. "Do you think the Imperial Retinue of Wizards would be willing to transport the dukes to the city? I know not everyone has access to a capable wizard, but I'm sure Duveau could think of something."

"I'm afraid not, milord. None of the dukes would agree to attend without their families, servants, and a *mountain* of baggage. We can only urge them politely to make haste."

Best just buckle down and play by the rules, Arbuckle. He'd spent his whole life playing by someone else's rules. A few more weeks wouldn't kill him. *Unless the next assassination attempt does.* His stomach soured at the thought.

They stopped before the Great Hall's towering double doors, and Arbuckle drew a deep breath to quell his nervousness. Every noble on his list of potential masterminds behind the assassination attempt would be in this room.

As the doors opened, a herald cracked his staff twice upon the marble floor. "Crown Prince Arbuckle of Tsing, Heir to the Throne!"

With a slow, dignified step, Arbuckle entered the hall, mounted the low dais, and took his seat. Nearly a hundred senior nobles arced around the front of the dais. Arbuckle noted that many had brought their daughters with them, the young ladies unduly primped for a business meeting. As the unmarried heir to the empire, beautiful ladies swarmed to him like bees to honey, but Arbuckle had more important things on his mind than courting potential empresses.

Tennison opened his ledger. "Honored nobles of Tsing, you attend this assembly to cast your vote for or against an amendment to the law regarding punishment of commoners proposed by Crown Prince Arbuckle. In brief, this amendment stipulates that corporal punishment of a servant or commoner may only be carried out after the accused is found guilty of committing a crime, and only under the aegis of the Tsing City Constabulary. A two-thirds vote is required for—"

The chamber doors burst open, and two columns of blademasters strode into the Great Hall. They were led by High Priest Saepse, wearing long black robes embroidered with a silver sword and a grim expression. Parting the crowd, they advanced and stopped before the dais.

The hair rose on Arbuckle's neck. *Why were they here?* His eyes flicked around the roomful of nobles and their scions. *Some threat to my safety? An assassination plot?*

Captain Ithross hurried up, his face a mask of worry. "Milord Prince, I'm sorry for the interruption. They—"

Arbuckle raised his hand, trying to appear calm. "Don't apologize, Captain. I'm sure there's a good reason for this." Only then did Arbuckle realize that every off-duty blademaster bound to imperial service accompanied the high priest. "High Priest Saepse, what's going on here?"

"I will explain, Milord Prince." The priest's fingers flicked in the silent language of the blademasters.

Immediately, the bodyguards at Arbuckle's side strode from the dais to join their ranks of brethren, standing with eyes forward, expressionless faces, and hands on the hilts of their swords. The prince felt instantly and conspicuously vulnerable, as if he'd just walked naked into a room full of people bearing daggers and ill will.

"Milord!" Tennison's voice came in an urgent hiss. "You are without protection!"

"Guards!" Ithross waved the imperial guards positioned around the room to the dais, and they form a thin line around their lord.

"My Lord Prince." High Priest Saepse dropped to one knee and bowed his head. The rest of the blademasters clutched their fists to their chests and bowed in the sacred gesture they performed during their oath-taking ceremony, when they pledged their lives— and deaths—to their master.

Arbuckle's brow furrowed as he stood, a surge of fear clenching his gut. "High Priest Saepse, what's this about?"

Saepse looked up. "It is about *failure*, milord. The failure of my order, my faith, and my brethren."

Murmurs swept through the crowd of wide-eyed nobles and attendants. Ithross looked nervous, his knuckles white on the hilt of his sword.

"I don't understand."

"Please accept my deepest apologies, milord. The Order of The Sword failed the House of Tsing when our charge, Tynean Tsing II, was murdered." He raised a hand and flicked his fingers. As one, the blademasters drew their swords and formed a circle around their priest.

The nobles backed away from the bared weapons, murmurs of disbelief and concern rising like a whispering tide.

"Swords!" yelled Ithross, drawing his blade. The imperial guards mirrored his action, a fragile barrier between Arbuckle and the most deadly swordsmen in the empire.

At another gesture from the high priest, each blademaster lifted his sword in salute, then lowered the tip, touching the back of the man before him to form an unbroken chain of steel and flesh. Saepse drew a long dagger from his robe, gazed skyward, and placed the tip against the hollow of his throat.

"Failure is the ultimate sin," the priest said. "There can be only one atonement!"

Arbuckle couldn't believe his eyes. "No!"

High Priest Saepse sheathed the dagger in his flesh. In the same instant, the blademasters thrust in perfect unison, each sword piercing the heart of the next man in the circle. They all fell as one.

After an instant of shocked silence, a woman's scream pierced the air. The crowd of nobles scrambled back.

Arbuckle stared in slack-jawed horror at the bodies encircling the high priest, their life blood spreading slowly across the cool marble floor. Fear prickled every nerve in the prince's body. His blademasters—loyal, inviolate, invulnerable—were gone. He couldn't think of what to do, what to say.

Captain Ithross solved that problem for him.

"Clear the chamber! Imperial Guard, to me! Protect your prince! Herald, call the guards from the hallway to assist!" Ithross turned to Arbuckle, lowering his voice. "Milord Prince, this is not safe! We must take you to someplace secure until protection can be arranged. Please, come with me." He gestured to a side door.

"Yes, I…" Arbuckle stepped off the dais and nearly fell, his knees trembled so badly. He tried to subdue his pounding heart. The heir to the empire needed to act calm, even if he didn't feel it.

Someone grabbed the prince's arm, and he jumped. Tennison pushed gently, nodding to the impatient captain. "Go with them, please, milord. I'll take care of everything."

"Yes." Arbuckle nodded numbly. "Thank you, Tennison. Captain, lead on."

Surrounded by a cordon of naked steel, he fled the hall. Murmurs and shouts broke out behind him, answered by Tennison's steady voice, but Arbuckle couldn't catch a single word over the roaring in his ears. *I'm vulnerable! There's nothing between me and an assassin's blade now.*

"Hear the news! Hear the news! Blademasters of Koss Godslayer all dead!"

It took a moment for the town crier's words to register through Mya's fatigue. She had been studying the cult of Demia all morning in hopes of learning more about Hoseph, and her mind was swimming with religious details she wished she'd never learned. Now she stopped short. *Blademasters all dead? Are they releasing details of Tynean Tsing's death now, a week later?* That seemed strange. Why advertise that the vaunted blademasters were fallible? Their myth was a greater deterrent than the now-tarnished truth.

"All blademasters dead as high priest orders suicide!"

Suicide? What? Mya moved into the Midtown crowd surrounding the crier, enduring the push and shove of sweaty bodies as she listened to the dramatic recitation of how the entire Order of the Sword had taken their own lives right in front of the crown prince.

"That's impossible!" cried someone when the man had finished his message.

"It's true!" the crier insisted. "It happened in the Great Hall! Dozens of nobles witnessed it!"

Ignoring the cries of disbelief and catcalls about lying nobles, Mya forced her way free of the crowd. She doubted a town crier would shout out unsubstantiated rumors, but this sounded too incredible to believe. She sought out a posterboard—businesses all around town paid a modest fee to have the boards erected outside their doors in hopes of attracting customers—and shoved through the crowd of people to read the newly posted notice. The news was true.

It's got to be Hoseph...

The priest had made his move, removing the prince's sworn protectors to better access the target. It was the logical first step in planning an assassination.

Mya wracked her brain, assessing what she had learned about the cult of Demia. How a priest could be transformed into a power-hungry assassin remained an mystery. After all, the Keeper of the Slain was a God of Light. The faith regarded death as a gentle, natural experience, not a violent act. Demia's followers repudiated wealth and comfort, and sought no domination over others.

After she'd read all she could find in the city library, Mya had investigated Demia's temple. As spare in architecture as the religion's adherents were in their habits, it radiated a sense of peace. The priests and acolytes were soft-spoken and eager to provide testimony to Demia's solace for those on the cusp of death. The true intent of the divine laying on of glowing hands was to ease a tortured soul on its way. Hoseph had twisted the act of mercy into murder. Had he perverted another of Demia's blessings to drive the blademasters to suicide? Regardless of how he had done it, one thing was certain; without the blademasters' protection, the crown prince was a much easier target.

She walked away from the posterboard. *It's not my fight. I've got enough on my hands.*

All the way back to the inn, Mya took the pulse of the city. Word of the blademasters' demise spread quickly, and many considered it an ill omen.

"Why would they abandon the prince?" cried an old woman as she twisted her hands in misery. "He's done nothin' but good."

"Good for us means bad for the nobles. Bet they're behind this!" groused another.

Even the constables on the bridge to the Dreggars Quarter were subdued. For once, the familiar sergeant just waved her on without a question or comment to his corporal.

Mya barely paid attention as she pondered what this news meant to her. What would happen to the Assassins Guild if they succeeded in killing the crown prince? Would there be a struggle for succession? What would the common people do? Would there be rebellion, civil war, martial law? And what about the guild? Gaining control would be more difficult amid such strife.

"Got a coin, lady?"

Mya looked down at the grimy urchin standing with an outstretched hand. She hadn't noticed Digger sidle up beside her. *Focus, Mya! Lad's not watching over you anymore.* Digger's approach meant the urchins were assembled and hungry.

She gestured as if the boy's presence offended her. "No. Now scat!"

Digger scampered away, and Mya continued down the street, making a stop at a bakery, and another to buy several papayas from a fruit vendor. Striding on, she glanced around to make sure no one was watching, then ducked into the abandoned stable. Her urchins met her with wide eyes and hungry smiles.

Mya pulled the loaves of bread out of the bag and placed them on the ragged but relatively clean scrap of canvas they used as a table. She handed the papayas to Digger, who quickly cut them into pieces. It pleased her to note that they didn't attack the food as they had when she first met them, but shared it out and ate deliberately. Their cheeks were a bit plumper or, at least, not quite as sunken. It was amazing what improvement a few days of decent food made in a child.

"Wait a minute!" Mya realized that she didn't recognize one of the dirty faces. "Who are you?"

The girl stopped chewing, her eyes as big as eggs. She looked no more than seven or eight, her hair a rat's nest, the simple shift she wore filthy with grime.

"This here's Kit. She's…um…" Nails fell silent and looked down at the dirt floor, his face red with embarrassment or shame.

Another mouth to feed. Mya sighed, but realized that the addition also meant another pair of eyes watching her back.

"All right, Kit, but if you stay, you earn your keep. Understand?"

"They told me the deal. I knows the score." The stern frown on the little girl's face looked almost comical. "I ain't as young as I look."

Mya wondered how many more meals her shrinking supply of coins would buy. She distained outright thievery, but she'd soon have to resort to some sort of larceny to sustain herself until she managed to get the guild—and its coffers—under her control. For now, she needed information from her spies.

"So, has everything been all right around the *Dulcimer*?"

Thumbs flew up in answer to her question. That was good; no one had yet found her hiding place.

"Ya' heard the big news?" Digger asked with a full mouth.

"About the blademasters? Yes. It's all over the city." She cocked her head and regarded her little spies. She hadn't brought them into her confidence, but it might be useful to know their opinions of the pulse of the city. She'd only been in Tsing a couple of weeks, but they'd lived here their entire short lives. "Someone is planning to kill the prince. What do you think will happen if they succeed?"

The urchins exchanged glances then looked to their eldest.

"Real trouble." Digger shook his head. "Folks think he's a

good'un after he burnt up all the gallows. He promised 'em justice. They ain't gonna go back to the way it was."

"What do you mean by 'real trouble'?"

"More fires, I expect. Ain't enough soldiers or caps in the city to keep it from happenin'." He shrugged and grinned. "I might just help with the torches."

"You'd burn your own home?"

"I got no home, remember?"

"But if the whole city goes up in flames…"

"Well, I don't think folks'll burn much south of the river, but I'd bet my left foot there won't be a stick standin' on the north side if they kill that prince."

Mya thought about this ill prophesy. One thing was true enough: nothing could stop the commoners if they chose to burn the city. Midtown and the Heights Districts would be hit hardest. That meant no nobles or rich merchants, no business or big factories, no profit to be made for the Assassins Guild. At least, not the Assassins Guild she wanted to govern. The aftermath would be horrific for the survivors, as well. The city of Tsing might cease to exist, and if the city fell and the streets ran with the blood of nobles, would there even be an empire?

I could move guild headquarters to Twailin like Lad suggested.

Mya rejected the thought; Twailin was too far from the center of the empire. No, the Grandmaster must remain in Tsing, which meant that Tsing had to remain intact. But that wasn't the only issue. She didn't know why the priest wanted to kill Arbuckle, but she would bet he was ready to install his own choice for emperor. If he gained power over the empire, her efforts to take over the guild would fail. There was only one thing to do.

"Whacha thinkin'?" Gimp looked at her expectantly. The urchins had finished eating, and were all staring at her.

"I'm thinking that I've got to keep the crown prince alive." Mya sighed. "I've just got to figure out how."

"Kill them who's plannin' it first." Digger drew his rusty kitchen knife and brandished it. "Way you fight, wouldn't be hard."

"I don't know everyone involved." Mya recalled the names she'd overheard in Lady T's sitting room: Seoli, Ingstrom, Graving. She'd recognize some of the others by their faces, but didn't know their names, which would make it difficult to track them down, especially alone. "Killing just some of them won't stop their plans, and will make the rest more wary."

Hoseph has got to be the driving force behind this. Cutting off the head of a snake was one sure way to stop it from striking. Unfortunately, getting her hands on a man who could disappear in a puff of smoke would be like trying to catch a fart on the breeze. But she might be able to get some help…

"Anything going on at Lady T's? A handkerchief in her window?"

"Nope. She comes and goes in that big carriage of hers, but we can't follow it." Digger shrugged. "She's got guards watchin', so we can't ride on the frame, and it's too fast to run after."

"A fella came to visit late last night, and didn't leave 'til just before sunup." Nails grinned and nudged Digger. "I think she's got a boyfriend."

"She got somethin' to do with this?" Gimp asked.

"Yes, but she also might be trying to help me…I think." Mya wondered if letting the lady know that she was onto the assassination conspiracy had been a mistake. "I don't know if I can trust her or not."

Mya gnawed on her nails and thought, twisting the problem this way and that to consider all possibilities. Finally she settled on one potential solution: *If I can't stop the assassins, then perhaps I can warn the target.*

She couldn't help but laugh at the notion. *Just warn the crown prince! Right, Mya. Maybe you should attend a court ball to meet him.*

"What's funny?" Gimp asked. The urchins were staring at her.

"Nothing. I'm just thinking." *Thinking that I must be daft!*

Getting in wasn't the problem. The ring she wore would open the secret doors into the dwarf-wrought passage beneath the bluff, and there must be access to the palace proper from the dungeons. But the palace was enormous. She'd need a layout or floorplan to locate the prince.

Mya scrabbled through her bag and pulled out her guide book of the city, thumbing through the pages until she found the section describing the palace. She skimmed over the obscure facts that might be fascinating to a tourist—*Two hundred chamber pots? Really?*—

but irrelevant to an intruder. There were lovely sketches of the towers and turrets and the stained glass of the Great Hall, but no diagrams of the interior. The original structure had been built centuries ago, dwarf-wrought, the book said, though the labor of both men and dwarves had been used during periods of expansion or renovation. The last major work had been completed about a century ago.

"No *men* who worked on that construction would still be alive, but dwarves…"

"What about 'em?"

Mya snapped out of her reverie and looked at Digger. She'd forgotten where she was again. "I need to speak to some dwarves."

"Well, good luck with that. They're a closed-mouthed lot."

"Leave that to me. I've got jobs for the rest of you. Keep your eyes on the *Tin Dulcimer* and Lady T's house. If anything unusual happens, I want to know right away. And ask around to see if you can locate the homes of Duke Seoli, Duchess Ingstrom, and Chief Magistrate Graving." It never hurt to have a back-up plan in case things went awry, and she might pressure one of them into betraying their cabal.

Gathering up her book and bag, Mya ducked out of the stable and headed back to the library. She had to learn whatever she could about the palace, then she needed to find some dwarves who were willing to talk.

CHAPTER XII

Dee reined in his mount to a walk to give it a rest while he admired the impressive vista from the crest of Forendell Pass. Though the early morning sunlight had burned the fog from the high mountains, clouds still shrouded the valleys. A tide of mist flowed like a waterfall over a high ridge, spilling down into the vale below. Soaring peaks tinged with gold surrounded them, islands floating in a lake of fog. It was an eerie wilderness to someone city-born and raised, and Dee shivered with a chill that wasn't due entirely to the cool air.

Danger lurked behind the beauty. Despite the empire's tenuous peace with the ogre tribes that roamed this harsh landscape, they'd seen fearful evidence that all was not well. The skulls atop the grimly painted standards propped along the roadside were usually animal, sometimes human. Nobody took chances here. Caravans aplenty labored through the pass, always escorted by weathered men and women with crossbows, or mail-clad dwarves hefting axes. Only the fast couriers travelled the pass alone, relying on speed for safety.

"Hell of a view, ain't it?" Pax pulled up beside Dee and stretched in his saddle. The tough old innkeeper seemed to have settled into his torment with a resigned stoicism.

"It is." Dee checked his recalcitrant mount as it shifted impatiently. Despite its labored breathing from the climb, the shaggy beast wanted to run. "We must be nearing the next way inn."

"Gods of Light preserve us, I can almost smell the blackbrew." Pax gave his mount its head, and the beast lurched forward with a grunt, hooves pounding the hard and finally downhill track.

They descended into the mists. A little more than a mile on, the road curved around a bend, then dipped down into a snug dell sheltered by tall pines. In the center of a clearing stood a compound girded by a sturdy log palisade and an iron-bound gate that now stood open. Within stood a large stone building with a steep slate roof and smoke trailing from the chimneys. The horses sprinted forward with renewed vigor, no doubt envisioning buckets of oats and piles of sweet hay.

As they pelted toward the gates, a coach pulled by a matched team of four prancing horses surged out.

"Whoa!" Dee reined in hard to avoid a collision. "Gods damn it! Watch where you're—"

As the driver hauled the horses to a stop, Dee blinked in sudden recognition. He'd know that carriage and team anywhere; he'd picked them out himself. But it was the figure that stepped out of the carriage—the mop of unruly hair, startling hazel eyes, and impossibly graceful movement—that sent a thrill up Dee's spine.

"Lad!" Dee cursed silently at his outburst. The near accident had drawn the eyes of all in the stable yard, and who knew where Hoseph's spies might lurk. To cover his gaffe, he waved peremptorily at a stable boy and called loudly, "You there, lad! Come take our horses."

Dee dismounted and shot Paxal a warning glance, but the innkeeper was staring hard at the carriage, as if something was missing. He realized what it was. *Mya! Where is she?*

"Gentlemen, I apologize for my driver's carelessness," Lad said with a cordial nod. He gestured toward the inn, and Dee noticed his left hand swathed in bandages. "Please, let me buy you breakfast in amends."

"Thank you, sir. I'm afraid our horses were heading for the barn without much care for what might be coming the other way." Dee hauled his saddlebags off his horse before the stable boy lead it away. "We'd welcome the chance to break our fast. We left our own way inn rather early this morning."

It took all Dee's restraint to not pepper Lad with questions as the innkeeper led them to a private back room.

Lad beat him to the first word as the door closed behind them. "What are you two doing here?"

"Looking for you! We got word of the Grandmaster's death, and—"

"Never mind that!" Paxal's fists clenched at his sides. "Where's Mya?"

Lad met the innkeeper's ire with calm. "Mya decided to stay in Tsing."

"Alone?" Paxal looked skeptical. "Why?"

"I suggested she come back to Twailin, but she said that the Grandmaster belongs in Tsing."

"The *Grandmaster*?" Dee's gaze shot to Lad's left hand and the bandage there. "Master, please, tell us what happened."

Lad reached into a pocket and held out two rings on his open palm, one made for a master's finger, the other a guildmaster's. "I'm not your master anymore, Dee. I'm not in the guild anymore."

Dee stared at him in shock. There was only one way to leave the guild...death. But then, Lad had never been a true member of the Assassins Guild. He had never signed a blood contract.

"So...Mya took the Grandmaster's ring?"

"Not really. I put it on her finger." Lad rubbed his cheek and smiled. "She wasn't happy about it."

Paxal growled deep in his throat. "What's this Grandmaster's ring, and why would you put it on Mya if she didn't want it?"

"It means she's Grandmaster of the Assassins Guild, Pax," Lad explained. "It means she's *safe*. No assassin can touch her."

Paxal pulled up a chair and sat at the table, his anger apparently quenched by Lad's calm explanation. "All right. Now, all I know about this situation is that Mya is in Tsing and in trouble. To help her, I need some details, and your guild's secrets can be damned to all Nine Hells."

Lad told them all that had transpired in Tsing—their discovery of the Grandmaster's identity, his involvement in Wiggen's death, Kiesha's torture, and how Lad's injury had freed him to kill the Grandmaster—pausing only when a maid delivered biscuits and blackbrew. When he'd finished, Dee told him of Hoseph's visits to Twailin.

"But he didn't look like you described him before. He was bald, and wore gray robes."

"Was he injured?" Lad asked.

Dee shook his head. "He didn't look hurt, but there's no mistaking his intentions toward you and Mya. He's out for blood, rallying the whole guild to hunt you both down."

"We figured as much." Lad frowned. "Mya's spreading the news that I'm dead. I hope Hoseph believes it."

"He said he wasn't sure. If you lay low, maybe he'll buy it." Dee stared at the two rings Lad had laid on the table during his recitation. "You should send Sereth the rings by messenger. That way, everyone there can truthfully say that the last they saw of you was when you went off to Tsing."

"But what about Mya?" Paxal looked grim. "If she's declaring herself Grandmaster, then she's putting herself square in their sights."

"Yes, she is, but they can't touch her. She intends to take the guild. Hopefully she can get the Tsing guildmaster on her side. It depends on how cozy Lady T is with Hoseph."

"What about the new emperor?" Dee asked. "Won't he expect to inherit the Assassins Guild?"

Lad shook his head. "No. The emperor seemed to despise his own son. I doubt the prince knew what his father was. Tsing's an ugly place. The Grandmaster used the guild to terrorize the populace. If Mya can take the guild, she'll put a stop to that."

"Unless someone kills her first." Paxal scowled down at his cup.

"She's tougher than you think, Paxal. If anyone can turn the guild around, it's Mya."

The three men sat in silence for a while, sipping their blackbrew. Finally Dee threw back the last gulp, sighed gustily, and patted the bulging saddlebags. "So, Mas—Lad, how can we help you? We've got money…"

"I've got enough to get back to Twailin. Save it for Mya. She'll need it if she can't get Lady T's support."

"How do we *find* Mya?" Paxal asked. "Tsing's a big city."

"I don't know. I left her at an inn called the *Prickly Pair*, just inside the east gate. We assumed they'd be looking for us, so she'll be wary and may have moved." Lad smiled. "She'll be glad to see you two. She'd never admit it, but she needs friends. Someone she can trust."

"Well, then we better get on the road." Paxal downed another mouthful of blackbrew and stuffed a biscuit into his jacket pocket. "We're wastin' daylight."

"Pax is right." Dee stood and slung the saddlebags over his shoulder. "It was a pleasure working for you, sir."

Lad actually laughed aloud, something Dee had never before seen him do. Standing, he extended a hand. "No it wasn't, Dee. I was horrible. You helped me immeasurably, and I'll always be grateful."

In Lad's smile, Dee could see that something on this trip had healed his former master, perhaps finally solving the riddle of his wife's death, or maybe freeing himself from the guild. Whatever the reason, Dee was glad; Lad deserved some joy in his life. He wondered if his own trip to Tsing would have such a happy ending.

"Aye, been to the palace a few times, I have. Deliver quarried marble when they feel like they need a new staircase or balustrade." The dwarf quaffed ale and squinted over the rim of his tankard at Mya. "Why you want ta know?"

"I'm writing a guide book." Mya pulled from her bag the one she had been using—The City of Tsing, Heart of the Empire Past and Present—to show the dwarf. "This one covers the city pretty well, but has hardly anything on the palace."

"Why don't you ask at the palace? That seems like the place ta start."

Mya shook her head. "I want a different perspective, a *dwarven* perspective. I don't think your people get enough credit for their work. I mean, dwarves *built* the original palace, right?"

"O'course we did!" The dwarf puffed up with pride, as had the three previous dwarves she spoke with. Hopefully, this one would be able to provide her with some useful information. "Did you know that the flagstones were laid over a thousand years ago?"

Oh, dear gods, here it comes. Mya withered at the thought of another lesson in fine stonework. She dare not be rude, for dwarves were quick to take offense, and if she angered one, she'd never get another to even say "Hello". Instead, she pulled out a small journal, pretended to scribble notes, and tried to steer the conversation.

"Really? That's fascinating! But let's start at the beginning. Dwarfs designed—"

"The beginning! Well, fact is, dwarves lived in that hill long before Arianus Tsing plopped his arse in a chair and called it a throne. Good mining it was once, and good transport out, what with the river and ocean at hand." The dwarf finished his tankard and waved a thick hand to the bartender for another.

Mya fished a coin from her dwindling supply and put it on the bar. "Yes, but—"

"So Arianus shows up, thinks the hilltop's just the spot for a castle, and negotiates with the dwarves. Dwarves got easy access to stone, iron, copper, lead, and men got easy access to crops and timber. Mutual benefit, you see. So they make a deal, and live happily ever after!"

"So the dwarves who lived beneath—"

"Dwarves *still* live beneath the palace, forging, crafting, working on the palace whenever somethin' needs doin', but the good stone's long played out."

Mya's ears perked up. Now she was getting somewhere. "So, there must be dwarves who know the palace inside out."

"Oh, that there are." The dwarf accepted his tankard from the bartender and sipped, thick foam whitening his moustache. "Know every stone, they do."

"And how might I speak to one of these dwarves? I'd like to get the entire layout of the palace for my book."

Silence prompted Mya to look up from her journal. The dwarf stared at her with narrowed eyes and one bushy brow raised, his tankard poised halfway to his lips.

"And why might you be wantin' a layout of the palace?"

Suspicious little toadstool... She tried to look innocent.

"I'm hoping the new emperor will be willing to have visitors, escorted tours to show the common folk what a beautiful and historic structure the palace is. But to interest people, I need floorplans and drawings of the grand rooms."

The dwarf's eyes remained narrow, as hard as stone and every bit as yielding.

"Well, if you don't know anyone I can speak to..." She started to rise from her barstool.

"Now hold on a second. You don't have ta leave just yet." He raised two fingers to the bartender. "I never said I didn't know anyone who could help ya."

Mya sat back down and stared at him, trying to figure out what kind of game he was playing. Was this just a ploy to get her to keep buying him ale? A moment later, the bartender delivered two new foaming tankards. Mya held up a coin.

"Who?"

"Just pay the man, lassie, and don't get yer knickers in a wad." The dwarf pulled both tankards close, waiting until Mya had paid and the bartender walked away before speaking again. "Now, I don't know what you mean ta do with this information, and frankly, it don't matter ta me, but I won't involve dwarves in any shifty plots."

"Shifty plots? I don't under—" She stopped at his raised hand.

"I don't care, and I don't want ta know. But I can give you a hint where ta start."

"So…you're saying there's someone *else* who can help me? Someone not a dwarf?"

"Oh, aye, there is. He's not a dwarf, he's a scoundrel." The dwarf quaffed half a tankard of ale. "Now, I'm not accusin', but I ain't born yesterday, either."

"Scoundrel?"

"Aye, scoundrel. They call him the Gnome. That little rat probably knows the layout of every building in the city. Least ways he's burgled most of 'em, some probably more'n once!" The dwarf laughed hard, finished his tankard, and started on the next. "The Gnome's been burglin' this city longer than most tall folks been breathin'. It's said he stole a jewel from Tynean Tsing I's very crown not five feet from the man sleepin' in his bed!"

"Oh, come on!" Mya rued the notion of plying a dwarf with alcohol for information. All she was getting was tall tales.

"I'm tellin' ya true, I am!" He looked indignant. "Look it up in yer books!"

"So what's this gnome's name?"

"The Gnome. That's all folks know him as. You want to talk to him, you ask around a few tinker shops in the Dreggars Quarter and tell 'em where you can be found. The Gnome'll find you if he's interested. It'll cost you, though; he don't do nothin' fer free."

"All right. Thanks for your time."

"And thank *you* for the ale. You ever need a nice marble

headstone, you let me know."

"I'm sure I'll need one someday, but hopefully not soon." Mya jingled her much-lightened purse as she left the tavern. Buying ale for dwarves had turned out to be expensive, and she'd still have to pay this gnome, if she could find him.

Maybe he needs someone killed, and we could barter services.

Turning up an alley, Mya froze. Two figures struggled in the shadows. A heavy-set man pressed a slim woman against the rough brick wall, her dirty skirts lifted to expose one grimy leg. Her face turned toward the street, and she saw Mya watching. With a smile and knowing wink, she let out a particularly enthusiastic shriek of encouragement.

Mya turned on her heel and hurried away, the parody of lovemaking fixed in her mind's eye.

Prostitution seemed to be a major trade in Tsing. She'd seen both men and women peddling flesh all over the city. At least she'd never have to resort to selling herself for money. Killing was easier than sex with strangers. *Besides, who would pay to have sex with a tattooed monster?*

Mya strode back toward the *Dulcimer*, not knowing what else to do. Should she canvas the entire Dreggars Quarter, knocking on gnome-sized doors? And if she did find the Gnome, how could she afford him? She wouldn't steal, wouldn't whore, and plying her trade as a killer required contacts she didn't have. She needed a solution that would allow her to maintain her dignity.

Lady T... Just one of the woman's jeweled necklaces would support her for months. It wouldn't be stealing...not really. As Grandmaster, the guild owed her a cut of the profits. She would demand her due or take it out in broken bones.

But right now, I have a gnome to find. For that task, at least, she had help.

She stopped at street vendors to buy sausage and a head of cabbage on the way back to the stable. She found her urchins awaiting her there, but their number seemed to have increased once again.

"Wait." She scanned the faces and noted a little boy even smaller even than Kit who she didn't recognize. "Who's this?"

"That's Tiny, Miss." Digger stepped up, unrepentant about

adding another to his cadre. "He's quick and quiet. Knows the streets, and he don't eat much."

Mya thought that the boy probably hadn't eaten much in months. His eyes were sunken, his cheeks hollow, and the shift he wore hung on him like a tent. She gritted her teeth. She didn't have time or resources to train and support the city's entire urchin population.

"Okay, but no more new friends, Digger. We have more than I can manage already, and the more of you there are, the more chance someone's going to figure out that you're working for me. Now eat. I need to talk to everyone."

"Yes, Miss Mya."

That was one instruction they never failed to follow. When they'd eaten, and she had their undivided attention, Mya told them what she needed.

"I have to find a burglar called the Gnome. Have any of you heard of him?"

Eyes went wide all around. "Oooh, he's a legend! They say he can steal the skin right off a cat."

"Good. I was told to ask for him at the tinkers' shops around the Dreggars Quarter. Do you know where those are?"

"Oh, aye, Miss Mya." Heads bobbed in affirmation.

"Good! Point them out to me." Mya opened her guide book to the map of the Dreggars Quarter. No one came forward, and she looked up into puzzled eyes.

"What's that?" Digger leaned forward, tracing the thin lines with a grimy finger.

Mya closed her eyes for a moment. What she wouldn't give to have her Hunters once again at her beck and call. *Work with what you have, Mya.*

"It's a map," she explained. "It's a picture of all the streets of the quarter. Each line is a street. See, we're right here." She pointed to the location of the stable.

"How do you know?"

"All the streets have names. See, this is 'Willow Way', and this is 'River Bend Road'."

Digger stared into her eyes. "We *know* the street names, but how can a street be a line on a piece of paper? That don't make no sense to me at all. How can we show you anything on *that*?"

Mya sat back on her heels, disheartened by the boy's bewilderment. "All right, if you can't show me on a map, can you take me to them?"

"Oh yeah! We can *show* you! We just have to actually," Digger pantomimed pointing, "*show* you."

Mya nodded in understanding. "That'll work. We start first thing in the morning."

As the urchins assigned to watch Lady T's house trooped out, those assigned to watch Mya sleep tonight waited expectantly. There would be more whistling practice, and probably more staring at the ceiling before she slept. She hadn't been sleeping well again, but not out of fear now. She'd dreamt of Lad a few times, and had a nightmare about her tattoos coming alive. She knew they were just dreams. She needed to focus, to put her past behind her and think of what she had to do. *Find this gnome, cut a deal, and figure out how to warn the prince.*

Easy…

Hoseph emerged from the Sphere of Shadow and released Chief Magistrate Graving's arm. The man stumbled and shook his head.

"Gods of Light, I despise that." Graving collapsed into a plush chair, pressing an embroidered handkerchief to his brow. "Feels like I'm being dragged to the bottom of the sea."

"As I've told you before, it's perfectly safe." Hoseph banished his dizziness and the nagging headache by sheer force of will as he regarded the gathered magistrates and nobles with veiled disappointment. It had taken untold trips through the shadows to convince them that this meeting was even necessary, and ferrying them to Lady T's home had taxed him even further. The mounting fatigue pressed on him heavily. This so-called conspiracy had, so far, consisted of him doing all the work, and the nobles and magistrates doing nothing but complaining about his inability to kill Arbuckle. He was in no mood to put up with any more grumbling.

"Wine, Chief Magistrate?" Lady T smiled and proffered a decanter, playing her role of gracious hostess.

Hoseph regretted the need for all this posturing, but Lady T's poise helped moderate between the pompous nobles and surly magistrates. Left to his own devices, Hoseph would motivate them quite differently.

"Now that we're all here, what is the *dire* emergency?" Duke Seoli demanded.

"The *emergency*, Milord Duke, is our need for information from you. You might have noticed that Arbuckle's blademasters are no more." He allowed himself a smug smile.

"You arranged that?" Duchess Ingstrom stared at him in disbelief. "How?"

"Are you complaining, milady?" Graving narrowed his piggish eyes at the duchess and sipped his wine. "What does it matter how Master Hoseph accomplished the feat? They're gone, and the plan can move forward."

"I was *there*, Magistrate Graving." The duchess' hand trembled as she lifted her wine glass. "It was a dreadful spectacle."

"It was a stroke of genius, and leaves Arbuckle vulnerable." Graving raised his glass to Hoseph in salute. "So, when do you put the bastard in his grave?"

"That is, indeed, the next step," Hoseph acknowledged. "We need information from within the palace. Since I'm obviously not welcome there, and minor nobles"—he nodded toward Lady T—"must await an invitation to visit, it's up to you senior nobles and magistrates, who can access the palace freely, to glean what we need. We simply want you to—"

"*Spy* for you?" Magistrate Ferrera reached for the decanter conveniently placed beside her and poured another whiskey. The woman obviously substituted alcohol for courage. "We're *not* your spies!"

"We've been doing exactly what you asked us to do by opposing Arbuckle's attempts to change the law." Duchess Ingstrom glared first at Hoseph, then Lady T. "Now you're telling us we have to do *more*?"

Seoli flipped his hand dismissively at Hoseph. "It's *your* job to rid us of the Arbuckle."

"We're not asking you to put a dagger in his heart, Milord Duke." Lady T maintained her calm demeanor. "We simply need information. We have no resources in the palace."

"What about this secret constabulary of yours? Have them infiltrate the palace staff." Graving smoothed his jacket over his ample belly and glowered.

"That's impossible at this juncture." Hoseph shared a glance with Lady T. They had agreed not to disclose the failed assassination attempt. No need to invite more criticism. "After the loss of the blademasters, security has been heightened. We've learned that all menials are being questioned by the Imperial Retinue of Wizards." Hoseph noted their discomfort at the mention of wizards. "You, however, are beyond reproach and can come and go as you please."

"Then you should have put someone in place *before* you did away with the blademasters!" Ferrera's sneer would have curdled milk. "Instead, you want to risk our lives!"

Graving shook his head, his frown doubling his number of chins. "My colleague is correct. We're not your spies. We've opposed Arbuckle on every turn, as instructed. Asking too many questions would be dangerous."

"Asking the *proper* questions of the right people need not be dangerous at all," Lady T explained. "Besides, we're interested in what's going on at the highest level, behind the scenes. Installing someone as a lowly maid won't tell us how to get close enough to the crown prince to kill him."

"He's still surrounded by the Imperial Guard. Getting near him will be impossible." Magistrate Ferrera downed her whiskey and reached for the decanter again.

"But imperial guards are not blademasters." Hoseph paced the room and all eyes followed him. *Good; at least they're listening.* "We need to identify and make contact with someone willing and able to assassinate Arbuckle, someone with access who can be recruited or pressured into complying with our wishes."

Duke Seoli frowned and shook his head. "And risk our necks for daring to suggest regicide to the wrong person? Don't be ridiculous!"

"I must agree with Duke Seoli." Duchess Ingstrom wrinkled her nose. "Whoever approaches a potential collaborator is as good as dead."

"You misunderstand," Hoseph said. "I would be the one to

actually broach the subject. All you need do is identify the person and deliver a message—discreetly, of course. A simple invitation to an unspecified meeting will not put anyone in danger."

"Until they refuse your offer and report the meeting and the origin of the message to Arbuckle." Seoli shook his head again. "It's too risky."

Hoseph raked the conspirators with a reproachful look. "So far, I've taken *all* the risks in this. If we're all to benefit from our association, the risk must also be shared."

"You're able to flit around like a breath of wind, Master Hoseph." One of the lesser nobles glared at him accusatively. "If one of us is approached by the Imperial Guard, we can't simply vanish!"

"And we have much more to lose than you." Duchess Ingstrom frowned at the signet ring on her finger. "Nobles convicted of treason forfeit their estates. An entire noble house can be disavowed, our families thrown into the street, our titles and lands sold to the highest bidder." She glanced toward Lady T and said, "No offense intended, my dear."

"None taken." Lady T's calm tone belied the fire in her eyes.

"Have a magistrate find your conspirator. All they stand to lose is a *job*." Seoli pronounced the word as if it were personally repugnant.

"This's *insane*!" Magistrate Ferrera quaffed yet another whiskey. She hadn't stopped since she arrived, and had begun to slur her words. "We're all gonna end up dead! I wish I'd never joined this plan, and I want no part of it anymore!" She lurched to her feet and started for the door.

Hoseph's patience snapped. *That's enough!*

He flicked the silver skull into his hand and grabbed her arm, her scream of protest fading as he dragged her into the Sphere of Shadow. Through the gray veils he perceived Ferrera's soul, wan and colorless, like the woman herself. She couldn't struggle, couldn't escape, but he could sense her panic through their connection. Ferrera had feared travel through the Sphere more than any of the others. She would learn very shortly that her fear was well founded.

Travel with me no more, he thought, releasing his connection to her incorporeal being.

Hoseph felt her drift away as the shadows shifted and swirled. Demia's grace protected him and those with him in this realm of banished godlings and demons. Not so the unfortunate magistrate. A looming presence, darker than the surrounding shadows, thickened around her, enveloped her struggling essence. With a wrenching jolt, Magistrate Ferrera was gone. Without a twinge of guilt, Hoseph returned to Lady T's sitting room.

"Now, let's get back to business."

Seroli stared aghast. "What did you do with her?"

"What else could I do? Hoseph shrugged. "You all heard her. She no longer wanted to be a part of our group, so…she's not."

"Did you kill her?"

"No, Duchess Ingstrom, I did not. I left her in the Sphere of Shadow." Hoseph smiled as they shrank back in response to his blasé admission. *Perhaps now they'll cooperate.*

Graving put down his wine to avoid spilling it. "If we should all disappear there'll be an investigation."

"But you won't, because everyone here is thoroughly committed to our cause. You should have taken more care in recruiting Magistrate Ferrera. She was unstable, undependable, and a liability to us all. Now, who will be placing our inquiries within the palace?"

"There will be compensation for this service." Lady T stepped up, flashing Hoseph a warning glance before she sweetened the pot. "Whoever brings us what we need will receive a boon: a title, lands, whatever they wish. *We're* the ones putting Tessifus on the throne, and we'll control his every move. Whatever you want, we can grant."

Silence hung heavy in the room, and Hoseph measured their avarice against their fear. As he knew all too well from working with the Grandmaster, fear nearly always won, but their fear of Arbuckle evidently exceeded their fear of him. Not one person—magistrate or noble—met his eye.

"You disappoint me." Hoseph glowered at them, but even his wrath seemed inadequate to motivate them. *Cowards and fools, all of them.* "If we don't succeed before the coronation, the task will be much more difficult. Perhaps when Arbuckle has replaced all of you with *commoners*, you'll realize your error."

CHAPTER XIII

Arbuckle stepped from his bedchamber into the sitting room as and immediately felt cramped by the press of people. Ten imperial guards and an armored knight snapped to attention. Ithross had insisted on the increased security, determined that the loss of the blademasters wouldn't put his sovereign at risk. The captain had chosen the guards not only for their loyalty, but also for their lack of familial ties.

"Loved ones can be used for coercion, Milord Prince," Ithross had said in explaining his choices. "Even the most loyal guard might succumb when given the choice between their child's life and yours."

Arbuckle appreciated the sentiment, but felt overwhelmed. *As long as they keep me breathing…*

Unfortunately, more guards meant many disturbances—a sniffle here, the creak of armor there. The guards weren't as unobtrusive as blademasters. Consequently, Arbuckle had begun using his bedchamber for meals and solitary work. It was the only place where Ithross allowed him to be alone.

"What's on the agenda this morning, Tennison?"

"No audiences until after lunch, milord. Just these reports from Lord MalEnthal." Tennison handed him a sheaf of papers. "His reviews of the cases you sent him.

"Excellent! I'll see to these first thing." A pen scratched behind him, and Arbuckle turned to find Verul sitting with his ledger instead of Renquis. "Verul! I'm pleased to have you back, my good man! You've straightened out the archives then, have you?"

"Pleased to be back, milord, and no, not quite yet. It's a catastrophe, if you don't mind my saying. It'll take some time to straighten out properly, but we're well on the way."

"As long as we're making progress, I'm pleased." Despite the potential embarrassment of his every word being recorded for posterity, Arbuckle wanted future scholars to be able to trust that the material they were reading was accurate.

What will history make of my father? he wondered as he returned to his bedchamber. Forty years of lies in the archives, with no way to determine the veracity of any of it. *A legacy of lies...*

I won't be like him, Arbuckle vowed. *If I survive long enough...*

Banishing his maudlin thoughts, Arbuckle settled down to his reading. The work progressed quickly. MalEnthal's reviews were spot on. Without exception, their judgments concurred. Unlawful assembly, disorderly behavior, looting, and minor destruction of property comprised the majority of charges. He rubbed his eyes before starting in on the last case.

"Arson?"

That dispelled his fatigue. Any fire in a city like Tsing could be disastrous. Many of the nobles' homes were stone-built, but most of the city was constructed of wooden buildings that would flare up like bonfires. Arbuckle didn't even want to think of what might happen if the Wharf District or the shipyards caught fire. With the Night of Flame still painfully on his conscience, he flipped the page to read the case.

There was a piece of paper inserted with a note.

> Milord Prince Arbuckle,
>
> May I beg that you see me before dealing with this case? I have information that may be pertinent to the outcome.
>
> Ever loyally yours,
>
> Lord Paladin MalEnthal

"How odd." Arbuckle flipped to the back, but found no review or further notations, simply the case of three commoners arrested for burning a noble's home. "I wonder what he means by this."

Gathering up the case, he strode into the sitting room.

"Tennison, we need to go see Lord MalEnthal."

"At once, milord." Tennison gathered the clattering entourage of guards, and they accompanied Arbuckle to the residential wing.

At the paladin's door, he stopped, considering the cryptic note about the case. He turned to the knight in charge of his guard detail. "Wait here, Sir Yanli. There's not room enough for everyone, and Lord MalEnthal is loyal to me."

"Very well, milord." The knight stationed his guards along the hall.

Tennison and Verul accompanied Arbuckle inside. They found Lord MalEnthal propped up in a chair by a window reading yet another case file.

"Milord Prince Arbuckle. Welcome!" He nodded respectfully, which was all he could do without lower limbs. "Please, take a seat. I see you got my note." MalEnthal's expression darkened.

"I did. What is it about this particular case that troubles you?"

"Have you studied it yet?"

"No. I know only that it's arson."

"Baron Ledwig's home was burned two days ago. The home was offset from its neighbors by a sufficient distance to allow the fire brigades and volunteers to keep other buildings from becoming involved. The home itself, however, was a complete loss."

"Was anyone hurt?"

"There were only minor injuries." The paladin's frown deepened. "Three culprits were caught in the act and arrested. An entire squad of constables witnessed them set the fire, so there can be no question as to their guilt. They knew what they were doing, and the act wasn't random."

Arbuckle cocked his head. "I don't understand what the problem is."

"This detail troubled me." MalEnthal flipped through several of the pages. "See here. The accused all have the same surname. I wondered how they were related, and what bearing it might have on this case, if any."

Tennison spoke up. "It's not unknown for criminality to run in families."

"I know," MalEnthal agreed. "I saw a lot of that when I was in the mountains hunting down bandits. Whole clans gone bad. But something nagged my gut on this one, so I sent Jamis here out to ask some questions. It turns out that they're brothers, and have never before been in trouble. Their sister is a chambermaid in the baron's home."

Arbuckle felt a chill. "And…"

"And that's all he could find out." The paladin shrugged. "But I've still got a bad feeling about this. You see, Baron Ledwig used to be a knight. I served with him for several years."

"And what's your opinion of the baron?"

MalEnthal glowered from beneath bushy brows. "Far be it for me to denigrate a noble, but may I just say this: Sir Ledwig enjoyed working for your father. He was awarded his title and lands by the emperor for his deeds putting down an uprising in the south."

Arbuckle sat back in his chair. This didn't bode well. MalEnthal was a veteran of countless campaigns, with a sharp mind and a sterling reputation. His opinion meant something. "Thank you for bringing this to my attention, Lord MalEnthal. I'll get to the bottom of it."

"I hope so, milord. It stinks like rotten fish to me."

Arbuckle stood. "Tennison, summon the chief magistrate."

Arbuckle reviewed the case twice while he waited in a small audience chamber. When Graving arrived, he could tell by the man's manner that he was annoyed at being summoned, but Arbuckle didn't care.

"Chief Magistrate Graving, thank you for coming. I've got a few questions about the arson case at Baron Ledwig's home that I hope you can clear up."

"I'll try my best, Milord Prince."

"These three brothers are relations of one of the baron's servants, I believe."

Graving's eyes narrowed before he assumed a thoughtful expression. "I believe you're right. A chambermaid, milord."

"I'd like to speak to her. Have Chief Constable Dreyfus bring her in."

"I'm afraid that's not possible. She passed away recently."

"Passed away?" An alarm tolled in Arbuckle's mind. "How did she die?"

"I'm not sure, milord." Graving's lie shone clear on his face.

Anger flared through Arbuckle's veins. "Chief Magistrate Graving, I believe that this woman's death has something to do with this case, and I intend to investigate thoroughly, starting with the accused, the constables who caught them in the act, anyone who interrogated them, and Baron Ledwig's entire household. I *will* discover how this woman died, and if I learn that you knew and withheld that information from me, I will arrest you for withholding evidence. Do you understand?"

Graving turned white, his triple chins quivering as he spoke. "I *understand*, milord. I was *not* withholding anything, as I am not *sure* exactly how the woman died. I was told the baron was displeased with her in some way. She supposedly died from…injuries resulting from her punishment."

"Her punishment?" Arbuckle felt sick. "What type of punishment?"

"Flogging, milord." Graving's eyes remained fixed upon the table.

"When did this happen?"

"Some days ago, milord." Still Graving averted his eyes.

"How *many* days ago, Chief Magistrate?"

"Three, milord."

"*Before* the arson. So why isn't that case here? Why haven't I reviewed the judgement against Baron Ledwig?"

"No crime was committed, milord. It was simply a case of punishment that—"

"No *crime* was committed?" Arbuckle surged to his feet, no longer able to restrain his rage. "A woman was beaten to death, and you say no crime was committed?"

"Milord, this is not a case of—"

"It's murder, Chief Magistrate!"

"Milord!" Graving's voice quivered with anger. "She was a *commoner*. Her brothers are commoners. The law states that a commoner cannot charge a noble with a crime. Therefore, there *was* no crime. The law—"

"The law is *wrong*, Chief Magistrate! When commoners feel they have to take matters into their own hands because they can't trust the authorities to seek justice, there's something wrong with the law! The common people of this empire have just as much a right to justice as any noble! Until it's given to them, this entire city—this entire *empire*—is wrong! *You* are wrong!"

Graving replied with tight lips and a furrowed brow. "No charges were filed, so this sad accident was not brought to my attention as an official matter. It's not my responsibility. My duty is to execute the law, not moral whims."

The prince couldn't believe his ears. How could Graving sleep at night if he regarded pursuing justice for murder as a whim?

"No, I guess it's not your responsibility, but it *is* mine. As this crime of arson must be answered for under the law, so must this crime of murder." Arbuckle sat back down, still fuming, but at least able to think straight. "Tennison, summon Chief Constable Dreyfus and tell him to place Baron Ledwig under arrest. I'll conduct a trial as soon as it can be arranged. Send word to all the senior nobles and magistrates in the city to attend. No excuses. Also, the baron's family, his household staff, and any other witnesses to the beating of his servant and to the act of arson are ordered to present themselves at the trial as witnesses."

"Yes, milord."

"Milord Prince, I—"

"Will attend the trial also, Chief Magistrate, or I'll find you derelict of your duty and strip you of your office. Do I make myself perfectly clear?"

"Yes, milord." Graving glared, whirled, and strode out, followed by a bustling Tennison.

The door closed behind them, and the room fell silent, save for the creak of a boot as someone shifted, Arbuckle's pounding heart, and the scratch of his scribe's pen.

"Did you get all that, Verul?"

"Every word, milord."

"Good. Have it written on my headstone." Arbuckle stood, and his guards closed in around him. "If they wanted me dead before, they'll *really* want me dead after this."

Mya looked at the note in her hand—

> The *Mug and Muffin*. Two hours after highsun today. Alone.
>
> The Gnome

—then up at the sign swinging in the afternoon breeze. This was the place.

Situated near the top of the Long Stair, the *Mug and Muffin* catered to the longshoremen and shipwrights who made their way from the Dreggars Quarter to the shipyards and docks below the bluff every morning. Thankfully, the smell of wood dust and tar drifting up on the breeze didn't overwhelm the aroma of strong blackbrew and fresh-baked pastries that wafted through the shop door as it opened. Mya's stomach growled.

The man exiting the shop tipped his hat to her. Mya ignored him; he was too tall to be the person she was here to meet.

The note had been handed to her at the third tinker's shop she revisited that morning. The shopkeeper denied knowing who had given it to him, and she hadn't pressed the issue, afraid that undue curiosity might scare off the Gnome.

Pausing at the door, she scanned the tiny café professionally, but neither saw nor heard anything that raised her suspicions. *No turning back now, Mya.* She walked in with one hand on the dagger secreted in the pocket of her dress.

"Help ya, Miss?" The proprietor's pearly teeth gleamed as he grinned at her.

"Just a cup of blackbrew and a nibble, if you please." She looked at the pastry case. "One of those sweet rolls will be perfect."

"Cream and sugar in your blackbrew?"

"Just cream."

"Sit anywhere you like. With you in two shakes."

High-backed booths lined one wall, a long counter with stools the other. There were three other customers, one at the counter near the door, and two sharing the nearest booth. None were gnomes. The only other door was behind the counter. Mya picked the far booth and sat with her back to the corner and a view of both doors and the entire room.

A moment later the shopkeeper stepped up with a tray. "There you are. Three pennies, if you please."

"Thank you. Here you go." Mya placed four pennies in his outstretched hand.

Pulling her guide book from her bag, she settled in as if stopping for a snack and a little reading. She sipped her blackbrew, piping hot and strong, and popped a bite of the sticky pastry into her mouth. It was delicious. Licking her fingers, she chased the bite with another swallow of blackbrew, and opened her book.

"Ye must be new ta Tsing."

The voice startled Mya so badly she slopped blackbrew over the edge of her cup. In the corner of the booth across from her sat a diminutive fellow who seemed to have materialized out of thin air. He was so short that his chin barely cleared the edge of the table, so she could only see a nose big enough for someone thrice his size and a gray cap pulled low to shade large eyes.

You let down your guard, Mya—for a sweet roll, no less—and you could've been killed.

She wiped up the spilled blackbrew with a napkin and put her cup down. "Yes, I am new to the city. How did you know?"

"One, yer readin' a book what tells ye about the city, and two, ye tipped." He reached across the table and nipped a bite of her pastry. "Where ye from?"

"Why does that matter?"

His dark eyes gleamed up at her. "I'm a mite choosey about who I work for, so if ye won't be answerin' me questions, I'll just be leavin'…"

"Twailin." Giving a truthful answer went against Mya's instincts, but she needed this information. Gimp had reported more flickering lights at Lady T's last night. The conspirators had apparently convened another meeting. Mya couldn't spend her life dangling from the mansion windowsill in hopes of catching them planning.

"Long way ta come fer a visit."

"I'm not visiting. I'll be staying." She tried to appear calm, sipping her blackbrew and pinching off another bite of her pastry.

"Why?"

"I've secured a position here that may turn out to be beneficial, but I find myself in need of your services."

"So I understand." He nipped another bite of pastry. "Wha'da ye need?"

"I was told you know the layout of the palace."

His oversized eyes widened. "Why'd ye want ta know that?"

"That's my business."

"No. You hire me, it becomes me business." His eyes narrowed and flicked over her, lingering here and there, then following her left hand as it moved from her plate to her mouth. "Yer ring. That what I think it is?"

"What do you think it is?"

"I think it means yer a killer. How'd ye get it?"

"I killed someone."

"Yer a killer, and ye want me ta get ye inta the palace? Ye must be daft." He started to move, but she held out a hand.

"Wait. I already know how to get in. I just need to know the layout of the upper floors."

"Yer lyin'."

"No, I'm not. And I don't need the layout so I can kill anyone. I need it to *keep* someone from being killed."

His eyes narrowed again. "Who?"

Mya took a deep breath and prayed that he'd believe her. "Crown Prince Arbuckle."

"Horseshite!" The gnome made a face of disgust, derision, or disbelief, Mya couldn't tell, but he didn't' get up and walk out. "Hold out yer hand."

With some trepidation, she complied. He reached out one finger to touch the Grandmaster's ring, then snatched his hand back as if he had touched hot iron. He shook his head, muttering in a language Mya didn't know.

"I only know two rings anythin' like that. One's on the finger of a blueblood north of the river, but it ain't quite so fancy. This one I ain't seen in fifty years. Why is that?"

Again, telling him the truth felt wrong, but it might just convince him to help her. "Because the emperor was wearing it."

"I don't believe ye."

Mya laughed. "I didn't quite believe it myself, but if you've lived in Tsing that long, it shouldn't be too much of a surprise. Think about how the empire's been run during his reign. Think of what's happened to the Thieves Guild. Think of *how* it happened." She'd learned that the Thieves Guild had been expunged from Tsing long ago, run out by the Assassins Guild and the constabulary combined. "And think how…" she wiggled her ring finger, "this guild has been terrorizing commoners but leaving gentry and nobility alone. It was the perfect set up, and I ended it."

"Aye…" He rubbed his prodigious nose and sniffed. "Mayhap yer tellin' me the truth, and mayhap yer full of shite. Either way, I got no reason to help ye."

"You've got two excellent reasons to help me."

"Oh? And what might those be?"

"First, I'll pay you." Mya hoped he didn't ask for any money up front; she still had to figure out how to get some. "Second," she lowered her voice and glanced at the proprietor, but the man seemed to be fully involved in cleaning his blackbrew pots, "if the plot I've uncovered to assassinate Prince Arbuckle is successful, everything north of the river will burn to the ground. If that doesn't put a damper on your earnings, I don't know what will."

"Aye, ya got that right enough." The gnome made another face, equally unreadable. "And how do ye plan ta stop his murder if I give ye what ye want?"

"I plan to tell the prince who's out to kill him."

"Why not just kill them plannin' it?"

"Because it's not that easy. If I miss just one, or if bodies start showing up, they'll know I'm onto them and make it even harder." *Not to mention the fact that I can't even* find *Hoseph!*

"Aye, good point." He chewed his lip and rubbed his nose. "But if yer who ye say ye are, then why not send yer people after all these folks at once?"

"My people *are* these folks." She wiggled her ring finger again. "I didn't get this the usual way, and we don't quite see eye to eye yet."

The Gnome chuckled and squinted up at her. "And why should I trust ye?"

"You shouldn't." Mya ate another bite of pastry and licked the sugar off her fingers. "You'd be a fool to trust an assassin you just met. Look into it. I'm sure you have your sources. But I can't tell you everything I know until I'm sure we've got a deal."

"What about yer name? Can ye tell me that?"

Mya hesitated for only an instant. If the Gnome wanted to betray her, he'd do it with or without her name. There was only one assassin from Twailin wearing the Grandmaster's ring. "I'm Mya."

"I'll look inta this and get back to ye."

"Don't take too long. They may act soon."

"Aye. Watch fer me note." The Gnome slipped out of the seat, dropped below the table...and vanished.

Mya had been listening, but it was like she'd gone momentarily deaf. One moment she could hear the gnome's heart beating in his chest, and the next, it and he were both gone.

"Sonofabitch..." The only other person she'd ever met who could move with such stealth was Lad.

Finishing her blackbrew and pastry, she considered the little man. Such a combination of stealth and caution were admirable, and she smiled to think of the Gnome prying a jewel from the imperial crown while the emperor slept. After meeting him, she had no doubt the story was true.

Maybe he can teach me *to move like that.*

CHAPTER XIV

$\mathcal{A}$rbuckle entered the Great Hall to the herald's ringing announcement, feeling for all the world as if he was the one on trial. Sweeping his gaze across the dozens of attending nobles, he wondered who among them might be plotting his death even now. Days had passed since the assassination attempt, but his stomach still quivered with the memory. Despite being surrounded by imperial guards and knights, he felt naked without his blademasters.

Don't let them see your fear, the prince reminded himself as he strode onto the dais and took his seat.

The hall had been arranged to accommodate the trials. To Arbuckle's right, a waist-high wooden rail surrounded three men sporting an undeniable family resemblance. Manacled at wrist and ankle and surrounded by constables, they stood with shoulders slumped and eyes downcast. To his left stood another railing, but the prisoner behind it couldn't have been more different. Baron Ledwig was a tall man with salt-and-pepper hair, the muscle of his youth still evident in his broad shoulders. He stood with his head held high, staring at Arbuckle defiantly. Though guarded, his hands and feet remained unfettered as a privilege of his rank. A row of witnesses sat between the two boxes.

As far as Arbuckle could tell, all the senior nobles and magistrates had obeyed his order to attend. Disapproval painted their faces. Only one noble in the past thirty years had been charged by the crown, and that for treason against the empire. To charge Baron Ledwig with the murder of a commoner probably seemed blasphemous to them, considering how many were either directly or indirectly guilty of similar crimes. If their gazes had been daggers, even a cordon of blademasters could not have saved the prince.

Fortunately, all save the guards had been disarmed before entering the Great Hall, one of the few of his father's edicts of which Arbuckle approved.

"Lords and ladies of Tsing, honored magistrates, thank you for attending. I have called you to witness these trials—two crimes irrevocably linked—to demonstrate how justice will be rendered during my reign. No longer will imperial laws be twisted to serve only the ruling classes. *Anyone* charged with a crime will be called to answer for his or her actions."

Mutters swept through the nobles, low and dangerous. The imperial guards shifted, but remained in place. Arbuckle didn't think there would be any trouble from the crowd, but Captain Ithross had insisted on additional security. Even more guards were stationed in the corridor in case violence broke out.

With a deep breath, Arbuckle commenced the proceedings. "Tennison, read the first charges."

"Yes, milord." Tennison unrolled a parchment and read in a voice loud enough to reach the far corners of the chamber. "Raul Walls, the charge of arson. Vance Walls, the charge of arson. Torance Walls, the charges of arson, assault upon a constable, and resistance to arrest."

Arbuckle turned to the accused. "Raul, Vance, and Torance Walls, how plead you to the charges levied against you here?"

The three men looked at one another in surprise, then back to the prince. "What do you mean, milord?" asked one.

"Milord Prince," interrupted Graving, heaving his bulk out of his chair. "The accused were caught red-handed by a squad of constables. What's the use in asking them how they plead?"

"Because the law states that they have the right to do so, Chief Magistrate." Arbuckle tied to maintain his composure. "The protocols require that the accused enter a plea, so they will. Now, please sit down."

The Chief Magistrate obeyed, glaring first at the prince, then at the nobles as someone tittered in amusement. He had thrown the law in Arbuckle's face, and having it thrown right back at him undoubtedly galled Graving no end.

Turning back to the Walls brothers, the prince explained, "You may plead innocent or guilty to the charges. If you plead innocent, know that you must present evidence to support your claim."

The three looked at one another again, then the man who appeared to be the eldest stepped forward, his broad workman's hands gripping the rail of the box. His knuckles were scabbed with dried blood, and his face was bruised. "I'm Torance Walls, milord, and I speak for me and my brothers. We plead guilty." He looked at Baron Ledwig with unabashed malice. "We burnt that pig's fancy house for what he did to our sister, Macie, and we'd do it again."

"Hang them!" came an anonymous shout from amidst the nobles.

"Silence!" Arbuckle glared the hall to an uneasy quiet. "The assembled will remain quiet, or I will charge the offenders with contempt of the crown!" He turned back to the brothers. "Now, Torance Walls, what do you believe Baron Ledwig did to your sister?"

"He killed her, milord." The words caught in his throat.

"And why did you not report your sister's death to the authorities?"

"Because, milord, as far as the *authorities* was concerned, beatin' a chambermaid to death ain't a crime." The man squared his shoulders and met Arbuckle's eyes, sure of his fate and resigned to it. "You say there's gonna be justice for commoners, but there ain't. Everyone knows that. The only justice we ever see is what we take for ourselves."

Arbuckle sat silent for a moment, allowing Torance Walls' words to reverberate around the cavernous chamber and watching the assembled nobles for their reactions. He saw only disgust, fear, and malice in their eyes. It was time to show them what they truly feared.

"*This* is why, lords and ladies, there must be justice for *everyone*. A brother will avenge his sister regardless of the law, so the law must be the *means* of his vengeance. Without equal justice, without the same laws governing nobles and commoners alike, we live by tyranny, risking rebellion and anarchy."

"Only because you're too weak to enforce the law!" A young man stood, his face livid. He pointed his finger at the Walls brothers. "Hang that rabble for the rest to see! Show them what comes of breaking the law, and you'll have order! Your father knew that, and ruled for forty years in peace!"

"The baron's son, milord," whispered Tennison.

Arbuckle saw the family resemblance in the young man's hard eyes and cruel twist to the mouth.

"Rest assured, Lord Ledwig, these men will be sentenced for their crimes, as will *all* who break the laws of this empire! Now, sit down."

The young man seethed, but sat.

"Tennison, since these three men have pled guilty, please continue with the other charges."

Once again, the secretary's voice boomed out. "Baron Uldric Ledwig, the charge of murder."

Another murmur swept the assembled crowd.

"Baron Ledwig." Arbuckle turned to the accused noble. "You are charged with murdering your chambermaid. How do you plead?"

"Point of Law, Milord Prince!" Chief Magistrate Graving once again rose.

Arbuckle sighed. "State the precedent, Chief Magistrate."

"In year four of his reign, *Emperor* Tynean Tsing II instituted the Law of Justifiable Punishment. That law states that a noble may punish, by any means they see fit, any servant or commoner for dereliction of duty, insult, assault, or impugnment."

"I'm familiar with that law, Chief Magistrate. Are you familiar with the Articles of the Foundation, laid down by Arianus Tsing I when he founded this empire?"

Graving's gloating expression fell. "I am, milord."

"And you no doubt know that *all* imperials law must comply with these basic tenets?"

"I do, milord."

"State for me the third Article."

Reluctantly, the chief magistrate recited, "No person of any station or class may take the life of another, barring only conflict during war, insurrection, in the defense of one's self or property, or in the lawful pursuit of justice."

"Thank you, Chief Magistrate." Arbuckle turned his attention to the rest of the crowd. "Lords and ladies, the Law of Justifiable Punishment does not—*cannot*—supersede the Articles of the

Foundation. Murder is wrong, no matter the rank of the perpetrator or victim. When a murder victim has no advocate, it's the duty of the Imperial Court to seek justice. It was the court's duty to charge Baron Ludwig with murder. In the court's dereliction, as ranking noble, I have done so."

Graving apparently interpreted Arbuckle's statement as an accusation. "It's been this way for forty years, milord! Nobles are not to be prosecuted for their actions against commoners. That is the order that came directly down from your father the emperor. That is how every magistrate is trained to execute the law!"

Trying to cover your fat ass. Arbuckle swallowed his disgust; this was neither the time nor place to deal with Graving.

"My father may have tolerated violations of the Articles of the Foundation, but I will not. Murder is a prosecutable offence for all. *Any* violation of the Articles of the Foundation will be prosecuted. If the court neglects to do its duty, be assured that I'll personally take up the slack."

Murmurs broke out again, louder this time, "Preposterous!" and "Anarchist!" among the exclamations. Arbuckle raised a hand, and the herald banged his staff hard upon the floor.

"Lords and ladies, we must all live under the governance of the Articles of the Foundation, nobles and commoners alike. If we do not, *that* is when we risk anarchy. Now, let's continue. Baron Ledwig, how do you plea to the charge of murder?"

"I have no plea, milord, because no crime was committed. It was justifiable punishment."

Frustration threatened to choke Arbuckle. "Did you not hear what I just said? Murder is a violation of the Articles of the Foundation. These apply to *everyone!*"

"If I had done this a month ago, it wouldn't have been a crime."

"It *would* have been a crime, whether you were charged or not! Now, answer me: Did you flog Macie Walls to death?"

"I did, milord, as an example to the rest of them." The baron sneered at the Walls brothers. "When a bitch bites the hand that feeds her, she must be put down, or she'll bite again."

"You filthy piece of—" The Walls brothers surged forward despite their chains.

"Silence!" Arbuckle surprised himself with the volume of his command. "The accused will remain silent until they are asked to speak, and you, Baron Ledwig, will be civil."

"I was unaware that I was required to be civil to *commoners*, milord." Ledwig's lip curled back from his teeth. "Is *that* a law?"

Arbuckle seethed. Ledwig was just as arrogant as Lord MalEnthal had said. "You were a knight before you were given a barony, were you not?"

"Yes."

"And before that, a squire?"

"Yes."

"And before that?"

"I was a soldier in your father's army."

"A *common*, solder. You held no title, and were commoner before you became a squire. Tell me, do you feel it was your right as a soldier to be treated with respect?"

"Yes. I was a soldier! A representative of the Crown!"

"And before you joined the army, as the son of a *tailor*, did you deserve respect?" He'd looked into the baron's past with care.

The muscles of Ledwig's smooth jaw writhed. "I *earned* my nobility in service to this empire! They didn't." He pointed accusatively at the Walls brothers.

"Then try to *act* like a noble! Now, what did Macie Walls do that resulted in her...punishment."

"Destruction of my personal property, assault of my person, and impugnment of my honor, milord." The baron nodded to a group of servants seated before them. "There were witnesses."

"Very well." Arbuckle surveyed the witnesses, apparently the entire staff of the baron's house. "Who among you saw Macie Walls assault Baron Ledwig?"

Three of the assembled tentatively raised their hands, one man, and two women.

"You there." The elder woman stiffened at being singled out. "Please stand, tell us who you are, and give us your account of this assault."

"Milord Prince." The woman stood and curtsied. She had a scar on the right side of her face, from the corner of her eye to her jaw. She fixed her eyes firmly on the floor. "I'm Libby, senior maid in the Ledwig household. Macie was serving tea for the baron and his friends. When the baron...touched her, she slapped his hand. That was when she dropped the tea service."

"He touched her?" Arbuckle's stomach writhed in disgust. "How did he touch her?"

"I...didn't see exactly, milord." The woman stood trembling.

"Did either of you others see what happened?" Arbuckle needed to know the truth of this, despite his disgust.

The younger man and woman looked at one another, then the woman stood, her jaw set defiantly. "Milord. I'm Hanse, the baron's house maid. I seen it."

"Tell us exactly what you saw."

"Yes, milord. Macie came into the baron's parlor with the tea service, and me with a tray of tidbits. He, the baron, that is, grabbed Macie by the arm, and put his other hand...on her...bottom."

"That's a filthy lie!" Baroness Ledwig shot to her feet. "I refuse to have this slander spoken in public!"

"This is not slander, Baroness Ledwig, it is testimony. Sit down!"

The baroness sat at Arbuckle's command, her face flushed with rage.

"Now, Hanse, tell us the rest of what happened."

"The baron did that a lot to the younger maids. It's kind of a game he played when he had his friends over for cards. He did...more sometimes, but this time, Macie slapped his hand away, lost her grip on the tray, and it fell. She said that he was a beast and had no right to touch her, that we had rights, and was gonna have a new justice soon. We talk about that all the time. But the baron, he knocked her down, called her a...a...bitch, and kicked her hard."

"Kicked her?" Arbuckle bit back his rage. "I thought she died from flogging."

"Oh, aye, milord. She died from the flogging right enough, but that came later." The maid glanced at the baron, tears running down her cheeks. "He dragged her into the courtyard and cinched her up on a post. Then he stripped her and beat her with a coach whip 'til it broke. Then he used a piece of knotted rope. He made us all watch. Said we better learn a lesson not to talk back."

Arbuckle felt sick, but forced himself to continue. "What about the baron's friends?"

"Sir Hambley, Lord Vosk, and a merchant fellow, Master Templeton. They laughed at first when Macie talked back, but they left when the baron dragged her to the courtyard."

"Hambley, Vosk, and Templeton, please stand," Arbuckle ordered.

Captain Ithross stepped forward. "Milord Prince, we sought them, but were told that all three men left the city when the charges against Baron Ledwig were announced."

Arbuckle gritted his teeth. "Well, *someone* recognized that what was being done was wrong. Baron Ledwig, do you have anything to say on your behalf?"

"Only that I have broken no law. A commoner struck me, impugned me, and destroyed my property, and I punished her accordingly and justifiably. If you charge every noble who has struck a commoner with a crime, my *lord*, you will find yourself with no nobility."

"I will not charge anyone for violations of the Articles of the Foundation that occurred prior to my ascension to ranking noble of this empire, Baron Ledwig, but I will see justice done under my authority!"

The crowd of nobles stared at him in stunned silence. Well they might; half of them were probably as guilty as Ledwig for past offenses, and he'd just let them off with a warning.

"Baron Ledwig, do you deny that you beat your maid, Macie Walls to the point of her death?"

"No, I do not. It was my right and duty to do so."

Arbuckle fumed at the man's arrogance and contempt for life, and saw his disgust mirrored in the faces of a number of nobles. Another low murmur swept through the room, but now, some of the whispers declaimed the baron's actions.

He turned to the accused, both commoners and noble. "Sentencing for your crimes will take place tomorrow morning in the Imperial Plaza for all to witness. Baron Ledwig, as the ranking imperial noble, I hereby revoke your title for behavior unbefitting a noble, but I won't punish your family for your reprehensible conduct. Baroness Ledwig, you are now matriarch of your house. Teach your heirs to behave better than your husband has."

The woman glared at him defiantly, but said not a word.

Arbuckle stood, and the crowd came to their feet. "These proceedings are finished. Commander Ithross, you will post announcements for tomorrow's sentencing so that all may bear witness."

"Yes, milord!"

Arbuckle departed through the side entrance and headed back to his chambers in the company of his entourage.

"Your pardon, milord, but do you think passing sentence in the plaza is a wise thing to do? It's apt to draw a large crowd." Tennison's brow wrinkled with worry.

"Wise?" Arbuckle considered the question. "I don't know if it's wise, but it's necessary. They've got to see that I'm serious about equal justice for all."

"The common folk?"

"Everyone." Arbuckle quirked a weak smile. "Besides, after I burnt all the gallows and pillories in the square, I'd probably face more danger at a cocktail party of nobles than I would walking the streets of the Dreggars Quarter."

"If I don't see another gods-be-damned saddle for the rest of my life, it'll be too soon." Paxal dismounted and rubbed his backside, then pulled the saddlebags off his horse.

"I'm with you on that one, Pax." Dee hefted his considerably heaver bags and followed Paxal out of the inn stable, his knees wobbling with every stride. "I'm for a hot meal and a warm bed."

"Add a cool pint, and you've got a winner, my boy."

Their last day had been their longest. Though they'd planned to arrive tomorrow, the good roads and lack of traffic had urged them on, and they'd ridden well into the night to reach Tsing. They were both shaking with fatigue, but they could start their search for Mya first thing in the morning.

A lamppost illuminated the door and bawdily illustrated sign of the *Prickly Pair*. The painting of a porcupine in congress with a cactus brought a smile to Dee's lips. He wondered if Mya would still be here.

Not likely.

If the guild had accepted her as Grandmaster, her new quarters would be far more luxurious. If they hadn't, she would have moved to evade Hoseph.

Unless he found her first. Dee shook off the disturbing notion, refusing to believe that their long trip had been for naught. In his musing, he almost ran into Paxal, who had stopped and was scrutinizing the posterboard mounted beside the inn's front door.

"Well, there's somethin' you don't see every day." Paxal rubbed his stubbly jaw and shook his head.

"What?" Dee stopped beside him, squinting at the collage of notices. "Something about Mya?"

"No." Paxal tapped a broadsheet embossed with the imperial crest of Tsing and pinned front and center on the board. "Least ways, I hope not. Looks like the crown prince is sentencing some noble for killing a commoner. It's gonna be public, too; in the Imperial Plaza tomorrow morning."

"Is that unusual? Duke Mir has publically sentenced criminals."

"It ain't the public sentencing that's unusual." Paxal pulled open the inn's door and they staggered inside. "Under the last emperor, nobles could do as they pleased to commoners, and nobody gave a flyin' bat fart. That's why I left. Maybe this crown prince's got new ideas."

"Can I help you gentlemen?" The man seated behind the small counter in the entrance hall tried to hide a yawn as he stood to greet them. "You look road weary. Do you need a room?"

"And a hot meal?" Dee asked hopefully.

"I'm afraid all we got is soup and bread, but you're welcome to it. And the bar's still open."

"Bless you, good man!" Pax looked relieved. "It'll be like mana from heaven."

"We'll probably be staying a few days." Dee fished a gold crown from his purse and dropped it on the counter, then jerked his thumb toward the front door. "What's that news we saw about the crown prince sentencing a noble tomorrow?"

"Oh, our new prince is a right firebrand, he is!" The man grinned and snatched up the coin, peering at the mint. Pocketing it, he waved them into the inn's common room. "Things are changin' for the better around here. He actually arrested some baron for whippin' one of his maids to death, and he's already held a trial! All anyone can talk about is what kind of sentence the prince might pass."

Dee looked around as the innkeeper led them to a table. He'd seen too many inn common rooms lately, and there was nothing special about this one. All the tables were empty, since it was well past meal time, but several late-night patrons still sat at the bar. No Mya. Gratefully depositing his heavy bags beside a chair, he sat. "You've roused my interest. Maybe we'll attend the sentencing."

"Not wise, my friend. Not unless you like a good fight and a night in the lockup."

Paxal raised his brows. "The lockup?"

"The last time Crown Prince Arbuckle had a gatherin' in the Imperial Plaza, more'n a few folks ended up behind bars for startin' fires. No, I'd advise you to stay well away. We'll hear soon enough what happened." The innkeeper waved toward their bags. "Do you mind takin' your own bags up? My boy's already gone to bed."

"We don't mind." Dee patted his gold-laden saddlebags. Innkeepers had been trying to unburden him of its weight all week, and it was a relief to not have to make yet another excuse to keep it beside him. "For now, I'll bless your name to all the Gods of Light if you pour us a pint of ale and bring us a meal. And if you've got a minute, would you mind filling us in on what's going on around the city?"

"Of course! I'll be right back."

Dee nodded at the man as he hurried away. "He seems helpful."

"Not much to do on the night shift," Pax explained. "Probably glad for the distraction. So, what's our first step to finding Mya?"

Dee nodded toward the inn's front door. "That posterboard gave me an idea. Mya's a Hunter; she deals in information. She'll be keeping an eye on the news."

"You want to post a flier to find her?"

"Yes, but we've got to word it so nobody else knows who we're looking for."

Mya reveled in the cool night air and the shadows that rendered her all but invisible. It felt good to be out at night for a change, dressed in her comfortable dark trousers, shirt, and soft boots instead of a bulky and restricting dress, not to mention the heeled shoes. Here in the dark—her daggers at the ready, her continued existence dependent on her skills as a Hunter—life made more sense. Alone, stalking the deep shadows, she felt right, alive, a monster in her natural habitat.

Sure as hell beats staring at the ceiling trying to sleep!

Ducking around a corner, she paused to listen as another squad of constables clanked past. They seemed intent on making noise, as if by sheer bluster they would keep the peace. *Good luck with that.* Not since the news of the blademasters' mass suicide had the city been so charged with nervous energy. Rumors of the sentencing had spread like wildfire. Crown Prince Arbuckle was being true to his word. Baron Ledwig had gone too far, and there would be hell to pay.

Unless someone makes the prince pay it first.

Mya wondered again if she had miscalculated by planning to warn the prince instead of concentrating on killing Hoseph. Now Arbuckle was coming out in public, and she knew that the Assassins Guild wouldn't pass up the chance to try to kill him. Lady T might promise to aid Mya, but until Hoseph was dead, she had to play along with the conspiracy.

As she made her way down an alley, Mya considered what she knew of the Imperial Plaza. It seemed the perfect setup: wide-open with thousands of people to serve as distractions for the guards, and an unwitting target. At least she assumed the crown prince was unwitting, for only a fool would show his face in the public if he knew someone wanted him dead. Ignorant or foolish, his public appearance had forced Mya's hand.

So she was out tonight doing what she was trained to do, surveying the scene, picking out the best vantage, the most likely approaches and lines of fire, evaluating obstacles, planning the hit. But this time she would be trying to *save* a life, pitting her skills against Lady T's Hunters, hoping to outguess the Tsing assassins.

Mya stopped short and pressed herself against the wall as another patrol stomped by. *They're as thick as flies on a horse's ass tonight.* But she knew they had been thicker during the day. Constables, soldiers, and imperial guards had surrounded the plaza until sunset, a deterrent to onlookers who attempted spy on the activity in the plaza. They had erected tall canvas barriers around the north end of the square, even cleared out the adjacent buildings for a time, angering those who labored in the factories and shops there. Wagons hauled lumber and other building materials in, and sounds of construction could be heard until the workers dispersed with the setting sun.

Noise alerted Mya to two patrols converging on her position. If she didn't want to be seen, she'd be forced to backtrack. The delay frustrated her. She had to get to the plaza, see the layout, anticipate where an assassin might be placed, and plan her countermeasures. *But how, with so many constables tromping the streets?* She looked left and right as the clattering caps neared.

Think like an assassin, Mya. Think like… No, think like Lad! She looked up.

Window, drainpipe, window, cornice, eaves and up. Her eye picked out the path like she was casing it for Lad. She wondered if she could do it without falling. The guards closed, leaving her no choice. She swarmed up the vertical path, making it to the top with surprising ease. Hunkering on the rooftop, she peered down at the passing constables and smiled.

Easy as pie…

Mya glanced around. She was still one street over from the plaza, and the roofs of the buildings here were flat or pitched at low angles. She had a better vantage from up here, but the path to the plaza presented some challenges. *I can do this.*

Mya rose from her crouch and dashed across the roof toward gaping space of the street, gauging the distance to the next building. Banishing the thought of what would happen if she missed, she leapt. Her landing wasn't as graceful as Lad's would have been, but she had made it safely. A couple of the roof tiles slipped askew under her feet, but none fell to give away her position. She edged up to the crest of the low-pitched roof and lay flat to look out over the Imperial Plaza.

The public space was enormous, two city blocks long and one wide. Since the Night of Flame, the plaza had been utterly bare, scoured clean of soot, ash, and the persistent bloodstains of four decades of brutality. It was no longer empty.

What in the Nine Hells?

A broad platform had been constructed at the north end of the plaza, about six feet high with stairs at the back and both sides. That was to be expected, but in the center of the platform stood a canvas-shrouded rectangle the height of three men. It wasn't big enough to be a gallows, and was too big to be a pillory.

Never mind that. She directed her attention to the surrounding buildings. *Where would I place assassins?*

Mya recalled all the troops accompanying the crown prince the last time he came here. Without his blademasters, the number of regular guards would be increased. They would surround the entire platform and seal off the streets on that end. There was no way anyone—even Lad—could get through such a cordon on foot. The attack would come from a distance, but from where?

Too close and you risk getting spotted. Too far and you risk missing. Too low, you're obstructed. Too high reduces your angle to the target.

Three buildings closest to the platform were the most suitable. She ruled out the roofs as being too exposed. A yarn factory and two storefronts with apartments above lined the street directly north of the platform. To the east stood a warehouse with high, vented windows, and to the west a chandlery, also windowed. A sniper could get a decent shot from any of the third- or fourth-floor windows. That narrowed the field somewhat, but still left plenty of possibilities.

I can't watch them all alone, but I don't have to. Mya would station her urchins as high as she could for the best view. She would tell them what to look for, and they could use their whistles to alert her of anything they spotted. She'd been practicing their whistling system for days, memorizing what each call meant, though she still needed a lot of work to master the calls herself.

So, where do I watch from?

Mya needed to hear their whistles, see everything, and still be able to act to save the prince's life, or at least shout a warning if she couldn't reach the assassin.

Where will a sniper be? She rose to her elbows and peered through the darkness, trying to think from the assassin's point of view. *Where would I—*

Something moved; a figure at the crest of the chandlery roof backlit for an instant by the glow of Hightown. Mya froze and held her breath. There were constables aplenty on the streets below, but would they set a rooftop watch? Squinting, she caught a glimpse of black on black as someone edged forward to peer down at the square.

Not a constable, she realized, *but an assassin.*

Lady T had sent one of her Hunters out to do exactly what Mya was doing.

Mya watched for a short while as the figure scanned the plaza, the buildings, and the surrounding rooftops with a spyglass. She held perfectly still, considering her options. Killing the assassin might actually thwart the assassination attempt by depriving Lady T of information. Moreover, if done correctly, the dead body might also tip off the constabulary that someone was planning to knock off the prince.

Before Mya made a decision, the sweep of the assassin's spyglass halted abruptly, the lens aimed right at her.

Was she backlit? What was behind her? The lights of Midtown perhaps? She stared at the gleaming lens, willing it to move, to sweep past her, but it didn't. She swallowed, and the lens suddenly shifted. The figure moved away fast in a crouch, over the crest of the roof. Gone... Somehow, she wasn't sure how, the assassin had spotted her.

Damn... Whoever it had been was good. Even if she'd been silhouetted against the light, picking out the shape of a human head on a skyline in the dark was something she'd only expect from someone with Lad's skills.

"Magic maybe?" It didn't matter. She'd surely been spotted.

Still, they had no way of knowing it was her, only that someone had seen them casing the plaza. That might make them more careful in their choices, but it wouldn't prevent the assassination attempt. She'd just have to make sure that she covered all the possibilities.

Mya headed for home. She'd seen everything she needed to see. Tonight she'd outline the most likely positions for a sniper targeting the prince on the platform, and tomorrow morning she'd instruct her urchins what to look for and place them in the nearby buildings.

Pitting me and my army of urchins against the Tsing Assassins Guild... It would have been laughable if it wasn't exactly what she was going to do.

CHAPTER XV

Arbuckle grunted as the weight of the chainmail shirt fell onto his shoulders. It felt wrong to be armoring himself to face his people, but Ithross had insisted. Thinking of the poisoned blackbrew, Arbuckle hadn't argued.

Not wise, but necessary... Maybe that should be my new mantra.

He held up his arms so Baris could slip the surcoat—elegant in imperial blue and gold—over his head and place the thin platinum circlet on his brow. Finally ready, he stepped into his sitting room, took his place with Tennison and Verul amongst the ring of imperial guards and knights. The walk to the courtyard was silent, as if the gravity of the situation stilled everyone's tongues. The future and wellbeing of the empire rode on this day. Everything depended on how his judgments were received by noble and commoner alike.

Am I doing the right thing?

Arbuckle squinted as he passed through the palace doors into the sunlit courtyard, paused until his eyes adjusted, and blinked at the size of the procession. Knights and squires on horseback, a phalanx of cavalry, and ranks of imperial guards in blue and gold waited to escort the three carriages. Two of the carriages were plain transport for the prisoners. The third shone like a gem-studded crown. The body of the carriage was blue, elaborately embellished with gold leaf, and the wheels were studded with glittering blue sapphires. A team of six perfectly matched white horses pranced and pawed at the cobbles, their gilded headdresses and harnesses flashing in the sun.

"Oh, Tennison, no. That's my *father's* carriage."

"No, Milord Prince, it's the *emperor's* carriage." He regarded the prince solemnly. "You may not yet have the title, but you will. Today you'll show yourself to be a true leader of the people—*all* the people."

With a sigh of contrition, Arbuckle mounted the carriage and settled back into the plush seat. He understood Tennison's point, but wanted to protest. *What kind of message does it send that I ride in a carriage more valuable than the yearly wages of a thousand commoners?*

Mya felt a curious sense of familiarity as the crown prince's entourage pulled into the Imperial Plaza. Hopefully this event wouldn't end as badly as the last. Of course, this had the potential to end much worse. If she didn't manage to stop Lady T's assassin, the ensuing conflagration would make the Night of Flame look like a campfire.

Mya blew an errant strand of hair out of her eyes and turned her gaze upward. She had stationed her spies atop the three northernmost buildings. When she asked the urchins if they could manage to get to the rooftops, they'd laughed.

"Ain't nowhere we can't go," Digger had told her proudly. "'Cept maybe the palace."

She picked them out one by one amid the crowds lining the buildings' rooftops. *Good; all in position.*

Mya stood equidistant between the eastern and western buildings, fairly close to the platform. She'd dressed herself as a young man once again. The disguise was both for safety—the Assassins Guild knew her as a woman—and utility—pants were easier to maneuver in than a dress. She had also slathered her borrowed jacket with manure, hoping the smell would give her a bit more room to work. No such luck. People were packed into the plaza like herring in a barrel.

Mya dug in her heels to hold her place as the crowd surged forward, and checked the most likely windows once again. She'd been surveying the best vantage points for an hour, scrutinizing movements, memorizing faces and attire. She'd seen no one so far whom she could tag as an assassin. That was the crux of the problem: what did an assassin look like?

Mya could generally pick out that certain something that identified someone as a professional killer, but it took years of practice. She considered the diversity just in the Twailin guild: the little old woman who could put a knitting needle in your eye before you blinked, the beefy thug who could tear your arms from their sockets bare handed, the dandy with the poisoned sword cane, the whore with needles in her garters... Assassins didn't generally look like assassins, but their actions often gave them away.

"Look for people doing things that don't look right," she'd told her urchins. "Look for someone out of place, not smiling, or smiling too much, someone with a broom or shovel in their hand who doesn't look like a maid or a workman, someone alone in a window when every other window has two or three people..."

She watched as the procession of cavalry, infantry, and carriages came to a halt behind the raised platform. The lancers positioned themselves on either side of the structure, their weapons gleaming in the sun as their horses snorted and fidgeted. A contingent of resplendently uniformed imperial guards mounted the platform and formed ranks right and left. Next came the four accused escorted by more guards. It wasn't hard to pick out the baron in his fine clothes.

Lastly, Crown Prince Arbuckle mounted the platform surrounded by a tight group of knights and more guards. Though his dress was regal, he walked stiffly. Mya wondered if he wore chainmail, and thought he might not be as foolish as she'd guessed, although, surrounded by enough steel to deter a dragon, personal armor seemed redundant.

The guards shifted, looking this way and that, but didn't survey their surroundings as systematically as blademasters would have done. Prince Arbuckle looked like he missed their constant presence.

Like I miss Lad's.

"He's like a god come down from the heavens!" a nearby woman cried out.

"Don't look like no god to me," another groused. "Just some rich bugger what thinks he's better than all the rest of us."

"No, he's not like that!"

Mya ignored the argument, watching her windows and listening to the bird calls that sweetened the air of the plaza. *That's Gimp,* she thought. *And that's Digger. Nails. Kit.* Mya interpreted their tweeting messages as "All clear." So far, so good.

219

The crowd's shouts and murmurs died away when a tall man in imperial livery banged an even taller staff on the platform. His voice carried impressively.

"Crown Prince Arbuckle, Heir to the Throne and the Empire of Tsing!"

Cheers rang out as the prince stepped forward. A pair of armored knights bearing broad shields stepped up beside him, with two more behind. It made for good show, but Mya doubted that they could react quickly enough to intercept a poisoned dart or arrow.

Where are you? She inspected the surrounding buildings again, checking the most-likely windows. Hundreds of onlookers leaned out all around the plaza. It seemed as if some people had turned the event into a party, everyone crowding to see, pushing and jostling for the best view.

"People of Tsing!" Arbuckle's voice carried almost as well as his herald's, booming over the crowd's sudden silence. "The last time I was here, I told you that justice would be served under my reign. Today, I will show you that I spoke the truth."

The few catcalls were quickly shushed.

"I bring you justice, but I tell you, justice must be impartial. Three of the convicted prisoners that I have brought before you today are commoners who took vengeance into their own hands. Vengeance is *not* justice! Only the law can bring justice, and therefore these three men must answer for their crimes."

The prince's words caught Mya's attention, and she glanced to the platform to see the three commoners brought forth, the chains on their wrists and ankles rattling. She listened for bird calls and watched the windows as the prince spoke.

"Raul Walls," intoned the prince. One of the men stepped forward, looking nervous. "You are convicted of arson, a crime that you admitted to of your own free will. I hereby sentence you to five years imprisonment."

The man's eyes widened with surprise, and a murmur swept through the crowd. Five years in prison for arson was lenient compared to the swift hanging that would have been his punishment only a month ago.

"Vance Walls." The next man stepped forward. "Like your

brother, you freely admitted to committing arson. I hereby sentence you to five years imprisonment."

The prince paused as more murmurs swept through the crowd. Mya checked the windows again and noticed a woman with a broom in her hand she hadn't seen before, but then two other maids also joined the crowded space. She heard a whistle of all clear.

"Torance Walls." The third man stepped up. "You are convicted of arson, assault of a constable, and resisting lawful arrest. Like your brothers, you admitted freely to your crimes. Therefore, I hereby sentence you to seven years imprisonment."

Though the man's jaw was set in a hard line, his eyes shone with unshed tears.

Watch the damn windows, Mya, not the spectacle! She swept her eyes around the plaza, but saw nothing untoward. Was she wrong? Had she scared the assassins off simply by scouting the scene last night?

"What about the noble?" someone shouted

"Yeah! What about his sentence?" another cried. A roar went up from the crowd, and Ledwig's upper lip curled with derision.

Prince Arbuckle raised his hands high, and silence fell. "Uldric Ledwig."

Mya's brows arched. *They stripped him of his title?* That would be punishment enough for some of the nobles.

Unlike his fellow prisoners, the former baron refused to step up, and had to be thrust forward by his guards.

Prince Arbuckle's expression remained impassive, but she could hear the distaste in his voice as he called out, "You are convicted of the murder of Macie Walls, a maid in your household."

"Justice!" someone cried, and the demand rang from the crowd until it echoed off the walls of the surrounding buildings. Only when Crown Prince Arbuckle raised his hands again did the cries subside.

Mya listened and watched the windows, but heard no whistles. She hoped her urchins were watching what she told them to watch.

"There *will* be justice," the prince assured them, his repressed rage clearly audible. "Uldric Ledwig, the title of Baron has been struck from your name, and your name will be struck from the Imperial Register of Nobles. Your family will wear black for the span of one year in shame for their tacit support of your actions. A blood price will be garnished from your fortune and provided to the family of Macie Walls, though no coin can ever replace a beloved daughter and sister." The prince paused. "And lastly, your head will be struck from your body, and you will be buried in an unmarked grave."

"Justice!" the crowd roared.

Well, I'll be damned. Mya thought that she just might like this new ruler, and she now understood why Hoseph and his conspiracy of nobles and magistrates were trying to get rid of him. Woe to the status quo when this prince was crowned emperor. *If he can stay alive that long…*

At the prince's nod, two imperial guards pulled on the ropes that secured the cover to the mysterious structure on the stage, and the canvas fell aside. The base of the frame looked like an unfinished set of stocks, a rack with only a single hole to hold someone's head, topped by a tall rectangular frame. At the peak of the frame hung a great steel blade, held in place by a latch hook. One tug on the attached cord would open the hook, and the blade would plummet.

Though Mya was no stranger to violent death, her stomach quivered at the sight of such a brutally efficient implement of execution.

"Know that if you deliberately take someone's life, you'll pay with your own," Prince Arbuckle said to the hushed crowd. "But when the ultimate justice is required, this new device will assure that punishment is swift and precise. No longer will anyone suffer a slow, torturous death on the gallows or whipping post." He turned to the doomed former baron. "Uldric Ledwig, may the Gods of Light have mercy on your soul."

The sneer on Ledwig's face dissolved into disbelief, then fear, and he began to struggle in earnest as his guard dragged him to the apparatus.

An owl hooted once…twice…thrice, and Mya dragged her gaze from the spectacle on the platform to the rooftops. The call meant they'd spotted something. Other calls rang out in as if all the birds in the city had converged on the plaza.

What? Where? Mya caught sight of Nestor atop the westernmost building, hooting away at the top of his lungs. To the east, Digger did the same. The urchins chirped and whistled, and they all pointed at the building to the north, the building directly behind the platform...and the prince.

Mya's heart leapt as she scanned the windows. *There!* On the fourth floor, in the fifth window from the right, an old man in a red shirt had sat alone for an hour. He was gone. Now there stood a tall man in plain workman's clothing. There was nothing remarkable about him except that he wasn't leaning out the window. He was standing back about three feet. Slowly, he raised a long, narrow rod.

Gods damn it all to the Nine Hells! He was going to shoot while everyone's attention was on the execution.

Mya might have reached an assassin in the eastern or western buildings before they could carry out their lethal task, but the northern buildings were blocked by a solid wall of soldiers, guards and constables. She had only one hope to prevent the attack.

"Assassin!" she screamed, pointing at the window. A few people nearby stared at her curiously, but her warning was drowned out by the roar of the crowd as Ledwig was locked into the contraption.

Damn! She looked back to the assassin, and movement caught her eye. Just above the assassin's window, Knock peered down from the rooftop. Her oversized teeth prevented the girl from whistling as the other urchins did, but she understood the twittering language. She waved to her friends, turned, and pushed her way through the rooftop crowd and out of Mya's sight.

Oh, no! Mya's intention had been to use the urchins as spies, never for them to actually confront anyone. As good as Knock was with her club, she was no match for a professional assassin.

She cried out, "Assassin! In the window! Look for the gods' sake!" but no guard looked. They scanned the crowd, but not the windows behind the stage.

The prince stood with one hand uplifted. The crowd pressed in around Mya, cheering madly, bloodlust in their cries. Shoving aside a portly man to her right, she raised one arm to wave wildly.

"Assassin! In the window!"

One of the imperial guards on the platform looked at Mya and turned where she frantically pointed.

Prince Arbuckle slashed down with his hand, signaling the knight to pull on the restraining cord. The gleaming blade fell.

In the window, the assassin heaved a deep breath and put the rod to his lips...and blew. Mya watched the dart fly, incapable of changing its trajectory.

Movement on the stage. Mya watched the guard she had alerted throw himself at the prince. The dart struck him in the neck. Crown Prince Arbuckle stumbled, but retained his feet, turning to stare at the guard who fell writhing to the platform.

Four armored knights tackled the crown prince.

Mya glanced up and saw the assassin grimace at his fouled shot and load another dart. He drew a deep breath and took aim, but then jerked around toward something in the apartment behind him.

Oh, no... Knock! Mya's heart leapt into her throat.

Suddenly, the assassin hurtled backward out the window, arms windmilling. The platform blocked Mya's view, but she heard something that sounded like a melon smashing on the cobblestones. When she looked back up to the window, there was no one there.

Knock?

The crowd's collective gasp drew Mya's gaze back to the platform. She didn't know if the crowd's reaction had been due to the falling assassin, or the Ledwig's head being struck from his shoulders. She could see little except the crowd of knights and guards hustling the prince down the stairs and into the waiting carriage. At least he was alive.

With a sigh of relief mixed with trepidation, Mya turned and started weaving her way through the crowd. Her plan hadn't worked out the way she'd expected, but it had worked nonetheless. Now she had to find out if all her urchins were still alive.

Arbuckle grunted as the knights slammed into him, dragging him down behind a ring of tall shields. He couldn't see, but he heard shrieks and cries shrilling from the crowd. He'd seen the guard fall after knocking him aside, but didn't understand what had happened. He'd been looking at Ledwig when the blade fell.

Close by, Ithross shouted orders. "To the carriage! Shields up! Guard the prince!"

"What's going on?" Arbuckle struggled to keep his feet as the knights hauled him bodily from the platform, down the steps, and toward his waiting carriage. "What happened?"

"An assassin, milord," replied one of the knights grimly. "Rebley's down. I think he saved your life."

"Gods of Light." Arbuckle's knees felt weak as they thrust him up into the carriage.

Verul came in next, propelled by Captain Ithross. The scribe landed on the floor and stayed there, scratching madly in his ledger. Two imperial guards trundled in next, planting themselves on either side of Arbuckle. A knight was the last to enter, sitting on the opposite seat and slamming shut the door. With a crack of the whip and the clash of hooves on cobbles, the carriage surged into motion.

As they passed the platform, Arbuckle peered out the carriage window at Ludwig's headless corpse lying behind the guillotine. A little farther on, he saw a man lying on the street, his head misshapen and drenched with blood. One of the guards grabbed Arbuckle's shoulder and thrust him gently back against the seat while the other drew the curtain.

"Best not show yourself, milord. There might be another assassin."

Arbuckle swallowed hard. "Gods..." He blinked and swallowed again, bile burning the back of his throat. "Do they hate me so?"

"Not the commoners, milord." Verul looked up from his ledger. "You just won the heart of every commoner in Tsing. They'll love you as they've not loved an emperor in generations."

"They'll love me for killing a man." Arbuckle closed his eyes, but all he could see was Ledwig's head as it toppled into the waiting basket. Ledwig might have been a murderous fool, but that didn't change the fact that he had just died at Arbuckle's command.

"They'll love you for bringing them justice, milord. It was long overdue."

"I don't understand how anyone gets used to seeing someone die, even if they deserved it." He swallowed hard. "I feel like I'm going to be sick."

"Comes with practice, milord." It was the knight who spoke, low and sad. "You get used to seeing death. Guilty, innocent, rich, poor...it doesn't matter. Death is death."

Arbuckle hoped he would never become inured to seeing such

things. If he did, he might think there was nothing wrong with lopping off a man's head. He mused as they rode in silence back to the palace. This was the second attempt on his life, and his second stroke of luck. He tried to ignore the old adage that kept whispering in his head.

Third time's the charm.

CHAPTER XVI

Mya checked to make sure she hadn't picked up a shadow on her way back to the Dreggars Quarter. Satisfied, she ducked into the stable, muttering a silent prayer to no god in particular that she would find all her urchins safe and sound. She's seen none of them during her way back across the river, but the streets were pretty crowded. After recovering her stashed clothes and changing back into a drab dress, she'd stopped at several shops to pick up something special to celebrate their success.

If they're all alive.

Digger met her just inside, his face split in a grimy grin. "We did good, didn't we?" His eyes gleamed as he took the parcels and handed them over to the others. "You brought us a right *feast!*"

Feast was a relative term: a bottle of cheap wine, a loaf of bread, a dried sausage, and a wedge of sharp cheese. Mya scanned the faces as they started dividing up the food. They were all there, all alive, and all grinning as if they'd just saved the entire empire of Tsing. Who could know? Maybe they had.

With the weight of concern lifting from her stomach, she fixed them with a stern look. "Well, you didn't exactly follow the *plan...*"

The fallen smiles and wide, worried eyes twisted Mya's gut. A flash of memory surfaced: a sharp rebuke, not pretty enough, not fast enough, not smart enough... Her urchins didn't deserve that from her.

"...but you *did* save Prince Arbuckle's life, so yes, you did well. In fact, you probably saved the whole city. You know better than anyone what would have happened if the prince died."

Their renewed grins seems to light up the entire stable, and they resumed divvying up the food. Nails drew the cork from the bottle

227

with his teeth, and they laughed at the rich pop.

"That's why we saved him, ain't it?" Nestor happily stuffed bread and cheese into his mouth and spoke as he chewed. "Don't give a fart for them rich types, but he's a good'n, ain't he?"

"I hope so." Mya honestly didn't know much about the prince, aside from seeing him during his two appearances in the plaza.

"He lopped off that baron's head right enough!" Nails took a swig from the bottle and passed it to eager hands. "Kept his promise to bring justice."

"That he did." Mya cared less about the prince's promises for justice than she did about making Assassins Guild into the organization she wanted it to be. To do that, she needed the city not burned down. And to keep it from burning, she needed the prince alive. That, of course, begged the question of how her urchins had managed to accomplish that feat.

"How did you spot the assassin?" Eyes flicked up to her as they continued to gorge themselves. "And for that matter, how did you tell Knock what to do? I didn't quite follow your whistles."

Digger shrugged. "We did what you told us. We looked for people who weren't doin' what they should be doin'. That old man in the window was watchin', then he just disappeared, like he fell off his chair or somethin'. Then another man was there, but he didn't look right. He wasn't smilin', stood back from the window instead of leanin' out like everyone else, and he had that stick in his hand."

Gimp took up the tale. "So Digger whistled at us, an' we whistled to each other. Knock was right near the bloke, so she went after him."

"Knock! Knock!" The half-breed girl leapt up, hunched her shoulder, and pantomimed giving a great shove. The twisted smile on her face no longer seemed gruesome to Mya. She supposed she had become accustomed to it.

"You could have gotten hurt," Mya argued. "He was bigger than you."

Digger grinned and shrugged. "We're used to everyone bein' bigger than us."

Mya had to admit that he had a point. Survival on the streets meant constant danger. Growing up homeless, poor, and starving, the urchins had probably seen more evil than most people did their entire lives. Still, that didn't mean she wanted to put them in even more danger. That they would throw themselves at assassins, risking their lives in return for a few pitiful meals, made her feel cold for recruiting them in the first place.

You've got a good heart... She wondered if Lad's claim had been just wishful thinking.

"Here." Tiny held a slice of sausage and hunk of bread out to her, a smile on his grimy face. "You have some, too."

Startled, Mya stared at him, at all the children. They had so little—only what she brought them—yet they were willing to share with her. They might not have homes in the proper sense, but they all cared for one another. They were a family, not of blood, but of necessity, and they considered her a part of that family.

"No." Mya cleared her throat and stood. "No, the feast is yours for a job well done. Good job today, all of you. Now, eat hearty and get some rest. I'll see whoever's on night watch at the back door of the *Dulcimer* after sunset."

"Yes, Miss Mya," they chimed, grinning and munching happily.

Mya stalked the Dreggars Quarter, intending to get a feel for how the commoners were responding to Ledwig's execution, but she couldn't get the children off her mind. *Don't get too attached. Caring for someone will only get you hurt.* That had been true her entire life: her mother...the guild...Lad... Why should now be any different? Gradually, she calmed her thoughts and put her mind to her task. *You have a job to do, Mya. Stop being maudlin and do it!*

The Dreggars Quarter buzzed like a kicked bee hive. Rumors of Ledwig's execution had spread like wildfire, and the mood varied from disbelief to awe to outright revelry. Even those skeptical of Arbuckle's promises of justice and rights for commoners couldn't deny that he'd kept his word. Many couldn't believe a noble had actually been executed for murdering a commoner, having never seen the like. Those old enough to remember the time before the reign of Tynean Tsing II had known justice once, when commoners were treated like people, not livestock. The populace had gotten a true taste of justice, and weren't about to revert to the way things were.

Before Mya knew it, the afternoon had passed to evening. Dusk washed the sky with color, incongruously beautiful above the shabby neighborhoods. She arrived back at the *Tin Dulcimer* as evening deepened to night. As usual, she stopped at the door to survey the posterboard for news of the day. The announcement of the sentencing was gone, probably taken as a souvenir. It had been replaced by the announcement of Ledwig's execution. She scanned the other news, and was about to go in when her eyes settled on a new flier, a simple personal notice with a most curious headline.

Golden Cockerel Lost

Seeking experienced Hunter to recover this valuable creature. Must be familiar with Golden Cockerels.

See Paxal at the Prickly Pair Inn

"Paxal?" Mya's heart hammered.

It couldn't be a coincidence. *But it could be a trap.* Who in Tsing could possibly know of her affiliation with the *Golden Cockerel* and Paxal? *Hoseph?* Her blood chilled. The priest could have wafted off to Twailin, discovered where she lived, and learned of her relationship with the old innkeeper. Her Hunters would never talk to a stranger, but the whole neighborhood knew her, and they knew she cared for Pax. *If he's harmed Pax, I'll…*

You'll what? Kill him? That task had already proven more difficult than she'd thought.

"Think, Mya…" Biting bit her lip, she stepped into the *Tin Dulcimer*. Something about this wasn't right, and she quickly realized what it was. *The* Prickly Pair… Of all the inns in Tsing, what was the chance that someone would set up a trap *there*? The only person who knew she'd stayed there was Lad, and he was still on the road somewhere…wasn't he?

Mya considered going to the *Prickly Pair* immediately, but restrained her curiosity. Going off half-cocked was a good way to get killed. She'd think about it tonight and deal with it in the morning when she was well rested. Besides, she didn't have to do this alone. She had her little spies, and today had given her an entirely new appreciation of their capabilities. If this was a trap, her urchins would be able to smoke it out.

Arbuckle ran his fingers over the device that had nearly ended his life. The long tube was disguised as a walking stick, hollow and fitted with a cap on the bottom and a concealed mouthpiece at the top. Three slim darts lay beside it. The tips of two were smudged with green, the third with dried blood.

Rebley's blood.

The brave imperial guard had given his life for his prince. Ithross insisted that the man was only doing his duty and would have been proud of his sacrifice. That didn't make him any less dead. Arbuckle sighed at the cost of his continued beating heart.

"The assassin also had these." Ithross placed two daggers on the table then held up a garrote. "*This* he used to murder the man who lived in the apartment."

Yet another death on my conscience.

"Professional, milord, without a doubt." Chief Constable Dreyfus picked up one of the darts. "Poisoned, of course, and the toxin is—"

"Put that down, if you please, Chief Constable." Captain Ithross' knuckles whitened on his sword hilt, and Arbuckle's guards stepped between Dreyfus and the prince. "The prince's life is *my* responsibility, and I'm feeling a little twitchy right now. None but imperial guards and knights may possess weapons in his presence."

Dreyfus reddened and clenched his jaw, but put down the dart. "As I was *saying*, the toxin is deadly in even a tiny dose, and the tips of the darts are hollow and thin enough to pierce chainmail. This fellow had resources. Nobody we've talked to recognized him. Of course, his face was…um…distorted from the fall."

"I don't think a professional assassin would be clumsy enough to fall," Ithross said. "He either jumped or was pushed."

"Jumped?"

Dreyfus shrugged. "A possibility, milord. He might've jumped to avoid capture and questioning."

Arbuckle grimaced as he remembered the blood from the man's shattered skull staining the cobbles. Then there was his wine steward, dead by his own hand. What kind of loyalty or fear could provoke suicide? "If someone did push him, maybe they'll come forward. Should we offer a reward? Fifty gold crowns might prompt someone to—"

Dreyfus' harsh bark of laughter grated on the prince's nerves. "Pardon, milord, but if you offer a reward, you'll have every dung-kicking roustabout in the city on the palace stoop swearing they saved your life. They'll lie, cheat, and steal for a single silver crown, much less fifty *gold*. We got one vague description of a short, ugly fellow running out of the building after the incident. Maybe a dwarf. We're still questioning people, but most were watching the...um...the execution." Dreyfus swallowed, looking decidedly uncomfortable.

"Keep asking questions, Chief Constable. If someone did save my life today, I'd like to thank them." Arbuckle gestured to the door. "You're dismissed."

"Thank you, milord." Dreyfus bowed and left the room, obviously relieved to vacate the royal presence.

Arbuckle turned to Ithross. "Captain, what's your opinion of Chief Constable Dreyfus?"

The captain's eyes widened. "My opinion, milord?"

"Do you think he'll pursue this investigation to the fullest extent of his capabilities? I must admit, he doesn't impress me. His opinion of commoners is barbaric."

"He is on the crude side, milord, but he does his job."

"Don't you think that you and your own people might do a *better* job investigating this?"

"No, milord." He shook his head emphatically. "My investigation of the first assassination attempt was logical. My people know the palace intimately and are familiar with the staff. But Dreyfus and his constables know the city high and low: the streets and alleys, who makes trouble, who's an informer. They're experienced canvassing the neighborhoods. The skills of an imperial guard are not those of a city constable."

Arbuckle rubbed his eyes. It hadn't been a physically strenuous day, but his nerves were stretched tighter than a harp's strings. He felt as if someone plucked a note, he'd snap. "I don't mean to disparage Dreyfus, Captain, but he and I are just...very dissimilar. I have few people I can trust implicitly, Captain Ithross. I'm sure you understand that."

"I understand perfectly, milord."

"Good. Now, back to this would-be assassination. Tennison and I drew up a list of those who would benefit most from my death or have been most displeased with my leadership. It's reads like the Imperial Register. What do you think about arranging private interviews with each of the senior nobles and magistrates with Archmage Duveau present to verify the truth of their statements?"

"I think we can do that, milord. Who would you like to see first?"

"Respectfully, milord, I would like to suggest you rethink that strategy." Tennison stepped forward, looking distraught. "It would be dangerous in the extreme."

Arbuckle laughed shortly. "More dangerous than the assassins already trying to kill me?"

"Perhaps not physically, but politically, to both you and the empire. An emperor cannot see to every detail of his empire. You must rely on your nobles to enforce your laws and carry out your will. If they so choose, they can stonewall you and undermine your authority at every turn. To be successful, you must *engage* them, not estrange them with interrogations."

Arbuckle shook his head and crooked a wry smile. "Of course, you're right, Tennison. Fear and paranoia seem to be getting the better of me. I'm not thinking clearly."

The secretary nodded sympathetically. "You have every right to be worried, milord."

"Perhaps it would be wise for you to refrain from public appearances in the near future." Despite his polite tone, Ithross didn't look like he was making a suggestion. "The palace is safe, at least."

"And look like a coward?" Arbuckle clenched his jaw.

"Captain Ithross has a point, milord," said Tennison. "You have no public events scheduled, and it's well known that we're busy planning the coronation. No one expects you to be out and about the city."

Ithross nodded gratefully to the secretary. "Milord, you can still make appearances in the safety of the palace where we can control the situation. You have a dinner scheduled this very evening. I suggest you make an appearance and show everyone you're safe and unafraid. We can't disregard the fact that attempts *have* been made on your life, but we needn't keep you locked in your chambers."

Arbuckle nodded reluctantly. Right now, being locked in his chambers had a certain appeal. He waved at the weapons on the table. "Get these out of here." The last thing he needed was a reminder that someone wanted him dead.

"You missed again!" Hoseph paced Lady T's sitting room, livid at the lost opportunity. "You complain that we can't kill Arbuckle because we have no one in the palace, but when he shows himself in public in front of thousands of people, your assassin *still* failed. What kind of incompetents do you hire?"

Lady T sipped a glass of pale wine, her poise intact. "Foirin was the best shot in the guild. He could shoot a sparrow out of the air. You know nothing of the difficulties of pulling off a proper assassination. A crowd of thousands makes a job *more* difficult, not easier."

"Then what went wrong?"

"His shot was true, but an imperial guard stepped in front of Arbuckle at the last moment, intercepting the dart."

"So, his failure was not in marksmanship, but in his inability to remain unobserved?"

Lady T shook her head. "He shouldn't have *been* observed. I had people posted throughout the plaza. The guard was looking forward until someone in the crowd yelled something that drew his attention to the windows. Apparently, the guard looked right at Foirin before diving into the path of the dart."

"So, why didn't he take a second shot?"

"He…" The guildmaster paused, pursing her lips. "…fell."

Hoseph stared at her, openmouthed. "He fell out of the *window?*"

"It seems more likely that he was pushed, but my people saw no one." Lady T threw back the rest of her wine in a very unladylike manner and slammed the glass down on the table.

"How could anyone have even known he was there? Who could

have pushed him?"

"I don't know." She turned away to stare out her window at the city.

"What about your people in the crowd? Couldn't they have acted?"

"That was not the plan."

"Well, the *plan* obviously didn't work. Couldn't they improvise?"

Lady T rounded on him, her carefully cultivated patience gone. "You weren't there! You're not an assassin! If you think we're so incompetent, then why not do it yourself? You could have popped in behind Arbuckle and killed him before any of his guards could react."

"And get myself skewered in the process?"

"Ahhh!" Lady T raised an eyebrow. "So, it finally comes out. You value your own *skin* over the guild. I thought as much."

"I don't see you putting yourself out there."

"It's not my *job* to put myself out there! I have people for that, and I lost one of my best today!"

They faced off, two predators regarding each other with narrowed eyes.

Hoseph breathed deep. *Blessed shadows of death, soothe me.* "Regardless of blame, the failure remains."

Lady T shook her head. "I don't think it was a *failure*, actually. I think we were thwarted."

"What?"

"Someone spotted Foirin and pushed him. There were only so many windows from which he could get a clear shot. I had a Hunter scout the plaza out last night, and he reported seeing someone else there on a rooftop. I think someone figured out where we would place our marksman and stationed their own assassin in the building."

"Who?"

The lady looked scathingly at Hoseph. "Who do we know who has a vested interest in thwarting the guild right now?"

There was only one possible answer. "Mya?" Hoseph was confused. "Why should she care about Arbuckle?"

The lady shrugged. "She wants control of the guild. Until she does, she may simply choose to oppose us at every turn. Since you've failed to kill her…"

Hoseph flushed at the implication. "I can't *find* her, and *you* refuse to have her followed. If she's actively opposing us in this, then she's gone far beyond being a mere nuisance."

"You know," Lady T arched an eyebrow, "though the assassination was foiled, we may yet salvage something from the day's events."

"What are you talking about? What can be *salvaged*? Arbuckle's alive and more wary than ever."

Lady T's eyes flashed. "Yes, but he executed a *noble* for doing what nobles have been doing for decades! Each and every one of them must be wondering whose head will roll into a basket next. If that's not incentive for our conspirators to be more cooperative, I don't know what is."

"Yes." Hoseph nodded as he considered the lady's words. "This might be exactly what we need to convince them to help us find someone who can be persuaded to kill Arbuckle."

"Precisely."

CHAPTER XVII

$\mathfrak{A}$ pretty little girl skipped out of the door of the *Prickly Pair* and up the street, a small brown bottle clutched in one hand. A blue ribbon fluttered from blond curls that flipped and bounced with every skip. Her dress, though it didn't fit perfectly, shone clean and bright in the sunlight., and her cheeks were rosy and freshly scrubbed. Passersby either ignored her or smiled at her jaunty manner.

Halfway up the next block, she turned into a dry goods store. The bell on the door jingled and the proprietor looked up, then away. He'd seen the girl only minutes before when her mother sent her up to the inn for a pint of sherry. At least, that was what he thought he'd seen.

"There you are, Kit. That was quick." Mya leaned down and took the pint bottle from the girl's hand. Lowering her voice to a whisper, she asked, "What did you see?"

"Saw that old codger just as you described him: not fat and not skinny, near bald with some white hair around the sides and stickin' out his ears, and a hook nose what looked like it had been broke a while back. Couldn't see if he'd a gap 'tween his front teeth 'cause he wasn't smilin'. He's sittin' at a table in the common room."

"Anyone else around?"

"A few." The girl rolled her eyes up as she thought. "A fat man at the desk where you come in. A old man and lady sittin' in the room on *that* side." She wiggled her right hand. "An' then in the common room along with your fella, two more men at a table and a lady behind the bar flirtin' with a dark-haired gent with a face ta make a maid swoon."

Mya grinned at Kit's description, so mature for a girl who

237

couldn't have been more than seven. "Perfect. Thank you, Kit."

So, it sounded like Paxal was really there, but that didn't mean it wasn't a trap. She had seen Hoseph transport a woman into Lady T's sitting room, so he could have brought Pax to Tsing to use as bait to lure her in for the kill. She might be paranoid, but paranoia had kept her alive through years of danger.

Paranoia and Lad. She snapped her mind back to focus as Kit tugged her skirt.

"Do I get to keep the dress?" Kit twirled and the bright material billowed. "I like it."

"That depends on if this works out, Kit. If this is a trap, and I'm dead in five minutes, then yes, you can keep the dress. Otherwise, no, because I'll have to sell it back so we can all eat. Do you understand?"

"Yes." Kit's lower lip stuck out and she fingered the ribbon at her waist, as if trying to equate how many meals she was wearing.

"Now, we need to go, okay?"

"Okay."

Out on the street, Mya held Kit's hand, hoping that nobody would expect an assassin to be dressed as a matron walking with a little girl. With her other hand, she fingered the dagger in her pocket. She had two more strapped to her thighs under her dress.

Over by the seawall, she spotted Digger, Twigs, and Nestor throwing stones into the river. Beyond the *Prickly Pair*, Nails and Gimp posed as beggars. The urchins had been keeping watch to make sure no obvious ambush awaited her. A couple of birds twittered from the alley behind the inn, Tiny and Knock signaling all clear.

She had given them all strict orders to stay out of the inn no matter what happened. Their job today was only to watch and whistle if they saw anything, hopefully giving Mya adequate warning.

Hopefully.

One last adjustment of her dress to make sure her weapons were in easy reach, and she let go of Kit's hand. The girl stepped aside on the inn's porch with her back to the wall, just like she'd been told to do. Mya nodded to her with a smile, then opened the door to the *Prickly Pair.*

As her eyes adjusted to the dim interior, she paused to listen.

The chatter of unfamiliar voices, the clatter of pans in the kitchen, and the clink of plates in the common room all seemed innocuous. She heard no whisper of steel leaving a sheath, no unconscious scuff of boot leather on the floor as someone shifted an uncomfortable position.

The innkeeper no longer sat at his desk, but that wasn't unusual. There was more to running an inn than waiting for new customers to walk through the door. Mya glanced into the small sitting room to her right. As Kit had told her, an older couple sat there, the woman knitting, the man shelling nuts. Neither looked spry enough to be assassins. Mya trod softly down the short hallway to her left toward the common room, halting just before the entrance. Leaning forward, she saw two unfamiliar men sitting at a table, then...

The breath caught in Mya's throat. Paxal sat at a table in the far corner, cradling a mug between his veined hands.

Focus, Mya! Look for the trap!

She leaned farther to scan the rest of the room. The barmaid polished the counter of the stool-lined bar, but there was no sign of her paramour. Mya slipped her hidden dagger from her pocket. Hiding the blade behind her arm, she stepped into the room. Neither the barmaid nor the two men at the table even glanced at her.

Softly, she called, "Paxal?"

His eyes flicked to her and widened, his mouth splitting into a gap-toothed grin. "My—gods! Thank the Seven Heavens you're all right!" He rose to his feet, but stopped when she raised a hand.

"Are you all right, Pax? Is everything okay?"

"Oh, right as rain now that you're here!" He stepped around the table and no one else in the room seemed concerned.

One more glance behind her confirmed that no assassins had leapt from hiding, and no murderous priest had materialized to take her life.

There was no trap.

Relief unlike anything Mya had ever felt flooded through her. "Gods of Light, Pax!" Before she knew what she was doing, she was crushing the innkeeper in her arms. Laughter bubbled up unbidden. "Gods, you're a sight for sore eyes!" She released him and put away her dagger, then wrinkled her brow. "What the hell are you *doing* here?"

"Well, we're here to help, of course! We never thought to find you so soon, but—"

"We?" Mya whirled at the scuff of footsteps behind her, damning herself for dropping her guard.

"Nice hat." The slim, dark-haired man couldn't have been more familiar.

"Dee!" She flung her arms around him and hugged him tight. Never had two faces been more welcome.

"I think she's glad ta see ya."

Paxal's quip snapped Mya back to her senses, and she released her grip. "Sorry, I…" She straightened her dress

Dee staggered and gasped breath. "Any gladder and she'd have pinched me in half!"

A heavy thud brought Mya around with her dagger back in her hand, but it was only a scullery maid kicking open the kitchen door, her hands filled with a tray of clean mugs. Beyond her, a portly cook calmly stirred a pot on the stove with no assassins in sight. Finally, Mya's sense of self-preservation reestablished control over her wayward emotions.

"Is this place really safe?"

"As far as I could determine." Dee lowered his voice. "I might not be much of an assassin, but I know what one looks like."

Mya grinned at Dee's self-deprecating comment. "Maybe not, but you're a *hell* of an assistant. Now, how—"

"Ahem. I think we have company."

Mya followed Paxal's gaze.

Peering around the door sill, a little girl with a blue ribbon in her hair bit her lip. "I know you said not to come in, but we wanted to know if you were dead."

Mya didn't know whether to admonish Kit or laugh out loud at the girl's ill-concealed agenda. "No, Kit, I'm not dead, so you can't keep the dress. I need the cash."

"I think we can help with that." Dee kicked a saddlebag under the table, wincing at the impact. "Sereth sent a parcel for you. I think you'll be pleased."

Pax nodded toward the little girl, looking dubious. "She's with *you*?"

"I think we've all got a lot of explaining to do," Mya said. "I know a safe place to talk, and there are some people I want you to meet."

Hoseph ignored the pain behind his eyes and his pervasive fatigue; he didn't have time for it. He considered the nobles and magistrates seated around Lady T's sitting room. Their fear hung in the air like cheap cologne. Leaving Magistrate Ferrera in the Sphere of Shadow had caught their attention, and the death Baron Ledwig had them on edge. He had them just where he wanted them, backed into a corner. None had protested this hastily called meeting and, though they sipped their wine and cast glances at one another, but not a single eye rose to meet his.

Fear... Demia's shadow, it's sweet...

"Do you see *now* that I was right about Prince Arbuckle?" He let the question hang, watching, waiting.

Duchess Ingstrom looked up, her mouth set in a line so hard her lips shone white. "The man is a menace!"

"Why didn't you kill him when you had the chance?" Duke Seoli downed his wine in a gulp. "You had the chance and you failed!"

Not enough fear in that one...

"We did not, in fact, fail, Milord Duke." Lady T pursed her lips in an unpleasant moue. "We were thwarted. The two are entirely different."

"What?" Seoli looked like he'd been slapped. "Who thwarted you?"

Hoseph could have smiled...but didn't. He and Lady T had worked out this little lie beforehand, and she brought it into play with consummate timing.

"We don't know exactly, but we believe Prince Arbuckle has agents working throughout the city." Lady T put precisely the right amount of dread into her claim. "One of his operatives killed our man before he could deal the lethal stroke."

"Gods and devils, he has people *watching* us?" Baron Grenger, an impressively wealthy lesser noble, downed his wine and smacked the glass down on the table too hard, snapping the stem. He glared at the piece left in his hand as if it had betrayed him. "I thought all this hush-hush was supposed to keep us safe!"

"We don't think his spies know of our association," Hoseph interjected. "We've been careful, but we don't know where they might be looking. We must act before they learn of us. We need to devise a method to end this threat to our way of life. How long do you think it will be before each of you is forced into that evil device Arbuckle has constructed to have your head lopped off?"

"He can't have us *all* executed. An emperor needs the noble class to support him." Duke Seoli looked more affronted than frightened.

"You still don't see it, do you?" Hoseph stared at the man, amazed that someone could ignore such clear threats to his own existence. "As *emperor*, Arbuckle can hand out titles like prizes at a country fair! He'll replace you all with his commoner friends, and the empire will change forever. An anarchist state ruled by peasants! He must be removed!"

"Our argument has never been against his removal, Master Hoseph, but that's supposed to be *your* task." Duchess Ingstrom glanced sidelong at him. Of all the conspirators, she was the most level-headed and astute. "We are *still* not spies."

"You're asking one of us to put our neck under that dreadful blade." Duke Seoli protested.

"Information is all we're ask for," Lady T said calmly. "Tell us what you know about what's happening in the palace. Ask people who may know something about Arbuckle's state of mind, his confidants, anything and everything. Seemingly inconsequential details could give us the edge we need. Duchess Ingstrom, Duke Seoli, you both attended the banquet last night for the arriving provincial dukes. What occurred there? Was anyone disgruntled enough to take matters into their own hands?"

Seoli barked a laugh. "Only every noble there! Ledwig's execution didn't sit well with any of them."

"Not *every* noble there," Duchess Ingstrom said with a frown. "There were some…"

"Oh, Arbuckle gave his rote speech about justice, and some of them seemed convinced that he's right. They're fools!"

The duchess pursed her lips. "Arbuckle dismissed the captain of the Imperial Guard some days ago, and in public, no less. I should think that he's disgruntled, and he might have access to the palace through some of his former associates."

"And there's Toffey," added Seoli. "Tynean Tsing's former valet was let go out of hand. My valet tells me that Toffey was crushed by the implication that he was less than loyal to the throne. The poor man's drinking himself to death."

Lady T's eyes narrowed with interest, but she maintained her casual tone. "This is good information, but perhaps you can think of someone who *still* has access to the palace and Arbuckle."

"Tennison?" suggested Seoli.

The duchess waved as if flicking a pesky fly. "Phah! I thought he might be chafing under Arbuckle's righteous arrogance, but when I tried to schedule tea to introduce Arbuckle to my daughter, he just smiled at me and said that the crown prince had more important things on his mind right now than *courting*. What's more important than ensuring that the emperor has an heir?"

Hoseph gritted his teeth against his pounding headache and the frustration of dealing with these self-centered idiots. Not one had the foresight to consider what was needed here: access, opportunity, and ability. They were all caught up in their own tiny worlds of court politics.

Graving raised a finger, as if not to be outdone by the nobles. "I heard that Archmage Duveau was unhappy with the crown prince."

Hoseph's eyebrows arched with interest. "Duveau?"

The chief magistrate nodded, his chins jiggling. "Apparently, Arbuckle's overworking the fellow dreadfully. Has him running around doing maintenance on the palace wards, interrogating menials, all kinds of nonsense. He won't let Duveau delegate anything to the junior members of the retinue, insisting that the archmage do all the work himself."

Archmage Duveau... In Hoseph's years of service to the emperor, he had met Duveau numerous times. The man was arrogant and self-centered, but also clever and talented. As archmage, he had unquestioningly provided the emperor with many a potion and magical favor that would be considered dubious, if not outright illegal, on the open market. In return, Tynean Tsing had allowed the man to do as he pleased, sparing no expense to acquire whatever magical tome or implement the archmage desired. What pleased Duveau most was magical research, dabbling in whichever realm of arcane study struck his fancy. *And I know just what will strike his fancy…*

"I must meet with Archmage Duveau." Hoseph's statement met with blank stares except for Lady T, who shot him a sharp glance. "I need someone to deliver a message to him."

"How did we go from giving information to delivering messages?" Seoli shook his head. "This risks not only the message bearer's life, but the rest of ours, as well. Duveau can compel the truth with a wave of his hand!"

Hoseph knew that all too well.

"There would be little danger of discovery." Lady T assumed the argument in her most persuasive manner. "The message would be worded carefully to be non-incriminating, and sealed before we give it to the message bearer. If Duveau refuses our offer, the deliverer of the message can truthfully disavow knowledge of its content and origin."

Graving frowned. "Legally, that might not—"

"This is *ridiculous*." Duchess Ingstrom put down her wine glass and surged up from her seat with an alacrity that belied her years. "I'll deliver your message to Archmage Duveau, and to all Nine Hells with the consequences! Now take me home, Master Hoseph. I have an appointment with a glass of *decent* wine and a book of poetry that I simply cannot forego." Scowling, she held out a hand to him.

"Very well, Duchess." He gently grasped her hand, smiling in satisfaction. "Thank you for—"

"Thank me by making gods-*damned* sure that Duveau takes your offer, Master Hoseph. Otherwise, our heads will all roll into the same basket as Baron Ludwig's."

Hoseph nodded politely as he invoked Demia's gift, already pondering the best way to convince Archmage Duveau to betray his master.

Dee peeled the last of the sweet pulp from an orange wedge and pitched the peel into the growing pile in the middle of the ring of grimy children. He considered the motley collection of street urchins sitting in the straw as they nibbled on their fruit, unexpected treats that they had accepted with a reverence more worthy of a priceless gem than a simple orange. He couldn't believe the tales Mya told of them, how she'd trained them to spy for her, and how they'd saved the life of the crown prince.

"*They* thwarted a professional assassin?" He hadn't thought it was possible.

"They did." She grinned and tousled one boy's hair. "Luck, more than skill, no doubt, but the prince's heart beats today due to their heroism."

The children all beamed with pride.

Only a little less surprising was the pride in Mya's voice when she spoke of their deeds. He'd expected her to be alive, maybe even in charge of the guild by now, but this... *Leave it to Mya to build an army out of nothing.*

Employing street children as spies was a stroke of genius. They could go anywhere without being noticed, and cost only food to fill their bellies. Mya had adapted the kids' skills to meet her needs, and they had responded amazingly. She would make a fine Grandmaster...if the Tsing guildmaster would only accept her.

Dee sighed and wiped his hands on his trousers. A month ago he was living in a mansion, assistant to the Twailin guildmaster. Now he stood in a filthy, abandoned stable surrounded by filthy, abandoned children. *Not exactly moving up in the world, are you?*

"Does seem like you're paddlin' upstream until you can off this priest fella." Paxal picked his teeth with a splinter he'd whittled into a toothpick. Next to him, a boy with a nail-studded stick—Nails, Mya had appropriately called him—picked up the knife Paxal had laid aside, and started whittling his own toothpick.

"Finding him's the problem." Mya flicked her finger and thumb, her nails ticking faintly.

Dee understood her problem, having seen Hoseph fade into mist in the blink of an eye, but thought she might be missing the real issue. "I hate to say it, but I don't think it's a matter of finding Hoseph as much as making sure that he doesn't find you."

"So far, I seem to have dodged him." She shrugged. "Lady T promised to set him up for me, but I'm not sure yet if she's on my side or his."

Dee paced as he thought, until his foot encountered a noisome lump in the straw. Cringing, he scraped the bottom of his boot on a board. "The first order of business, Miss Mya, should be to find a better base of operations. If you want any hope of earning the respect of the guild, you shouldn't be living in a third-class inn and conducting business in squalor."

"They don't know where I live or do business," Mya protested. "That would be an invitation for Hoseph to kill me."

"I understand that, but in time the guild will come to recognize you as Grandmaster." Dee hoped he sounded more confident than he felt about that eventuality. "By that time, you'll need to be well-established somewhere...well...better than this. Someplace north of the river would be best, a nicer neighborhood, and certainly more convenient for the work you're doing now."

"A better headquarters would help," Mya conceded. "And now we have the money. An inn, maybe. Someplace like the *Cockerel* back in Twailin."

"How we gonna do that?" Digger looked down at his grimy hands. "Street kids ain't welcome in fancy inns."

Dee was about to suggest that the urchins were fine where they were, when Mya nodded in acknowledgement. "Don't worry, Digger, we'll find someplace we can all stay together."

"Everyone can wash and get new clothes like me!" The pretty little Kit twirled to make her skirt spin out around her.

"Problem is, street kids stick out anywhere they're not on the street. You put us in some fancy house, and everyone's gonna know somethin's up. You pretty us all up like Kit, and we stick out on the street unless we're walkin' with a grown-up." Digger shrugged. "Seems to me yer buggered either way."

"And it seems to me," Paxal flicked his toothpick into the straw and plucked his knife from Nails' unwilling fingers, "that you're already runnin' an orphanage. Why not make it official?"

"An orphanage?" Mya's eyebrows arched.

Dee considered the idea and sighed. He'd never been partial to children, but it looked like Mya wasn't going anywhere without her army of urchins. To be honest, it made sense. He and Paxal might be here to help, but the two of them couldn't do much, and certainly not what these children did. His job should be to advise her, not thwart what she'd already built.

"An orphanage sounds good. We clean some of the kids up for times when you need them for cover, like you did with Kit today. Others we can leave...as is...so they can continue to do what they're doing."

"Easy enough to dirty up for street work." The little girl, Gimp, wiped her nose with her arm. "Harder to stay clean than it is to get dirty."

"We might be able to lease an inn that's been abandoned." Paxal's forehead wrinkled above raised eyebrows. "Quite a few folks left the city when the trouble started, if the traffic on the road was any indication. I'll find you a place."

Mya bit her lip. Dee had seen her like this before, weighing the pros and cons of a plan. "We'll have to think up a cover story. Who am I and why am I doing this?"

"That's simple." Paxal levered himself up off the floor and dusted off his trousers. "You can be the widow of some landed gentry who never liked the country. You come back to Tsing to find so many kids on the street that it broke your heart. You want to change things, but kids have to work to support themselves, right?"

"Work?" Nails sat up straight. "I ain't gonna—"

"Not real work, boy. We just tell 'em what they want to hear, ay?" Paxal tousled the boy's grimy hair. Turning back to Mya, he said, "The powers that be will be thrilled to have the kids off the street, and you and your little army of spies can come and go as you please without a hitch." With a wave, he started for the door.

"Pax!" Mya looked dubious. "Are you sure you want to get so involved in this?"

"Sure as rain falls and taxes rise, Miss Mya." Paxal left without another word.

"Well! It looks like we're going to have a new home." Mya stood, brushing the straw and dust from her skirt.

"Knock!" The half-breed girl's face twisted into a misshapen frown.

Kit frowned and patted her friend on the shoulder. "Knock

thinks she'll stick out like a turd on a silver platter north of the river."

Dee chuckled at the girl's language. Even dressed up, she was still a street urchin.

Mya smiled reassuringly and ruffled Knock's hair. "Don't worry, we'll figure something out."

The kids clustered around her, chattering and smiling and tugging on her skirts.

Dee bit his lip to keep from laughing at the sight of Mya, the stone-cold killer, holding hands with a little girl with ribbons in her hair and affectionately teasing the other children. He thought at first that it was an act put on for the kids' benefit, but she actually seemed sincere. He'd sooner have expected her to be hobnobbing with nobles and gentry, plying her assassin skills amid the political turmoil that inevitably followed assassination, than setting up an orphanage for street children.

Dee wondered what he'd gotten himself into and where it would take him. Knowing Mya, it would be someplace dangerous.

CHAPTER XVIII

Mya stepped down from the carriage and looked uncertainly at her new home. Pax had returned the previous evening with a lease in hand. A former inn, its proprietors had fled during the Night of Flame. The place might have been pleasant once, but hadn't seen a new coat of paint in years, and the boards on the lower windows made it look mean. It wasn't even as nice as the *Twin Dulcimer*. A nondescript building on a nondescript street in a nondescript Midtown neighborhood. It was perfect for their needs, but Mya felt vaguely disquieted.

So much for moving up in the world.

As delighted as she had been when Dee had up-ended his heavy saddlebags onto her bed at the *Tin Dulcimer*, she knew the money would go quickly. Rent, food, whatever payment the Gnome demanded for plans to the palace... They couldn't afford to be frivolous.

"Problem, Mistress?" Dee asked as he climbed down from the driver's seat.

"It's just so...dreary." She kept her voice low.

"Paxal thought it best if we didn't draw attention, and I agree. Besides, it was inexpensive, and he said the inside was clean, with hardly any rats."

"Wonderful." Mya knew Dee was right, but the place looked like a worn pair of shoes, with no character or charm.

It's supposed to be an orphanage, not a brothel, Mya. Get over it!

"I like it!" Little Kit hopped down from the carriage, showing off her pretty dress. "Mommy." She grinned up at Mya and grasped her hand. Kit had flatly refused to take the dress off, so they'd decided it best if she posed as the head mistress' daughter. She seemed to be enjoying her role a little too much.

"Whoa, you mangy critter!"

Paxal's hoarse cry and several stifled giggles drew her attention to the rented wagon pulling up behind her rented carriage. The mule pulling the contrivance had proven difficult, especially at the bridge, where it balked and refused to cross. Paxal had proven even more determined, however, convincing the recalcitrant beast to proceed with much cursing, lashing of reins, and finally bribing it with a carrot. Mya's urchins found it all very entertaining.

"Time to play our parts." Mya had noticed curious glances from the shops lining the streets, and she didn't want to arouse suspicions. Tugging her plain black dress straight, she cracked the tip of her parasol hard on the cobbles. "All right, you lot. Out of the wagon and line up. No nonsense!" She bustled forward, finding the padding beneath the dress both restricting and cumbersome. That, along with a hat, a lace veil, and some simple makeup to age her youthful features, transformed her into the middle-aged widow she was attempting to portray. "Paxal, get the door. Dee, my bags."

"Yes, Mistress Bouchard." Dee opened the boot of the carriage while children lined up. Paxal hurried to the door with his ring of keys and opened the door.

"Caps comin'," Kit whispered, squeezing her hand.

"It's all right." Mya stepped forward and regarded her urchins. They'd cleaned up a bit, but still looked rough, which was exactly how she wanted them to look. *Let's see how well this cover story holds up.* "Now remember. You're here at my pleasure, so if you misbehave, you're right back across the river. Our first order of business is to make this place livable."

"You've got quite a passel here, ma'am."

Mya turned and craned her neck to look the tall constable in the face. "Good morning, Constable. Is there a problem?"

"Just wondering where you're goin' with so many..." He surveyed the children with a skeptical eye, "...young ones."

"My name is Bouchard, and these are my charges." She waved at the urchins. "I've leased this inn with the intent to begin an orphanage."

"An orphanage?" He looked dubiously at her, the children, and the building. The five bored caps behind him chuckled and shook their heads. "You're taking on quite a responsibility."

Nosey nuisance, she thought, fixing him with a glare. "Yes, I am, Constable. My late husband left me with a child to support, finite funds, and a limited set of skills. I am *quite* capable of disciplining children, however, as well as teaching them to read, write, and do their sums." She cracked the tip of her parasol on the cobbles. "Inside now, all of you! Paxal, put them to work."

"Yes, ma'am." Paxal herded the children inside.

"No offense meant, ma'am, but how are you going to support such a...your orphanage if you have limited funds?" The constable rubbed his stubbled jaw, obviously puzzled.

"The children will work, of course, as all children must." She cracked her parasol on the street again with an exasperated sigh. "As you know, many children traverse the bridges every day to work in the shops and factories here in Midtown, only to go back across to live in squalor every night, barely earning enough to survive. Here, I'll pool their meager pay and provide a roof, food, and education. Everybody wins."

"I see." He arched an eyebrow. "Well, as long as you understand that you're accountable for their behavior while their under your roof. If we catch any of them stealing, you'll be held responsible."

"I understand, Constable. Now, if that's all, I have children to attend to."

"That's all, ma'am. Have a good day." He touched his cap in deference, and waved his patrol on.

"Thank you." Mya turned to go, but not before she caught Kit sticking her tongue out at the constables. "Kit! Behave now."

"Yes, *mother*."

Mya hurried the little girl up the steps and into the inn. She cast a glance at the constables as Paxal closed the door behind her, but none of them were watching. In the entry hall stood all of her urchins, grinning like fiends in the dim light.

"He bought it hook line and sinker, ma'am." Digger patted Knock on the back. The girl had simply kept her head down and gone along with the crowd.

"They did." Mya looked around at the drab but clean interior. "Well, let's get to work. Boards off the windows first, and let's air things out. Dee, check the place over and assign rooms, then return the carriage and wagon. The cook and scullery maid won't arrive until this afternoon, and I'd like us to look like an orphanage by then. Remember, I'm Mistress Bouchard, and if I'm not wearing this getup when someone comes to the door, then you tell them I'm out on business."

"I'll tend to the kitchen and stock the larder, Miss Mya." Paxal knew more about running a place like this than anyone else.

"Good. Supper at sundown. We won't bother with a watch on Lady T's house tonight." Her spies had not seen anything untoward through the guildmaster's windows lately, though Mya knew she and Hoseph must be having fits over the thwarted assassination attempt. "We'll sleep in three rooms, each adult with two children in the room, one awake at all times. Two more down here will keep watch on the doors."

"Yes, Miss Mya."

Dee lifted Mya's trunk and started up the stairs. "Would you like to pick out your room?"

"Pick one for me on the third floor." She looked around. "Where's the office Pax told us about? I need to draft a letter."

Dee stopped and nodded toward the back hall. "Through there and left. Who are you writing to?"

"Lady T." Mya took off her hat and scratched under it. She hated disguises, and planned to wear this one only when necessary. "I'm going to hit her up for a donation to support our fine charity work here."

"You're kidding." He gaped at her as if she'd told him she was planning to steal the crown jewels.

"Yes, I am." She flashed a grin and started for the office. Gods, it felt good to have an adult around who she could joke with. "I don't want to barge into her home again, and I need to speak with her. She needs to know why she shouldn't be trying to kill the crown prince."

"You're not inviting her *here*, are you?"

"Don't worry, Dee." Mya raised her voice over the banging of hammers as the urchins began removing the boards covering the windows. "I'm still not sure she's on my side. The last thing I want is for her to know where I live."

Arbuckle sipped chilled lemonade as he watched the small contingent approach his table across the lawn. Halting, the herald bowed, then announced his charge.

"Duke Nythes of Miravore, Sovereign of the Southern Province."

"Crown Prince Arbuckle." Nythes bowed low.

"Please join me for some refreshment, my good cousin." Arbuckle gestured to the chair across the small table.

With little support from the local nobility, the crown prince had shifted his attention farther afield to the provincial sovereigns who had begun to arrive for his coronation. Nythes seemed a likely hope for an alliance, second cousin on his mother's side, and Arbuckle's childhood companion during his infrequent visits to Tsing. He had inherited his dukedom ten years ago when his father died in a hunting accident. Arbuckle now doubted it had been a hunting accident after all, considering his father's association with the Assassins Guild, but hoped that Nethys would support him.

"I'm sorry I wasn't able to greet you personally upon your arrival, but the affairs of state are drowning me."

"Thank you, milord. You've been most welcoming." Nythes sat stiffly.

"I hope your trip was uneventful."

"It was fine, milord."

"How are things in the south?" Up close, Arbuckle noticed the fine lines around Nethes' eyes, his wan features, hair gray at the temples. The man boasted only a few years more than Arbuckle, but he seemed to have aged drastically since they'd last met only a few years ago.

A far cry from the dashing figure of his youth...

Arbuckle recalled his tenth birthday party, when they first met. Nythes had seemed such an adult then, strong and straight, blissfully ignorant of the onus of his title. They had had such a good time until—

The remembrance dredged up another memory. That was the birthday when Arbuckle's father had presented him with a live elephant. The young prince had been elated until the next gift arrived—a gilded hornbow.

"Aim here!" his father had instructed, prodding the restrained beast with a long pole. "Kill it!"

Horrified, Arbuckle had dropped the bow and refused, only to see the elephant slaughtered anyway. *Another memory of dear father.*

His stomach roiled. He wondered if part of Nythes' discomfort were his own memories of the day. His cousin's voice cut off his musing.

"We are having some…difficulty in the south, milord. Your edicts," Nythes paused, looking increasingly uncomfortable, "have caused unrest among the upper classes, and elicited violence from the commoners."

"Revenge violence, I assume." Arbuckle sighed. "Yes, we've seen a bit of that here, but it's settling down. You'll see the same, I'm sure."

"I doubt it, milord." Nythes eyes slipped sideways toward Arbuckle's guards standing at his shoulders. He licked his lips and sipped his lemonade. "There's too much hatred among the commoners. I fear we can't keep order without drastic action. The rebels must be put down."

"Force is not the answer, cousin." Arbuckle looked curiously at the man. He could see his fear as plain as day, and he sounded as if he were reciting words that he had learned by rote.

"We…" The duke's eyes flashed up to Arbuckle's for the first time, then at the guards behind the prince. He looked away. "As you say, milord."

Enough of this. Arbuckle gritted his teeth. He had to know why Nythes was so terrified. "Sir Calvert, take your detail for a stroll. Servants, all of you, leave us."

The duke's eyes snapped to his, surprise clear on his face. "But milord, there has been an assassination attempt…"

Arbuckle smiled to mask his own nervousness. He was taking a chance here, but he had to know. "My good duke, I count you my friend and ally. Let's reminisce about old times. Verul, you go, too. Duke Nythes and I have a lot of catching up to do, and there's no sense in cluttering up the archives with nonsense about our personal lives."

It pained him to dismiss his scribe after his declarations of a totally open and honest reign. But he was realizing that some things were too dangerous be recorded in the archives.

"Milord?" The knight assigned to his guard detail stepped forward, his hand on his sword. "You're sure, milord?"

"I'm sure, Sir Calvert." Arbuckle wasn't sure at all, but he needed to allay Nythes' fears. He waved them away casually. "We'll be fine, and you'll not be far away. The gardens are secure." He didn't know that for certain, of course, but they had taken every precaution they could think of. *I can't live my life in constant terror.*

"Very well, milord." Sir Calvert gathered up his detail by eye and they moved away. The footmen and maids retreated as well, Verul with them.

"You needn't have done that." Nythes' gaze dropped to his untouched plate.

"No? Well, I sometimes get tired of them looming over my shoulder while I eat."

"But...the attempt on your life..."

"That's why I need to speak to you privately, Nythes." He laughed loudly and waved a hand as if sharing a humorous anecdote, surprised how easily the deception came. He leaned forward, imploring the man to open up. "My father was a *monster*, which you undoubtedly know, and involved in crimes against the Empire of Tsing that I could not let come to light. But he's gone. You're safe. You can speak to me."

"It's...not my safety I'm worried about, milord." Nythes swallowed, his face pale.

"Who then?"

"They've...taken people. My youngest daughter and a few others."

"What?" Arbuckle fought down the horror threatening to rise up his throat. "Who took them? What's being done to get them back?"

"People..." Nythes swallowed hard and clenched his jaw. "Milord, there are factions in this empire who use kidnapping and murder to control things. If one doesn't go along with their demands, their loved ones are returned a piece at a time. It's happened before!"

"The Assassins Guild." Arbuckle gritted his teeth. His father's legacy had risen from the grave to haunt him. "Yes. My father was…involved with them."

"Then you know that just by telling you this, just by speaking with you in private, I'm putting my daughter's life…*more* than her life at risk. They have people everywhere! Probably in your own personal guard!"

"Not in my guard, or in my palace. I've made sure of it."

"You have?" Nythes looked astonished, as if such a feat were impossible. "How?"

"I can't reveal my methods, cousin, but let me assure you, the people I have retained are loyal to me." Arbuckle grinned ruefully. "My own nobility however…I'm unsure of."

"You must understand, milord, I *have* to publicly denounce your policies or they'll…" Nythes words caught in his throat, emerging only in a wracking cough. "I'm sorry, milord."

"Gods of Light…" He couldn't imagine the man's plight, a daughter held by such fiends.

The reason for the abduction seemed obvious: they were pressuring his nobles to oppose his new policies. The legacy of terror continued…spreading like a cancer through his empire. Throughout his upbringing, the isolated prince rarely heard any news from the provinces, but the duke's confession prompted a memory, a series of murders some years back in Twailin, nobles killed in their beds, but they had stopped before Duke Mir called for imperial assistance. *Damn it, I should have asked Norwood about that.* Was Duke Mir under pressure from these criminals as well? Were all his dukes? What could he do? He clenched his jaw in determination.

"Nythes, you must outwardly go along with their demands, but know this: I *will* fix this. Once I'm emperor, I will wipe these vile criminals from the empire for good." He had no idea how he would accomplish this, but resolved to do so. He would end his father's legacy.

"Can you, milord?" Nythes sniffed and clenched his jaw. "I don't know how. I've tried. I swear it, milord, but each time I do, someone beloved to me dies, or worse. They're invisible and untouchable. You say your palace is safe. Mine is *not*. My own City Guard is certainly compromised, and I fear my Royal Guard too."

"It goes that deep?"

"If a member of my own entourage saw me talking to you thus, someone would suffer." Nythes looked down at his untouched food. "I can trust no one, milord."

"You can trust *me*, Nythes. Trust me to never become the monster my father was, and to wipe this vile stain from our empire. I swear to you, I'll do it."

"I believe you, milord." Nythes straightened in his chair, a measure of calm returning, though the fear still lurked under the surface. "I believe that you'll try, at least. You're lucky, you know. You've no one they can take; no family. You were wise never to marry and have children."

"Was I?" Arbuckle realized that the man was right. He had no one, and nothing to lose but his life.

Hoseph materialized in Lady T's sitting room to find her pacing the floor. He steadied himself with a deep breath. He'd been resting quietly in his reclusive abode, martialing his strength and trying not to use his talisman except when necessary.

So many matters vied for his attention, he seemed to be stretched a dozen different directions. He was exhausted from trying to tie up all the loose ends, and needed rest, but a summons from the Tsing guildmaster trumped his needs.

Lady T gave a start, but didn't point a crossbow at him this time. "Good. You got my summons." She put down the tiny chime he'd given her, the one he'd recovered from the late Baron Patino, that sounded a note in the priest's mind when struck. "I didn't know if the thing would work."

"It works perfectly." This was the first time she'd used the simple device. He'd made it clear that it was only to be used in emergencies. "What's happened?"

"Your chance to kill Mya has arrived." She snatched a sheet of cheap parchment from her desk and held it out for his examination. "She wants to meet with me."

"Excellent." He couldn't suppress a smile as he read the note. They were to meet in a tea shop, of all places.

Things were finally coming together. Lady T had set Mya up for him. It would be dangerous, but Hoseph was patient; the usurper was as good as dead. Which reminded him of their other plans.

"Tessifus' youngest son. How is that progressing?"

She frowned at his question. "Master Lakshmi knows her job and is good at it. The first phase of his conditioning is progressing as planned. By the time we need him, the boy will be ours."

"Good." He rubbed his eyes, trying to scour the pain away. So many issues... "There's another question I've been pondering: Duke Mir is the only provincial duke we have no control over and the Twailin guild is rebelling. He's going to be here for the coronation. Is there a reason we shouldn't kill him?"

"*Numerous* reasons!" Lady T seemed irritated with him. "Can we *please* focus on the matter at hand?"

"There are numerous matters at hand!" he snapped back. "Which one?"

"Killing Mya, of course! That's why I *asked* you here!" She glared at him. "How are you going to do it?"

Blessed shadows of death, soothe me... The woman had such a one-track mind. She couldn't think of more than one plan at a time, while he had to consider everything at once.

Hoseph dropped the parchment on her desk. "This is too public a venue, but once I spot her, I'll follow her. She'll never see me, and I can complete the task when she thinks she's safe." He retrieved his talisman. "Keep your appointment with her. This is just the opportunity I've been waiting for."

"Good." Lady T took a deep breath and let it out slowly. "Very good."

CHAPTER XIX

Lady T entered the elegant little teahouse like an empress into a ballroom, her armed guards lumbering in close escort. The hostess greeted her with a curtsey. Unfortunately, even with her keen hearing, Mya couldn't hear what was said over the clatter and chatter of Tsing's gentry taking their afternoon tea.

She hated busy places like this. The crowd impeded movement, while noise and constant motion dampened her ability to scan for threats. Unfortunately, she'd chosen the place for the exact same reason; the crowd might keep Hoseph from popping in and murdering her. The constabulary was still looking for him in connection with the emperor's death. Materializing in a teahouse and murdering someone would banish any chance of him ever clearing his name. At the very least, there would be screams to warn her.

And that's the only warning you'll get, because you told your spies to stay home.

After her urchins had disregarded her orders at the plaza, and again at the *Prickly Pair*, she'd decided to leave them out of this one. She couldn't worry about them when she was worrying about her own safety. And Hoseph had seen Dee up close, and might recognize him loitering, so having him help was out. Paxal had offered, too, but she'd simply told him no, flat out. She'd do this alone.

Lady T's gaze swept the room as the hostess gestured her guards to a nearby sitting room. Mya felt gratified when the guildmaster's gaze passed her over without recognition. Her matronly disguise was holding up. Only as they approached the table did Lady T finally recognize her, her eyes widening in surprise.

Mya stood and curtsied respectfully. "Lady T. Thank you so much for accepting my invitation."

"My pleasure, my dear." She took her seat. When the hostess had gone she continued in a lower tone. "That's a different look for you."

"Do you like it?"

"No. It's positively dowdy."

"Good. That's just what I was hoping for." Mya had actually been trying for sedate elegance, and Dee had helped alter one of her traveling dresses. As long as she didn't stand out, it worked. She couldn't care less about Lady T's opinion. "We need to discuss a few things."

"Yes, we do." Lady T smiled at the waitress as she came to take their orders, and continued without missing a beat once she'd left. "The most pressing of which is Hoseph."

"I would think the most pressing would be your recent attempt in the Imperial Plaza." Mya narrowed her eyes at the woman. "It's good that your man was sloppy. He gave me enough time to intervene."

"So that *was* you." Lady T raised an eyebrow. "I thought it might have been."

"The important issue is that you don't seem to realize what would have happened if he had succeeded."

"I know *precisely* what would have happened."

"Really?" Mya allowed her lip to curl in derision. "So, you and your conspirators have plans to evacuate the city?"

The woman's upper lip twitched. "What are you talking about?"

Mya lowered her voice and leaned forward. "I'm talking about everything north of the river going up in flames, and I mean *everything*. The people of this city are not going to just sit by and watch if their only hope for a future is destroyed."

"They already tried that once, and were put down by the constabulary." Lady T cast a sneer across the table. "If it happens again, the result will be the same."

"You think the Night of Flame was an all-out revolt? The commoners were *happy* then. They were celebrating! Just try making them truly angry, and you'll think you've died and gone to the Nine Hells." Mya sipped her tepid tea with a thin smile. "You haven't been listening to the rumors. I have. They love this prince of theirs, and won't stand by if he's taken from them."

"And you think the constabulary, military, and Imperial Guard are going to simply let them wreak havoc?" Lady T fell silent as the waitress returned with a pot of tea and two glazed raspberry scones. When the waitress had gone, the noblewoman raised her cup and sipped. "You think I don't have people listening to all the scuttlebutt and rumors? You think I'll let a revolt take place in this city and do nothing to prevent it? How amusing."

"Tell that to Baron Ledwig." Mya pinched off a bite of scone and popped it into her mouth. "A skin of oil and a torch are very simple to wield. If you think the guild or the authorities can stand against the entire populace, you're delusional."

"I would *not* let it happen. We would nip it in the bud before the first—"

Mya's laughter cut her short, earning a glare. "You *are* delusional. You've spent too much time in your fancy house, Lady. The Night of Flame saw a few hundred troublemakers with torches. There are a quarter *million* commoners in this city who have been given a taste of justice. If that's taken from them, they'll all be wielding torches. You have perhaps five hundred guildsmen in this city, maybe twice that. Can you stand against two-hundred times your number?"

Lady T pressed her lips together so hard that they blanched white even through the rouge. "The plans to eliminate the…this *person,* hinge on Hoseph, not me. Eliminate him, and you end the threat to your precious prince."

Mya didn't need to be told the obvious, but Lady T hadn't been forthcoming in setting up Hoseph for the kill. Mya had already decided that warning the crown prince was the best route to prevent the assassination. She just needed Lady T to give her the details of their plot. She needed more than just the few names she had picked up from observing their meeting.

"I don't give a *damn* about the crown prince; I care about the *guild!* Half of the city reduced to ashes will be bad for business. *Our* business. You're going to tell me every bit of the plan Hoseph and you have concocted. Who's involved and when and how are they planning to do it?"

Lady T fell silent for a moment, sipping her tea, her eyes fixed on Mya and her features set in a frame of consternation. "Very well." She fished a cylinder the length and width of her finger from her bag and put it on the table. "Here are the names of all the conspirators. They plan to use Archmage Duveau. I don't know exactly how, but it'll happen before the heir is crowned."

Mya raised an eyebrow and picked up the cylinder. "You came prepared."

"I'm *always* prepared." Lady T smiled. "In fact, I brought you exactly what you need to solve your greatest problem. Hoseph knows I'm meeting you here."

Mya nearly dropped her teacup. "You *told* him?" She fought to keep the panic out of her voice.

"You *asked* me to set him up for you, and this is the best I could do. I don't know where he lives, and he pops in and out at the most unpredictable times." She sampled her scone and made a face, pushing the little plate away as if the luscious morsel was not utterly delicious. "He won't try to kill you with so many people around, but given the opportunity, he *will* try. When he does, kill him."

Mya tried to swallow her fear, tried to think, and failed. "You make it sound simple!"

"It *should* be simple. If you can fight blademasters, you can certainly kill a priest before he can touch you." The lady finished her tea and dropped her napkin over her plate. "He doesn't know you'll be ready for him. Give him the proper opportunity, then strike first."

Lady T obviously didn't know all of Hoseph's capabilities. If he used the same magic that had incapacitated her in the emperor's torture chamber, she'd be a sitting duck. Mya glared at Lady T, trying to transform her terror into anger.

"He's going to *kill* me." The words came out before she could stop them.

"I doubt that." Smiling, Lady T stood, then leaned down to whisper in Mya's ear. "When Hoseph is dead, I'll name you Grandmaster."

As the guildmaster walked away, Mya thought, *If I didn't need you, you would be so dead.*

Unfortunately, she did need Lady T if she hoped to be

Grandmaster, but for that to happen, she had to survive. Her worst nightmare had just come true: Hoseph was waiting for her, ready to pop in with his glowing hand of death and kill her.

Mya tried to press down her fear, to think, but the memory of that soul-wrenching jolt of magic dredging up the darkest moments of her life all at once left her shaking.

Think, Mya… She sipped her cooling tea, trying to appear calm as she considered her slim options. *How do you get out of this?*

She might be able to slip out the back, maybe abscond with a cook's outfit, but such an obviously evasive move would alert him to Lady T's warning, and the guildmaster's life would be forfeit.

"Did the lady not like the scone, ma'am?" The waitress startled Mya out of her thoughts, nearly earning a dagger in her eye for it.

Moving her hand away from the blade hidden in the bodice of her padded dress, Mya smiled. "Lady T has no taste when it comes to fine confections. The scones are delicious."

"Thank you, ma'am." She removed Lady T's plate and cup, leaving Mya to think in peace.

I'm safe in here for now, but I can't delay. What will he expect me to do? Where should I go? How do I lose him without looking like I'm trying to? Where will he watch from? How will he attack?

If she stayed in busy public places, she might be able to thwart him, but that would only get her so far. He would expect her to go home, but she couldn't let him follow her back to the orphanage. As a Hunter, she could usually spot someone prowling, but Hoseph wasn't an assassin. He wouldn't just walk down the street, not with every constable in Tsing looking for him. He could blink around at will, giving him an immense advantage.

His most likely strategy seemed obvious: pop in behind her, cast that gut-wrenching spell to stun her, and then kill her with a touch. Against that, she had no defense.

Or do I?

She knew the spell's debilitation lasted only a few seconds. But the magic hadn't affected Lad at all. When they discussed it later, his answer had taken her aback.

"It didn't show me anything I hadn't already been reliving for weeks."

In the midst of his despair for Wiggen, heaping his heart with more guilt had been like throwing a lit match into a bonfire. She knew now what to expect if Hoseph used the magic on her again. Could she ready herself for it? How?

You've faced impossible odds before, Mya. Twice, in fact!

But both of those times, against the combined might of the masters of the Twailin Assassins Guild, and against the emperor's blademasters, Lad had been with her.

Now she had to face it alone.

When her scone was gone, and the tea cold—she really preferred blackbrew—Mya had in her mind a simple plan. Stay in the midst of as many people as possible, and don't go home until she was sure she'd evaded any possibility of pursuit. As far as preparing for Hoseph's attack, she would just have to be vigilant. She knew that Hoseph wasn't exactly a skilled assassin. Even Dee had managed to knock him down before he could invoke his killing magic, but his ability to flit around like smoke on the breeze made him impossible to predict. She knew from Dee's account that he didn't appear in an instant, but formed from mist and shadow. If she caught a glimpse of his telltale arrival, she needed to stay out of his reach and put a dagger in his heart, no matter what horrors from her past his magic dredged up in her mind.

Simple.

Mya left a gold crown on the table, got up, steeled her nerves, and walked out the front door as if she hadn't a care in the world. Suppressing the desire to look around for Hoseph, she made her way up the street, alone amid the bustle of the city. She strained her senses against the cacophony of a hundred footsteps clattering on cobbles and wood, hooves clacking and iron-shod wheels rumbling on the streets. Voices called out, motion everywhere, a thousand smells and drafts of fetid air...

Focus! She sifted through the morass, trying to detect her would-be assailant.

With her senses heightened to a fever-pitch, Mya turned right at the next street, up into the Heights District instead of down into Midtown toward home, the tip of her parasol clicking on the cobbles with each step. *Don't give him an opportunity... Stay in the crowds... Focus! If he pops in, move, and kill him before he can touch you!*

A pair of workers exited a swanky shop ahead carrying a rolled rug between them, and the foot traffic bunched up. Someone jostled Mya from behind, and she started, her hand going to the hilt beneath her bodice.

Calm down! Not here…he's not going to attack in a crowd…

She turned to cast an admonishing look at the tall gentleman who barely acknowledged her glare. She took the opportunity to scan the street, the buildings, the rooftops, but saw no sign of Hoseph.

Where are you?

The men moved, and people surged, forcing her eyes forward. She strode on, tapping her parasol and suppressing the chill up her spine. *Just a proper gentlewoman out for a stroll, not an assassin in fear for her life.* She continued up the hill, thinking of one familiar place where she might be able to lose her deadly escort.

"Where are you going?" Hoseph watched Mya turn the corner from the street of the teahouse and head toward the Heights District. He doubted she would be staying in the most expensive district in the city. Alone, without resources or support from the guild, how could she afford it? No matter; there was nowhere she could go where he couldn't follow.

From the top of the building across the street from the teahouse, Hoseph scanned the nearby rooftops, picking out a nice flat roof next to the street Mya had turned onto. He faded into the shadows and reappeared exactly where he wanted, on a level spot far in from the roof edge. The now-constant headache and dizziness made falling a real danger, but standing on a flat roof hardly required preternatural agility. Also, this was the only way he could be sure that Mya wouldn't spot him.

He leaned forward just far enough to view the street four floors below. If he fell, he might have time to invoke his talisman before he died.

Scanning the shifting crowd, he picked Mya out easily. All of her clever disguises could not fool a high priest of Demia, sorter of souls. He could pick out her particular soul anywhere. She paused with the crowd as some menials moved a carpet across the walkway.

Someone jostled her, and she turned, looking around, probably watching for Lady T's assassins. The guildmaster had been right; Mya was careful. He leaned back until he could barely see her over the edge of the roof. Finally, she moved on.

Six more transitions through the shadows left his head feeling like daggers had plunged into his eyes, but he remained stoic. Mya had ventured deep into the district, and turned into the one place he never thought she would go: the *Drake and Lion* inn, the very place she and Lad had stayed.

"Returning to the scene of the crime?" He wondered how she could be so foolish, but then considered his own reaction to her coming here. He certainly hadn't expected it. Could she be so bold? "Your arrogance will be your undoing, traitor…"

Hoseph settled down to wait, rubbing his temples as he watched the inn. He had never been inside, so couldn't follow her using his talisman, but this might just be a ruse, too. Mya was nothing if not wily. He would wait to be certain this was truly where she was staying. If it was, he would have Lady T find out which room she was in. From there, he would find a way in to kill her while she slept.

Patience… Sweet shadows of death, sooth me… Patience…

There were four armed guards stationed beside the doorman at the *Drake and Lion*. They gave her a cursory glance, but a frumpy gentlewoman evidently didn't warrant a confrontation. Granted, most of the swanky inn's clientele were much more elaborately dressed, but she didn't look like a commoner, which was enough to get her past. The doorman nodded to her and did his job.

The inn wasn't very busy, but nobody gave her a second glance as she strode purposefully forward, using the age-old practice of looking like she knew where she was going to avoid questions. Picking a bellboy of about the right size, she stepped into his path.

"You there, young man. I require your assistance. Follow me." She crooked a finger and started for the stairs.

"But, ma'am, I'm busy with another—"

She fixed him with an intolerant stare. "*Must* I report your disrespect to the manager and have you fired?"

"Um…no, ma'am."

"Good. Now, follow me!" Mya ascended the sweeping staircase, and he fell in behind, conditioned by a lifetime of subservience to simply do as he was told. At least she hoped so. At the fourth landing he was out of breath. She hurried down the deserted hallway to the last door and stopped. "I've lost my key. Open this."

"I don't have any keys, ma'am. I'll have to go check with the manager." He turned to go.

Whether he was telling her the truth or had keys and wasn't about to open a room for someone without approval of his boss, didn't matter in the slightest. Mya struck him carefully just at the juncture of his neck and shoulder. The blow didn't quite snap his neck, but dropped him like a steer in a slaughterhouse. She caught him before he hit the floor, and lowered him gently to the floor, senseless, but still breathing. Pressing her ear against the door, she listened.

Nothing…no voices, no breathing, no heartbeats. Good.

Mya gripped the shiny brass handle and twisted hard. The lock gave way with a crack, and she pushed open the door. She'd chosen well; the room was small, ornate, and unoccupied. She dragged the unfortunate young man inside and closed the door.

Work fast, Mya.

She stripped out of her dress, shoes, and wig, and scrubbed the makeup from her face with her pettiskirts. Next, she stripped off the man's uniform, and put it on. The shoes were too big, but she stuffed his socks into the toes and put them on anyway. Next, she bundled her clothing into one of the bed's sheets, tying the corners tight. Her daggers she secreted under her dapper bellboy's jacket. She lifted him into the bed and tucked a pillow under his head. He was going to wake up with a splitting headache and quite a story to tell, but probably wouldn't be able to identify her. Mya picked up the bundle and hurried out, confident that Hoseph would never spot her dressed like a hotel employee.

267

Hoseph materialized on yet another rooftop and pressed his thumbs to his temples to scour away the pain. If it got much worse, he would have to abandon his pursuit or risk falling to his death. He blinked and focused, edging close to the tenement's roof to watch Mya enter yet another inn. This was her third since leaving the meeting with Lady T. The woman truly was paranoid, changing first into a bellboy's uniform at the *Drake and Lion*, then back into her dress at another inn. Now this unassuming place only a few blocks from the river.

He sat down to wait, muttering a prayer to help ease the agony inside his skull. If she left this inn under a new guise, he'd have to try to follow. Hoseph knew his own limitations, and he was far too fatigued to try to kill her today. He would have to wait. He'd long considered his strategy, knowing firsthand how dangerous she was. He had one weapon that would give him the opportunity he needed: the invocation of soul searching. Intended as a means to show sinners the errors of their pasts, the invocation also had the effect of momentarily overwhelming the recipient. Hoseph had used the magic to great effect before, once against Captain Norwood, and again in the palace dungeon. He didn't know why it hadn't worked on Lad, but that creature was more magic than flesh anyway. It had, however, knocked Mya to her knees, and should do so again. If he could get close enough to render her senseless, he could send her soul to Demia and be done with it.

He spotted two children slipping out the inn's servants' entrance and up the alley. One was almost tall enough to be Mya in disguise, but neither possessed the assassin's peculiar twisted soul. Moments later, two more children left the inn.

What's going on here?

Curtains moved in a top-floor window, but not enough for him to get a glimpse inside. In fact, in every window above the ground floor, the draperies were pulled closed. On the first floor, slatted shutters blocked his view.

Patience…

Hoseph waited. Two more children left, then one he hadn't see before returned, then an old man—the first adult he'd seen—left through the front door and strode up the street. Another rough-looking child approached and entered the inn again by the back door.

Is this some kind of school or home for street children?

Regardless, though many had come and gone from the building, Mya was still inside. This appeared to be her refuge. Hoseph would have laughed if he'd possessed anything resembling a sense of humor.

She's hiding behind children?

Mya must truly be desperate if she had resorted to recruiting the dregs of the Downwind Quarter for cover. Hoseph smiled through his pain. Now that he knew where Mya lived. He would get a glimpse inside when the next person came or went. Then he would use his gifts to slip inside and kill Mya in her sleep. Not tonight; his fatigue hung too heavily on him. *Perhaps tomorrow.* It was only a matter of time, and he could wait.

Dee held up the bellman's jacket Mya had stolen, suppressing a grin of admiration. The disguise had been quick thinking, and had probably saved Mya's life. Good thing she had the slim figure to fit into the uniform, and short enough hair to pass for a boy. He hung it in her clothes press, thinking it might come in handy later. He'd take in the seams here and there to make it fit better, and add some padding to hide her feminine curves.

"I don't know if Lady T was just trying to scare the shit out of me with this, or if I'm just good at disguises, but I'm still alive." Mya bit her lip, pacing as she removed her disguise. "I must have lost him at the *Drake and Lion*."

"You think she would lie to you?" Dee took her hat and placed it on the rack. She hadn't put her makeup back on, of course, but the lace veil hid her features well enough.

"Not really, but it's possible." Mya held up a small tube. "I was thinking about this on the way back, too. She had it ready. The names of the conspiracy. I keep thinking it's too good to be true. What if she's playing me, giving me a list of people she's hoping I'll kill? I don't know Tsing's politics. Some of these could be Arbuckle's supporters."

"But you know three of them, right? Seoli, Ingstrom and…what was the magistrate's name?"

"Graving. Yes, they're on the list, but I have no way to confirm the others. I couldn't see faces well through her draperies."

"If the whole thing's a lie, what about Duveau? Could she be trying to get you to kill him, too? Remove Arbuckle's protection, like the blademasters?"

"Maybe, but I don't see how." She shook her head. "It doesn't seem likely to be a lie for two reasons: one, if I found out, she knows I'd kill her; two, I have no way to get to Duveau."

"So, if it's *not* a lie, you're still planning to take the list to the prince?"

"Yes." Mya finished with the buttons of her dress and stepped behind her dressing screen. The dress flew over the top of the screen, followed by her pettiskirts. "I'm sorry about the pettiskirts, but I had to use them to scrub off my makeup. Hand me my robe will you?"

"No worries, Miss Mya. It'll launder out easily enough." He plucked the dress from the screen and handed her the robe. As her hand reached around to take the garment, he saw that her wrist and forearm were wrapped in close-fitting black cloth. *Strange undergarments...* He wondered if it was a bandage or something, but she'd mentioned no injury. Well, he wasn't going to ask. Mya had her secrets, and he wasn't about to pry.

She stepped out from behind the screen, covered her from neck to wrist to ankles by the voluminous robe, and held up the tiny scroll case. "So, we assume this is genuine and get it to the prince."

"You're sure about breaking into the *palace*, Miss Mya? It seems so..."

"I'm sure, Dee." She bit her lip, and Dee didn't think she was sure at all. "I'll leave word at the tinker's shop that I need to see the Gnome again. I can't wait any longer."

"As you wish, Miss Mya, but..."

"But what?" She fixed him with a pleading look. "*Tell* me, Dee. I want your opinion."

Well that's a first... "All right. It's too dangerous. You shouldn't trust a thief. He could give you false information, set you up."

"That's funny, he said the same thing about trusting an assassin." Mya smirked and nudged him toward the door. "Don't worry, Dee.

I'm not trusting him implicitly, and I can take care of myself. Now get out of here. I've got to get cleaned up."

"Very well, Miss Mya. I've put hot water in the wash room." He left with her soiled pettiskirts draped over one arm and his concern for her undiminished. She took horrible chances, and he could tell she was afraid, especially of Hoseph, but she insisted on going on. He had failed Mya once, and she'd still trusted him. All he could do was to try his hardest not to fail her again.

CHAPTER XX

$\mathbf{Y}$er late."

Mya suppressed the urge to whirl and lash out. Even when she knew he was going to show up, she hadn't heard the gnome's approach. She turned casually and put the little jade carving of a duck back on the shelf. "I've been waiting for ten minutes. How could I be late?"

The gnome squinted up at her from under his cap and wrinkled his prodigious nose. "Hand me down that bag 'o cherry wood blend, would ye?"

"Sure." She retrieved the bag of tobacco and handed it down. "Must be challenging being so short."

"Only when I'm in a shop run by one 'o ye longlegs." He picked a pipe off a lower shelf, examined its workmanship, and sniffed the bowl. "Follow me, but keep yer distance."

"All right." She picked the jade duck off the shelf and strolled to the front of the smoke shop while the gnome paid for his pipe and tobacco. At the counter, the shopkeeper greeted her with a smile.

"Half a crown. Would you like that wrapped up?"

"No, thank you." Mya paid for the little carving and left the shop, duck in hand.

She had little difficulty following the gnome. The streets of the Dreggars Quarter were busy, even though most people displaced by the Night of Flame had moved back to Midtown, but his size and distinctive cap marked him well. Of course, he wanted her to follow him. She imagined he could vanish readily enough if he so chose. Three blocks from the smoke shop, he paused at a stair that descended to the basement of a brick building. With a discreet glance back, he trundled down the steps.

Mya paused to examine something through a shop window, then followed. At the bottom of the stairwell stood an iron-bound door with a shiny bronze handle, only four feet tall. *Gnomes...* She hoped the height of the building's interior didn't match the door.

The door swung open. "Come in."

She ducked through, stepping down into an airy cellar full of rows of crates, barrels, and shelves of tiny bins all lined up in precise order. At least the ceiling was high enough that she wouldn't have to stoop. "Nice place you've got here."

"Ain't mine." He regarded her as he strode to the middle of the room to lean against a shelf. "I still don't trust ye enough to take ye to me own place, let alone the palace."

"You've had almost a week."

"Aye, and yers ain't the only job I've got."

She had one thing that might jog him into action. "I have the names of the conspirators who are planning to kill the crown prince." She enjoyed the surprise on his face at her pronouncement. "I know who they're going to use to assassinate him, and I can warn him. If you don't help me, they'll probably succeed."

"Tell me, and I'll get a note to him." Mistrust hung on his homely features like a mask.

"Not a chance." She shook her head. "You've given me no reason to trust you that much."

"So, I don't trust ye, and ye don't trust me." His prodigious nose wrinkled.

"But both of us want to save this prince's life, even if it's only so we both have customers to fleece. So, how do we do it?"

"We'll have ta go in together, but I want some insurance that yer not gonna just murder the man, then me as well."

Mya squinted down at his inscrutable face. He'd clearly thought this through, and she knew this wouldn't be a trifling point. "What kind of insurance?"

"This kind." He pulled a small metal ring from a pocket. It looked like a cheap steel bracelet.

"What's that?"

"My insurance." He whispered a word with the guttural intonation of his mother tongue, and the ring expanded in radius.

Pulling a stout shaft of hardwood from a nearby bin, he looped the ring over it and spoke another word. The ring constricted to fit snugly around the post.

"Ye wear this around yer neck, see." He tapped it with a finger. "Won't hurt ye unless I want it to."

Mya swallowed. "And if I betray you…"

Holding the shaft upright, he said another word in gnomish, and the metal ring suddenly constricted, sheering off the top of the post. He caught the end before it hit the floor and put it on a shelf, then proffered the shaft in his hand. Atop it sat the metal ring, now barely large enough to fit a pin through.

Mya swallowed. She doubted even her magical tattoos could save her from the constricting metal ring. "That's asking me to trust you a lot."

"Aye, but no more'n I'm trustin' ye." He nodded to her skirts. "Ye don't move like a thief, but I don't doubt fer a second that ye could put one 'o them daggers in my eye before I could blink it."

"Even before you could kill me with that thing." She nodded to the ring in his hand. "So, that won't save your life."

"No, but it'd take yers right enough." He shrugged and pocketed the ring. "And if I don't come home, me wife says that word."

"You're married?"

"Aye?" He squinted at her. "What of it?"

"Just surprised."

"Why?"

"Because loved ones can be used against you. They're a liability."

"Fer killers, maybe. Not so much fer burglars." He shrugged again. "Ye gotta trust someone eventually."

Mya thought about that. Who did she really trust? The list was depressingly short: Lad, Dee, Paxal, and to a lesser extent, Sereth. The other Twailin Masters even less. She trusted her urchins not to stab her in the back, but not enough to confide her deep, dark secrets. Trusting this gnome with her life grated against her innate paranoia, but she couldn't think of a motive for him to murder her out of hand, and with his lack of love for the Assassins Guild, there seemed little chance of him conspiring with someone to kill her.

He put the ring in his pocket. "Ye in or not?"

Mya had little choice. "Fine. We go in together. I can get us into the dungeons, but I'm not going to tell you how yet."

"The dungeons?" His face scrunched into a mass of wrinkles. "Why couldn't ye have a nice tunnel into the loo?"

"Blame the dwarves who built the place. Is that a problem?"

"Not really."

"Good. Now, how do we find the prince?"

"Aye, well, there's only two or three places he could be sleepin'."

"And we're just going to walk in?"

"Nay, lass!" He squinted at her and winked. "We're gonna use one of the secret passages, but I'm not gonna tell you where they are."

Mya really shouldn't have been surprised. If there was a secret passage into the palace, there were probably more within. "When?"

"Ye busy tonight?"

"I am now." She couldn't suppress a grin.

"Meet me here an hour before midnight, and dress proper." He nodded to her hard shoes. "No toe pinchers."

"I'll be here."

Hoseph paced the roof of the Tsing Library, fingering the tiny silver skull that hung within his sleeve and wondering if he'd been betrayed. He'd picked this spot as a place the archmage would undoubtedly know of and could easily access, and where they wouldn't be seen. The Library was one of the tallest buildings in the Heights District, it's wide, flat roof visible only from the distant palace walls and a few lofty temple spires.

But Duveau was late.

He reviewed all the reasons Duchess Ingstrom could have to betray him. She might barter Hoseph's life in exchange for a provincial rulership or even an empress' crown on her daughter's head.

Motivation indeed…and Archmage Duveau could be the one they send to take me.

If there was one person in the empire who could subdue

Hoseph with little trouble, it was Duveau. Hoseph could vanish in a moment, but he didn't know what magic the archmage could wield. He'd seen what the wizard had done to the seemingly impenetrable door to the imperial dungeons.

Hoseph paced, clenching his talisman and considering his own level of paranoia—*Too much, or not enough?*—when suddenly Archmage Duveau emerged from one of the ornate merlons that girded the rooftop. The priest remembered what it had felt like to travel through the dungeon stone and shivered.

Mild surprise registered on the wizard's face. The note hadn't specified who he was meeting here.

Hoseph nodded respectfully. "Archmage Duveau."

"Master Hoseph." The archmage remained where he was, regarding his host with a blank mien. "Forgive my tardiness, but one cannot be too careful."

"I understand completely. Rest assured, I mean you no harm."

"You'll forgive me if I don't take your words as…gospel. You're implicated in the emperor's death, you know."

"Yes, and the notion is utterly preposterous." Hoseph stifled his irritation. "I had no motive, no means, and couldn't have fought His Majesty's blademasters. If I had killed the emperor, why would I call for help? Also, I was injured."

"Yet you fled."

"Yes, to avoid answering questions under your compulsion. I know things that can't be divulged."

"I see." Duveau pursed his lips. "Your note stated that you had an offer to make. Make it."

"You're familiar with the legendary runemage, Corillian, I assume."

Duveau's eyes widened with interest. "I was not *familiar* with Corillian, I knew him personally. An brilliant runemage. He personally taught me the rudiments of rune magic. Unfortunately, before we could proceed farther, he sought seclusion. No one I know has heard from him in years. It was rumored that he was dead, but the rumors were never confirmed."

"He is dead." Hoseph smiled without mirth. He'd gauged the Archmage correctly. The fish was circling the bait. "And I know *where* he sought seclusion."

"Krakengul Keep?" The wide eyes narrowed as interest evolved into avarice.

"Yes." Hoseph had gauged the archmage correctly.

"How did you learn that? Many have sought his refuge and failed."

"An associate of mine did business with Corillian. When our people found his body, we contracted a mage to identify him, then backtrack to his keep. The structure was completely sealed in an impenetrable magical field, but he reported its location to us."

"What was this mage's name?" Duveau's demanding tone and stiff body language spoke volumes. He wanted the secrets of the runemage. He wanted them very badly.

The fish taken the hook. Now to set it.

"That doesn't matter. The mage is dead. But I know where the keep is. I've seen it. It's quite...impressive." On the Grandmaster's orders, Hoseph had ventured to Krakengul Keep to confirm the mage's report. Perched on the rim of the vast caldera of the Bitter Sea, it was indeed impressive...and impenetrable. Once the mage had been killed, only Saliez, the Grandmaster, and Hoseph had been privy to the location. As the only survivor, Hoseph saw no reason not to barter this valuable information for the good of the guild.

Duveau frowned. "And what do you want from me for this knowledge?"

Avarice tinged with suspicion, Hoseph decided. Now to see exactly how badly Duveau wanted the magic of his dead associate. He fingered Demia's talisman, ready to flee if the conversation took a dangerous turn. "I want you to assassinate Prince Arbuckle."

Duveau snorted in disbelief, then sobered. "Good gods, you're serious!"

"I am." Hoseph raised a forestalling hand. He had to persuade Duveau that his motives weren't simple revenge or the lust for power. Since the wizard could discern truth through magic, Hoseph chose his words carefully. "Please, hear me out. During Tynean Tsing II's reign we had order. He was the only emperor in history to have control over his own empire, not this chaos that Arbuckle is inciting. I intend to reestablish that order and control."

"How? By putting Duke Tessifus on the throne?"

"Initially, but his reign will be short. We are

currently…preparing his youngest son to assume the position of emperor."

"We?" Suspicion blossomed again. Duveau might be the most powerful mage in the land, but he could no more hide his moods than he could sprout wings and fly. "Who is 'we'?"

"A secret organization to which our former emperor belonged, and which I now administer in his stead." True enough, though he wouldn't dare say that in front of Lady T. "This organization was one of the ways he kept order."

"And you plan to reinstate this organization's control of the empire by placing a person you have…prepared upon the throne." Duveau was no fool. He knew a power grab when he heard one, but Hoseph had more persuasive points to make.

"I plan to place on the throne capable of proper *ruling*. Arbuckle is unfit. He murdered a member of his own nobility for an offense that's been condoned in this empire for decades. He gives commoners free reign to pillage and seek vengeance upon those who rule them. He invites anarchy. I offer order." *Once I'm in control…*

Duveau pursed his lips again, pausing long before he continued. "I care little for politics, Master Hoseph, but I do care about my *own* welfare. I've been archmage for decades, and I don't wish to lose that position."

"And Arbuckle has been treating you like peasant labor! Do you think anything will change once he's crowned?"

"Probably not, but there is a certain *prestige* in the position."

"And if I promised you the position back in twenty years or so?"

Duveau scoffed again. "You think *any* emperor would allow the man who committed regicide to assume the post of imperial archmage?"

"Oh, come now. I may only be a humble priest, but I'm not unacquainted with magic. After mastering the secrets of the *legendary* Corillian, you can forge yourself an entirely new body. Age means nothing to a runemage of that caliber, and flesh is malleable." He paused, considering the man once again. Duveau was a brilliant wizard, but he seemed to lack the ability to look into his own future. That made him vulnerable to manipulation. *I could use a man like him.* "If you remove Arbuckle for us, I'll take you to Krakengul Keep. It's mysteries should occupy you until our new emperor is established, then you return wearing a new face, maybe Corillian's, and assume the role of archmage. You stand to gain a great deal, and lose nothing in the long run."

"In the long run…" Duveau scowled. "Twenty years of exile and a death sentence on my head are not trivial sacrifices."

"Twenty years of *studying* the secrets of rune magic is hardly exile. You know as well as I do that the death sentence is meaningless. Who in this empire could deliver that sentence?"

Duveau considered again, his brow furrowing in thought. "And when would this assassination occur?"

Yes! Hoseph bridled his elation. "Before he's crowned. As emperor, Arbuckle can change laws without approval of the nobility, and may even change the line of succession. If he revokes Duke Tessifus' title, our preparations will be for naught. We leave the details up to you, but we prefer there be witnesses to the assassination."

"Why?"

"Because, if people see *you* kill the prince, there's no guilt to be laid elsewhere." *Namely on me.*

"You've thought this through quite thoroughly."

"Yes, I have." Hoseph did smile then, allowing himself the pleasure of a job well done. "It's what I do best."

CHAPTER XXI

The tunnel under the river came as a surprise. The Gnome had led Mya through a locked cellar door behind a cobbler's shop, then a concealed panel in the cluttered basement. Two flights of steps and a long narrow tunnel that sloped down for a quarter of a mile, then up again, put them in the basement of an ironmonger's shop. He closed the concealed door and motioned her toward an exit onto the street. A glance around confirmed they were somewhere in Midtown.

"That was handy." Mya fingered the steel band around her neck as he relocked the door. Was it her imagination, or was the damn thing getting tighter? At least the rest of her clothes were comfortable: trousers and shirt, soft boots and daggers, her trappings of old.

"Bridges mean caps, and we don't need anyone seein' us." He looked up at her, his pupils large in the dark. "Where to?"

She'd withheld the location of the secret entrance into the palace as a last safety measure. He, in turn, had refused to give her any information about the secret passages within the palace. Trust still ran thin between them.

"Vin' ju' Tsing. Do you know it?"

"Sure. Hoity-toity wine shop up Hightown." He wrinkled his nose as if he found affluence distasteful.

"I'll follow you."

"Aye. Try not to make so much noise, ay? Don't they teach you how to *walk* in assassin school?"

"Evidently not to *your* standards." The jab stung a little. Lad had never complained about her lack of stealth. "Go ahead. I'll try not to trip."

"Humph." The gnome started off at a quick pace considering his short legs, as quiet as a mouse.

Mya matched his pace with no trouble, trying her best to stay quiet. It was near midnight, so they shouldn't meet too many late night wanderers, but stealth seemed prudent. They'd covered a dozen blocks before she caught the sound of a constable patrol.

"Ssst!"

"What?" The Gnome turned with an irritable look on his face, but then, he looked perpetually irritable.

"Constables." She tapped her ear and pointed ahead and to the right. "Two, maybe three blocks."

He cocked his hear and listened. She could discern the tromping of boots and jingle of armor clearly over the occasional clink and clatter from apartments, the skitter of a rats, and their own breathing and heartbeats. To the gnome's credit, he didn't doubt her, but just kept listening. Finally, he nodded and motioned down an alley to the right. She followed him around the noisy patrol. After they were past, he stopped again and looked up at her.

"Ye got good ears fer a human."

"Who said I was human?" She flashed him a predatory grin. *Let the little git chew on that one.*

He snorted quietly. "Well, ye certainly *smell* human enough. Come on."

"I don't smell!" She followed, muttering curses under her breath.

When they finally reached Vin' ju' Tsing, they found another obstacle. Four guards patrolled outside the building. Mya had cased the shop it earlier that day, and only saw two. Evidently someone was being careful about uninvited nighttime visitors. Other affluent business had posted guards, so this wasn't unusual. However, the guild owned this shop. The guards might have been hired to keep commoners from pillaging, or they could have been sent by Lady T to prevent Mya from sneaking into the palace. Regardless, they had to bypass them.

The Gnome tapped her arm and pointed around the side of the building. She followed, placing her feet where he trod and keeping her breathing slow and quiet. They hunkered in the shadows on the darker side of the building, watching the nearest guard walk to and fro. Mya counted; for twelve seconds his back was turned away from the corner where the building abutted the face of the bluff.

"Second floor window?" she whispered an inch from the gnome's ear.

"Can ye make it up there quiet?"

"Yes." She'd already picked out a path that used the rock face as well as the building. If Lad could do it, so could she. "But the window's closed, maybe locked."

"Let me go first and get the window. Once it's open, wait fer him to make a pass, then come up when he turns away again."

"Right." Mya saw no reason not to let the burglar burgle. She hadn't brought him along for his witty repartee.

When the guard next turned, the Gnome slipped away. He moved like a wraith. Her eyes picked him out of the shadows easily enough, but she doubted that the guard would have seen him if he'd been looking right at him. The gnome climbed the wall like a spider, hands and feet finding purchase where she wouldn't have guessed they could. When the guard turned back, the thief hunkered where the building and rock face met, as still as stone.

The guard turned again, and the Gnome worked his way over to the window, clinging to the building like a bug climbing a pane of glass. She squinted, and saw that he wore some kind of climbing devices on his hands and feet, though she hadn't seen him put the things on. Beneath the window, he removed one of the climbers and tucked it in a belt pouch, then fiddled at the window. It opened silently, and he slipped inside.

Mya waited for the guard to turn his back, then moved.

Her dash and leap took her only halfway to the height of the window, but she used her momentum to propel herself up the rough stone of the bluff before bounding back to land on the window sill. Not quite as silent as the gnome, but quicker by far. She slipped inside before the guard made half his circuit.

The Gnome stared at her from the dark of the room, his eyes wide. He pointed to the window, and mimed closing it. She complied, working the latch silently.

"Maybe ye ain't human after all," he whispered as she turned back. "How'd ye make that jump?"

"Magic. Let's go." She'd be damned if she would explain her

abilities to him. Lad was the only living person in the world who knew about her runic tattoos, and she intended to keep it that way. "First floor, back of the shop, there's a door into the aging cavern."

He made a face. "Stay close. They may have guards inside, too."

She followed him downstairs, grateful there were no guards to evade inside the shop. At the door, he made short work of the lock and oiled the hinges with a tiny can from his pouch. It swung open silently and they slipped inside.

"Ye need light?" he asked as the door closed behind them, plunging them into deep darkness.

"No. You?"

"I'm a gnome," he said, as if that explained everything. "Dunno quite what ye are if ye can see in this."

"I'm a *monster*." She grinned maliciously. "Now hurry up! Eighteenth barrel on the left."

The Gnome muttered something in gnomish and led the way. At the eighteenth barrel, they stopped. Mya stepped forward and pressed the Grandmaster's ring into a niche in one of the support wedges, and the huge tun rolled aside to reveal the passage beyond.

"Go ahead. I've got to close the door."

"Aye." The gnome slipped through the narrow opening and waited patiently in the small room.

When the barrel rolled back into place, she turned to find him examining the walls despite the utter darkness. "Do you see the door?"

"I see two doors." He pointed to the one Mya knew of. "One there, and another there." He pointed to the adjoining wall, which looked featureless to Mya. "Which one we usin'?"

"Huh. I only knew of one. This one." She pressed her ring to the secret catch and the door she'd used before slid aside without a sound.

"Dwarf work these." He stepped through and didn't flinch when soft white light blossomed around him, sourceless and casting no shadows.

"Yes." Mya stepped inside and closed the door. "They were probably built when the palace foundation was laid."

"Or before." The Gnome ran his fingers over the wall and

shrugged. "Wondered how the beards came and went. Now I know."

Mya started out at a steady pace. "You think the dwarves use these to come and go from the palace?"

"Well, not this one, but if there's one dwarf tunnel in this rock, there's dozens." He matched her pace until they arrived at the end of the tunnel. "Now what?"

"This opens into the dungeons." She nodded to the door. "The last time I was here, two of the emperor's blademasters were stationed there waiting for me, so I know at least some people knew about this passage." She shrugged. "Now that the blademasters are gone, I don't know if anyone does. Seems like they would have sealed it if they knew, but it looks just like it did before."

"From *this* side. They could've walled it up from the inside. Try that ring 'o yers and we'll see."

"And if there are guards?"

"Then close it again. I know another way in."

She knew without asking that he wasn't about to tell her what it was unless it was necessary. "All right." She raised her hand to press her ring into the niche, but he stopped her with a tug at her shirt.

"One thing about guards. If we're spotted, we run. No fightin' and no killin'."

"With your short legs, I don't think we're going to be outrunning anyone."

"I'm faster than ye think, lass."

"Call me Mya. I'm not a lass. And if we get cornered?"

"We don't get cornered."

"Fine. If we have to run, you go as fast as you can and I'll follow." She lifted her hand, then stopped again to look down at him. "Or I could tuck you under my arm and carry you."

"Don't even think about it, la—er, Mya."

She grinned at him and pressed her ring to the niche. The light winked out, and the two heavy stone slabs slid aside.

The corridor beyond was blissfully empty.

"Now I'm following you," she whispered as they stepped through. She closed the door.

"Right. This way." He turned to the right and she followed.

He opened the same locked door she and Lad had passed

through with the emperor, his hands moving so fast that she barely had to pause, then moved down the corridor lined with cells. The odor of confinement was less rank than she remembered, and there were lamps at regular intervals. Many of the cells were full, but everyone slept, and their passage made no stir. To Mya's horror, he continued on until they stood before the two very familiar doors of the emperor's torture chamber.

"Bugger!" The Gnome peered at the heavy padlock that hung from twin ringbolts set into the stone beside the door. "Well, we'll have to use another way up."

"Can't you unlock it?" She regretted her words as soon as she said them. She had nearly died in that room, and would sooner have walked into a dragon's den than step into it again.

"O'course I can unlock it, but we can't lock that chain behind us, and the jailor on rounds might see. Then we'd be double buggered, so it's no good. Not to worry. I know another way."

Mya said a silent thanks to whatever sympathetic deity seemed to be watching over her. She suppressed a shiver as she turned her back on the door and followed him. They retraced their steps all the way, then continued on to the room where she and Lad had dined with the emperor. Instead of a dining table set with silver and porcelain, however, the room was bare.

The Gnome strode across the far wall and eased a slim metal blade into a tiny crack that looked like a seam in the stonework. Something clicked, and a panel slid up. The opening was barely two feet square.

Though less cunningly hidden than the dwarf doors, Mya hadn't detected it. Immediately, she knew its purpose. "A dumb waiter?"

"Aye. Didn't plan on climbin', but you shouldn't have any trouble."

"And if I couldn't climb it?" She looked up the narrow shaft. It wouldn't be as difficult as climbing across the portcullis bridge with Lad.

"I know other ways, but not so easy on the other end." He slipped climbers onto his hands and feet, ingenious little devices with metal tines for fitting into the seams of brick or stonework. "Next stop, the kitchens. Come along."

He scrambled in and up the shaft. Mya followed.

A half hour later, she was completely lost. They'd traversed the kitchens, two more secret passages, and a bedroom with a sleeping couple, evaded a strolling pair of imperial guards, slipped into a library, and finally into another secret passage behind a bookcase. She wondered how he kept it all in his head.

"Now we're back on the right track." He patted the dusty stone wall and grinned. "This'll take us right to the royal chambers. All seven."

"Seven?"

"Aye, the emperor's, the empress', and five more for princes and princesses. They called this passage the Emperor's Eyes. Word is, he spied on his family usin' this."

"Which emperor?"

"Dunno. One of the early ones, when they were still buildin', I guess. Come on."

They tried two bedchambers to no avail. At the third, he stopped at the door and glanced at Mya. She pressed her ear to the stone and heard breathing.

"Someone's sleeping inside."

"Right. Quiet now. Not a sound."

She nodded, and he worked the catch that opened the door. It swung silently inward. Dim lamplight revealed a wide fireplace, a four poster bed, several dressers and cabinets, and a small bookshelf. It also revealed a sleeping crown prince.

Finally!

Mya eased forward and retrieved the note she'd prepared from the list Lady T had given her. She'd included a few details about Hoseph as well.

The prince half reclined against his pillow, a book open in his lap. The flame in his bedside lamp barely sputtered.

Mya regarded him for a moment. He looked younger close up, his beard lighter, the lines around his eyes smoothed in sleep. She placed the bound note against his book and eased her hand away.

The Gnome tugged at her sleeve and jerked his head toward the secret passage, impatient to go. She hadn't known he was right behind her, probably ready to lop her head off if she tried to assassinate Arbuckle. She nodded, but looked back at the crown prince again, wondering why this man was so different from his father, the tyrant?

The crown prince stirred in his sleep. The book shifted, and the note rolled away. His eyes fluttered in the dim light, and one hand groped for the lamp.

Shit!

Without willful thought, Mya's hands moved. One extinguished the lamp, and the other clapped over the waking prince's mouth.

CHAPTER XXII

Shadows invaded the darkness and coalesced into a man.

Hoseph stood perfectly still, an ear cocked close to the building's back door to listen. Other than a persistent ringing in his ears, he heard only a faint murmur of voices from inside, but not loud enough for them to be just inside the door. He didn't know if this was a school, orphanage, or if Mya had simply invited street children to live there as cover, but he had little doubt that she would post a night watch of some kind. There were no lights to be seen now, but earlier, from the burned-out building across the street, he'd watched three lights on the third floor wink out. He felt sure that Mya slept in one of those rooms. None of the drapes had been open, and the old man had closed the shutters on the first floor at sunset, so Hoseph had gained only a bare glimpse into the back hallway when one of the children returned. A glimpse was all he needed. Steeling his nerves, he stepped into the Sphere of Shadow, then into the inn's back hallway.

After a brief bout of dizziness, he heard a clink of crockery and a whisper from an opening to his left. The kitchen, no doubt. At this time of night, the cook wouldn't be working. Hoseph didn't care who was making the noise unless it was Mya was sneaking a midnight snack, but, he had to make sure. He'd check every room in the place until he found her.

Invoking the talisman, he rematerialized just beyond the kitchen door. Waiting until another surge of dizziness and a stab of pain behind his eyes subsided, he peered around the corner.

Low lamplight revealed two rough-and-tumble children at the kitchen table. They tore chunks from a loaf of bread, trading a knife back and forth to slather on butter from a pot. Happily, they munched away and chatted in whispers.

Some sentries. Hoseph suppressed a sneer. *If this is the best Mya can do, killing her will be easy.*

The memory of the fight in the emperor's interrogation chamber tempered his confidence. There would be nothing easy about killing Mya. Anyone who could survive a fight with blademasters could murder a priest of Demia in an instant. He needed to remain vigilant.

Hoseph took a step down the hall, and a floorboard creaked faintly underfoot. He froze. The two children in the kitchen seemed not to notice, but he couldn't risk discovery. Despite the effects invoking his talisman was having on him, he had to use it.

Hoseph flicked in and out of the shadows to the bottom of the servants' stairs, then again up to the first landing. There he steadied himself, pressing his thumbs to his temples to massage away the pain behind his eyes, and listened again. Nothing penetrated the persistent ringing in his ears that seemed to grow louder now in the silence.

Leaning out into the hall of the second floor, he saw no one in the faint glow of a street lamp through the draperies at the end of the hall. Foregoing his talisman for now, he crept down the hallway, testing each board as he put his foot down. The first doorknob turned easily in his hand, and the hinges creaked faintly as he opened the door. The room was too dark to see anything, so Hoseph flared Demia's pearly radiance in his palm. Empty. The bed was without linens, the curtains drawn closed.

Hoseph checked every room on the second floor. All were empty and unused. This wasn't a school or orphanage after all, not with so many empty rooms. Mya was simply using a few street children as cover and cheap security.

Back at the stairs, he doused the glow of magic and flicked in and out of shadow to the next landing. At the top, he paused again until the pain faded, then peered into a hallway lit by a wall lamp turned low. The doors here were farther apart, the rooms apparently larger.

Naturally, she'd pick the best for her own.

He considered the lighted windows he'd seen from outside and discerned which of the doors must belong to those rooms. Three rooms: Mya, the old man he'd seen earlier, and…who else? The only other adults he'd seen were the two servants who had left with the setting of the sun. No matter. He would find Mya. If the others got in his way, he'd kill them as well.

He blinked through the shadows to the nearest of the three doors and put his hand on the knob. It wouldn't turn. Bending, he peered through the keyhole. The dim lamp on the bedside table illuminated a bed. The coverlet draped across a sleeping body topped with a mop of dark hair.

Mya!

Movement drew his gaze to a small boy sitting cross legged beside the bed. He rocked gently forward and back as he bent over something in his hands. The child was watching over her, a human guard dog to alert Mya if anyone broke into her room.

What a vile creature you are to use children so.

The child presented a problem. He might be small, but he could not doubt sound an alarm, waking Mya. Hoseph saw only one solution.

It's her own fault, he rationalized. *A woman who uses children to guard against assassins must expect them to be treated as combatants.* She left him no choice.

Hoseph flicked into the room behind the boy and invoked Demia's blessing. *May your soul find its final home.*

A quiet gasp of surprise and a brief stiffening were all the boy could manage before his soul fled his body. Hoseph lowered the tiny corpse to the floor. He had done what he had to do. The child was in a better place now, free of pain and the life of ridicule and prejudice that he would have had to endure.

Hoseph felt no such pity for Mya.

Stepping over the child's body, a floorboard creaked faintly underfoot. He winced, but Mya didn't stir. Demia's blessing flared in Hoseph's hand as he prepared to send her soul to whichever of the Nine Hells best suited her. But as he reached out, the pearly light illuminated the angular features and strong nose of a man.

Not Mya!

In fact, Hoseph recognized the man as Lad's assistant. The man who had foiled his attempt in Twailin to kill the traitorous Sereth.

How did he get here? Where—

"Knock!"

Hoseph whirled. In the pearly light of Demia's power, he glimpsed a hellish face, contorted and snarling. Then something smashed into his shoulder with stunning force, pulping flesh and snapping bone. His magic faded, and the darkness of the room spun around him for an instant before he hit the wall and slid to the floor. Pain blazed through his shock as the broken bone in his arm grated. He heard a shout, then the dreadful creature loomed out of the darkness.

"Knock!" it screamed as it raised a club high, ready to smash Hoseph's skull.

The invocation of soul searching burst from Hoseph's lips as if Demia herself raised a hand to intervene. Divine magic pulsed outward from the priest, lashing through the fearsome creature. Its scream rattled Hoseph's ears, but the club fell from its grasp and it stumbled back. Hoseph struggled to stand, and noticed Dee flailing in a tangled blanket. If he could dispose of these two quickly, he might still be able to kill Mya when she came running to help her friends. Death glowing in his hand, Hoseph stepped forward.

Arbuckle stirred as the book started to slide off his chest. He'd fallen asleep reading again.

Oh, bother... Barely awake, he struggled to open his sleep-gummed eyes as he reached out for the bedside lamp. Before he could touch it, the room plunged into darkness and a hand clapped over his mouth.

Terror lanced through the prince like a bolt of lightning, wrenching him to total wakefulness. He drew breath to scream, clawing at the hand on his mouth, but couldn't budge the iron grip. Grabbing the slim wrist, he strained to pull it away, but it moved not an inch. At any moment, he expected a knife to slit his throat.

"Quiet, prince!" The bare whisper so close to his ear fueled the fear already ripping through him.

Arbuckle lashed out blindly, but another hand caught his wrist and forced his arm down to his side. The sheer strength of his attacker chilled his blood. What was this creature?

"Stop that! We're not here to kill you, just to deliver a message." The grip on his wrist eased and let go. "If we wanted you dead, you would be, so just hold still."

The prince froze, his mind racing. We? How many intruders were there? And if they weren't here to kill him, then what? Kidnapping, torture, ransom? He could see nothing in the darkness, only sensed the shape beside the bed. If he could knock over the lamp on the bedside table, maybe his guards would hear and come to his rescue. Before he could act on the plan, the voice whispered again.

"We didn't intend even to wake you, but brought you a note." He heard the rustle of paper beside the book on the bed, and a roll of parchment was pressed into his hand. "It lists those involved in the plot to assassinate you."

That stopped Arbuckle cold, and he stopped struggling. *Assassination?* There had been two attempts on his life already, and this person knew who was behind them. He reached up and tapped the hand covering his mouth. He had questions…so many questions.

"No, prince. I can't stay to chat." The voice was clearer now, feminine with a sardonic lilt. "You must martial your allies, keep them close, and trust *no* one on that list!" The iron grip on his mouth eased a trifle. "I'm going to release you, but if you cry out, we'll have a problem. Trust me, prince; we're here to help you. Nod if you agree to remain quiet."

Arbuckle didn't want to know what she'd do if he refused, so he nodded.

"Good. So long, prince. Try to keep that royal head on your shoulders." The hand slipped away, and the shadow in the darkness moved.

"Wait!" he whispered. "Who are you? What—"

No answer. No sound of a footfall or a door closing, either.

Arbuckle fumbled for the matches on the table and struck one.

The room was empty. Not a single sign that anyone had come or gone other than the roll of parchment on the bed.

"Gods of Light…" Arbuckle lit the lamp, his hands shaking so badly that he burned his fingers. He turned up the flame and cast about the room, looking for any sign of his visitors. Nothing. No gaping hidden passage, no open window. *How in the Nine Hells did they get in?*

Arbuckle drew breath to shout for his guards, but held it as the whispered words came back to him. "Trust no one on that list." He glared at the parchment tied with black ribbon lying on his bed. Did he dare open it? Could it be a trap? Some dire magic to murder him?

If we wanted you dead, you would be…

Don't be an idiot, Arbuckle. He snatched up the scroll and slipped off the ribbon. The note didn't say anything the shadowy woman hadn't already, but the list of names brought him up short.

Five nobles and three magistrates… Graving he would have guessed, but Duchess Ingstrom and Duke Seoli had both been trying to marry their daughters to him. It disturbed him to learn that people he'd met with over the past week—actually had dined with— were planning to kill him. He'd suspected, but now he knew…or thought he knew. Could he trust this shadowy visitor?

She didn't kill you, Arbuckle…

The last lines of the note made his blood run cold.

> High Priest Hoseph is their ringleader. He seeks to regain the power he lost with the death of your father. They plan to employ Archmage Duveau to kill you. We don't know how or when, but the attempt will be before you are crowned emperor.

"Duveau?" Arbuckle couldn't believe it, didn't want to believe it. The archmage was the most accomplished wizard in the empire. How could anyone defend against someone of that power?

The answer to that question was simple, something Arbuckle had learned from innumerable history books. It was the reason the Imperial Retinue of Wizards had been assembled in the first place: Fight magic with magic.

Martial your allies, keep them close…

Arbuckle went to his desk and penned a note. To martial his allies, he had to be sure exactly who they were. The list of people he trusted implicitly was very short indeed.

Dee bolted awake at Knock's bellow. A pearly glow filled the room.

Hoseph!

The glow disappeared with the sound of a meaty crack, then a crash and gasp as someone hit the wall.

Dee lunged, struggling to free himself from the sheets and reach the crossbow propped against the night table. As his hand closed on the weapon's stock, his foot caught in the sheet and he tumbled to the floor.

"Pax!"

Cursing his clumsiness, Dee fought to his feet and aimed the crossbow at the crumpled bundle of dark cloaks against the wall. Then Knock stepped in his way, her club raised high. Before the blow fell or Dee could tell the girl to move, a pulse of deeper darkness slammed through him.

Moirin died in his arms... His father shouted in rage, his belt lashing... Mother's bloody split lip... Cruel laughter as his dagger misses the target...

Every dark moment of Dee's life—ridicule, loss, failure— crushed his soul. His knees folded, and he pitched forward onto the bed. The stock of the crossbow smacked him in the mouth, and the familiar tang of blood touched his tongue.

Knock's anguished wail shivered the air, drawing his gaze. The girl dropped her club and fell to her knees. Her eyes swam with horrors unknown. Dee dared not guess what haunted the poor girl so; his own humiliations were bad enough.

From amidst a rumpled pile of robes, Hoseph struggled to his feet. The pearly glow flared again, and the priest reached down for Knock.

No.

Dee squeezed the crossbow's trigger.

The bolt vanished into the dark robes, and Hoseph staggered back, gasping. The glow vanished from his hand, plunging the room into darkness. Dee's despair eased, allowing him to fumble for another bolt. Recalling how Hoseph blinked in behind Sereth, he flung himself back against the wall, his hands working mechanically, cocking and fitting the bolt in the crossbow by touch. He shouldered the weapon and scanned the darkness, his fingers trembling on the trigger, waiting for that pearly glow.

Nothing. No light, no sound save Knock's soft sobbing and the thunder of footsteps outside in the hall.

"Dee?" A key rattled in the door's lock.

Dee lowered his crossbow as lamplight swept in. Paxal stood there with several urchins. Some stared at him, others stared at Knock curled in a fetal ball on the floor, sobbing and rocking back and forth. Gimp stared at something beside the bed, out of Dee's sight.

"Oh, no." Dee vaulted over the bed. Tiny lay there as still as a stone. Dee touched the skinny chest, probed the side of the thin neck, but felt no pulse. The boy's heart had stopped. *Hoseph...* "Gods take that sonofabitch and send him to the hottest hell there is!"

"He *dead?*" Gimp jostled her friend's shoulder to no effect.

"Knock!" Kit rushed in and wrapped her arms around her friend's heaving shoulders.

More urchins arrived, feet pounding on the wooden floors. Pax handed his lamp to Nestor. "Dee! What happened?"

"Hoseph." Dee stood, his teeth clenched so hard he could feel his pounding heart between them. "Knock saved my life, but Tiny must have been in the way. Is everyone else okay?"

Paxal looked around. "Everyone's here but Mya. She's still out."

"I was just in the kitchen with Twigs havin' a bite." Nestor stared down at Tiny in horror. "We didn't see nothin'."

"How'd he get up here without us hearin'?" Twigs gripped his sticks so hard his knuckles turned white. "Doors are still locked closed."

"He must have used magic to get in. I've seen him do it before." Dee rose and went to where Hoseph had stood and reached to turn up his bedside lamp. "Knock tagged him with her club, but then he did...something. Some spell or curse that knocked both of us flat. He was going to kill Knock, and I..." Kneeling, he felt around, found a wet spot. Dabbing it with a finger, he examined it in the lamplight and confirmed his suspicion. Blood. "Yes, I put a crossbow bolt into him, but he got away."

"I'm thinkin' *we* got away." Paxal's frown made him look old. He knelt beside Gimp and lay a hand on little Tiny. "Or most of us did."

CHAPTER XXIII

In the Sphere of Shadow, he felt no pain. Of course, that made returning to the real world a dread, for Hoseph knew there would be pain aplenty waiting for him. His arm was broken, and the assassin's shot had struck him in the side of his hip, the iron head lodged in bone. Neither injury would kill him right away, and Demia's grace would heal his wounds in time, but the bolt would have to be removed.

Where to go?

Could he trust anyone? The authorities were still searching for him, and there would be questions at any temple in the city. What about another city? There would still be questions, surely, but at least his likeness wasn't pinned to the posterboards empire-wide...yet. Then there was the matter of trust; someone was going to have to cut the bolt out of his hip. Who did he trust to hold that knife?

Lady T?

Did he trust her to cut the bolt from his hip? He had botched her perfect setup. The guildmaster might just pull the bolt and stick it in his heart for failing to kill Mya.

No. Hoseph dared trust no one but himself. That left him only one option.

Pain snatched the breath from his lungs as he returned to the real world, safe in the guild archive. His right arm hung limp, the bone broken just below his shoulder, but he could still flex his fingers. Rest and Demia's grace would suffice to heal it, but he couldn't wait for the pain to ease before he tended to his other, more serious wound.

The crossbow bolt had struck him in the left side, and putting

297

weight on that leg sent agony lancing through his hip. Struggling to keep from screaming with every movement, he lit a lamp and eased himself down onto the chair at the desk. Here, the tools he used to prepare scrolls for inscription lay gleaming and awaiting his need.

The scissors intended to trim fine vellum worked equally well to cut his robe from around the crossbow bolt. Hoseph gritted his teeth, careful not to bump the bolt as he worked or move his broken arm. Once the bloody material was cut free, a cleaning rag wiped away the blood.

Gingerly, Hoseph probed the wound. The shaft protruded from his flesh just above of the hip joint. The bleeding wasn't bad, thank Demia, but the head of the bolt had lodged in bone. Just touching the shaft felt like a knife being twisted in his hip. And he couldn't just pull it out; if the head was barbed, it would snare muscle and skin. It had to be cut free. Hoseph uttered a prayer for strength, and felt Demia's grace steady his hand and still his fears.

I must do this.

He picked up his razor from his kit and checked its edge. It was made for shaving, not for parting flesh, but it would do. Next he placed a roll blank vellum between his teeth. It wasn't likely that anyone would hear his screams, but he couldn't take any risks. Biting down hard, he positioned the razor's edge where the bolt's shaft met his skin.

With a deep breath and another prayer to Demia, he pressed the blade into his flesh.

His scream didn't quite escape the vellum, and the soft material saved his teeth. When the edge of the razor met bone, he dropped the blade and plunged his fingers into the bleeding wound, probing for the head of the bolt. Dark blood flowed freely, slickening his fingers, but he could feel the barbed head. His incision had freed it of tissue, but the tip was buried deep in bone. Gripping the steel head as best he could, he pulled, but his fingers slipped and the shaft remained lodged in place.

Dizziness threatened to overwhelm him, darkness edging into his vision. *No! Please, Demia! Give me strength!* If he fainted and fell out of his chair, the bolt might break and he would be even worse off. He should have lain on his pallet to do this, but couldn't move now.

His vision cleared, but still, he couldn't get a grip on the bolt to pull it free. He'd have to use both hands.

Moving his broken arm sent more pain lancing through him, but he was able to grip the shaft. Slowly, careful not to break it off, he levered the bolt back and forth. Every movement elicited agonizing stabs through his arm and leg. Closing his eyes against the torture and biting down to stifle his screams, he pried the bolt's iron head free from bone and flung the bloody shaft aside.

Yes!

The agony eased to mere pain, and he could breathe again, he could think. Hoseph clapped the bloody rag onto the wound to staunch the bleeding and let the roll of vellum fall from his mouth.

Rest now. I need rest. That's all. The priest pushed himself up out of the chair and took a step toward his bedroll. Standing, however, turned out to be a bad idea. Darkness swam up from the floor to overwhelm him. For a moment, Hoseph wondered how this could be; he hadn't invoked Demia's talisman. He felt himself falling, but not into the Sphere of Shadow. His bedroll felt as hard as stone when he hit, but his mind was already spinning away into a black pit of oblivion.

Mya tapped the Gnome on the shoulder when they crossed into Midtown. "I don't need to go back across the river. Follow me, and I'll get you your money, then you can you take this thing off my neck."

"Eh?" He squinted up at her. "You live north of the river now?"

"Yes." Mya grinned down at him. A few hours ago, his knowing where she lived would have bothered her, but he'd done right by her, kept their bargain, helped her warn the prince. "You followed me to the *Tin Dulcimer*, didn't you?"

"Aye." He grinned back. "Ye said to check into yer claims. I was just bein' careful."

"So follow me now, and I'll get your money."

"Ye can keep yer money." He muttered a word in gnomish and the metal encircling her neck expanded.

Surprised, Mya slipped the ring over her head and handed it to him. "Thanks, but I'll pay you what we agreed on. Nothing personal, but I don't like to owe anyone favors."

"Ye don't owe me nothin'." The Gnome shrugged. "Ye already paid plenty by savin' that blue blood's life."

A thief who doesn't want money… Mya couldn't deny that she could use the funds herself, so she didn't push it. "Have it your way, as long as were even."

"We're even."

She started to turn away, but paused. "You're not so bad for a thief, Gnome."

"Me name's Torghen." He muttered another word and put the now-tiny ring into a pocket. "And ye ain't so bad either, fer a murderer."

"Thanks, Torghen."

"Think nothin' of it. Let me know if ye need anthin' lifted for ye. I get thirty percent of appraised value, and I do the appraisin'."

"I will." Mya didn't think she'd ever need anything stolen, but one never knew.

She turned and walked away. When she looked back, Torghen was gone. She wondered if he'd follow her home, and realized that it didn't really matter. She'd already trusted him with her life.

Mya only detoured twice on the way home to circumvent patrols of caps. Fatigue and grime from the dusty passages in the palace seemed to have invaded her bones, but she felt good. Maybe she'd saved the prince's life. She turned her key in the back door, dreaming of a bath and a bed. Inside, however, she found Dee standing in the hall with a loaded crossbow in his hands, the weapon not quite pointed at the door.

Her stomach lurched at the expression on his face. "What happened?"

"Hoseph came to kill you while you were out." He motioned her toward the common room. "You should sit down for this."

Dread hollowed her stomach as she followed Dee into the common room. Pax and the urchins sat all around, loaded crossbows in hand, faces like headstones, grim and cold. She looked from one to the next and did a quick count. They were short one urchin. The dread opened into a pit of despair.

"Who…"

Paxal nodded to a small, blanket-wrapped bundle. "Tiny got in his way."

"Tiny? No!" Mya dropped to her knees beside the bundle, her hands shaking as she reached out.

"Mya, don't." Dee put a hand on her arm. "He's gone. There's nothing you can do."

Brushing the bundle with her fingertips, she envisioned the little boy and his crooked smile as he offered her food. Then what Paxal said came to her. *In the way…*

She'd ordered the urchins to watch over the adults as they slept. Her order had cost Tiny his life. Mya had seen an inordinate amount of death for her years, and dealt no small amount of it herself. She'd even seen dead children before. But never had she caused a child's death. The pit of despair within her filled with guilt, overflowed, and spilled into her soul.

"It wasn't your fault, Mya." Dee's hand closed on her arm.

"It was." Standing, she brushed off his touch and the tears that had sprung to her eyes. "He was coming after me."

"You don't' know that," Paxal said. "He could've been after Dee for kickin' his ass in Twailin."

"He *was* trying to kill me." Dee shrugged and took a step back from her. "He was in my room."

Not likely… Hoseph might kill Dee if he recognized him, but he had been here for Mya. But none of that mattered. Tiny was dead, and it was her fault. She'd accept the responsibility.

"Tell me what happened. I want details, Dee."

"I was sleeping in the third-floor, back-corner room when Knock's shout woke me. Hoseph was right beside the bed." Dee swallowed and cleared his throat. "His hand was glowing, but Knock smacked him with her stick. Before I could get a shot at him, he…cast a spell that knocked us both down. It felt like…like my mind had been kicked in the gut."

"Like every bad thing that had ever happened to you happened again all at once." Mya gut clenched as she remembered that feeling.

"Yes, exactly that." Dee continued. "Hoseph got up and reached for Knock, and I managed to put a crossbow bolt into him. I don't think I killed him, but I hit him. There was blood on the rug.

He vanished before I could reload, and…then we found Tiny. He was on the floor beside the bed. That's just about it."

Mya's mind raced. Hoseph knew where she lived. He must have followed her from the teahouse yesterday. But if so, why hadn't he attacked her last night? It didn't matter. He'd come here to kill her, and all he'd managed to do was murder a little boy.

A sudden thought tweaked her mind. Might the priest have learned where she lived from someone else? Torghen? If the gnome had betrayed her, Hoseph would have known she was out tonight… Why would he attack? She looked back at Dee. *Was he here to kill Dee?* Had he planned to destroy her support system by killing her allies? *By killing Tiny?* No. She had no way to know why he'd chosen this night to attack, but she felt sure that she'd led him here, and he'd come to kill her. It was her fault.

There was only one thing to do.

"Pack everything up. We're out of here first thing in the morning." She started for the stairs. "Pax, I'll need you to find—"

"We ain't leavin'."

"What?" She turned back. "Who said that?"

"I did, ma'am." Digger frowned and shook his head. "We never had no place like this before, and we ain't gonna let nobody run us out."

"You don't understand, Digger. It's not safe here. We've got to leave. If we don't, Hoseph will come back and one of you might get in his way again. I won't let that happen." She looked from face to face, but none of the urchins moved.

"That's what I was going to tell you." Dee dropped into a chair. "I thought we should leave, too, but they all said no."

"This isn't up for a vote! We're leaving!"

"There ain't nothin' to say he won't find that place, too. What we gonna do if he does, just run to another?" Digger shook his head. "Nope. Ain't gonna happen."

Mya stared at them in open-mouthed shock. In five years as Master Hunter, never had a subordinate refused an order. Now she was being contravened by a bunch of kids. "We can't stay! It's too dangerous!"

"*Everything's* dangerous, Miss Mya." Gimp bit her lip, looking to her friends, then back to Mya. "You can't run from it. You gotta

302

face it. You gotta fight it."

"Right. That's why we're a gang. We fight." Digger drew his knife, a real dagger this, not a rusty kitchen knife, and buried the tip in the table top. "We don't run when some rat kills one of us. We kill him right back!"

"Knock!" Knock slapped her stick into her hand with a loud pop.

"You can't fight Hoseph!" Mya bit back the desperation honing her temper. Yelling at them wouldn't help. "He can blink in anywhere now that he knows where we live."

Dee shook his head. "Not anywhere, I think. He was in my room, and the door was still locked, but I don't think he can just materialize anywhere he wants. The first time he came to Lad's house, he knocked on the front door. The second time, he appeared in the front hall. I think he has to see where he wants to pop in at least once. Maybe he saw my room through the drapes."

"All the more reason we should leave. He's been in here, and can pop in any time he wants." Mya raked their faces with a glare. "We can't fight that!"

"Master Dee shot him, and Knock whacked him good." Digger retrieved his dagger and brandished it. "He ain't immortal. He pops in, and we pop him."

"And if you don't, another one of you dies." The last thing she needed now was a rebellion. Mya glared at them, but the urchins just glared right back.

"Might want to think it through, Miss Mya." Paxal furrowed his brow. "They got a point. Yeah, he knows where we live, but he'll also know we're ready for him. Knock and Dee hurt the bastard. We can have more hurt waitin' if he tries it again."

"And when do we sleep?"

"Different room ever night, and leave lamps on so he don't know which one we're in." Nails examined the tip of the nail protruding from his stick. "And we rig up trippers to tangle him up if he uses that magic to pop in here."

"He's the wasp, but we's the spider!" Gimp nodded and the others with her. "We done that before, too."

Mya's brow furrowed at their chatter. "What are trippers?

"This." Digger pulled from his pocket a ball of heavy waxed

catgut, the kind fishermen used. "We rig our webs, and put broke glass on the floors where we don't walk. He pops in, gets tangled, and maybe even falls and gets cut up. We take turns sleepin', just like Knock watchin' over Master Dee." Digger put the twine away and patted the crossbow on the table. "Buy us some more of these pig-stickers and we'll stick this pig for you."

"Crossbows *are* easy to use. We could train in the cellar." Dee suggested.

Mya looked from face to face once again, and saw no way to fight them. Some Grandmaster she turned out to be. She couldn't even control a pack of street kids.

Rubbing her eyes, Mya cursed under her breath. The fatigue and stress of her foray into the palace wore on her, and now this. She felt grimy and tired, but she doubted she'd be able to bathe or sleep. The former required privacy, for she couldn't let anyone see her tattoos, and the latter required calm, which she knew wouldn't come tonight. She saw Tiny's crooked smile behind her closed eyelids.

Damn it!

"Okay, fine. If we're going to do this, we're going to do it right." Lessons from her long-dead master flicked through her mind. Traps, snares, alarms...a Hunter's stock and trade. "We set up your nets, and broken glass in likely places, and rig bells on the wires, but nothing on the first floor. That has to be clear if someone knocks on the door. And we have to have escape routes. If Hoseph torches the building, we have to be able to get out. Dee, set up watch schedules and sentry posts. Nobody's alone at any time, and someone's always watching over *anyone* who's asleep. If you're on watch, you sit with your back to a wall so he can't pop in behind you. He's more likely to try at night. Darkness favors his tactics, so daytime's probably safer for us to rest. Pax, outfit everyone with whatever weapons they're best with. Crossbows are good if they don't have to reload, and we can set up a target in the basement for practice. Digger, you clear your ideas with me before you do anything beyond what we've discussed. Is everyone clear on this?"

"Yes, Miss Mya," they all said.

"Everyone get busy," Digger ordered, gathering his urchins. "Master Pax, we need more catgut, hammers and nails. Nestor, you get us as many broken bottles as you can scrounge." He tossed his ball of twine to Nails and said "Start with what we got. Gimp, you set up our routes if there's a fire. Oh, and rope would be good, too, if we gotta go out a window. Master Pax?"

"On my list. I'll go out shopping as soon as it's light." Pax got up and looked at Mya. "Don't you worry about Tiny, Miss Mya. I'll take care of him when I go out."

"Fine." Mya clenched and unclenched her fists. This would put them all in danger, but setting traps seemed somehow more satisfying than running away. She'd been hiding for weeks. It was time to face her fear.

"You look like you could use a mulled wine." Paxal started for the kitchen, grabbing an urchin in passing. "Come on, Twigs. Nobody's alone!"

"No wine, Pax." Mya met his questioning look. "Blackbrew. I need to stay sharp. I will, however, wash up. I've been crawling through musty passages all night."

"Water's already on to boil." He continued toward the kitchen.

"I'll watch for you." Dee stood and picked up his crossbow.

Mya opened her mouth to argue with him, but there were no arguments left in her. "Fine. I'll just get my things and—"

"I set your things out in the washroom before I went to bed."

She scowled at him. "Dee, your efficiency would be irritating if it weren't such a comfort."

"Lad always just found it irritating." He tried to smile, but it fell short.

"He would." Mya took another long look at Tiny's wrapped body and gritted her teeth. "Come on."

Dee closed the door to the washroom and flipped the bolt. The air in the chamber was already thick with steam, moisture beading on the stone walls. The cave-like room was centrally located in the inn's cellar, with a fireplace in one wall, a huge copper tub, and a drain in the floor. It had an earthy scent, but had been well scrubbed to keep the constant damp at bay. He swept the room with his eyes one last time as Mya sat down on the dressing chair and started removing her soft leather boots, then turned his back to her and focused on the door, crossbow at the ready.

"Thank you for watching for me, Dee."

A boot fell to the floor, and the chair creaked.

"I knew you'd be keyed up and tired. I thought a bath would be welcome." He concentrated on the swirling patterns of the woodgrains in the door.

"I'm filthy, too. We crept through about a hundred miles of dusty passages."

The other boot fell, and he heard the rustle of cloth.

"So you got the message to the prince?"

"Yes, but he woke up." Mya's snort of laughter almost brought Dee's around but he stopped himself. "I think I scared him half to death, but I don't think he got a good look at me."

"I sure hope not."

Silence stretched, and he heard more cloth rustling.

"I'm sorry about Tiny. It was my fault. Hoseph was after me."

"I think you should blame Hoseph, not yourself." As Dee traced the swirls of woodgrains with his eyes, a flick of motion in the burnished brass doorknob drew his attention. "I remember Lad mentioning the glowing hand when Hoseph tried to kill his informant, and I saw it when he tried for Sereth. I woke up to that glow and thought I was dead." A dark reflection moved in the burnished brass and Dee looked away. Maybe he should have had Gimp watch over Mya. "That's how he tried to kill Sereth. But that other magic...the thing that brought all the horrible memories... Is that what happened when you and Lad were fighting the blademasters?"

"Yes." She sighed and the chair beside the tub creaked again. "It knocked me on my ass. Lad saved my life. I couldn't move for a moment, but he seemed to be less effected by it." Her voice always sounded different when she spoke of Lad.

"That's odd." Cloth rustled again. How long did it take disrobe? He remembered the dark cloth he'd seen on her arm and wondered what it was. Dee refused to let his eyes drift to the reflection in the doorknob. Even though he could discern no detail, Mya deserved her privacy. "With all he's been through, I would have thought having it all dredged up at once would kill him."

"He was already in pain." There it was again, that twinge in her voice.

"I know." Dee had seen Lad's pain, so Mya's words made a morbid kind of sense. To someone suffering from a horrible wound, the pain of a scalpel might go unnoticed. He suspected that Mya harbored her own pain. Dee considered what he knew about her. She was a loner with no apparent friends or family. No lovers, though, at least once, she'd paid for the services of a prostitute. That secret would go to his grave with him. All he knew about her past was what Paxal had told him, and he wasn't about to ask Mya for details. "He seemed...better when we met him on the road."

"Did he tell you about Kiesha?"

"Yes." Dee heard the splash of water, and his eyes flicked involuntarily toward the doorknob. A dark shape moved there, and he wondered if the wrappings he had seen on her arm covered her whole body. Was it armor of some kind? Did she never take them off, even to bathe? Was that part of her secret? "I can't believe they did that to her. Why?"

"The Grandmaster was...he was worse than Saliez." More splashing, and he looked away. "The two were cut from the same cloth. No wonder the guild's a mess when it's run by maniacs who torture for recreation."

"No wonder..." Dee rubbed his eyes and blinked away the desire to yawn. His nerves felt like they'd been dragged through broken glass. "Good riddance to—"

Something clacked on the stone floor, and Dee whirled, visions of dark mists and murderous priests flashing into his mind. He swept the crossbow in an arc, looking for something to shoot, but Mya had only knocked the scrub brush from the bathing table. Her arm and shoulder were out of the tub, reaching for the brush. A fine tracery of black runic tattoos shone on her skin, twisted shapes hard to focus on. They writhed like snakes before his eyes, as if possessing a life of their own...but not.

The crossbow started to slip in his sweaty grasp. He caught it before it fell to the floor, though his jaw might have followed it there if he hadn't clamped it closed. Then his eyes met Mya's and he whirled away.

"Sorry!"

Silence, then a splash and sounds of Mya scrubbing. Not a

word. Dee's mind spun. He wondered if he should say something, apologize again. What had he really seen? Dark symbols on her skin that seemed to move... *Magic*! *Of course*! That explained all the rumors of the fight at Fiveway Fountain.

Dee kept his mouth shut and his eyes focused on the door. Another splash, the rustle of a towel, then more silence.

"Dee, I need to explain something to you."

"You really don't, Miss Mya." He swallowed, his hands sweaty on the crossbow. Would she kill him for learning her secret?

"I really *do*. I need to tell someone, and I know you'll understand. Turn around."

"Miss Mya, I don't—"

"Turn around, Dee. *Now*." Command edged her tone.

Dee didn't know what to expect. He was still her subordinate, but he remembered the eagerness in her face when she greeted their arrival. Something had changed in their relationship, though he wasn't sure how. Dee turned slowly

Mya stood wrapped in a towel, her arms, shoulders, and legs exposed. Black tattoos writhed on her exposed skin from neck to wrist to ankle, every inch of exposed flesh covered in magic.

"This is how I survived the fight at Fiveway Fountain and the fight with the blademasters. I know you've heard how Lad's wife cut my throat. It wasn't fake. The blademasters did worse." She brushed one inked arm with the fingers of her other hand. "These are my secret. This is how I survived."

"They're..." Dee couldn't tear his eyes away from the black tracery on her pale flesh, how the lines moved and blurred.

"I know." Her voice ached with pain. "I may not be exactly human anymore, but—"

"*What?*" He looked up into her anguished eyes. "No! You're..." How could he say it? How could he tell her what he really wanted to?

"What I am I made myself, Dee, and I'd do it again!" The pain had transformed to defiance, her eyes flinty. "If I hadn't done it, I'd be dead."

"You don't understand!" It came out harsher than he'd intended, and her eyes narrowed. "That's not what I *meant*."

"What *did* you mean then?" Mya's eyes were narrow, and her

voice accusative.

I'm walking on dangerous ground here. She might kill him for it, but Dee couldn't lie to her. *Maybe it's the truth she needs to hear.*

"They're…beautiful."

Mya's face flushed, and her lips pressed together hard. She stared at him for a moment as if she thought he might be mocking her or lying outright. He opened his mouth to explain, but she shook her head, one sharp jerk of negation.

"Turn around, Dee."

"I'm sorry." Dee whirled and fixed his eyes on the door. He wanted to explain what he meant, but he knew that tone. He listened to more splashing, then she brushed past him, dressed in her voluminous robe, her secret hidden once more, a bundle of dark cloth in her arms.

"Get some sleep." Mya opened the door and slipped through without looking at him. "We've got a lot to do tomorrow."

"Yes, Miss Mya." He followed without arguing, without saying what he really wanted to say. What else could he do?

CHAPTER XXIV

Nothing, sir." The guard brushed his knees of dust and looked chagrinned. Two of Ithross' most trusted people had spent the small hours of the morning going through the prince's chambers with a fine toothed comb looking for any sign of a secret passage. "If there's something there, it's got to be hidden with dwarf magic."

"Very well." Ithross turned to Arbuckle. "I'm sorry, milord."

"There's *got* to be a passage somewhere, or they travelled using magic and the palace wards are useless. Of course, I guess we have to consider what the note says, and who conjured the wards." The prince resumed his pacing, refusing to sit. He had also refused to eat and sleep. This had not been a restful or productive night.

"We'll search again, milord."

"Yes…please." Arbuckle had only shared the truth of the intruders' visit with the few he trusted: Ithross, Tennison, Baris, and his scribe, Verul. Ithross had been apoplectic at first, then enraged that someone had invaded the imperial chambers. The captain had handpicked a few guards and knights to entrust with the information. Most of those were in his sitting room now, while a few others covertly searched the palace for signs of entry. Arbuckle paced and obsessed. *How…how had they gotten in?*

Then something the guard said stopped the prince in his tracks. "Dwarf magic! That's got to be it. Dwarves built the palace. They've know every stone! Summon *them* and have them search!"

"We'll summon the clan elders, milord, and post guards tonight."

And I spend another sleepless night… The captain had suggested that he move to another room, but Arbuckle had refused. Moving might alert Duveau.

Fight magic with magic… It was Arbuckle's only hope if Duveau was truly planning to kill him. That was why he'd invited one more person to potentially entrust with the information he'd received last night.

A knock at the door halted the prince's pacing. He nodded, and a door guard reached for the latch.

"Master Keyfur, milord," the hall guard said.

"Admit him." Arbuckle clenched his hands behind his back and tried to look calm.

"Milord Prince." Keyfur stepped into the room and bowed gracefully, his rainbow-hued robes brushing the floor. "You summoned me?"

"I did." Arbuckle's eyes flicked to the guards manning the door behind Keyfur. Their hands rested on their swords. Should this turn out badly, they were ready. The prince was betting his life that they could react fast enough to save his life if Keyfur started to cast a spell. "Come in. Can I offer you something?" He waved a hand at a table laden with all manner of food and beverages.

"Actually, I have not yet broken my fast, and that blackbrew smells absolutely heavenly. Thank you, milord." The wizard stepped to the table and poured a cup from the silver service, adding three cubes of sugar before reaching for a spoon. Keyfur seemed perfectly at ease, though his eyes flicked from face to face. "Something dire has occurred from the look of your guests' dour faces, milord. How may I be of service?"

"I'll be blunt, Master Keyfur. I've received information revealing another plot to take my life." Arbuckle watched the wizard sip his blackbrew. The cup remained steady. The previous two attempts on his life were known to the mage, so the revelation of a third had evidently come as no surprise. "I asked you here because I'm in need of magical protection."

"I see. And why, may I ask, did you not summon Archmage Duveau?" Keyfur sipped again and reached for a scone from the silver tray. His face remained utterly guileless. Either he was a very good liar, or knew nothing.

"Because the conspiracy to end my life reaches deep into the palace."

The cup in Keyfur's hand wavered ever so slightly, and the scone paused halfway to his mouth. "But, milord, we interviewed *everyone*."

"Yes, I know. You say that you personally determined the truth of questions put to Archmage Duveau."

"I did." For the first time since Arbuckle had known Keyfur, the wizard's amiable demeanor faltered. He put the scone down on a porcelain plate and brushed his fingers on his robe. "You suspect Archmage *Duveau*?"

"I find myself in need of people I can trust, and Archmage Duveau is *not* among those people."

"He...*isn't*?"

The shock on the wizard's face seemed genuine, but that didn't mean Arbuckle's plan couldn't still fall apart. He had no idea how close the two wizards were. They seemed very different, Duveau, dour and irascible, Keyfur, flamboyant and gregarious. The prince was betting that the two had only a professional relationship, not a friendship. He couldn't remember ever seeing them in the same room at the same time save for a few state functions attended by the entire retinue.

There was also the possibility that this midnight warning was nothing but a plot to sow discord and suspicion among the Retinue of Wizards, denying him their full protection, just as the blademasters of Koss Godslayer had been taken from him. There was only one fact to counter that theory—Arbuckle was still breathing. If his midnight visitor had wanted him dead, he would be. Why go to the trouble to sow convoluted plots to weaken his defenses when a dagger in the dark would have done the deed all too easily? That made the list of conspirators in his pocket difficult to refute.

"No, I'm afraid he is not." Arbuckle took a steadying breath, letting it out slowly. "I've received information that states plainly that the archmage has been recruited by a conspiracy of nobles and magistrates to end my life."

"That's..." Keyfur's cup trembled in his hand until blackbrew slopped over the side. He cupped his hand beneath it to catch the dribble, then put the cup down. "Pardon me, milord, but this is unprecedented. I...don't know what to say."

"Say that you're loyal to both the empire and me, and that you can keep me alive." Arbuckle fixed his gaze upon the wizard, watching for any sign of evasion.

"On the first two points, milord, let me assure you that I am your loyal servant." Keyfur bowed carefully, glancing sidelong at the stern guards, apparently cognizant of the position he was in. "As to the last, I'm unsure if I or any other wizard in the Imperial Retinue could oppose Archmage Duveau."

"Why?"

"Because he is *archmage*, milord." Keyfur shrugged as if that explained everything, but everyone in the room just stared at him blankly. "The entire retinue united might be able to stand against him, but individually…"

"I can't *trust* the entire retinue, Master Keyfur. I'm trusting *you*. Now tell me why Duveau is so invulnerable."

"Not invulnerable, milord, but he has earned his position as archmage. Duveau is learned in many spheres of magic, and is more proficient in most than any other among the retinue, perhaps in the empire."

"Yes, but I don't know what he's *capable* of." Arbuckle pursed his lips. "Can he bring the whole palace down on my head, stop my heart with a wave of his hand?"

"He could not, milord. He cannot manipulate dwarf-wrought stonework, and is not versed in death-magic. That I *do* know. He's also not immune to the effects of his own magic." Keyfur looked around the room as if unsure how much he should say.

"Please be frank, Master Keyfur. I trust everyone in this room with my life. We need to know what we're up against."

"Very well. His greatest prowess is in the manipulation of earth-based elements." He gestured toward the ceiling, the knights, the window. "Stone, metal, even glass, which is, after all, nothing but fused sand, he can bend to his will. He could easily fend off a sword, but he would have to know the stroke was coming. If a rock fell from a parapet and he didn't see it, its impact would kill him."

"Well, that's good news," Sir Calvert said.

"Forgive me, Sir Knight, but it is *not* good." Keyfur gestured at the armor clad warrior. "Duveau could easily wad your armor into a ball…with you inside it." He turned back to the prince. "And do the same with any metal-clad guard or warrior."

"Bloody hells…" Sir Calvert muttered, then nodded

apologetically to Arbuckle. "Pardon, milord."

"No, I want everyone here to speak freely. Please, Master Keyfur. What else?"

"Most of the palace itself is dwarf-wrought, and therefore beyond his skill to manipulate. He's less apt with magic that manipulates the other elements; fire water, air, life, and death."

"*Death* is an element?" Ithross looked aghast.

"It is, but necromancy has been banned in the Empire of Tsing for centuries, Captain, and rightly so. Duveau will not be raising armies of undead to assail us. He's also not as learned as some of us in the more esoteric disciplines of magic. I can bend light and create some pretty illusions, for instance, that he can't penetrate. Mistress Ellis is more proficient with runemagic. However, none of the retinue would last long in a duel against Duveau, I'm afraid." Keyfur looked around at the crowd. "He is…formidable."

"What might we use against him?"

"As I said, metal weapons would likely not reach him if he was aware of the attack." Keyfur furrowed his brow as the knights and guards traded worried glances. "Fire can certainly burn him. Bone, wood, ivory, and horn are likely materials for more useful weapons and armor."

"The swordmasters of the far west wear wicker armor, milord," Ithross said.

"Yes, and it's no match for a decent weapon," Sir Calvert countered with a frown.

"Your pardon, milord, but if Duveau has been named as an assassin, why not send him away?" Keyfur lifted his abandoned cup of blackbrew and downed it at a single swallow. "Once outside the palace, even *he* can't breach its magical barriers."

"Even though he's the one who put those barriers in place?"

"Yes, milord. A door or wall is a barrier, after all, even to the one who built it."

"Well, that's something." Arbuckle chewed his lip and resumed pacing. "In answer to your question, I have no actual evidence against him or the conspirators save a scrap of paper from an unknown source. Though I doubt it, this could be an elaborate fabrication to discredit me or lower my defenses. If I have Duveau or the other conspirators arrested or expelled without charges or evidence, there would be repercussions."

"I see." The wizard looked thoughtful. "And do you know when the attack will occur?"

"The note said that he would strike before I'm crowned emperor."

"That leaves us little time to plan." Keyfur nodded. "You must wait for him to make his attempt, then thwart him."

"Or find hard evidence of this plot."

"That's not likely, milord. Duveau is an intelligent man. If he's going to strike, there'll be no warning." The wizard's eyebrows rose. "Which begs the question of how he plans to accomplish the task and escape the palace. You're rarely without company, milord. There would be witnesses."

"Well, I won't be without guards even when I sleep, I'll tell you that!" Arbuckle thought of his midnight visitors and shuddered.

"Could he make it look like an accident, or frame someone else?" Ithross asked.

"That's entirely possible." Keyfur nodded. "Yes, if it appeared as if someone else committed the crime, he would remain blameless."

"But how do I keep him from killing me if we don't know when or how he'll strike?"

"Keep some guards close who wear no metal, milord, but they must not appear unusual in any way. Also, I should remain at your side whenever possible." Keyfur nodded to Ithross. "I can tell your guard captain what to look for if Duveau should attempt to strike using a doppelganger or cause a distraction with a simulacrum."

"You mean a *disguise?*" Ithross asked.

"A magical disguise, yes. Duveau's aren't as good as *mine*, but they are convincing."

"But you can't stay by my side constantly without tipping our hand that we know something."

"Your pardon, milord, but I can." Keyfur smiled and withdrew a tiny crystal from a pocket. "With your permission, milord, I'll demonstrate."

Arbuckle tensed, and Ithross stepped between him and the wizard. At the captain's hand signal, several more guards formed around the prince.

"I want to see this, Captain." He had to trust someone. "Proceed, Master Keyfur."

"Thank you, milord." Keyfur pressed the crystal to the center of his forehead, and uttered a phrase that seemed to evaporate in the air before the mind could grasp its meaning.

Keyfur vanished.

Everyone in the room stirred uncomfortably.

"I'm still present, milord, and standing in the same place. I can maintain this as long as I concentrate on the spell. If anything happens to me, or I have to cast another spell, the bending of light that renders me invisible will fail."

"I understand." Arbuckle nodded, and the mage suddenly reappeared.

"A doppelganger might look like someone you know, but be Duveau. A simulacrum is a construct that can act like a person, but won't stand up to close scrutiny. They can't speak, have no bodily functions like sweat, tears, or body odor, and they don't bleed." Keyfur pursed his lips. "I can't best Duveau alone, but I should be able to hold off his magic for a time. A minute, maybe two, at most. I might surprise him with a trick or two long enough for someone else to kill him, but not while I'm protecting you."

"We'll have wooden armor and bone weapons made, milord." Ithross said. "Archers with bone tipped arrows will ward you whenever possible."

"A fine idea, but it will take time to attire the entire knighthood in wood and horn." Calvert still sounded skeptical. "And it'll cause rumors. Squires will talk."

"We begin with those of us close to the prince, then anyone else in close proximity, but only those we trust absolutely. Word mustn't get out that we're doing this." Ithross looked grim. "And we must limit your exposure, milord."

Arbuckle nodded, and looked down at the rings on his fingers, then fingered the golden circle on his brow. "By the Nine Hells, I'm wearing enough metal right now to sink a skiff."

The knights chuckled nervously, but Arbuckle's valet, Baris, stepped forward and bowed. "Pardon me, milord, but you needn't if you don't wish to."

"What?" Arbuckle looked to Baris questioningly. "What do you mean?"

"I mean you needn't wear metal, milord. There are paste mock-ups for display. Your grandfather had them made after the theft of a jewel from his crown."

Arbuckle knew the story; there were few who didn't. "Well, I suppose that would fool a casual glance, but I can hardly wear them at court."

"You could, milord, and nobody'd be the wiser. They're quite convincing. Your father used to wear the paste crown for formal occasions because it's so much lighter than the real one."

"He did?" Arbuckle tried—and failed—to picture his tyrant father wearing a paste crown. He had never suspected.

"Yes, milord."

"That solves part of the problem, but hardly the rest." Sir Calvert rapped his metal-clad knuckles against the breastplate of his armor.

"Is there no way to neutralize Duveau's magic?" Arbuckle asked.

"None that I know of, milord." Keyfur shrugged helplessly.

"Wonderful." Arbuckle resumed pacing, chewing his lip and wracking his brain for some idea that might save his life. "We must all try to think of some way to thwart Duveau. There's more of concern here than my life. There is an empire at stake, ladies and gentlemen."

Hoseph woke to the cloying taste of old blood and a persistent ache between his temples. That he woke at all came as a cold comfort. He blinked eyes gummy with sleep. The lamp had burned low, revealing only dim shapes. Nausea threatened as he tried to rise, but he swallowed it down. He worked his tongue around his mouth and found no broken teeth, though he must have bitten his tongue or cheek when he fell. Demia's grace had healed his wounds as he slept, but he was still sore and his head ached, either from the trauma of his wounds or his use of the talisman.

What time…no, what day *is it?*

Forcing himself up, he paused on hands and knees to allow the dizziness and nausea to ease, then stood. Leaning on the desk for support, he turned up the lamp. The amount of dried blood on the floor, chair, and his ruined robes explained his weakness. His failure, however, weighed even more heavily upon him than the aftermath of his injuries. Mya had slipped his grasp. Once again, a task he had thought straightforward had turned out to be more than he had anticipated. This time, he'd nearly lost his life as a consequence.

You're no assassin… Forcing himself to realize that simple truth could only aid his cause. There was no shame in admitting defeat in the face of a competent adversary. Mya had cleverly surrounded herself with crude but effective defenses. He had neutralized one child defender, not expecting a second one wielding a club. Fortunately, Hoseph had other resources he could draw upon to deal with her precautions.

He stripped out of his blood-crusted garments and poured water into the basin, then scrubbed himself thoroughly. The cool water washed away the scabbed blood to reveal a livid pink scar on his hip. The wound was healed, but Demia had left him a reminder of his failure. *Good…I won't underestimate my adversary again.*

After toweling dry and bundling the bloody clothing to be discarded later, he knelt on his bedroll to shave. His hands shook enough with his lingering fatigue to nick his scalp a few times, but he took that small pain as another reminder of his failure. Finished, he donned a new robe, sat on the floor, and recited his morning prayers, giving thanks to the Keeper of the Slain for his gifts, for every beat of his heart, and for the solace he knew he would receive when it beat no more. A cool calm spread through him.

He ate a meager meal of bread, cheese, and hard sausage, washing down with water. While he ate, he thought of his next step. When he stood once again, his knees barely trembled, though his head still throbbed. Was that also a reminder?

Hoseph withdrew the silver skull from his sleeve and gazed into its deep black eyes. Demia's gift stared back at him without judgment. His prayers had brought comfort; how could the use of Demia's gift bring such discomfort? He felt as if he was missing something important. He couldn't deny that his headaches and fatigue were getting worse. Demia would not harm her disciples, but she might remind them of their failures, or punish if one misused her blessings. Was Demia displeased with him?

The Keeper of the Slain cares not for the machinations of kings, queens, wizards, or commoners. The old mantra brought comfort. Though his hip still ached, and his head throbbed in time with his heartbeat, his injuries had been healed by his goddess' grace. He was still one with the Demia, and his use of the talisman was necessary.

Hoseph invoked it once again and felt the mists devour his physical form, sensed the swirling nothingness of the Sphere around him. He took solace in the brief abeyance of his nagging aches and pains before reluctantly continuing on to his destination. Lady T's sitting room coalesced around him. Midmorning light streamed through the windows, and he realized that he'd slept late.

Lady T looked up from a sheaf of papers. She'd apparently become used to his frequent comings and goings, for she didn't even start. "You're as pale as death warmed over. Did something frighten you terribly?"

"No!" Hoseph bristled. "I found Mya's refuge. However, her defenses are considerable, and I was injured."

One immaculate eyebrow arched. "Is she…"

"As far as I know, she's alive."

"You mean you *missed.*" The guildmaster's lips pressed together in a hard line. "You said you could kill her, so I helped you find her, and you *missed!*"

"I was attacked and had to flee." Hoseph said it matter-of-factly, as if the memory of being bested by a child and a common assassin wasn't humiliating. "I need you to assign some Hunters to track her. After last night, she'll probably move her base of operations, and I need to know where she goes. Also, contract some mercenaries outside of the guild. She'll be wary, and I'll need people who can actually raise a hand against her. The time for subtlety is over. She's already brought at least one assassin up from Twailin. She's marshaling her forces."

"No." Lady T returned her attention to her papers.

"*What?*"

"I've told you, I'm not going to assign any member of the guild to spy on Mya. She's a skilled Hunter, and likely to spot anyone following her. She'll track them back to the guild, and I'll be implicated. She knows where I live and would kill me. I'll not allow *your* ineptitude to cost me my life." Lady T scratched a signature on a paper and flipped it onto another pile. "If you want to contract someone outside the guild to kill her, you'll do so without my help or knowledge. I can recommend someone reliable and supply funds, but you will *not* use my name."

Hoseph seethed, but could hardly refute her logic. "That will suffice. But time is of the essence."

"Here." She scrawled something on a blank sheet and flipped it across the desk. "Speak to a man named Dagel." She opened a drawer and withdrew a small leather pouch. It jingled when she dropped it atop the paper.

Hoseph tucked the heavy pouch in his pocket and glanced at the paper. The address was in the Wharf District. He wasn't familiar with the exact location, but knew someplace close enough that he wouldn't have to walk far.

Lady T flicked her pen between her fingers, clicking it annoyingly against the desk top. "I wish you'd forget about Mya. We've ignored her this long; a little longer won't matter."

"It will if she thwarts another assassination attempt."

"She can't get into the palace, and even if she could, Mya couldn't stand against the archmage. The coronation is in three days. When is Duveau going to fulfill his end of the bargain?"

"I don't know exactly, but he'll do it before Arbuckle is crowned."

"And if he betrays us?"

"He won't. I have something he wants very badly."

The guildmaster cocked her head. "What did you offer to induce an archmage to commit regicide?"

"It's not something you need to know."

Lady T pouted prettily, then flicked her pen again. "Fine. Keep your little secret, but I think—"

Hoseph didn't stay to hear the lady's thoughts. He invoked his talisman and faded into the Sphere of Shadow. He had to hire some mercenaries.

Mya rubbed her eyes and tried to think. The hammers seemed to be pounding within her head. It didn't help that she hadn't slept well, even with two of her urchins watching over her. Thoughts and worries scurried around her mind like a nest of rats, denying her rest.

Tiny dead...

Hoseph knows where we live...

Crown Prince Arbuckle...

Lady T...

They're beautiful...

Dee's comment befuddled her more than anything else. She knew how to respond to a threat to her safety, an insult or warning, but Dee's compliment had completely blindsided her. She'd always thought her tattoos made her a monster, and he thought they were beautiful? She didn't know how to handle that.

Mya shuddered. She'd spend a lifetime protecting her secrets, keeping herself apart to stay safe. *So, why did you explain your tattoos to him? Why did you show him?* She didn't know, but those questions and a hundred more wouldn't let her rest. Finally, with the first light of dawn, she'd risen, dressed, and begun fortifying their ridiculously vulnerable fortress. The urchins had pitched right in, working as if their lives depended upon it. Which, of course, they did.

Mya could hardly believe what they had accomplished during the course of the morning. If Hoseph appeared suddenly, he'd be in for a surprise.

"We's spiders..." Gimp had said, and her fanciful description seemed apt.

Taut strings of catgut webbed every corridor and room above the first floor. A labyrinth of narrow passages—hard to discern unless you knew where they were—twisted through the tangle. Bells hung from the trip wires at odd intervals, tinkling alarms when disturbed. Three bedrooms were kept free of obstruction, but that would change every night. Dee, Paxal, and Mya would each have two urchins armed with crossbows sleeping in shifts in their rooms. Digger and Nestor would patrol the halls of the second floor. In case of fire—*Gods of Light, please don't let them try to burn us out*—rope lay coiled at each window, and buckets of water and sand were positioned at the bedroom doors.

At midday, Pax called out that lunch was ready, and the urchins bolted through the maze of strings for the kitchen hall. Mya found them stuffing their grinning faces with bread, stew, and sliced fruit.

Dee motioned to her from the kitchen door. "Pax dismissed Cook for a few days, but she made a pot of stew before she left. When that's gone, he's going to make our meals himself."

"I didn't know Pax could cook," she whispered before stepping into the kitchen. The air was still and humid—the windows were all shut tight—but redolent with the aroma of peppers, garlic, and spices. A pot simmered atop the stove; the lunch Cook had left for them. Beside it sat a much larger pot into which Pax was dumping a curious assortment of chicken, potatoes, onions, peppers, and chunks of bacon.

"Can't cook," Pax admitted, "but I figured it best to get the help out of harm's way. If that bastard of a priest comes at us again, it'll be soon." Wiping his hands, he filled three bowls from the smaller pot and nodded to the table. "Have a seat."

"Good thinking." Mya tore off a hunk of fresh, dark bread heavy with nuts and raisins. "We're just about as secure as we can be. I'd like everyone to get some sleep this afternoon. I need to go out."

"Out? Why?" Dee paused in the middle of buttering a piece of bread, concern plain on his face.

"Other than the fact that all the hammering's driving me crazy, I thought I might check the neighborhood for threats." She bit into her bread. Paxal already played mother hen to her, and now it seemed that Dee had picked up the protective attitude.

"That sounds dangerous." Paxal placed the stew on the table and joined them.

"Maybe, but if we're surrounded by assassins, I need to know."

"Can't argue with that." Paxal ate a bite of stew and grimaced. "Damn cook thinks red pepper's a vegetable, not a spice."

Dee reached for a pitcher and poured three cups of lemonade. He placed one before Paxal. "That'll cut the heat."

"Thanks." Pax shortened the contents of his cup by half.

"I'm just wondering what to do if I spot assassins. If they're guild, that means Lady T sent them." She sampled the stew, a heady concoction of sausage, garlic, onions, lentils, and a slurry of spices.

"Do you think she'd do that?" Dee asked.

"Not really." She nibbled bread and sipped lemonade, clicking her nails under the table.

"Stop fidgeting and eat." Pax pointed to her bowl.

Mya glared at him. "I feel like I should be doing *something*."

"You are. You're eating lunch." Pax pointed at her bowl with his spoon, his face set in stern lines of disapproval.

"He's right. We've done all we can." Dee ate, but didn't look at her. "All we can do is wait."

"Like a spider…" The problem was, Mya hated waiting. Dee was right, if the information Lady T had given her was true, if the prince believed her, if they could foil the plan, if…if…if… She thought seriously about murdering the conspirators in their beds, but that would require preparation she didn't have time for, and if she missed one, the others would know she was onto their plot. She couldn't kill Duveau, and couldn't find Hoseph.

You know where I live, you bastard. Come and get me.

"Exactly." Dee ate more stew. "And we should buy you some clothes."

"What do I need? I'm a spinster mistress of an orphanage."

Dee finished his stew and took his bowl to the wash barrel. "If Duveau doesn't kill Arbuckle before the coronation, I think you should go."

"To the *coronation*?" She stared at him as if he'd sprouted wings. "You want me to sneak into the palace in the middle of the coronation?"

"No, I think you should pose as an eligible young lady looking to catch the eye of the emperor-to-be, and go with your noble aunt, Lady T." Dee looked her in the eye as he returned to the table. "Every noble in Tsing will be there, and every single one with a daughter of the right age will bring them along. There hasn't been an unwed emperor in three hundred years, so he's quite a catch."

"And you think Lady T will go along with that?"

"I don't think she can refuse if you show up at her door unannounced."

"He's got a point." Pax nodded.

Mya glared at the old innkeeper. He wasn't helping. "You really think Duveau will make his attempt during the *coronation*?"

"I have no idea, but he's a wizard, not an assassin." Dee shrugged. "I don't think either of us has a clue what he'll do, but he's not supposed to let the prince be crowned. If the prince is still breathing the morning of the event, where else will he be able to be in the same room with him?"

"So he'll do it in full view of hundreds of people?"

"Maybe he'll use magic to make it look like someone else kills the prince." Dee shrugged again. "He could conjure a demon in the middle of the whole show for all I know."

"I don't even know what he looks like." Mya knew little about magic, but she knew some of what it could do. She was evidence of that. "In fact, he can probably look like whoever or whatever he wants."

"And he doesn't know what *you* look like." Dee finished his lemonade. "He certainly won't be expecting the lovely young lady on Lady T's arm to thwart him."

"He's got a point." Paxal looked from Mya to Dee and back.

Mya glared at them both. "There's *also* the point that I don't really want the new emperor to know what I look like." She held up the ring on her finger. "I'm wearing his father's ring. He might actually recognize it."

"A little gold paint will fix that."

"You have answers for everything, don't you?" She didn't want to admit that the notion of walking into the palace in plain view of every noble in the city made her skin crawl. "Answer me this? If I do have to kill Duveau in front of hundreds of nobles and the gods-be-damned emperor himself, how to I get out of there?"

"You tell everyone that you were hired as Lady T's bodyguard, and when the lady saw her emperor in danger, she ordered you to intervene." Dee smiled innocently.

Mya felt the perverse desire to wipe that smile off. "You were never this imaginative when you were my assistant, Dee."

"You never asked me for my opinion." He shrugged and looked down at his hands. "Except with your correspondence."

As much as she hated to admit it, Dee's plan had merit. There was no harm in preparing. "Fine. If the prince and Duveau are both still around for the coronation, I'll go."

CHAPTER XXV

Hoseph looked over the five mercenaries with a mixture of disgust and satisfaction. Three men, a dwarf, and a lanky woman stood ready, armed with short blades and hand axes, torches, oil, and crossbows. They'd not balked at the notion of killing children if they got in the way, nor burning an entire block of Midtown if necessary. For a sword-for-hire, gold trumped morality.

"Ready?"

"Don't know why we can't just bash in the door." One of the men thumbed the keen edge of a hand axe. "Don't like magic."

"Because, you brainless git, they'll be ready and fill you full of crossbow bolts." The woman cocked her crossbow and loaded a bolt. "I like the priest's plan. Pop in, kill everyone, light a fire, and pop out. Clean and simple. No witnesses."

"Don't you call me—"

"Shut up, Rance. Yurty's right." Maul, their thick-necked leader, glared down the other man. "We're ready."

"Good." Hoseph wiped his palms on his robe and tried to ignore the persistent ringing in his ears, pervasive headache, and fatigue. Transferring five through the Sphere of Shadow would be taxing. *Soon, it'll be done, and I can rest.*

He'd been surprised to find Mya and her people still occupying the same building at nightfall. He'd watched for hours that evening. Lights blazed in every window, and he'd caught a glimpse of shadows moving on the third floor. She was dug in, ready for him. Well, he wasn't going in alone this time, and his mercenaries might surprise her. They could touch her even if guild assassins couldn't. And if some of them were killed in the process, well, no great loss. They were mercenaries. Their lives were full of risks.

"Remember, we'll be appearing in the third floor hallway. Mya is deadly. Kill whoever you have to, but she's the target. Distract her long enough for me to get behind her, and the job is done."

They nodded and readied their weapons; Yurty and Rance lit torches. Maul clamped a heavy hand on Hoseph's shoulder, and the rest did likewise in succession. When they were all thus connected, the priest invoked Demia's talisman.

They entered the Sphere of Shadow, and Hoseph knew instantly that this would be more difficult than he'd anticipated. Transferring a single additional person through the Sphere taxed him. Five dragged at him so heavily that he felt as if his soul was being drawn and quartered from the inside outward.

Focus! It will pass as soon as we materialize.

Hoseph envisioned the third floor hall and started the invocation, but felt as if a spectral hand restrained him. Something had changed. He'd experienced this before when trying to materialize in a room where furniture had been moved or people stood about, interfering with his intended destination. He shifted his point of arrival in his mind and tried again, but still felt resistance.

The pressure on his soul dragged at him. He felt as if he might fly apart any moment. Unaccustomed panic threatened. Hoseph shifted his destination closer to the wall near the end of the hall, and the resistance eased. *Finally!* The priest pushed through into the real world.

Screams and gasps of shock greeted him, and for a moment, Hoseph thought one might be his, so fiercely did the pain blossom behind his eyes. He blinked hard to clear his vision, wondering if the incongruous jingle of bells was some strange auditory hallucination. Maul's fingers dug painfully into his shoulder. Something was dreadfully wrong.

Wrenching himself free of the mercenary's grasp, the priest rebounded off of something resilient, certainly not a wall. He flailed an arm for balance, and felt a taut cord catch his hand. *What in the name of...* Hoseph turned and beheld a scene reminiscent of a painting he had once seen in the temple of Xakra the Tangler, Mistress of Webs.

The entire hallway was crisscrossed with strands of heavy twine. The feeling of resistance had saved Hoseph from materializing within the convoluted web, but not so his companions. Maul struggled against the half-dozen strings that pierced his torso and legs, fighting to reach a belt knife. The dwarf hung without a twitch, four strings intersecting his head at various angles, his eyes bulging horribly and blood oozing from his nose and ears. Yurty waved her torch, trying to burn through the strings that pinned arm and legs, grimacing against the pain. The other two men twitched and moaned with taut lines through their chests. Rance lost his grip on his torch, and the flaming brand hung in the air, the wooden shaft transected by a string.

Hoseph had woefully underestimated Mya once again. The shadows he had spied earlier in the evening in the third-floor windows had seemed carelessness to him, not calculated to draw him in. He'd blundered right into a trap seemingly designed to thwart the very attack he had chosen to employ. *How could she have known?*

"Ding a ling! Ding a ling!" came a shrill shout from behind one of the closed doors. A chorus of similar calls rang out, and the priest knew the rest of the trap was about to be sprung.

Hoseph reached into the web of taut catgut and wrenched the dagger from Maul's hip sheath. One slash severed the strings transecting Maul's arm, and he handed over the knife. "Cut yourself free, then the others."

"We're buggered! Get us out of here!" Yurty demanded through gritted teeth as she wrenched severed strings from her body.

"Free yourselves!" Hoseph wouldn't give up yet. "We can still—"

Three doors opened, and small grimy faces peered into the torch-lit hall. Feral grins preceded the glint of loaded crossbows, the nearest only feet away from Hoseph and his immobilized mercenaries. Before Hoseph could react, two of them fired. Thankfully, the urchins apparently had little training. One bolt thudded into the wall, and the other only tugged at Hoseph's robes.

"It's that priest!"

Several more crossbow-wielding urchins surged into the hall, crouching among the maze of twine to aim their weapons.

Maul was almost free, his face contorted in pain and fury. Yurty had managed to burn enough of the strings to reach her crossbow. The weapon, however, was tangled. She twisted and fired at the nearest door. Missing an urchin by inches, the bolt vanished into the darkness. Rance hung limply, his face pale, while the other man struggled feebly to reach a blade. Hoseph had to intervene or they'd all be shot down and his chance to kill Mya would be ruined.

The priest cast forth his soul-searching invocation, sending a pulse of darkness through the hallway. Cries of despair rang out from urchins and mercenaries alike, and weapons clattered to the floor. Yurty dropped her torch into the pool of volatile oil that had leaked from the pierced skin at her hip. The liquid ignited with a whoosh, engulfing the woman in flames. A horrible scream tore from her throat as her clothes blackened and hair shriveled. Tongues of flame licked at the ceiling.

This wasn't going according to plan at all.

Another crossbow cracked, and the bolt buzzed past Hoseph's ear. In the gloom at the far end of the hall, a grizzled old man reloaded a crossbow. Beside him, two more urchins raised their own weapons. Still, there was no sign of Mya.

Hoseph dissolved into the Sphere of Shadow and visualized the hallway behind the old man. Resistance inhibited him again. He shifted his destination again and again, but everywhere he tried, he was blocked. He even tried the room he'd been in before, but no, it, too, must be trapped. He had nowhere to go in the hallway except back where he had been standing, nowhere safe from which to attack. If he returned to the same spot, he would die. He had no choice but to flee.

Perhaps the fire will do the job for me.

Picturing a new destination, Hoseph coalesced on the rooftop across the street, the perch he had spied from earlier in the evening. He sank to his knees as he head swam, gripping the tiles as he fought off the dizziness, and tried to ignore the pain and ringing in his ears. Lifting his head, he watched the growing glow of fire behind the drapes of the third-floor windows.

The first shout snapped Mya out of a fitful, dream-filled sleep. Lurching out of bed, she fought a dizzying disorientation, not quite sure where she was. Then the door opened, and a flickering light outlined Nails and Gimp, crossbows at the ready. The urchins fired their weapons into the hallway without hesitation, then backed into the room.

"It's that priest!" Nails shouted, reaching for another bolt.

Mya snatched her daggers from the night table, dodging as a crossbow bolt zipped through the door and thudded into the far wall. Halfway to the door, a wave of darkness swept through the wall toward her. *Dear gods, no!*

Hoseph's soul-wrenching magic folded her knees.

The sting of a slap across her cheek, hateful words burning into her soul—*I wish you'd never been born*—blood on her hands, blood on the knife, the astonished look on her mother's face as blood pulsed from the severed artery in her neck.

Not real... It's just magic! Focus or you're dead!

Screaming, Mya gripped her daggers so hard she felt the sinews and bones of her hands cracking and popping under the strain. She pressed herself to her feet. Lurching for the door, she tripped over Nails, curled and sobbing on the floor, and slammed into the doorjamb. The impact rattled her teeth—*No pain*—and she blinked as a wave of hot air washed against her face.

Fire... The sight of flames outside the door burned away the lingering despair. A human shape writhed in the inferno. Was it Hoseph? No, the screams were a woman's. Others hung limp, taut strings of catgut piercing their bodies. One hulking man slashed with a knife, trying to fight free. Hoseph must have materialized his assassins right in the midst of their web. *Spiders indeed.* Hoseph was nowhere to be seen.

Damn! She spun, but no killer priest lurked behind her. *But the fire...*

"FIRE!" Mya grasped the bucket of wet sand beside her door and flung the contents onto the burning woman. The flames dimmed, but still spread along the floor. *Oil... They brought oil to burn us out.*

Paxal strove through the maze of strings with another sand bucket, but slowly. Dee emerged from his door, his face pale and sheened with sweat, but his eyes clear and determined. He leveled a crossbow at the assassins and fired. The bolt caught the big man in the chest and he went down with a guttural cry.

But the fire...

"Dee, get your fire bucket!" Mya whirled back into her room and jerked the coverlet from the bed. "Nails! Gimp! Keep an eye out for Hoseph! Everyone watch your backs!"

Mya dashed into the hall, cutting through strings with lightning strokes of her dagger. Leaping over the assassin Dee had shot, she barreled into the burning woman, wrapping the blanket around her to keep the flames from spreading. Together they crashed to the floor. Using the edges of the blanket, she patted out as much of the fire as she could reach. She felt the heat on her hands, the skin blistering and healing before her eyes. *No pain...*

Wet sand spattered across the floor, smothering more of the flames. Then Dee and Paxal were there with blankets, dousing the last remnants of the fire. Mya levered herself up and surveyed the damage. Smoke filled the corridor, and their maze of strings hung in tatters.

"Anyone hurt?" She raked her gaze down the length of the hall. Everyone was accounted for, and all shook their heads to her question. She heaved a sigh of relief and coughed as the acrid smoke filled her lungs.

A gurgling sound came from beneath the smoldering coverlet at her feet. Mya pulled back the blanket and cringed. The woman's face was a mass of blackened blisters, and sooty blood oozed from her shriveled lips.

"Aside from this lot, you mean?" Paxal fired a crossbow point blank into one twitching figure, and reached for another bolt. Reloading, he aimed it at the intruder at Mya's feet and gave her a questioning look.

Mya looked down at the smoldering wreckage that used to be a woman. A memory surfaced—Kiesha, tortured and bleeding. Lad had shown his wife's killer mercy, how could she do any less? A crossbow bolt would be a kindness. Nodding at Pax, she winced as he fired, ending the woman's torment. *Mercy...*

Mya looked to the other trespassers. They were all dead save one. The man lay face down, his legs scorched by fire, but he was breathing. "Leave that one, Pax. I want to ask him some questions."

"Ask him how he wants to die."

Mya looked up, startled by the cold malice in Dee's voice and the bloodlust in his narrowed eyes. He'd never struck her as bloodthirsty, but he seemed to have no problem killing in defense of their home. She held up a restraining hand. "I want to know what faction he works for, so I can visit his boss."

Several strings protruded from the man's torso, and frothy pink blood bubbled from his mouth and nose. Mya wondered if he could even speak. Stepping over a corpse, she reached down, gripped the man's shoulder, and rolled him over.

She jerked at the crack of a crossbow. *Who did Paxal shoot now?*

"Mya!"

At Dee's shout, she looked down. A triangle of feathers stood out from her shirt. It took a second for her to realize that it was the fletching of a crossbow bolt buried deep in her abdomen.

"Son of a—" Mya stood up. A peculiar tugging in her gut sent a wave of nausea washing over her. She felt no pain, but thought she might puke.

Reaching back, she felt the barbed head protruding from her back. This bolt would only come out the way it went in. Mya gripped the head and jerked, felt the length of the bolt pass through her. Another wave of nausea and some dizziness washed over her. She wavered on her feet, and felt Dee's hand on her shoulder.

"You're..." He swallowed hard, his eyes fixed on the bloody bolt in her hand. "Are you all right?"

Paxal was at her side then, his eyes wide and shining. "Mya! Oh, dear Gods of Light!"

"It's okay, Pax. I'm fine. Really. I'll explain later." Mya glared down at her attacker's blood-flecked lips, twisted in a grotesque semblance of a smile. "Well, that answered one question." Flipping the crossbow bolt in her hand, she thrust the bloody point through his eye. The corpse twitched, then stilled.

"He wasn't guild." Dee nodded to the ring on Mya's finger.

"Exactly." Mya thought she should be relieved. "At least this means that Lady T didn't send them."

"Miss Mya?"

Mya looked up. Her urchins were staring at her, some aghast, some grinning. She tried to smile reassuringly. "You all did well. We'll clean this up in the morning. For now, wrap the corpses in blankets. We'll move down to the second floor."

Turning to Dee, Mya clapped him on the shoulder. "Nice shot, by the way."

"Thanks." Dee tried to smile, but it didn't reach his eyes. He glanced down at the spot where she'd been shot, then away.

Mya's stomach flipped. She'd let down her guard and told Dee her secret, and now he had seen for himself what the magic inscribed in her skin could do. It didn't take much to guess what he was thinking. *Monster...*

"Might make an assassin out of him after all." Paxal grinned and turned to the urchins. "All right, you little heroes. You heard her. Go grab some blankets and let's get downstairs. I need some sleep tonight."

CHAPTER XXVI

Arbuckle tensed as the door to the small audience chamber opened. Lately, every time a door opened, he'd half-expected Duveau to walk through and kill him. Now, the day before he was due to be crowned emperor, he was still breathing, but thought he might die of heart failure from the strain. He turned from the view of the gardens and saw that it was only Tennison.

Still alive...

His secretary bowed politely. "They're here, milord."

The prince checked his preparations one last time. There seemed an inordinate number of guards in the room, and two glowering knights as well. Such an imposing security presence might put off his visitors, but if anyone in the empire understood the need for protection, it was Duke Mir. Besides, the clandestine invitation to the duke and his mage, Master Woefler, would have told Mir that this was not a usual greeting for a visiting provincial duke. Princes didn't invite wizards to tea.

"You're sure about this, Master Keyfur?" The meeting had been the wizard's idea, but Arbuckle didn't know Mir well. He'd only met the man once, more than a decade ago. Mir's entourage had arrived only the day before, and Keyfur had informed him that the duke had brought his mage along as a precaution for the dangerous trip over the mountains. Then he'd proposed the idea to ask Mir for help.

"Not *sure*, milord." Keyfur's voice came from thin air only a step away. Arbuckle was just learning to not let the mage's invisible presence unnerve him. "But of all the provincial dukes, Mir opposed your late father's policies most vehemently. If any will support you, he seems most likely. And Master Woefler is a *highly* proficient mage."

333

"But he knows Duveau."

"Only through correspondence, as far as I'm aware."

It seemed strange to put so much trust into people he barely knew, but with his own court conspiring to kill him, strangers might be safer than close associates.

"Very well." Arbuckle faced the door and nodded. "Tennison, show them in."

"Yes, milord." His secretary opened the door and admitted Duke Mir and Master Woefler.

The two approached and bowed low. Mir looked much older than Arbuckle remembered. His wizard, on the other hand, looked rather mischievous, with a wide, boyish smile. The prince hoped Keyfur hadn't overestimated the mage's skills.

Mir straightened. "Milord Prince Arbuckle. You're looking well."

"I am well, thank you. I hope your trip wasn't too arduous."

"It was lengthy, but comfortable, milord."

"I've arranged tea for us." The prince gestured to a small table set with tea. "I'm afraid you've missed most of the balls and dinners leading up to the coronation, but I felt the need to greet you personally."

"Thoughtful of you, milord, but, if I might ask, why have you invited Master Woefler to this?" Mir glance at his mage. "Do you seek some magical consultation?"

"As a matter of fact, yes." He gestured again to the table. "Please."

"Of course, milord."

The three of them sat, and Tennison poured their tea with surprising alacrity for a secretary.

"You'll pardon my secretary serving us, but what we need to speak of here is not for the ears of servants."

"I surmised as much." Mir looked grave as he poured cream into his tea. "We've heard of the attempts on your life, milord. I daresay I was most elated to see you well upon our arrival."

"Were you?" Arbuckle watched Mir closely, but the man seemed sincere.

"I *was*, milord." Mir sipped his tea, meeting Arbuckle's gaze with frankness. "You know that I've opposed your father's policies for years. Your messages and edicts were the most welcome correspondence I've received from Tsing in decades. I've prayed to all the Gods of Light for deliverance, and it seems I have an unknown assassin to thank for it."

The guards stirred around them at the audacious comment, but Arbuckle couldn't suppress a smile. No one plotting against him would say such a thing. Keyfur's assessment seemed to be spot on.

"My father was a monster." Arbuckle dropped a cube of sugar into his tea and stirred it. "My reason for asking you here is in hopes that you might be able to help me live long enough to expunge his legacy from this empire. I've received information that revealed a plot to—"

"Milord, if I may interrupt." Woefler raised a forestalling hand.

"Yes?" Arbuckle tensed again and regarded the man, slim and angular, not young, but not old either. His face looked much younger than his hands, in fact, and that face looked suddenly worried. "Is there a problem?"

"I don't know exactly, milord, but you seem to have taken pains to keep this meeting confidential, and I'm concerned that we may be under some kind of magical surveillance. I don't know what's afoot, but there's magic about or I'm no wizard."

Arbuckle stiffened. For a moment, he didn't know what to do. Had Woefler detected some kind of spying spell, or had Keyfur's magic simply alerted him to the presence of another wizard?

"Milord." The whisper sounded right in Arbuckle's ear, so close he could feel Keyfur's breath on the nape of his neck. "I should reveal myself to avoid any misunderstanding."

"Yes." He nodded to Woefler. "Yes, there is magic about. Master Keyfur, if you please."

The wizard blinked into view at Arbuckle's left shoulder. The only person who started at the sudden appearance was Duke Mir.

"Good gods!" The duke nearly dropped his tea cup.

"Please be at ease, my good duke. Master Keyfur is here to secure my safety.

"Master Keyfur." Woefler nodded to the wizard in greeting. His boyish smile beamed for a moment, then dropped into a look of consternation. "But why are *you* acting as the prince's magical security instead of the archmage."

"Because, if the information I've received is accurate, the next attempt on my life will *come* from my archmage." Arbuckle tried to sip his tea, but found his hand shaking. "Master Duveau has been named specifically as the assassin, recruited somehow by a conspiracy of high nobles and magistrates."

"That's..." Woefler looked utterly stunned. "Pardon me, milord, but that's not good at all."

Duke Mir simply turned pale.

"Yes..." Arbuckle put his cup down. He felt nauseous. "If the attack doesn't come tonight or tomorrow morning, it will come during the coronation. It's supposed to occur before I'm crowned emperor, and the ceremony is the only time Duveau will be in my presence. He hasn't even asked for an audience so far."

"This is dire indeed, milord. Duveau is...a formidable wizard." Woefler looked grave.

"Do you know him well?" Arbuckle asked.

"Only by reputation, milord, but he *is* archmage. That means a great deal!"

"So Master Keyfur has told me." Arbuckle leveled a stare at his visitors. "Frankly, we've made all the preparations we can, but still feel inadequate to the task of defeating him. I asked you here for your help. You, Duke, to allow your mage to aid me, and you, Master Woefler, because you're less likely to have been swayed into this conspiracy than any of the other members of my retinue of wizards. Master Keyfur speaks highly of your abilities."

"Of course you have my permission, milord." Mir looked to Woefler, then fixed Arbuckle with a stony gaze. "Anything you need that is mine to provide, be it my mage or my life, I'll give."

The man's vow struck Arbuckle deeply. It felt good to have someone unreservedly on his side. He took a deep breath and let it out. "Thank you. So, I'm asking for some sound strategy that will foil the plot or some magical aid to thwart or destroy Duveau when he strikes."

"Postpone the coronation." Mir looked at Arbuckle imploringly. "Gods, milord, have him sent away! Have one of your men put a *dagger* in his heart! Even archmages can be killed, they say."

"I can't postpone the coronation without causing major strife to the empire. There are laws my father enacted that must be changed, and I've been thwarted by my own nobility in every attempt to do so." Arbuckle frowned and dropped his napkin onto his plate. "As for dismissing him or having him killed... Though I trust the information I received to a certain degree, I'll not spend a man's life on another's word without hard evidence. If I try to dismiss him, and he *is* intending to kill me, he'll know I've learned of the plot. I doubt he'll go quietly. He would lose everything and gain nothing. If confronted, he could very easily make every effort to kill me regardless of who gets in his way. Hundreds could be killed."

"Pardon me, milord, but won't hundreds die if he strikes at the coronation?" Mir looked ill.

"*Will* he resort to physical attacks?" Woefler asked. "I don't know the archmage's forte', but there are many ways to kill a man with magic. Some are quite subtle."

"Master Keyfur knows his capabilities, and the two of you should speak privately of specifics, but we believe that if he tries to kill me, the attack will be direct and physical. We hope to thwart him and limit the damage." Arbuckle looked to Woefler. "What we really need is some means to immobilize, distract, or kill him quickly."

"I certainly can't stand against him directly, milord." Woefler twitched his lips. "But I have something that *should* distract him. Master Keyfur and I should speak of this."

"Yes, we should." Keyfur looked intrigued. "Milord, if I can protect you for a time, and Master Woefler can distract Duveau, we may give the guards an opportunity to kill him."

"Well, that's something." Arbuckle looked at Keyfur. "We don't have much time to plan. Master Woefler, please speak with Master Keyfur."

"Milord." Woefler stood, and he and Keyfur strolled away from the table, conversing in hushed tones.

"I wish there was more we could do, milord." Mir shook his head. "Captain Norwood said some very good things about you when he returned. I see that his assessment of you was accurate. You're not your father's son in anything but blood."

"No, I'm not." Arbuckle tried to smile. "I trust the captain's well."

"Yes, save for a bit of a limp, and that damned *dog* of his that won't leave his side." Mir laughed shortly. "It crapped a pile the size of a dinner plate in my garden the last time the captain visited."

Arbuckle laughed. He couldn't remember the last time he'd laughed. "I'm glad he's well." The prince rose from his seat and gestured for Mir to remain. "Please, enjoy the tea. I'm afraid I've lost my appetite."

"Milord." Mir stood and bowed. "Thank you for your confidence. We should speak after the coronation, if you would. I think we have much in common with regard to our theories of governance."

"I'd like that." Arbuckle thought that he could probably learn a lot about statecraft from Mir, things that his father never deigned to tell him. He left the room with his guards cordoned around him, heartened that he had formidable allies willing to give their all to save his life.

"Why did I let you talk me into this?" Mya cursed under her breath as Dee tightened the laces girding the bodice of her new dress.

"Because I'm right." Finishing the laces, he retrieved the hat and wig she would wear with the gown. "If the prince is still breathing in the morning, then the assassination attempt has *got* to happen during the coronation."

"True, but that doesn't mean I have to like it." Mya glared at herself in the mirror as Dee fitted the wig on her head. She didn't care for the gown's bright purple color, but trusted Dee's judgment in this more than her own. With the blonde wig and a matching hat and veil, it worked. Black lace sleeves and neck over a flesh-colored sheath covered her wrappings. "Attending this coronation without any weapons will be like going to battle wearing nothing but my scanties."

"But if the guards find any kind of weapon on you, not only will you miss the coronation, you'll probably end up in that new beheading contraption."

"Only if they catch me." Mya frowned at the dark circles under her eyes.

She hadn't slept well since Hoseph's attack. When she did sleep, she dreamt of fire, probably because the scent of smoke pervaded the place. She'd been downing cup after cup of Pax's strongest blackbrew to stay sharp, and her nerves were singing like harp strings.

Now I'm going to walk into an imperial coronation and try to save a crown prince from assassination by a gods-be-damned wizard.

Mya had killed a wizard once before, but the runemage who inscribed her tattoos had known Mya, had trusted her enough to welcome her into his home. Then it was just a matter of shoving a dagger into the back of his skull quicker than he could blink. Duveau, on the other hand, would be ready for a fight.

I must be crazy.

"Well, you might not be armed, but you look *good.*" Dee adjusted the lace ruffles on her sleeves and the drape of the skirt. "Remember to walk like a lady."

"I will." She turned and checked the mirror again. Dee was right; the dress looked good on her. She just hoped it was easier to get off than it had been to get on. She fingered the tiny tabs at her hips. "You sure these will work?"

Dee shrugged and stepped back. "Try it."

"Are you serious? It'll have to be restitched."

"Sure. The stitching's easy, and you really should make sure you can get out of it quickly. Just don't pull too hard. If you break the tabs, you'll have to fight in it."

"Right." Mya bit her lip. Fighting the emperor's blademasters in a gown had nearly been the death of her. *One more thing to worry about.* "Okay, I just pull, right?"

"Right."

Mya jerked the two tabs. With a zip, the specially constructed side seams split from hip to shoulder, and the bodice of the gown fell loose. Mya shrugged out of the sleeves, and the skirt dropped to the floor. She stepped free of the frothy heap easily.

"Well, that worked like a charm!" Dee grinned.

"I hope I don't have to use it tomorrow." Mya took off the wig and placed it on its stand, then ran her hands through her short hair. "What if this whole thing's a set up? What if Lady T fed me a big lie to get me to kill Duveau, making Arbuckle even more vulnerable?"

"That seems an elaborate ruse." Dee cast her a sidelong glance, then snatched up the dress and examined the stitching to be replaced. "You're thinking about this too much."

Mya knew Dee was eying her wrappings, but she didn't care; he already knew her secret. She started to pace, lifting a hand to bite her nails. "How can I *not* think about it?"

"*Don't* bite your nails! You'll ruin the lacquer."

"Oh." She looked down at her painted nails and cringed. "I forgot." She clenched her hands at her sides.

"Would you *please* stop worrying about it?" Dee fixed her with a stare like a disapproving governess. "If Duveau tries to kill the prince, you take him out. If he doesn't, you have a nice time and eat too many confections at the reception. Play your cards right, and you might even get to dance with the new emperor."

"Stop it!" Mya started pacing again. "Telling me not to worry is like telling fire not to be hot. I could be going up against a gods-be-damned *archmage*! I have no idea what to expect from him!"

"And he has no idea what to expect from you." Dee stepped into her path. "In fact, he doesn't even know you're coming. Surprise him, and he won't have a chance. Wizards bleed, just like regular folk."

She stopped and glared at him. "Since when have you been a tactician?"

He looked a little affronted by her comment. "Just because I was your assistant, doesn't mean I don't have other skills. I *am* an assassin, you know."

"I know." She turned away and stalked back and forth across the floor, her mind awhirl. Of course Dee had skills. He was smart and thorough, and had done fine against Hoseph's mercenaries. A wry thought flashed into her mind; if Moirin's boasts were to be believed, he had other skills, too. She glanced at Dee as she turned.

They're…beautiful,

Stop it, Mya…this is Dee. She paced faster.

"You're going to wear a rut in the floor. Would you please try to relax?" Dee stepped into her path again, his dark eyes pleading. "You haven't slept since Hoseph attacked the inn. If you don't get some rest, you'll be exhausted tomorrow!"

Mya sidestepped him. "I'll be fine."

"Fine!" Dee whirled and scooped up the dress. "Worry yourself sick. But if you get yourself killed tomorrow, you're not just letting yourself down; you're letting the whole guild down. The whole *empire*, maybe."

"And that's supposed to make me worry *less*?"

"No, it's supposed to make you realize that if you don't relax, you're *dead*!" He stormed out with the dress, leaving her alone with her worries.

Mya stopped and looked after him. Dee certainly wasn't acting like her normally mild-mannered assistant. But he was right. If she didn't relax, she was dead.

"Wine and a bath. That's what I need…" Mya donned her robe and snatched up her towel. She would pick up Gimp on her way down to the cellar to watch for her.

The scent of the scorched floorboards wrinkled her nose as she emerged from her room. The hall was a maze of strings once again. She bent and wove her way through the path toward the stairs, glaring at Dee's door as she passed.

They're beautiful…

The doorknob turned in her hand before she realized what she was doing. Nails and Nestor sat on the floor playing some game with sticks and stones, their crossbows within easy reach. Dee looked up from where he sat on his bed, her dress draped over his lap, a needle and thread in his hand.

"I need to talk to Dee in private." She held the door open. "Go get something to eat in the kitchen."

"Okay!" The urchins grabbed their weapons and left.

Mya closed the door and met Dee's gaze with eyes that wanted to look anywhere but at him. *Don't do this, Mya…*

"I need to ask you something, but you don't have to answer if you don't want to." She clenched her hands at her sides, trying not to fidget.

"All right." Dee put the dress aside and looked at her patiently. "Ask."

"After Moirin died, did you ever… Have you been with anyone else?"

Pain flickered across his face. "No. Not yet."

"You were in love with her." It wasn't really a question. She knew he had been.

"Yes, but she obviously wasn't in love with me." He crossed his arms and shifted on the bed. "Why the interest in my love life?"

"Because..." She sighed and looked away, unclenching her hands. She looked down at them. It seemed that all she'd ever done with them was kill. "Because I was in love with Lad for a long time. It was stupid. I was a fool, and he's still in love with his dead wife, so he's gone. I just wanted to know if you ever feel...over it." She looked back up at him, her teeth grinding together.

He showed astonishingly little surprise at her admission. "Over it?" He shrugged. "Not really, but it hurts less with time."

"Good." She fiddled her fingernails, longing to bite them. "I needed to know that I won't feel like this forever."

"You won't." He nodded to the towel. "Going for a bath?"

"I was."

They're beautiful...

"Mind if I ask one more question?" *Why are you doing this, Mya? Don't be stupid...* Her conscience was right, she knew, but the rest of her needed something that her conscience didn't.

"Not at all."

"You said...in the washroom...that my tattoos were beautiful."

One of his eyebrows lifted. "Yes, I did."

"Why?"

"Because they are, and I didn't want you to misunderstand me."

"Because you're afraid of me." She could see the fear in his eyes. At least, she thought it was fear.

"Partly, yes, but I wanted you to know the truth, too." He sat up straighter. "You might keep them covered because you don't want people to know your secret, but they're not ugly."

"You don't think they make me a monster?" *Don't do this, Mya...* She told her conscience to shut the hell up.

"No, they don't."

"Would you like to see them again?" She fidgeted with the tie of her robe. "All of them?"

"Mya, I..." Dee swallowed hard, then nodded. "I would."

Mya pulled her robe tie and shrugged out of the voluminous garment. She loosened the end of her wrappings at her wrist, then hesitated and looked at Dee again. His mien remained neutral, attentive, but his eyes gleamed.

"You're sure?" She had to ask.

"I'm sure."

Mya unwound her wrappings, balling the magical cloth as she bared one arm, her neck, the other arm. The air felt warm against her breasts as she unwound the fabric from her torso, her hips, and, finally, from her legs. She dropped the wad of cloth to the floor and stood straight. Dee's gaze roved over her from head to foot, his mouth slightly parted. He looked a little stunned, but not disgusted, as she thought he might be.

"Well?"

"Well..." He cleared his throat. "Well, what?"

"Do you still think they're beautiful?"

"Oh, yes!"

Mya walked up to Dee slowly, deliberately. He stared up into her eyes. Her conscience was blissfully silent.

"Would you like to touch them?"

His tongue darted out to wet his lips. "Very much."

Tell him the truth, Mya! Be honest. He deserves that much. For once, her conscience was absolutely right.

"I'm not in love with you, Dee. Love is a weakness I can't afford. Don't expect me to fall in love, or swoon like a maiden, or write you love notes. It's not going to happen." She met his eyes with firm resolve. "I'm not in love with you, but I need to be touched. I need someone to make me feel...human."

A sweet, peaceful smile graced his lips. "I can do that."

"Then touch me."

Dee lifted his hands from his lap and ran his fingertips up her thighs, her hips, her abdomen...light as feathers, smooth as silk. Mya shivered with the sensation, closed her eyes, and let his touch sooth her tortured soul.

CHAPTER XXVII

Mya stepped off the curb as Lady T's elaborate coach rounded the corner. As the matched team of four clomped past, she hiked up her gown, took two running strides, and hopped up to the running board. The gold latch turned in her hand, and she ducked through the door, landing in a frothy pile beside an astonished man in dress doublet and hose.

"What in the name of—"

"Sorry I'm late, but I simply could *not* make myself get out of bed this morning!" Mya flashed a smile at the man, then at the open-mouthed Lady T.

A cry from one of the coach guards above heralded a bellow from the driver—"Whoa!"—and the conveyance rumbled to a stop. One of the guards leapt down and jerked open the door.

The man beside her brandished his cane like a weapon. "See here now! You'll be out of this carriage this instant!"

"No, *you'll* be out of this carriage this instant, or I'll break that cane of yours and stick it up your arse splintered end first." Mya smiled sweetly.

He swung the cane's golden head at her, but she caught it easily. He tried to wrench it free, but she wouldn't let go. The guard tried to grab her arm through the door, but his hand stopped an inch from her. *Guild.* He couldn't touch her.

"Get out. Now." Mya jerked her head toward the door.

"Terrance!" Lady T's commanding tone drew the man's attention. "Please don't make a scene. My friend here intended to attend the coronation with me, but had a conflict in her schedule. That conflict has evidently been resolved. Please leave us. I'll make it up to you."

Terrance's face reddened, and he snatched his cane from Mya's eased grasp. "Fine!" Shoving past Mya, he dismounted the carriage, turning back to glare at her as he slapped his hat on his head. With his jaw clenched, he bowed to Lady T. "I'll contact you tomorrow, milady."

"Do so." Lady T nodded to the guard. "Drive on!"

"Goodbye, Terrance!" Mya twiddled her fingers and blew the enraged man a kiss.

The door closed and the carriage lurched into motion.

"You picked up on that very quickly. I'm impressed." Mya smiled at her hostess and settled back in her seat, relaxed and comfortable. It was amazing what a good night's sleep had done for her outlook. The rumors about Dee had proven wholly inadequate, and she'd told him so…many times. As sweet as it might have been to stay with him until morning, she had gone back to her own bed to sleep, guarded by her urchins. Mya woke refreshed, still not in love with anyone, and feeling wonderful.

"What in the Nine Hells do you think you're doing?" Lady T's face flushed scarlet, her crimson lips set in a hard line.

"I'm attending the coronation as your guest, just like you told your friend." She glanced back out the window. "He's gorgeous, by the way. Is he any good in bed?"

"Not that it's any of your business, but yes, he's absolutely fabulous in bed." The lady regained some of her composure. "What makes you think I'll take you to the coronation?"

"Two reasons: One, you need me to keep Arbuckle alive so the guild will have rich customers to fleece, and two, if you don't, I'll break your knees and tell *everyone* you had an accident while having intercourse with one of your horses."

"You *filthy*…"

"Stop playing the lady with me, *Lady*, and start thinking like an assassin." Mya jabbed a finger at Lady T. She was through with jokes and threats. "I *told* you what would happen if the prince died, and yet you seem content to keep playing along with Hoseph's mad plan. I've already warned the prince about the impending assassination attempt, so he'll have all kinds of protection. I probably won't have to intervene, but I'm here to make sure nothing goes wrong before he's crowned."

"You *warned* the crown prince? How?"

"I whispered in his ear." Mya enjoyed the woman's skeptical glare. "Now, I'm assuming your invitation to the coronation says something like 'Lady Tara Monjhi and guest,' so I'll be your niece, Moirin, visiting from Twailin for the coronation. I imagine there'll be whole flocks of young women being presented to the new emperor during the reception."

"And if there is trouble and you do have to *intervene*, as you put it, what do I tell the nobility of this realm? That my niece also *happens* to be a magically imbued assassin?"

"No, you tell them that you hired the very best bodyguard money could buy. You'll probably be given a duchy from the emperor for having the presence of mind to order me to save his life at your own personal risk." Mya grinned. "Are we thinking like assassins yet?"

Lady T glowered at her, her eyes flicking down to Mya's dress. "How did you know I'd be wearing lavender?"

"I didn't." Mya noticed for the first time that they matched hues nicely, her gown darker than the lady's by several shades, but close enough to complement one another perfectly. "Sometimes you just get lucky."

Arbuckle pushed aside his untouched breakfast. This was his second, actually. The first had gone cold and been replaced. It looked delicious, but if he ate it, he knew he'd be sick. His stomach clenched on nothing but blackbrew, a roiling pit of nerves and acid. He'd been awake all night, sitting in an armchair surrounded by guards, reading a book of fanciful stories in hopes of distracting his mind from the impending coronation…and the chance that he might not live through it. The dwarven clan elders had shown them the secret passages throughout the palace. Arbuckle's father had sworn them to secrecy, but their oaths had died with him. Arbuckle had ordered them to seal the passages, so there would be no more unexpected midnight visits. Still, he hadn't slept.

Now, a contingent of guards and knights stood quiet and grim, ready to escort him to the Great Hall at the appointed time.

For now, he waited.

"Milord?" The footman proffered the blackbrew pot.

"No, thank you. My head is about to explode already."

"Something stronger then?" The man smiled and produced a silver flask from his waistcoat. "A single malt from Fengotherond. The best, in honor of your coronation today."

"Bless you, my good man." Arbuckle nudged his blackbrew cup over and the man poured a double measure. The cup didn't crack, so it wasn't poison, and the prince could definitely use the whiskey's medicinal properties. He sipped and sighed in bliss, smiling his thanks. "Your name?"

"Getry, milord." He bowed.

"Thank you, Getry."

"My pleasure, milord."

"Milord, it's time."

Arbuckle turned to find Baris with a cushioned golden tray in his hands. Upon the red satin sat his princely accoutrements: a platinum band for his head, a necklace of office resplendent with rubies, and several rings. They were remarkable reproductions—all paste and wood—but they looked like the genuine articles.

"Very well." Arbuckle downed the rest of the smooth liquor in his cup and stood. With great solemnity, Baris placed the mock jewelry on the prince, his movements as deft and sure as ever. When he'd finished, Arbuckle grasped the man's shoulder. "Thank you, Baris. For everything."

"I look forward to seeing to your needs as emperor, milord." The tray under his arm, Baris bowed low and backed away.

"Ready, milord?" Tennison looked regal in his dress clothes and badges of office, his ever-present appointment book in hand. Only the strain around his eyes betrayed his apprehension.

"Hells, *no*, I'm not ready." Arbuckle hoped his sarcasm might break the tension. A couple of the guards hid tight smiles. "But ready or not, we better be at it. If I'm late, they'll probably hire someone *else* for the job."

A few more smiled at that, and Sir Calvert choked off a snort of laughter.

Arbuckle took a deep breath and let it out slowly. "Is the Great Hall in order?"

Tennison nodded, with a reassuring smile. "All is in order, milord, and the guests are entering as we speak."

Arbuckle glanced around the room. The footmen had gone, and only his trusted cadre of guards and attendants remained. "And Master Keyfur?"

"He's with us…in spirit, milord." Tennison winked.

Arbuckle jumped as something unseen brushed his shoulder.

"More than in spirit, milord," the mage whispered. "My simulacrum is in place with the rest of the Retinue of Wizards. It should fool Duveau. I'll be at your side throughout this."

"Good." Arbuckle allowed Baris to place the robe of his office on his shoulders. The chain and clasp had been replaced with gold-painted wood, but the garment weighed heavily on him. There were no more reasons to delay. "Ready then."

They proceeded through the palace in precise formation: knights in the van, Arbuckle with Tennison and Verul centered within a cordon of imperial guards. The sedate march seemed to take an eternity, and Arbuckle looked at things as he never had before. The palace had been his lifelong home, though he'd more often felt like a prisoner than a resident, always under guard, never allowed to leave except with a detachment of protectors, relegated to meeting only those deemed safe and appropriate for a crown prince's company. Only the last few weeks had opened his eyes to the lies he had been fed his entire life about what he should be, what being noble meant, and why his father considered him a failure.

I may have failed him, but no more than he failed the empire, Arbuckle thought. If he survived this day, the prince would become emperor, and the empire would change for the better. If he did not…

The crown prince winced. If he died today, Duke Tessifus—who had argued so vehemently against Arbuckle's reforms—would assume the throne. The laws would not change, the commoners would not receive the justice they'd been promised, and they would revolt. Martial law, oppression, violence, death… An empire of slaves, beaten like curs when they dare to bite their masters…

I can't let that happen. I won't let that happen. A cold resolve settled over Arbuckle as they descended the final flight of stairs to the main level of the palace. *I must survive this day. If I fall, Tsing will fall.*

As the procession turned into the narrow corridors that would bring them to the small corner entrance to the Great Hall, the weight of the mantle on Arbuckle's shoulders suddenly and unexpectedly felt lighter. He straightened and squared his shoulders. Every measure they could think of had been taken to insure his survival. His fate now rested in the hands of the gods and the intrepid souls who had pledged their lives to protect him. He had placed his trust in both, and would live, or die, with that decision.

The entourage paused at the door, and Tennison checked his pocket watch. "Just a few minutes here, milord."

"I'm ready, Tennison." Arbuckle realized with a start that he was telling the truth. He was ready to become emperor...or die trying.

Mya stepped out of the carriage into the inner court of the Imperial Palace, and another world. Never had she seen such grandeur, such a cacophony of color, light, and noise. A thousand people flowed like a river of rainbows, resplendent in colorful gowns and doublets. A low murmur of constant chatter dampened the occasional higher exclamation of wonder and delight. Perfumes and powders filled the air, cloying her senses and making her eyes water. Around the throng of courtiers, imperial guards stood like statues carved of marble, resplendent in spotless white dress uniforms. Servants in imperial blue and gold helped the guests from their carriages and guided them into the flow in an orderly fashion.

Don't stare, Mya! Reining in her awe, she scanned to evaluate her surroundings on a more professional level. Guards with gleaming halberds edged the immense courtyard. More stood atop the inner wall armed with bows. A few knights and squires stood at the gate and flanked the towering doors to the palace proper, gleaming in burnished armor. Of the nobles involved in the conspiracy, she saw nothing. Fingertips brushed her shoulder, and Mya suppressed the reflex to knock them away.

"Put your hand on my arm. That tells everyone we're related." Lady T held her arm out and smiled graciously. "And try not to gawk, my dear. People will think you're provincial."

"I *am* provincial." Mya fluttered her lace fan and tried to look overwhelmed, which wasn't difficult.

"Just don't embarrass me." Their carriage rumbled away, and they joined the flow of color, noise, and fragrance.

"Lady T!" A woman hurried up to greet Mya's escort with a fingertip embrace and kisses that didn't come anywhere near to touching skin. "You look *lovely*! And who's your guest? I thought you were bringing your new beau!"

"This is my niece Moirin, from Twailin." Lady T presented her with little aplomb, her face set in a neutral mien. "Please forgive her rather stunned expression. It's her first time to the city, let *alone* the palace. Moirin, this is Countess Grenfield."

"Milady." Mya curtsied and beamed as if thrilled to meet the woman.

"A *lovely* gown." The countess scrutinized Mya's dress. "Unusual, with all that lace. Is that the latest style in Twailin?"

"No, I had it made here." Mya made a show of turning. "I thought modesty best in the presence of our new emperor."

"No doubt." Countess Grenfield sneered and thrust out her daring décolletage before nodding to Lady T. "Tara."

"Countess." Lady T curtsied, and the countess moved on.

"If your shoulder had been any colder, the countess would have frozen to the cobblestones," Mya whispered.

"Politics, my dear. The countess may out rank me, but she has nothing I need. If I gushed, it would seem suspicious. If you intend to remain in Tsing, you would do well to remember that."

Mya glanced sidelong. "Don't have many friends, do you?"

"Lady T!"

"Baron Remson! Lovely to see you!" Lady T beamed and curtsied to a dashing man in a crimson and gold doublet.

"You're looking especially beautiful today." The baron kissed Lady T's hand, then turned to Mya. "And who's this lovely creature?

"Let me present my dear niece, Moirin." Tara nudged Mya forward, glowing with well-feigned adoration. "She's hoping to catch the new emperor's eye, of course. Her first foray into nobility is proving rather overwhelming."

"Well, she certainly caught *my* eye! Delighted!" The baron lingered over Mya's hand, eying her like a wolf deciding which portions of a lamb might taste best.

"I'm honored, milord." Mya curtsied and tried to look demure.

"Will you be in Tsing long, Miss Moirin? I would *love* to take you to an amusing little restaurant I recently discovered."

"Oh, I don't—"

"She would be *honored*!" Lady T gushed. "Please send your card to my house, Baron, and we can arrange the details."

"I will." He smiled to them both, perfect white teeth flashing before he turned away.

Mya dug her fingers into Lady T's arm. "What in the Nine Hells are you doing?"

"I'm introducing you to society," the lady said. "If you're my niece, it's expected for me to present you as a marriageable prospect. *You're* the one who insisted on accompanying me, so you'll have to play the part."

A continuous parade of carriages deposited more and more overdressed nobility, until the enormous courtyard began to feel crowded. Finally, the entire throng moved like a rising tide toward the towering open doors of the palace.

Mya smiled and curtsied as required, but never stopped scanning the crowd for the assassination conspirators. She would only recognize a few of them, but if they saw her with Lady T, there might be problems later. Soon, the crowd was too thick for her to scrutinize every face, which was both frustrating and comforting. If she couldn't spot them, they couldn't spot her.

As they approached the doors, and the crowd narrowed to a single file, Lady T suddenly turned to her with a worried expression and whispered, "Are you armed?"

"No, but—" Before she could ask why she wanted to know, they reached the door and were greeted by a tall woman in a tight red gown.

"Lady Monjhi! How nice to see you." The woman touched the guildmaster gently on the arm in greeting. "And who is this lovely young lady?"

"Mistress Jeffreys, this is my niece, Moirin, from Twailin."

"Such a pretty young lady." The woman brushed Mya's cheek with one warm hand. "Welcome, Moirin. This must be a big day for you."

"Oh, yes! I'm very excited." Mya couldn't recall ever being

touched like that, but the woman seemed so sincerely delighted to see them, she didn't find it untoward. It seemed almost motherly.

"Lovely, truly lovely!" Mistress Jeffreys waved them on and greeted the next guests in line.

"Well, *that* was close." Lady T eyed Mya with a cocked eyebrow. "Stepping out of line would have been…awkward."

"What do you—" Mya glanced back to see the woman greeting each and every guest with a casual touch. Lady T's question and the woman's curious manner clicked into place. "She's *frisking* everyone?"

"Magically, yes. She's one of the Imperial Retinue."

Thank you, Dee. His instincts had been spot on, as usual.

They passed through the foyer and an adjoining antechamber, both so grandiosely decorated that Mya found herself gaping once again. The sketches in her tour book didn't even start to convey the grandeur. "Will there be seats or pews in the Great Hall?"

"Not with this many guests. It'll be standing room only, I'm afraid." She looked askance at Mya. "Do your feet hurt already?"

"No, I just want to be as close to the front as possible."

"You and everyone else, my dear." Lady T smiled and exchanged pleasantries with yet another acquaintance.

Mya fidgeted as they shuffled forward. They'd never get through to the front of the hall at this rate. She leaned in close and whispered, "We need to get farther forward."

"Through all these people? You're dreaming."

"Work along the *edge*!" Mya couldn't believe she had to tell the Tsing Guildmaster how to work her way through a crowd. "What faction were you before you made guildmaster, anyway? Alchemy?"

Lady T's eyes narrowed disdainfully. "Inquisition."

"I should have guessed." *She'd get along great with Bemrin.* Mya had always considered the Master Inquisitor of the Twailin guild a pretentious fop. He and Lady T seemed to be cut from the same bolt of cloth. She pushed her way along the fringe of the crowd, dragging Lady T with her.

When they finally entered the cavernous Great Hall, Mya caught her breath once again. A jousting tournament could have been held in the room with floor space to spare. Two rows of columns marched the length of the chamber, fluted at top and bottom and inscribed with runes and symbols the like of which she had never seen. The columns soared a hundred feet to a ceiling of mosaic porcelain tiles that glittered in the blazing light of myriad chandeliers and sconces.

At the far end, above and behind a gilded dais, a balcony seemed to float before the legendary stained glass windows, which in turn soared almost to the ceiling. Sunlight ignited the glass and threw colors into the room that rivaled even the assembling crowd. Mya caught glimpses of the dais through the throng, a golden throne and small side tables at the back flanked by intricate scrollwork of gold and gems, all lit with glow crystals.

Torghen would faint dead away...

Mya and Lady T worked their way along the right-hand side of the room, then angled in toward the center, apologizing and excusing themselves as they displaced indignant nobles. When they could progress no further, Mya snugged up against one of the pillars, resting her back against the cool stone as she focused on where the coronation would take place.

Imperial guards stood at rigid attention along the walls and balcony, and knights in gleaming armor ringed the dais. High priests of the six Gods of Light lined up before the gilded steps, ready to bestow their blessings upon the new emperor. Mya cringed when she noticed the crimson-robed high priest of Demia, instantly reminded of Hoseph. Could he have infiltrated, posing as the high priest he once was?

No, he's not that stupid.

She whispered a silent prayer that the priests would have a chance to perform their duty today.

"It's something, isn't it?" Lady T had to lean in close to Mya's ear to be heard over the buzz of excited conversations, her voice vibrant with something Mya couldn't quite put a finger on: ambition, awe, or maybe even reverence?

"It is." Mya couldn't disagree, but saw the opportunity to make a point. "Wouldn't you rather have someone *sane* on that throne, or in charge of your guild for that matter?"

"Our guildmaster *wasn't* insane." Lady T glowered at her. "He was...unusual, but invaluable. He empowered our guild as it never had been before."

"He *perverted* the guild into something it was never meant to be. I saw what he did to a young woman who had displeased him, Tara. He flayed her alive, and *enjoyed* it." She eyed the woman critically. If she had been an Inquisitor, perhaps she had the same predilections. "Tell me you don't think that's vile."

"There's an intoxicating power in the dominion over others, Mya. Eliciting an utter surrender is a heady thing. You may not understand it, but it exists." Her eyes glinted. "And that power can be addictive."

Mya couldn't restrain a look of disgust.

"Provincial *and* naïve..." If Lady T hadn't been born with a noble's air of superiority, she certainly had adopted one. "Did you know there are people who derive sexual pleasure from the infliction of pain, and those who derive it from having pain inflicted upon themselves?"

"No, I didn't." Mya swallowed. "Torture for pleasure is abhorrent."

"Even if the one being tortured submits willingly?"

"Perhaps not then, but the Grandmaster's subjects were *not* willing." She stared into the lady's eyes. "Have you ever lain on a slab and felt a finger probing for the most sensitive spot to cut, knowing that the pain would come, and that there was nothing you could do to stop it? I've endured the blades of a sadist. I watched the gleam in his eyes as he cut me open. Have you?"

"No." Lady T wrenched her gaze away. "But he made me watch him do it to others. He...instructed me in inquisition."

"And that's why you feared him. You knew you could end up under his knife." And that was why Tara had become his guildmaster. He knew he could control her through fear, just as he controlled the rest of the empire.

"Yes."

"That's one thing that will never happen to you if you work for me, Tara." Mya met the guildmaster's renewed gaze openly. "If I ever kill you, you'll never know what hit you, and you won't feel the pain."

"That's such a *comforting* thought." Lady T's whisper dripped sarcasm.

"After working for your last Grandmaster, it *should* be."

Tara pursed her lips. "Perhaps I could—"

A fanfare of trumpets split the air, reverberating through the room and cutting off all conversation. The time for talking was over.

The coronation of Tynean Tsing III had begun.

CHAPTER XXVIII

Arbuckle started at the peal of trumpets. The stout shot of whiskey had set his mind wandering to the few truly joyous memories of his youth: chasing butterflies through the palace gardens…a favored book with pictures of dragons…listening to stories of knights in armor slaying evil ogres… The fanfare shattered his pleasant recollections and jolted him back to the real world and his duty to the empire.

"Milord, it's time."

"Of course, Tennison." Arbuckle watched his secretary bow and join the line of senior palace staff filing into the Great Hall.

Verul bowed and said, "I look forward to many years of recording your words, milord," then quickly followed Tennison.

"Thank you." Arbuckle swallowed a lump in his throat at the loss of the two men's company. The servants had become his closest confidants, friends, even, in the last few weeks. Something he'd never truly had before.

Another peal of trumpets, more prolonged and elaborate this time, announced his entry. Checking his accoutrements, Arbuckle nodded to the knights in the fore. "Gentlemen and ladies, let's be at this."

"Yes, milord!" They ushered him forward.

"Are you still with me, Keyfur?" Arbuckle whispered just before stepping through the door.

A hand rested on his shoulder for a moment, comforting in its solidity. "Yes, milord."

"Crown Prince Arbuckle, Heir to the Throne and the Empire of Tsing!" The herald's voice reverberated throughout the hall.

The prince entered to a rumble of polite applause from the

assembled crowd. The knights surrounding the dais snapped to attention and saluted, and the high priests and priestesses bowed. As Arbuckle mounted the steps, his guards peeled away and took up their stations. Only the emperor-to-be continued to the highest platform, where he could be viewed by all.

An easy target.

Turning at the prescribed spot in the center of the dais, Arbuckle swept the room with his gaze. To his left stood the senior palace staff, Tennison and Verul among a half dozen others. Some he knew by name, others only by sight, but all glowed with pride.

To his right stood the Imperial Retinue of Wizards.

It struck him as odd to see Keyfur's simulacrum standing among the other wizards, attentive and smiling, when he knew the man actually stood at his side. Arbuckle made certain his gaze didn't linger overlong on Duveau. He wondered how many of the mages' smiles were sincere. Duveau's seemed so. Not for the first time, the prince wondered if the warning he'd received was genuine or some elaborate fabrication to discredit his archmage.

Arbuckle looked down the length of the Great Hall at the assembled peers of the realm. The nobles and courtiers were draped in a veritable rainbow of hues, the jewelry dangling from their ears, necks, and fingers enough wealth to finance several wars. The provincial dukes sat in their elevated balconies. He caught sight of the Twailin contingent. Duke Mir appeared uneasy, in stark contrast to the mage Woefler, who smiled and bobbed his head to the excited chattering of the duchess. All eyes were fixed on Arbuckle, but not all gleamed with the disdain he had come to expect from his nobility. Maybe, once he wore the crown and they saw the good he intended to do, some would actually look on him with love, or at least respect.

High Priestess Arranal of the temple of Eos All-Father, stepped to the fore of the high clerics. The last of the crowd's murmurs withered beneath her incongruously deep-pitched voice as she recited the opening benediction. Her words recalled the glories of the empire past and extolled the promise of things to come. She might have been enumerating the ceiling tiles for all Arbuckle noticed. His gaze flicked here and there, always coming back to glimpse Duveau from the corner of his eye.

I must survive this day!

The mantra sounded hollow now, lost in the vast space of the Great Hall. Sweat trickled down his neck into the cowl of his mantle, and his stomach growled, soured by nothing but blackbrew and single-malt whiskey. Though attended by dozens of guards, Arbuckle had never felt so alone.

I'm not alone. Keyfur is with me.

"Why isn't he doing something?" he whispered, trying not to move his mouth as he spoke.

"Patience, milord." The whispered words hung in thin air inches from his ear. "If the moment *does* come, remember to touch no metal, nor any stone that's not dwarf-wrought."

Arbuckle waited, trembling with dread anticipation.

Arranal raised her hands, and her voice thundered in praise of her deity. "All Hail Eos! Father of All!" The very flagstones beneath their feet seemed to echo her blessing, trembling with divine power.

Or is it my knees shaking?

The crowd stood enthralled, their eyes gleaming and their mouths agape as they gazed upon the priestess. Their rapture turned to apprehension, then horror, when Arranal staggered, her face ashen, and the towering stained-glass windows behind them rattled in their casements.

Not my knees... Duveau!

Arbuckle couldn't help it; he turned to look at Duveau, and his heart leapt to his throat. The archmage stood with one hand pressed against a great stone pillar, his eyes glazed over slate gray.

"Gods of Light protect us!" Arbuckle hissed. "You said he *couldn't* bring the palace down!"

"He *can't*, milord!" Keyfur insisted. "Perhaps he's communicating with the bedrock beneath, but even Duveau can't manipulate dwarf-wrought stonework."

Keyfur's assurance was less than comforting. Arbuckle's mind screamed for him to flee, but his feet remained rooted. *Don't move!* He had to trust Keyfur. *If you move, you're dead!*

Keyfur's airy whisper of a spell touched his ear, and a breeze cooled the prince's neck. The air shimmered around him, muting the panicked exclamations of the crowd.

Don't move!

Arbuckle gritted his teeth against his rising panic as the dais around him erupted into a storm of chaos and blood.

At the first fanfare, Mya realized that she'd made a grave tactical error.

"I should have worn higher heels!"

Amongst the tall lords and ladies, she couldn't see the dais very well. She caught only glimpses of people moving, robed figures taking position before the dais, armored knights gleaming in their metal skins, the golden throne at the back of the platform reflecting the light of the lamps, and the glittering accoutrements of the ceremony awaiting use beside it.

"Which one's Duveau?" she hissed to Lady T.

"The retinue is lining up to the left. He's in the fore, wearing silver robes."

"Why didn't you tell me he'd be on that side?" Mya cursed under her breath. This is what came from not casing a target properly. She was on the far side of the room from the wizard. How was she going to get through the crowd?

"How was I to know which side they'd be on?"

Mya and Lady T exchanged glares as a second peal of trumpets rang out, and more figures entered from the right hand corner of the room. Knights, guards, and among them, the crown prince, resplendent in full royal frippery. She rose on tiptoe and glimpsed a silver-clad figure on the far side of the dais.

Duveau... Why in the name of the gods didn't the prince have him dismissed or arrested? Had he not believed her warning? Had he not made any preparations to safeguard against the wizard?

The prince's entourage took station, and the emperor-to-be stepped up on the dais alone.

Either he didn't believe my note, or he's a complete idiot exposing himself like that.

Mya forced down her apprehension. She'd vowed only to intervene if the prince's defenses proved inadequate, and the massed knights and Imperial Guard seemed like more than enough might to protect one man from one wizard. Still, he looked horribly exposed up there.

As the high priestess of Eos started her benediction, Mya tried to pick out a path to reach the archmage, just in case. If violence erupted, she would have to keep from being swept away with the panicked crowd. The pillar at her back served that purpose, but to reach Duveau, she'd have to get through the crowd and a mass of knights and guards quickly. That seemed impossible.

As the high priestess raised her arms and her voice, Mya felt the floor tremble beneath her feet. A murmur of worry swept through the crowd, people looking around for the source of the tremor.

This is it…

Every nerve in Mya's body sang. Her hand itched to grab a spear from one of the guards and throw it through the traitorous wizard, but she knew that would be worse than useless. She'd never hit him from so far away, and the guards would think she was attacking the prince. She'd be cut down.

Bide… Wait for it… You're the last resort, Mya. The prince isn't a fool. He'll be ready.

With a horrific screech, the golden throne, gilded accoutrements, and every bit of metal on or around the dais rose up like a bizarre living thing, twisting and forming into jagged implements of death.

"Holy…"

The crowd around her erupted in panic, their shrieks and screams rivaling that of the twisted metal that lanced inward from all directions at the seemingly unprotected prince. Rainbow light flared around the would-be sovereign, and a second man flickered into being before him, arms outstretched, colorful robes fluttering in a cyclone of wind. The storm of metal struck, and a scintillating sphere of light arced and flickered, deflecting the deadly onslaught.

Maybe he's prepared after all…

Mya braced herself against the pillar at her back, thrusting aside panicked nobles and courtiers as they fled in terror. She caught a glimpse of the Imperial Retinue just as a massive plate of gold sheared through the line of wizards standing beside Duveau. Five of them fell in a welter of blood, the tall woman in the red dress who had greeted Mya and touched her cheek cut cleanly in half. One, however, a flamboyantly dressed mage who looked like a mirror image of the one protecting Arbuckle, flew apart into a swarm of brilliantly colored butterflies.

What the hell? Mya had no time to wonder what had happened.

Shouts and screams clashed against the walls, and arms and elbows smashed against her, threatening to tear her away from the pillar. She fought against that tide, trying to see through the mayhem. She heard Lady T shriek a curse, and glanced back to see her huddling behind the pillar out of the chaotic flow.

Mya turned back. Through the thinning throng, she could finally see.

Knights and guards whirled with drawn weapons. The once-gilded dais had been stripped bare of metal, the gold flowing like a living thing, lashing out against the scintillating shield that protected the prince. Within the sphere, the wizard's hands glowed with rainbow light.

Three armored knights near the far end of the dais charged the archmage, but a flick of Duveau's hand sent two of them flying aside like ragdolls. The closest screamed in agony as his breastplate crumpled inward, splintering ribs and pulping organs. The dead knight didn't fall, however, but turned and lunged at the prince like a bloody marionette. His puppet-corpse smashed into the rainbow barrier and flew apart, fragmenting into a swirling storm of bloody metal and meat that clashed against the sphere again and again.

Most of the rest of the knights fared no better, lurching and stumbling as their armor crinkled and peeled away. Pieces of metal flew up to attack the prince, the knights, and the guards. A few protectors seemed unaffected by Duveau's magic. Three knights formed up around their prince, fending off the onslaught of animated metal as best they could. One's sword shattered into wooden splinters as the man tried to parry a sweeping golden blade.

Metal! Mya realized. *Duveau's only affecting metal!*

The wooden armor and weapons fared poorly against the storm of gold and steel, however, and two of the knights went down in moments as the shreds of their metal-clad brethren stabbed and slashed.

Imperial guards joined the fray, slashing at Duveau with gleaming halberds and firing bows from the balcony. Those close to the wizard found their own weapons turned against them, and although some arrows seemed to find their mark, the archmage remained unscathed. Wherever an arrow struck, his robe changed hue and texture, from silver cloth to polished stone, then back again. The shafts shattered and fell in pieces.

With another wave of Duveau's hand, the high balustrade above and behind the dais smashed back against the row of archers there. Several bowmen crashed through the lofty stained-glass windows in a shower of colorful shards.

The fleeing crowd of nobles and courtiers thinned, expanding Mya's view even further. Twin storms of metal now flew in deadly swarms around the prince and Duveau, the former lashing against the scintillating sphere, the latter slashing and stabbing at anyone who came near. Arbuckle's defenses had failed to kill the archmage, and from the look of the continued onslaught, the barrier surrounding the prince was slowly shrinking.

"Is it time for you to *intervene* yet?" Lady T peeked around the pillar for a glance, then ducked back, horror plain on her face.

"You *think*?" Mya grasped the release tabs of her gown and jerked. The dress fell away and she kicked off her shoes.

Unfortunately, Mya didn't see how she could get to Duveau without getting cut to pieces. If she simply charged him, she'd fare no better than the poor guards trying to fight through the flying swords, shields, and bits of armor surrounding him.

How do I kill him if I can't even get to him? Mya gritted her teeth. *Think! Think like Lad…*

"I've got to get over there!" Mya looked for a path that might not get her killed and didn't like what she found. *Nothing for it…* "Try not to die while I'm gone!"

"Your *concern* for me is touching!" Lady T hunkered behind the pillar.

"Don't flatter yourself, Lady. I need you alive!"

Mya ran straight at the next pillar and leapt. Planting one foot against the column's engraved surface, she launched herself up. Her fingers met the lower edge of a balcony, and a deft twist brought her up and over the balustrade. Nobles cowered among the seats, and she did a double-take when she recognized Duke Mir of Twailin.

Damn it, what were the chances of that?

The duke and duchess stared at her in terror.

"Sorry! No harm intended, milord. I'm trying to save the

prince's life, but I've got to get to Duveau." Mya crouched, readying herself to leap.

"Wait!" Another man—a wizard by his rune-embroidered robes—crouched on the balcony, incongruously unrolling a large painting on canvas. "I have a way to distract Duveau, but it won't last long."

She glanced at the dais and cringed. The shimmering sphere around the prince and his wizard was still shrinking. It wouldn't be long before Duveau's magical attack broke through.

"Whatever it is, do it now!" Without looking back, Mya launched herself from the balcony.

Bouncing off another lofty pillar, she landed in a sprawling heap among the seats on the adjacent balcony. *Lad would have done this much more gracefully.* Another duke and his entourage were fleeing, and barely noticed her. Mya disentangled herself from the broken furniture and took another running leap toward the dais, launching herself as far as she could.

Don't miss, Mya! If she fell, she'd plummet into a tornado of sharpened metal.

She caught the twisted balustrade above the dais in an iron grip and slammed into the wall. Thankfully, Duveau didn't seem to have noticed her, so focused was he on fending off the attacking guards while besieging the prince with flying steel and gold. Scrambling onto the balcony, she dashed along it, leaping over the twisted metal and several dead and wounded guards. In passing, she snatched a handful of arrows from a quiver, ignoring the daggers and swords. *Nothing metal...* She noted with satisfaction that the tips of the arrows were bone. The prince had prepared his forces after all.

At the far end of the balcony, she glanced back at Duke Mir's box, and her jaw dropped.

A tiny burning woman hovered in front of the now-blank canvas in the wizard's hands. No more than three-feet high, her skin shimmered orange, and her hair writhed in crackling flames. Blowing a kiss to Mir's wizard, she flipped around and soared straight at Duveau.

Mya gripped the arrows in one fist and gauged her target. A whirlwind of metal surrounded the archmage. *Timing, Mya...* If she leapt before the fiery woman distracted Duveau, he might direct the hail of steel at her. One blade through her heart, and she'd be finished. But if she waited too long, the crown prince would die. *Timing…it's all about timing.*

The flaming woman streaked right at Duveau's head. With a flick of one hand, the archmage sent metal lashing at her, but the shards that touched her burst into molten fragments. She was knocked aside by the impacts, but on she flew, stoically fighting through the storm of steel, eyes blazing and black teeth gleaming. Molten slag spattered the floor around the archmage, but the hail of metal thinned with every piece that fell in glowing hot bits.

It's now or never.

Mya leapt.

Arbuckle crouched behind Keyfur, gritting his teeth to hold his panic in check at the horrific onslaught. The scintillating shield reverberated as pieces of metal, and worse—pieces of bloody armor, pieces of men and women he knew—all torn apart and flung at him like weapons hammered against it. Duveau's powers exceeded anything he could have imagined. The men and women of the Imperial Guard, brave knights and squires, all sworn to protect him, fell in bloody tatters.

My fault…

He knew they all couldn't have been warned against wearing metal for fear of Duveau learning, but that gave the prince no comfort. They were dying because of him.

Metal sang against the shimmering shield, inches away now as it shrank with every resounding blow. His ears rang with the howl of impacts, the muffled screams of his dying guards, and the continued stoic chant of his brave wizard protector.

Keyfur…

The mage no longer stood straight over his charge, but crouched to remain inside the shield. His voice rang hoarse, his sweat dripping onto the floor as if he had been laboring for hours, though the attack couldn't have been going on for even a minute. The shield scintillated and shrank as missile after missile slammed into it. Arbuckle hunkered closer, pressing up against Keyfur's legs, and felt them trembling.

Suddenly the wizard's chant rose into a shriek. The mage didn't stop his recitation, but each word sounded as if it had been ripped from his throat. Arbuckle felt a warm spatter against his cheek and looked up. A rain of blood blinded him, but not before he saw that Keyfur's outthrust hands were now thrust *outside* the rainbow barrier into the tornado of metal.

As Keyfur's blood smeared the rainbow of light about them, Arbuckle prepared himself for death.

Mya plunged through the tornado of steel. Tattered armor and broken weapons pierced her without pain, knocking her off target. Twisting like a cat, she thrust the arrows down at the crown of the archmage's head.

Duveau moved.

The arrows pierced the wizard at the juncture of his neck and shoulder, just above the collar of his enchanted robe. The force of the blow drove the shafts down into his chest, and blood flooded over Mya's fists as the arrows snapped off in her grasp.

She smashed to the floor with stunning force, felt a sickening crunch as the bones of her knee and shoulder shattered on the unyielding flagstones. Her head cracked down hard as she rolled, and her sight faded to gray. Her subconscious would have none of it, screaming at her, *You missed! He's going to kill you! Move!*

Too late—shards of metal showered down on her.

Huddled on the cold stone, Mya wondered why she didn't feel the painless rending of flesh and organs, the sickening weakness of her lifeblood leaving her body. She knew what that felt like. Instead, she shuddered as bones began to snap back into place. She wasn't dead. Rolling over, she looked up at Duveau.

The archmage stood in open-mouthed shock, one hand scrabbling to stem the bright blood that pulsed from his neck. All the flying metal surrounding him had fallen from the air, inanimate as his magic failed.

Ha! I didn't miss... Mya bridled her elation as she noticed Duveau's other hand fishing something from a pocket, a small black sphere no bigger than a marble. Clutching it in trembling fingers, he raised it to his mouth.

Mya didn't know what the sphere was, but whatever Duveau meant to do with it couldn't be good for her. Knowing she couldn't regain her feet and reach him before the black sphere met his lips, she felt around desperately for some sort of weapon.

She never got the chance.

"Noooo, wizard!" The tiny burning woman darted in, her blazing hands closing around the archmage's wrist. Flesh hissed under her burning grasp.

Duveau screamed. His hand spasmed open and the black sphere fell into the mire of blood and metal. He tried to fling the fiery woman from his arm, shrieking arcane words. Frost formed around his other hand even as blood pulsed from his neck, and the little burning woman's eyes grew wide with fear.

Mya's fingers found a broken spear, the splintered tip of the shaft needle sharp. She took aim and threw it with all her strength.

This time she didn't miss.

The broken shaft pierced Duveau's left eye and exited through the top of his skull. The archmage's head snapped back, and he stood there for a moment like a bloody silver pillar, then dropped like a poleaxed steer.

Mya leaned back and heaved a sigh. It was over. Shifting as the last of her broken bones ground back into place, she started as the tiny burning woman flew at her, black teeth gleaming in a snarl.

"Sssilly woman! Master Woefler *promised* I could eat him, and you ruined it!"

"Sorry." Mya coughed, and felt a catch in her chest. Swallowing her nausea—*No pain*—she wrenched a piece of broken plate armor from between her ribs and dropped it to the floor. Plucking a few more pieces of metal from her flesh, she waved toward Duveau's body. "You can have what's left."

"Oh, he's no good now! There's nothing left but meat! No sssoul!" The flaming woman glared at her with eyes that blazed like Hades, then flew away.

Mya lurched to her feet and looked toward the dais, wondering if she had struck in time.

Arbuckle sat amid a pile of fallen metal and a heap of blood-soaked robes, his shoulders heaving. The crown prince of Tsing was alive. Unfortunately, she couldn't say as much for the prince's wizard. Bright blood painted the mage's flamboyant robes as he lay in Arbuckle's arms, his sweat-sheened face a deathly gray. His hands were gone, and blood pulsed from the stumps of his wrists. The prince was trying to staunch the flow, but to little effect. Mya shook her head. The wizard would bleed out in moments without a healer unless—

Duveau.

Mya dropped to her knees, searching the litter of bloody metal until she found what she was looking for. Plucking the black sphere from the gore, she glanced to the prince and his dying mage.

Maybe…

CHAPTER XXIX

Outside the magical barrier, steel and gold fell in a clangorous hail. Keyfur's lonely wailing chant against the sudden silence jolted Arbuckle out of his stupor. The wizard's voice broke, and the scintillating barrier vanished. Arbuckle forced his muscles into motion and caught Keyfur as the mage's knees folded. Blood pulsed from the ends of the poor man's ravaged arms.

"Help!" the prince screamed, clutching at the bleeding stumps to staunch the flow. "Get a healer!"

"My...lord..." Keyfur's eyes fluttered, his dark skin sheened with sweat. "I'm..."

"Hang on, Keyfur! We'll get you help." Arbuckle clenched his hands hard on the bleeding wrists and looked up to see Tennison and Ithross dashing toward him.

"Milord! Are you hurt?" Tennison fell to his knees, his eyes wide, Ithross at his heels.

"I'm fine, but Keyfur's bleeding. Get a healer, Tennison! Now!"

"At once, milord!" His secretary lunged up and dashed away.

"Imperial Guard, to me!" Ithross waved over a guard and gestured toward the bleeding mage. "Let us take care of him, Milord. You should be out of here. It's not safe for you."

"I'm *fine*!" Arbuckle snapped, looking around at the chaos of blood and twisted metal, nobles and courtiers still fleeing in panic. "I'll stay with him. Get a godsdamned healer here now!"

The strange elation of being alive clashed with the guilt that sustaining his life had cost so many others their own. He stared down into Keyfur's sickly gray face, at the drooping eyes and shallow breath, death hovering there. *No... Please...* He felt the man's thin pulse racing under his grasp, weaker every moment.

"Milord Prince!"

Arbuckle looked up to see a cordon of grim imperial guards surrounding a woman in snug black clothing spattered with blood. The sight of her seemed surreal, like a dark spirt or angel of death. Who was she?

"Milord!" Something glistened in her outstretched hand. "I may have something to help him."

Two guards made to grab her arms.

"Wait!" Ithross strode to her, sword in hand. "I saw you! You killed Duveau. Why?"

"Because I was *ordered* to!" The woman waved impatiently at Keyfur. "There's no time for explanations!"

"Let her through! If she killed Duveau, then surely she's not here to kill me!" Arbuckle felt the wizard's pulse weakening. "Now, Captain!"

"Give it to me!" Ithross commanded, extending his hand.

The woman pressed a tiny black sphere into the captain's palm. "I don't' know what it does, milord, but Duveau wanted desperately to put it in his mouth after I stabbed him."

Ithross quickly knelt and poked the sphere between Keyfur's lips.

Nothing happened.

"Why isn't it working?" Arbuckle looked at the woman hopelessly.

"I don't..." Glancing around, the woman hurried to the shattered tables that had held all the accoutrements of the ceremony. Snatching up a fallen bottle of sacramental wine, she handed it to Ithross. "Make him swallow it."

"Do it!" Arbuckle ordered.

Ithross pulled the crystal stopper and poured some into the injured wizard's mouth, then held his nose. Keyfur coughed and swallowed, then drew a ragged breath. His eyes suddenly flung wide.

"Lords of Light!" Arbuckle released his grip on the wizard's wrists and stared in shock.

Flesh flowed like melting wax, forming over the bleeding stumps. The skin there bulged into buds that grew into tiny hands. As the miniature members grew, Keyfur lifted his arms and stared in wonder. His newly forming hands fleshed out to their original size, hale and unblemished, in a matter of seconds.

Arbuckle breathed a sigh of relief. At least one life had been spared.

"Milord, I—" Keyfur's eyes suddenly widened again, and he retched. The black marble fell from his mouth to the floor.

"What in the names of all the gods..." Arbuckle stared as Ithross scooped up the mysterious sphere.

"It's a fleshforge, milord." Keyfur flexed his newly reforged hands and grinned in delight. "I had heard that Duveau possessed one, but I wasn't sure. How did you get it?"

Everyone turned to the mysterious woman in black.

"I...I didn't know." She shrugged and looked embarrassed. "I just saw him trying to swallow it and assumed..."

"Just who might you be that you come to my aid, then save the life of my only remaining wizard?" Arbuckle accepted the help of several guards to stand.

"Moirin, milord. Lady Monjhi's bodyguard." She curtsied and gestured toward a dark-haired woman standing all alone in the nearly vacated Great Hall. "I came as her protector, but she ordered me to aid you."

"It was...quite amazing, milord, how she dealt with Duveau," Ithross said.

"I've no doubt. Lady Monjhi!" Arbuckle beckoned her to approach. He remembered seeing her in the company of his father once or twice, but they had never been formally introduced. "Your action saved my life! You have my thanks!"

"It...was the least I could do, milord." She curtsied low.

Tennison hurried up with Master Corvecosi in tow

The healer stared at the blood on Arbuckle's clothes. "Milord! Are you injured?"

"No, my good man, but there are many who are. Please see to the wounded."

"At once, milord!"

"Might we use this, milord?" Ithross held up the tiny black sphere.

"It may help, but its power to heal is not infinite." Keyfur plucked it from the captain's hand. "If swallowed when its power is depleted, it'll be destroyed forever."

"Use it sparingly, then. Master Keyfur, accompany Master Corvecosi and use this fleshforge on anyone close to death." As the healer and wizard hurried off, Arbuckle took a deep and cleansing breath. "Gods of Light, I'm alive, thanks to you, Lady Monjhi, and your amazing bodyguard. Moirin, is it?"

"Yes, milord." The woman in black curtsied again, a sardonic smile on her lips. "I was just doing as I was told."

"Well, regardless, you both have my gratitude. As soon as we get this mess sorted out and a crown on my head, you'll know what the gratitude of an emperor means!" Arbuckle laughed. He'd been granted a second chance at life, and was determined to make the most of it.

"Milord, you can't seriously expect to continue with the coronation today!" Tennison looked aghast. "The place is a shambles, and people have died!"

"The Great Hall is a shambles, Tennison, and people have died for *me* today. They died to protect me, to keep me alive because they thought I would be a good emperor. If I delay my coronation, I risk wasting their dying efforts." Arbuckle felt more certain about this than anything he'd done. Straightening his mantle, bloody though it was, he fixed his entourage with a steely glare. "I *will* be crowned emperor today! Tell everyone that once I've changed clothes, we'll move the coronation to the south gardens and make the best of it! The injured will be cared for here."

"At once, milord!" Tennison bowed and hurried off.

"Lady Monjhi, I hope that you and your *amazing* young bodyguard will consent to be my special guests at the reception afterword."

"At your pleasure, milord. And please, call me Lady T. All my friends do." The lady's glance slid sideways as she curtsied. "May I request leave for my bodyguard to don something more appropriate for a coronation? Her gown was ruined in the fracas."

"Of course." He waved away the details. "Captain, have the ladies escorted to someplace appropriate and summon the imperial tailor."

"Yes, milord!" Ithross waved guards forward.

"Thank you, milord."

After the lady and her bodyguard curtsied and hurried away in the company of two imperial guards, Arbuckle allowed his cadre to usher him out of the Great Hall. Glancing back, he spied Duveau's corpse sprawled on the flagstones, encircled by guards.

What could have seduced someone as formidable and upright as Duveau into betraying me? Is no one above corruption?

The thought sobered him. His midnight visitor had been right about Duveau. What about the rest of the names on that list? If a conspiracy to assassinate him still existed, he dare not ignore it. Today, however, he would be crowned Emperor Tynean Tsing III, and rejoice in being alive.

Mya sank back into the plush seat of Lady T's carriage. It had been a long day, and she was both tired and wound as tight as a watch spring. She stared at Lady T as the footman closed the door, waiting until they had clattered through the gates of the palace and onto the streets of Tsing before she spoke.

"So, *Baroness* Monjhi, how did it feel to be personally toasted by the new emperor?" She raised her hand as if holding a goblet of wine. "'To Lady Tara Monjhi, who risked her own life when she ordered her bodyguard to leave her side in defense of her sovereign.'"

Tara still seemed a little stunned by all that had transpired, but managed a wry smile. "You didn't do so badly yourself."

Mya wasn't sure if the guildmaster was referring to the emperor's praise of Moirin the bodyguard, or Mya's timely murder of Duveau. It didn't matter. It was done. She had succeeded and survived, and even profited. Mya fingered the necklace that rested upon the lace at her throat—amethysts surrounded by diamonds—a king's ransom in jewels. It wasn't as great a gift as Lady T's new barony, but it would support her for a long, long time. And Dee had been right about one more thing: she'd danced with an emperor.

"So, Baroness," Mya grinned, "how do you plan to deal with your newly acquired fame and fortune?"

"Oh, shut up." The lady's glare was unfeigned. "This will cause me no end of strife with the nobility. Do you think they'll *welcome* the person who saved the emperor and ruined their lives? They'll curse me every time their servants act up and flout their newly acquired *rights*. My name will be 'Mud' for a very long time. And then there's Hoseph. He'll try to kill me for this."

"Yes, he will." Mya had been thinking about Hoseph. "I guess that means that you're on my side now whether you like it or not. I have a simple solution: help me kill Hoseph first, and we get down to *real* guild business. This city is ripe for fleecing, and with a baroness touting our services, we'll be raking in more gold from your blue-blooded peers than you've ever seen before."

"There is that," Lady T admitted with a frown. "But until Hoseph is dead, I'm going to need protection, and I mean *real* protection, every hour of every day."

Mya screwed up her face. "You've got the entire Tsing guild. Isn't that enough?"

"You don't understand. He knows where I live. Where I sleep! He could pop in any moment."

"Stay someplace safe until he's dead."

"I *can't* just disappear. I have a reputation to maintain, especially now that I'm a baroness. I'll have to live in fear until I see his corpse."

"Welcome to my world," Mya muttered, then added, "I suggest you keep your crossbow handy."

"I always do. But I don't relish sleeping surrounded by heavily armed Enforcers." Lady T turned away and looked out the window, watching the city roll past.

After a time, Mya asked the question she'd wanted answered for weeks. "So, were you playing both sides, waiting for either Hoseph or me to kill the other?"

Lady T looked startled, then shrugged in resignation. "What if I was? You've trumped my best card. I've got nowhere to go now *but* with you. Tomorrow I'll convene my people and name you Grandmaster."

"Good. I think we'll work well together, now that things are out in the open."

Lady T shrugged again, then her eyes narrowed slyly. "Would you like me to drop you at home?"

"If you wish. I live at—"

The baroness opened a tiny door and called up to her driver, "The corner of Tanner Street and Archer!"

"Yes, milady!"

Mya let the lady's little power play slide by without comment. It didn't surprise her that the guildmaster knew where she lived. Hoseph had undoubtedly told her.

They continued on in silence. There was nothing much more to discuss. Mya stared out at the setting sun, weary with the day's events, but satisfied. She'd won. With the guildmaster on her side, the guild was hers. She rubbed the ring Lad had put on her finger and smiled. The hard part was over.

The carriage rumbled to a stop before the orphanage, and one of the guards leapt down to open the door for Mya.

She got out, turning back to fix the guildmaster with a serious stare. "Be *careful*, milady."

"You know I will be."

"Good. I'll call on you tomorrow afternoon."

"That will be fine…" Lady T paused, then nodded respectfully, "…Grandmaster."

Mya smiled, nodded, and stepped back. The Enforcer closed the carriage door and clambered up to his post.

"Home, driver!" Lady T called up, and the man applied his whip.

Mya's keen ears picked up an excited yell from inside her orphanage—"She's home!"—and the sound of feet pounding down stairs and across squeaky floors. She watched the beautiful team of horses lurch into motion, then turned to see Dee and Paxal emerging from the doorway, flanked by smiling urchins. *Home…*

"No! Wait! I—"

Mya whirled at Lady T's cry of alarm. "Oh, gods…" She was moving before she gave it a second thought. *Godsdamned deathtrap of a carriage!*

The driver reined in hard, and a guard leaned down to peer through the window. "Milady?

The other guard leapt down, but Mya shoved him aside and wrenched open the carriage door. She caught a glimpse of black mist, quickly dissipating. Lady T sat staring at nothing, her face blank.

"No!" Mya whirled in case Hoseph popped in behind her, but

found only the guard staring wide-eyed at his dead mistress. Lunging into the carriage, Mya clasped Tara's wrist, but felt no pulse. No life. *No soul.* She stumbled out of the carriage. "Gods *damn* it to all Nine Hells!"

"What happened?" The guards looked at Mya, their dead guildmaster, then back to Mya. "Who killed her? How did they—"

"It was Hoseph. I saw him fading away into mist."

Recognition dawned in the guards' eyes. They'd worked for Lady T long enough to know of the high priest's preternatural abilities.

Dee and Pax hurried up, their eyes wide. "What happened?"

Mya nodded into the carriage. "That bastard Hoseph murdered her." A thought sparked, and she stepped up into the carriage once more. "Gods damn him! Her ring's gone! He must have taken it."

I had it! I had it all! Mya stepped out of the carriage and clamped down on her raging emotions.

Staring at the guards, she pointed to their dead guildmaster. "You heard what she said to me! When you opened the door and I stepped out, you heard it, didn't you?" They evaded her gaze. She strode up to the one who had opened the door and grasped his shirt front. "I don't *care* if you were eavesdropping. You heard! What did she say to me?"

"She…she called you Grandmaster."

"That's right! You're all Enforcers, and you *know* what that means. You have no guildmaster and I'm your Grandmaster, so listen closely. You!" Mya stabbed a finger toward another of the guards. "You're going to summon constables and report that Baroness Monjhi has been murdered by High Priest Hoseph, who is also wanted for questioning in Emperor Tynean Tsing II's murder."

They looked at her wide eyed. "Tell the constables?"

"Yes." She glared them down. "Do it now! Don't move this carriage until they're here!"

The guard ran off.

Mya pointed at the second guard. "You, send runners to all the masters. Tell them Hoseph murdered the guildmaster and took her ring. Also tell them what you heard, that I was acknowledged by Lady T as Grandmaster, and I'm naming Hoseph a traitor and enemy to the Assassins Guild. He's to be killed on sight. Anyone conspiring with him will also be considered a traitor. You got that?"

The guard nodded and took off running.

Dee sidled up to her, his voice low. "Mya, is calling in the constables a good idea?"

"I don't know, but I need all the allies I can get." Mya spoke through gritted teeth. She wanted to loose the scream raging to escape her throat. *It was mine! The guild was mine, and now it's gone!* Without Lady T to vouch for her, she'd have to start from scratch, win over the masters one by one. "I won't be cheated out of the guild by that lunatic priest. This is war!"

Emperor Tynean Tsing III settled into his comfortable armchair feeling a strange mixture of relief, trepidation, and crushing guilt. He had survived the day and gained his crown, but it had cost the lives of eleven members of his knighthood and Imperial Guard, not to mention the entire Retinue of Wizards, save one. He wondered if Master Keyfur would consider taking the position of archmage.

Many nobles had been injured in the panic, but all were slated to recover. Indeed, most had managed to attend the coronation and reception and regale their peers with stories exaggerated by the free-flowing wine. Arbuckle knew the cost could have been a lot higher. Thanks to an intrepid few, he was alive and finally emperor. Now it was up to him to fulfill his promises to his people.

Baris came help him get ready for bed. "Sleepy, Your Majesty?"

"Exhausted." The emperor rose and loosened his doublet. "I can't remember when I've been more spent."

"We, Your Majesty." At Arbuckle's raised eyebrows, his valet explained, "Your Majesty must use the royal 'We' when referring to himself."

"I must...er...We must?"

"Yes, Majesty." Baris smiled as he accepted his master's doublet. "It's *tradition*."

"Well, *We* mustn't break tradition!" Arbuckle chuckled and allowed Baris help him doff his shirt and pants and don his nightshirt. "Is there any tradition that states the new emperor can't have a nightcap?"

"None whatsoever, Majesty."

"Well, We're glad of that!" Arbuckle poured himself a whiskey and placed it on his night table. Climbing into bed, he picked up the book he'd been trying to read for more than a month. With everything that had happened, he'd lost his place. Sighing, he flipped to page one and started anew. This is how an evening should be spent, with a good book and an easy-sipping whiskey.

A knock sounded at the door.

The emperor looked up from his reading, and Baris looked up from his tidying. "Who could it be at this time of night?"

Arbuckle shivered as he realized that it was one month ago to the day, while reading this very book, when a late-night knock on his door had set recent events in motion.

"It must be important, Majesty. Word was left to not disturb you."

"Best answer it, then." The emperor put down his whiskey and book as Baris went to the door.

It opened to reveal a glowering Captain Ithross. "Pardon, Your Majesty, but I just received dire news that I thought you would want to know."

Arbuckle's mind flashed through a hundred possible sources of bad news. "What's happened?"

"There's been a murder. Baroness Monjhi was killed in her carriage this evening on her way home."

"Oh, gods! Who…"

"Her bodyguard witnessed the attack and reported that it was High Priest Hoseph, your late father's spiritual advisor, who committed the murder."

"Hoseph!" Arbuckle's stomach clenched. "Gods *damn* that man to the Nine Hells!"

"Yes, milor—er, Your Majesty." Ithross looked miserable. "The constabulary's been notified, but we've been seeking him for a month with no luck."

"Well, keep looking." Arbuckle reached for his whiskey and downed it in one long swallow. "Damn it! The baroness was a fine and noble woman. He killed her because she saved my life! There's no doubt of it!"

"It seems likely, Majesty."

The pieces fit together in Arbuckle's mind. "Hoseph could have been behind the other attempts on my life as well!"

"It's possible, Majesty. He *was* involved in this...guild of assassins, after all, according to Captain Norwood, and named in the warning you received as ringleader of the conspiracy."

"Yes. Thank you for bringing me word, Captain. We've got to consider this carefully. I— We want a full investigation." Arbuckle dismissed him with a nod.

"Of course, Majesty." Ithross ducked out, and Baris went with him.

Arbuckle got up and poured himself another whiskey. He knew he wouldn't be able to sleep after the news. Standing at the window, he sipped the smooth liquor and looked out over the city—*his* city, his empire—and wondered how many assassins were out there.

My father used to be one of them.

"Is anyone ever safe in this world?" Emperor Tynean Tsing III downed his whiskey and went to bed. He lay awake a very long time, wondering if he would ever be free of his father's legacy.

In the end, he knew it didn't matter.

It was time to make a legacy of his own.

EPILOGUE

Hoseph materialized in the soothing darkness of his refuge, staggered, and collapsed to his knees. Pain pulsed in his head, and waves of dizziness threatened to empty his stomach. Closing his eyes, he waited until the pain and nausea eased, then struggled to his feet. His knees trembled, but held him.

One more task...then I can rest.

He called on Demia's grace, and light flared and wavered in his trembling hand. The tiny skull hung from his sleeve on its chain, reflecting the pearly glow. He'd used the talisman extensively this afternoon, and paid the price. *Necessary... I can rest later.* He examined the silver skull, lurid in the flickering flame, and wondered, *Is it killing me?*

I fear not Death for she is my ally. She will claim me in the end, and I will stand at Demia's side. The ancient mantra calmed him, but he still had work to do in this world, and that work required him to travel through the Sphere of Shadow.

He'd waited for Duveau to bring word of Arbuckle's death, but the archmage never arrived. At the palace, he knew by the celebrations that something had gone dreadfully wrong. When he spotted Duchess Ingstrom's carriage leaving early, he went to her home to await word.

It arrived in the form of a livid Duchess.

"What in the Nine Hells does Lady T mean by ordering her bodyguard to save Arbuckle's life?"

"Bodyguard? What bodyguard?"

"The skinny woman who can leap around like a court acrobat! Moirin or something from Twailin, she said her name was! She killed Duveau!"

It took little imagination to realize who this bodyguard must be. *Mya!*

Hoseph had gone back to the palace to wait for the traitorous Twailin guildmaster to leave, and followed her carriage. When he materialized beside her, She'd tried to explain, but he was through listening to her lies. She'd paid for her treason with her soul and her ring. Next, Hoseph had visited each and every master of the Tsing guild to decry Lady T's betrayal and promise his support in the coming conflict. They had all eagerly eyed the guildmaster's ring he proffered as the promised prize for killing Mya.

Mya...

She had foiled him again and again, destroyed his elegant system of power, pushed him to the brink of collapse.

Never again... Hoseph lurched to his desk and started gathering his things. *One more thing to do tonight before I can rest...*

Into his spare cloak he piled a few essential items: his razor, personal effects, writing tools and parchment, and several priceless tomes from the guild archives. *So few possessions for one who will shape an empire.* He tied it tight and lay the bundle down in the center of the floor.

Demia's high priest gazed around the repository of dusty books and myriad scrolls. For decades he had preserved the guild's history here, plotted the future. No more.

No choice...

Hoseph lifted the lamp from the desk and removed the brass cap on the filling spout. With a flick of his wrist, he dashed oil onto the shelves of bone-dry vellum. In his conversations with the masters he had finally understood what must be done. He couldn't kill Mya himself, not with pain and fatigue plaguing him every time he traversed the Sphere of Shadow. He had to use the guild, but Mya wore the Grandmasters ring, so no guild-bound assassin could touch her. There was only one solution.

They'll be guild-bound no more.

Dropping the empty lamp, Hoseph plucked a match from the desk drawer. Flame blossomed in his hand with a flick of his thumbnail. He walked around the small room, touching the match here and there until the fire roared and smoke whirled.

Finally, Hoseph picked up his bundle and flicked the silver skull into his hand. How ironic it would be if this one time Demia's talisman failed him. He would burn here, consumed by his own cleverness.

He spoke the invocation, and the mists formed around him.

Thank you, sweet Demia...

Hoseph watched the blood contracts blazing and burning as the shadows consumed him. The guild assassins were free from constraint.

It was open season, and Mya was the game of choice.

ABOUT THE AUTHORS

Chris was born and raised in Oregon, Anne in Massachusetts. They met at graduate school in Texas, and have been together ever since. They have been gaming together since 1985, sailing together since 1988, married since 1989, and writing together off and on throughout their relationship. Most astonishingly, they have not killed each other, or even tried to, at any time during the creation or editing of any of their stories...although it was close a few times. The couple has been sailing and writing full time aboard their beloved sailboat, *Mr. Mac*, since 2009. They return to the US every summer for conventions, so check out jaxbooks.com for updates and events. They are always happy to sign copies of their books and talk to fans.

Other books by Chris A. Jackson
and Anne L McMillen-Jackson

From Jaxbooks
A Soul for Tsing
Deathmask

The Weapon of Flesh Trilogy
Weapon of Flesh
Weapon of Blood
Weapon of Vengeance

The Cornerstones Trilogy (with Anne L. McMillen-Jackson)
Zellohar
Nekdukarr
Jundag

The Cheese Runners Trilogy (novellas)
Cheese Runners
Cheese Rustlers
Cheese Lords

From Dragon Moon Press
Scimitar Moon
Scimitar Sun
Scimitar's Heir
Scimitar War

From Paizo Publishing
Pirate's Honor
Pirate's Promise
Pirate's Prophecy (February 2016)

From Privateer Press
Blood & Iron (ebook novella)

From The Ed Greenwood Group
Dragon Dreams (November 2015)